D0728306

THE STYCLAR SAGA

GABRIEL

Nikki Kelly

FEIWEL AND FRIENDS

NEW YORK

For Liz Szabla—Thank you for being "a shaft
of sunlight at the end of a dark afternoon."

A Feiwel and Friends Book
An Imprint of Macmillan

GABRIEL. Copyright © 2015 by Nikki Kelly. All rights reserved. Printed in
the United States of America by R. R. Donnelley & Sons Company,
Harrisonburg, Virginia. For information, address Feiwel and Friends,
175 Fifth Avenue, New York, N.Y. 10010.

Our books may be purchased in bulk for promotional, educational, or
business use. Please contact your local bookseller or the Macmillan Corporate
and Premium Sales Department at (800) 221-7945 ext. 5442 or by e-mail at
MacmillanSpecialMarkets@macmillan.com.

Library of Congress Cataloging-in-Publication Data is available.

ISBN 978-1-250-05153-0 (hardcover) / ISBN 978-1-250-07864-3 (ebook)

Feiwel and Friends logo designed by Filomena Tuosto

First Edition—2015

10 9 8 7 6 5 4 3 2 1

fiercereads.com

The night is darkest just before the dawn.
And I promise you the dawn is coming.

—District Attorney Harvey Dent,
The Dark Knight

INTRODUCTION

Tick. tock. tick. tock. Tock. Tick.

The hands of the invisible clock rolled over and over.

This was nowhere. But time did indeed subsist in this place. The sound of the clock reminded nowhere's company of the inescapability of nothingness. A form of torture to know that time continued to move forward for everything else—and everyone else—in a place where they still existed, while those who had gone lay lost, wrapped in the fabric of the unknown.

Thoughts, only thoughts, here at the center of a room. Only there were no walls, no floor, and no ceiling. No longer possessing a physical form, all that was here were my erratic, barely conceived thoughts.

Thoughts that wondered if this was nature. If this was what happened when everything you were just stopped and no other worldly force intervened.

But then, someone had put that clock in here.

All thoughts were fragmented and stifled, but they struggled on regardless—anything to block out the sound of the maddening *tick tock* by concentrating on the faintest smudge of an imprinted memory.

A strange image of an object—small and thick with a jagged edge around its top—flashed into thought.

Focusing on *it*, and yet no comprehension as to what *it* was.

The object started to fuzz and blur, but this mind wasn't going to release it so easily. Think and remember.

King. A word. Recognition. *King.* It had a name.

Now it existed.

The *tick tock* filtered back in and made it harder to concentrate. And, somehow, the sound of those malevolent hands was getting louder.

King. King. King. Its name now resounded in time with the strikes—balancing it, holding the image steady.

Check. A new word forming. *Check.* My king was in check. My king.

Me.

Me. I. I wasn't me. I wasn't anything. I didn't exist. And then the idea started to dissolve. . . .

Lailah . . .

The word almost whispered into life, and repeated: *Lailah* . . .

A name. Things that didn't exist didn't have names. But I had a name. One I swore I would never forget again.

Lailah . . .

Strange . . . at the end of the room, a circle appeared.

The *tick tock* quickened.

A window. A glass window with an image locked inside—someone beautiful sat at the foot of a bed. I knew him. On a table before him sat a chess set.

I concentrated on the king, and a spark of light flowed through my mind. Though I began to feel something, whatever it was quickly receded as the face before me dulled with a shadow of sadness.

"No." My voice bounced off the sides of the room that were now forming. "No!" I shouted again. As I did, the king moved for me; it moved itself out of check.

Command the choice to decide.

Command the choice to decide.

As the familiar words looped themselves in my mind, a chill crept up from below.

The room had a floor, and I had feet.

Tick, tock, tick, tock, tick, tock . . . The clock sped up, booming with every strike, almost deafening my mind into silence once again. And with every turn of the big hand, it was as if my head were being pounded and smacked against the newly formed wooden walls.

I was locked inside a grandfather clock. I was a nonexistent prisoner of time. But I was beginning to exist once more, so time would have to halt long enough to release me.

I could see my hands now, and as the floor started to fall away and the ceiling began to cave in, I placed my palms against the window in desperation, watching him.

The glass shattered as the space bounced and rocked from side to side, and his image left along with the shards, shortly to be replaced with a new window, a way back to the world.

Heavy chunks of wood came crashing down around me. I squeezed myself through, staring down into oblivion. I stood straight and teetered on the ledge of its gold pane.

Three perfect spheres lined up in a row. One was a luminous white. The second was an amalgam of sapphire blue and emerald green. The third was a black ball with gray clouds that swirled as though a storm was trapped inside.

I cast my gaze to my right, and as the prison broke apart, I saw a number: 9. Debris rained down from above, and I struggled to retain my balance. I snapped my attention to the left. Another number—3—cracked and fell away.

My head thumped and throbbed. I kept my balance, but the clock's hands twirled at an incredible speed, so fast everything was spinning.

I had commanded the choice; now I had to decide.

"I want to go home! I want to live!" I shouted at nothing and no one.

The heavy brass pendulum swung as the hands finally slowed and hovered at 12. The casing that had enclosed me broke away as the clock chimed for its last time, sounding the beginning of a new day.

I remembered his face as I closed my eyes. His name formed at the fringes of my consciousness, and I fell from the ledge of my prison.

The clock stopped ticking.

Every clock in every world stopped. Just for me.

PROLOGUE

ALTHOUGH IT WAS THE onset of a deeply bitter winter, a deceptive sheet of sunlight fell over the Emerald Isle—nothing but crystal-blue sky above.

Reverend Cillian O'Sileabhin noted this with annoyance. On a day such as this, the rain should have lashed down and the heavens should have cried. It was the least his son Padraig deserved.

O'Sileabhin carried the white lie on his shoulder, bearing the coffin's weight without flinching. He looked to his other—and now only—son, Fergal, who was struggling to balance the heavy wood on the opposite side. Fergal was weak compared with Padraig; perhaps he should have beaten Fergal as a child. It certainly seemed to have made a man out of his eldest.

Though O'Sileabhin had, on countless occasions, raised his hand to his youngest son, he had never been able to bring it down upon him. Fergal would cower, kneading his fingers through his messy blond hair around his temples, and peer up through the wayward strands with fear. And in Fergal's wide eyes, O'Sileabhin would see his wife's staring back at him. He would once again hear her whisper "good-bye" the night she had fled. And with Padraig only too willing to receive a beating on his brother's behalf, he had borne the brunt of O'Sileabhin's retribution.

But now, with Padraig gone, he would need to be harder—more stringent—with Fergal. An upbringing with a good balance of faith and discipline—that was what made leaders. Though Fergal was younger than Phelan, the son of O'Sileabhin's brother, Diarmuid, Fergal was still the offspring of the eldest O'Sileabhin brother, which meant he would become leader when the day came, even if Phelan happened to be better suited to leadership than Fergal. This was the way it had always been.

The task of protecting this town—this congregation—from the Devil's brood, as O'Sileabhin's great-great-great-great-great-grandfather would have expected, demanded nothing short of valiant and intrepid servants of God.

And Reverend Cillian O'Sileabhin led by example.

As the men approached the gated entrance to the long path that led to the coffered panel doors of the church, the sun rose just over the peak of the church turret and momentarily blinded Cillian.

Refrains of "Danny Boy" softly called them inside the place of worship. As the arched doors swung open and the sweet song sang down the long aisle, the coffin was carried through on a freezing breeze that swept its way over the silver hinges and fastenings, causing them to clank and clatter.

Cillian passed his beautiful daughter, Iona, who sat waiting for him in the pews. Her plump lips strained in a sorrowful smile and wistful tears fell from her gray-blue eyes as Cillian acknowledged her with a small nod.

Diarmuid delivered the service, though Cillian barely listened to his brother's words about the righteous who had fallen in the Lord's name. How Padraig had been an honorable and fearless young man. Words would bring little comfort on this darkest of days.

As the service drew to a close and the song replayed, Cillian took Iona's hand and squeezed it reassuringly. "'Twas a grand choice, munchkin. Padraig would have liked it."

Once the church had emptied, he allowed his daughter to guide him from the pews. She hesitated, and Cillian waited for her to speak. Instead, she unfastened her clutch purse and pulled out his gold cross.

Cillian had removed it, feeling disillusioned after Padraig had been lost to the Devil's servants. But despite his daughter's sadness, she had shown strength, and now she was asking him to do the same.

Iona dropped the gold cross into his palm, and he placed a kiss on her forehead in reply. Satisfied, she stepped into the aisle. The reverend considered the necklace and chose to tuck it in his pocket. He would wear it when he was ready to speak to the Lord once more.

Cillian took a moment to glance back, to see Fergal with his hand spread over the face of the closed casket, sobbing. Cillian shook his head in quiet irritation. Making a man, let alone a leader, out of Fergal would not be an easy task.

As was customary, the solemn service was followed by a wake at the local public house before the sun set. Cillian leaned against the wood-paneled wall and sighed. They had been here too often over these last few years.

Stories of Padraig's bravery and tales of his antics—his way with women, his loyalty and friendship—were swapped among the brave men that were still left. But with every story told, there was fear deeply set in the eyes of these soldiers as they, perhaps, recognized that it could be any one of them next.

Eventually the Reverends O'Sileabhin made their way to the gardens at the back of the pub, where they pulled out two fine cigars to smoke in Padraig's honor. A tradition, shared between them, to mark and show respect for those who had fallen for the cause.

The sun was nearly set and the dust of the land could be seen rising into the air where the light above the door illuminated a stripe ahead of them. The wind picked up, whistling toward the doorway, and the particles swirled and dispersed as day prepared to give way to night.

Cillian struggled to keep the flame from his match alive, but then the bitter breeze dropped. As the flame grew strong and high, the end of his cigar turned red. The reverends inhaled the tobacco while an eerie stillness crept over the gardens. The noise from the wake inside seemed to fade, and a figure stepped out from the shadows.

Neither O'Sileabhin brother was prepared for the golden-haired woman who suddenly presented herself. She was not human. No mere mortal could be so breathtaking.

"I need your assistance," she began.

Dumbfounded, the O'Sileabhin brothers glanced at each other before staring back at the beauty before them.

"You come to us from the Lord?" Diarmuid asked.

"I am what you would call an Angel, and *I need your assistance*." She repeated the phrase, the words gliding from her tongue. Though her features were soft, she had a look of steely determination beaming from her wide eyes. "There is little time. Reverend Cillian O'Sileabhin, are you still the leader of the band of men known as the Sealgaire?"

Cillian placed his hand to the top of the revolver in his waistband. "You know my name; tell me yours."

Diarmuid wrapped his hand firmly around the barrel of the revolver and pushed Cillian's arm down. "Brother, no! She comes to us from the Lord." He furrowed his brow and turned back toward the Angel. "That we are, Seraph. How is it we may assist you?"

"Your name?" Cillian demanded once again.

The Angel shifted her weight from side to side as she considered that the darkness was fast approaching. Finally she said, "Aingeal."

Cillian lurched backward, and his fingers tightened around the base of his cigar.

"There is a girl. . . ." the Angel began, her words pausing before rushing forth. "I need you to seek her out. I need you to save her."

"What girl, and what does she need saving from?" Diarmuid asked quickly.

"She needs saving from herself. She resides too closely to a large Vampire Army. If they find her, if they know her . . ." She trailed off. As the darkened shadows of night began to draw across the surrounding land, the wind returned, almost acting as a warning. "I must go. I will send word of where she resides."

"How will we know who she is?" Diarmuid pushed.

"I gave her the name Lailah. But she goes by many. If your heart is truly pure, you will find her; she will look like me." With that, she turned on her heel.

"Wait!" Cillian found his voice. Stepping forward, he reached for the Angel's arm and looked her square in the eye. "You knew her. You helped her. Tell me, did she make it?"

The Angel contemplated and then finally replied. "Yes. She is safe with the sea."

Diarmuid shook his head in confusion; he did not understand what it was his brother had asked the Angel nor the reply she had given.

The Angel's eyes darted around as the light above the door flickered, and she feared she had stayed too long. With no further hesitation, she proceeded to slink into the gray of night.

Diarmuid shouted after her. "Dear Angel, please, I don't understand!"

The Angel Aingeal stopped, grinding her heels into the grass. "Reach her, before they do." She tipped her weight backward and peered over her shoulder. "Or the battle line between the worlds shall be drawn here in the blood of mortals, and everything will turn to ash."

And then, she was gone.

Fueled with a new sense of purpose, Cillian stubbed out his cigar and hurried back into the pub to gather the men.

Diarmuid turned to follow, but the sound of brambles snapping in the tree line that bordered the gardens caused him to halt. Cautiously, he trudged through the bare undergrowth, pushing past the tangled, low-hanging branches. Nothing could have prepared him for who stood waiting.

The Angel was not the only one to deliver a message that evening.

ONE

THEY SAY THAT DEATH is a part of life. And that the only thing in life that is truly certain is death.

But "they" never met me.

I gasped and air filled my lungs, circulating some form of life back into my sleeping body. My senses were dulled. Everything around me seemed to move slowly, frame by frame. Or maybe it was just him. Not moving, merely staring at me with the most remarkable, utterly unreadable expression.

Rays of sunlight shone through the trees, creating shadowed stripes across his face, but nothing could darken those sapphire eyes.

Everything was utterly serene.

I released a steady breath and the frost of this new day tingled on my lips. It was as though I was blowing a bubble through a magical sphere, as the image of him and the snowy landscape behind seemed to stretch. Gently, as I exhaled, it expanded. He and the scenery around him became caught in my bubble.

I was holding the whole world trapped within my first full breath.

It was beautiful. He was beautiful. And I was home.

But then a dark, swirling cloud appeared, and when it dispersed, a new pair of mesmerizing midnight eyes blemished the beauty of the snowy scene. The stranger stood not far from the blond guy, where he watched me.

His black orbs pulled me in, sucking and destroying the light and peace I had felt. And before I knew what was happening, my gaze became imprisoned by his eyes.

Panicking, I inhaled sharply, and the bubble I had created rocketed back toward me. A strange new scent rode the breeze and rushed all around me, finally catching in the back of my throat. From zero to a thousand, the whole world slapped me in the face as the bubble burst.

Without warning, peace erupted into chaos, and everything became audible at once. The sound of a bird chirping miles away stabbed my eardrums; the distant noise of the wind hitting tree trunks felt like tidal waves smacking me underneath them. And that step he took toward me—the sound of his shoe in the snow down underfoot— almost caused my eardrums to rupture as the ice crunched from his weight.

I bolted upright, craning my neck toward the origin of the overwhelming scent. I regarded the shadowed stranger daring to look back at me, daring now to approach me. But my attention was drawn away from his dark eyes, to his elbow, where the smallest trace of blood was smeared against his pale skin and where I witnessed the final moments of a wound healing.

A strange sensation flooded me as my teeth fractured into fangs and my top lip quivered. My skin crawled with an intensifying heat, rising from inside me. I wasn't in control of what happened next. My legs swung off the large stone that I had been placed upon and found their way to the ground. I let out a low moan and my body attempted to stretch, but it wasn't fully awake yet and I stumbled down to the snowy blanket beneath me. I clawed my way to my feet, getting ever closer to that scent, as my body propelled itself in the stranger's direction. I came to an abrupt stop as strong arms wrapped themselves around my waist, turning me away from the stranger.

I struggled against the restraint, but he whispered, "Lailah, no," and the coolness of his breath skimmed my earlobe.

I paused, and my red-hot skin simmered against him. My gums ached as my new fangs receded. My body weakened, but he held me tightly and eased me to the ground, cradling me in a protective embrace.

"You need to go." His hurried voice cut through the jumbled noise invading my hearing.

"But . . ." The stranger's footsteps moved closer from behind me, and I growled and dug my fingernails into the earth beneath the snow.

"Go," my protector said. "Now."

The stranger hesitated for only a moment before the wind whipped against my warm cheeks as he sped away through the clearing.

My ears throbbed, and I covered them with my hands as I rocked back and forth, letting a scream escape from my lungs.

"Shhhhh," my protector said, "it's all right. I'm here, shhhhh. . . ." He cupped his hands over my own.

A trickle of liquid seeped between our entwined fingers, and I knew my eardrums were bleeding.

As the sun rose higher, the glow of twinkling stars moved around me. It was a sight I'd seen before. But, this time, the flashes of ice crystals came from my skin as well as his. His light wrapped itself around mine, and a sudden explosion of energy filled me. As the crystals from his skin and my own merged, our connection rekindled.

He held me for what felt like an eternity, and I closed my eyes, allowing the sun's rays to sink into my new skin. Finally, the noises dulled into a low hum, but I still didn't feel right; I was dizzy.

He helped me to my feet, and I hesitated, stumbling as I broke away from him. I sensed him following me, but I held my hand in the air, signaling for him to stay back. I stood, precariously balancing my weight, barefoot in the snow. I breathed in and out, forming a rhythm, taking my time. He waited patiently.

"I may not remember you, but I never forgot you," I whispered. "One shared light, split into two . . ."

As though I was staring through a kaleidoscope, memories, thoughts, feelings all took new shape, each becoming more prominent than the last as it moved into focus.

"Styclar-Plena," I said. "The third dimension. Earth. Home—choice. I had a choice. . . ."

The blur that filled the space in between the luminous charms brought with it a different type of memory: a scar, reimprinting itself, damaging me again.

Michael—a Second Generation Vampire, killed by his Gualtiero (Pureblood Master), Eligio—when his plan to hand me over to the Purebloods backfired on him.

Ethan—the fiancé from my first life, who had fled after accidentally killing me only to be changed by a Pureblood Vampire. After seeing me alive, over a hundred and fifty years from when he thought he had ended my life, he chased me down and ultimately met his demise in his attempt to seek revenge.

Frederic—the first Second Generation Vampire I could recall knowing. Whom I had foolishly befriended, and who had dragged me through the woods with a sharpened hook lodged in my back, and whom the girl in shadow—me—had then mercilessly killed.

Bradley—the not so gentlemanly gentleman in the club in Limoux. He had also fallen victim to my extreme dark side—to the girl in shadow. And just like the others who had crossed me, Bradley was no longer alive to tell the tale.

And now she was gone; the girl in shadow was ended. I had died, but I was back. He led me home—his face, the thought of him, and the thought of me.

I bowed my head and my bangs shielded my eyes. I turned slowly toward him. His dimples dipped at the sides of his cheeks as he frowned. His pupils expanded. He was anxious to hear what I was about to say.

"Gabriel." A small smile crept across my lips before I added, "My Gabriel. You waited for me."

The knots in his body loosened. He murmured, "I knew to wait for you this time."

Stepping cautiously toward me, he tilted my chin with his index finger. He swept my bangs away, clearing my vision, and then cupped my cheek with his palm. He looked me square, exploring my eyes. But he looked away—fast. Too fast.

I had fought my way back, and yet with that one silent glance, I knew a great chasm was already forming between us. What I didn't know then was that it wasn't the appearance of my new sapphire eyes flecked with black spots that had caused Gabriel to look away, but instead, it was his fleeting thought of what lay behind them.

I sighed heavily and began to pace through the clearing, oozing a false sense of confidence, as though I knew where I was going when really I knew nothing. But I was afraid that the longer I stood there the greater the unspoken divide between us would become.

He raced to my side and took my hand with his own. "Do you remember . . . everything?" he asked tentatively.

"I remember . . . I remember the last six years. I remember the memories and the dreams I have had for the same time. I can't recall anything before. And I know the things she did. The girl in shadow." I gulped. "Me."

"She was an extreme darkness, Lai; she's gone now. You accepted both sides of yourself before your heart stopped. It's probably why you haven't forgotten."

As we moved through the snow underfoot, the trees' bare branches seemed to bow, as though they pitied me.

"I'm different. Again, I'm different." I sighed and let my hand drift away from Gabriel's.

"No. It's just now, for the first time in your existence, you know where you come from. You know what you were born out of and into. You're you. What gifts you have, how they work on this plane, is something we will find out together."

I wasn't sure how right he was about that. I didn't feel human anymore. I was born into human skin, having been birthed here on Earth. And when I died at seventeen nearly two centuries ago, I awoke having inherited my immortal lineage.

"I smelled blood, and fangs broke through my gums, Gabriel." I paused to allow the weight of that fact to sink beneath Gabriel's sea-of-glass exterior. "I'm light and dark; I know it to be true now. And I don't even really know what that means for me yet. But Azrael said I could exist and keep my form in any of the three dimensions. So the Arch Angels will come from the first dimension, and the Pure-bloods will come from the third to find me. They will all seek me out, here in the second."

He stopped dead in his tracks; at last something I'd said had caused a reaction.

"Yes," he said, "they will. If they find out you are alive, they will hunt you down, and they won't stop until they have you. So, we cut all ties and we leave together. We'll hide. You have been through enough. It ends here." Gabriel's jaw locked and his eyes widened with conviction.

No longer softening the blow for my benefit, he seemed to have hardened. Either that or he was taking my choices away from me, perhaps for my own good. I wasn't sure.

We hadn't walked for long when a château fort came into view. It stood alone, with a brewing fog clouding its base.

I looked at Gabriel with raised eyebrows. "*This* is where you've been staying?"

Gabriel seemed to have more money than sense, and I made a mental note to ask him where his wealth came from.

"It's very small. I couldn't take you back to the barn. Han—" He stopped.

Hanora. The very suggestion of her name made my toes curl

instantly. Sadly, I hadn't forgotten her. In fact, there were a few things concerning that particular Vampire that I would have gladly left behind.

"It wasn't safe," he finished.

Standing now only meters away from the entrance, I rocked back on the heels of my feet dubiously. Gabriel halted and reached for my hand. As he slipped his fingers between mine, I knew he could sense my unease.

I didn't know how long I had been trapped between life and death, but he hadn't seemed to change. His broad shoulders and strong arms made me feel safe. He was an unbreakable wall, protecting me, and I knew he'd meet his end long before he'd let anyone pry me from him again. And God, he was gorgeous.

"I love you, Lailah."

Those words surprised me.

"I. Love. You," he repeated firmly. "I should have said it sooner," he continued. "I didn't think I had to, because I felt it. I have always felt it, and so I thought you knew it. Every day we have been together, I *should* have said it."

Right now, I had no inclination to debate the specifics of the love he was proclaiming for someone whose eyes he had struggled to meet only minutes ago or to question what that meant for us now. Instead, I smiled, though I was sure that the sadness at the edge of my lips was obvious enough for him to read. Having faced the end—the real end—and come through the other side, I was suddenly so tired. I was done with the complications of Pureblood Vampires, Arch Angels, and being a pawn in a battle between the two. I wanted it all to stop. I wanted my life back.

I had loved Gabriel in my first life, and though I had wandered this world for nearly two centuries without him, he had always been with me, buried in my memories and in my heart. I loved him still.

I tightened my grip around his hand and said, "And I, you. I'll do what you say; I will go wherever you want to take me, for as long as you will have me."

It was true. I'd woken from my cocoon a Hedylidae, not a Morpho butterfly like him. But if he felt for me even a fraction of what I felt for him, I would flap my confused wings as hard as I could and follow him to the ends of any and every world, without question.

I immediately felt a sense of angst swelling within him. As he tilted his head, his blond curls fell slightly into his vision, stopping me from being able to read the message his eyes were writing.

Finally he said, "Really?"

"Really," I said. I had no idea why he seemed so surprised.

Gabriel let go of my hand and began rolling his fingertips in circles within his palms. "What about Jonah?"

I scratched the tops of my arms pensively before I replied, "Sorry—who?"

TWO

GABRIEL STARED AT ME as though I had lost my mind. Granted, up until this point, losing my mind was a fairly normal occurrence for me. But unlike all the other times I had awoken, this time, I was aware of everything that had come before and the complicated worlds that claimed me.

There was Styclar-Plena: the first dimension. A world that existed in light, born from a crystal that resided at its center. The day the crystal started to lose its light, the darkness began to fall on the Arch Angels and the other inhabitants that had been created directly from the light of the crystal. Their world began to die.

But fortunately for them, there was also the second dimension: Earth. Seeking a way to fuel the crystal and bring light back to Styclar-Plena, Orifiel, the leader of the Arch Angels, passed through a rift to Earth. Upon witnessing a bright white energy leaving the body of a human in death, Orifiel found the solution to his problem. He collected the clean, light souls of mortals, and transported them back to Styclar-Plena to refuel the crystal.

With so many Arch Angels dying because of the extended period of darkness in Styclar-Plena, Orifiel could not wait for the crystal to organically create more of his kind. He began mating the Arch Angels—the same way human beings on Earth repopulated their world—creating Angel Descendants. The Descendants were tasked with moving the light human souls across the planes to keep the crystal fueled, preventing future bouts of darkness. The first of these new Angel Descendants were created as independent beings with no connection to one another. However, as these Angels traveled to Earth, their connection to the light of Styclar-Plena began to dull and, feeling disillusioned, many chose to stay in the second dimension. They became known as fallen Angels.

To give the Angels a reason to return to Styclar-Plena, Orifiel paired the Descendants through an exchange of light—of love. When two Angel mothers were pregnant with their Angel babies, a ceremony would be held. Harnessing the light from the crystal, it touched both unborn Angel children in their mothers' wombs, connecting them to one another forever. One light, split into two. It no longer mattered how often or how long the Angel Descendants were parted from Styclar-Plena, as long as they had their Pair, they had no reason to fall.

And finally, there was the third dimension: the opposite of the first—a world existing in darkness, from which the Pureblood Vampires emerged.

The Pureblood Vampires who came through the rifts to Earth fed from the dark souls of mortals and used their venom to change humans who possessed a light soul into Second Generation Vampires. This was how they built their armies.

And, there was me.

I was created as an Angel Descendant, paired with Gabriel by Orifiel through the exchange of light before I was even born. But still in my mother's womb, I was infected with Vampire venom by Zherneboh—the deadliest of all the Purebloods.

My Angel mother had given birth to me here, on Earth, and I was born into human skin. The fact that I was Gabriel's Angel Pair was kept from him by Orifiel. In 1839, Orifiel tasked Gabriel to find and kill me. But Gabriel did something that was forbidden: He fell in love with me despite thinking I was a mortal. He refused to kill me and instead protected me.

But he was too late.

The same year, when I was seventeen years old, Ethan, my child-hood friend turned fiancé, discovered that I was about to run away with Gabriel and, during a struggle where he had pleaded for me not to leave, had accidentally killed me. Gabriel found me lifeless, and so he left, thinking that the Arch Angels had discovered his plan to protect me and had sent another Angel to do what he would not. He then began a search for my lost soul.

Though I had died, I came back to life. I woke up, inheriting my immortal lineage.

And yet when I awoke, it was without the knowledge of all of this. And so I spent nearly two hundred years living, dying, and re-awakening, not knowing what or who I really was. All I knew was that I didn't age and that if I died, I would be resurrected.

But in the past few weeks, Gabriel and I had found each other again. I was traveling with him, now a rogue Angel Descendant, and the Second Generation Vampires whom he'd helped free from their ties to their Pureblood creators. Vampires who, despite their darkness, had found their lights once more. We were on the run from both the Arch Angels and the Purebloods, who each sought me out.

It was through my Angel father, Azrael, that we learned the truth of my heritage. Gabriel had found Azrael with help from a wise and old fallen Angel, Malachi. It had been far from the family reunion one dreams of, however. Azrael had tricked my friend the Vampire Ruadhan into plunging a sword through my chest when the girl in shadow—an extreme darkness hiding deep within me—had morphed through my skin to appear in the presence of Zherneboh.

Azrael had been working on behalf of the Arch Angels and had struck a deal that he could return to Styclar-Plena upon my true and final death. He fled the mountain as I lay in the snow dying, and Ruadhan made chase.

My father had believed that once I knew what I was—both light and dark—I would not be able to accept it, that I would meet my final end. This was what the Arch Angels wanted because they knew, as did the Purebloods, that I was the only being that could keep my form in all three dimensions. If my Angel and Vampire abilities manifested, I could pass through rifts into any dimension and potentially end their worlds.

Zherneboh hoped to use me as the ultimate weapon in a war he was waiting for me to wage against Styclar-Plena. He wanted me alive, and Orifiel wanted me dead.

But I had chosen to return to Earth, to live.

Jonah. I turned back to Gabriel, unable to recall the name. "Am I missing something?" I asked.

Gabriel straightened and without reluctance replied, "No. Nothing."

"Okay—"

"Lailah, I'm going inside to get your things. Then we're leaving. I want you to stay here. I'll ask Brooke to come and wait with you." He paused. "You remember Brooke?"

"I told you—I remember everything. That includes Brooke and her chip."

"Her chip?" His eyebrows arched.

"The one she wears on her shoulder." Something nagged at me: Brooke always seemed angry with me, but right now, I couldn't put my finger on why.

"Brooke!" Gabriel called.

A whip of chilly air skimmed my cheek as she appeared from nowhere.

"What's up?" she said, removing her sunglasses and placing them on top of her head. She did a double take when she saw me standing beside Gabriel. "Cessie?"

"Actually, my name is Lailah." My body shriveled a little as I recalled the charade Gabriel and I had kept up over my name. Not to mention the tiny detail about me being immortal.

Brooke's eyes flicked to Gabriel, and he nodded encouragingly at her.

"Yeah, right, Lailah," Brooke said. "So . . . how you been?" She pushed back her flaming red hair awkwardly.

"Well, dead," I said.

Brooke bobbed her head like one of those toy dogs you sometimes see in the back of a car. "Hmmm, sucks to be you, I guess."

"Sometimes."

"I need to collect Lailah's things," Gabriel said. "Then we're leaving. You, too, Brooke, like we discussed."

"Yes!" she cried. "Back to the sun, sea, and sand of the OC."

"Good. I will be two minutes, not a second longer. Don't move, okay?" Gabriel's instructions were directed at Brooke, and she rolled her eyes.

Before Gabriel left, he offered me a sumptuous smile, which put me at ease.

"So, we're going to the States?" I asked.

"No, you're going with Gabriel to England. I'm going back to the US. Seems like this is where we say au revoir."

I scratched my head; I wasn't comfortable enough around Brooke to ask too many questions. The more I tried to place where that sense came from, the more difficult it became. I cleared my mind, and then, from nowhere, it hit me.

She was upset with me over a guy. No. Not a guy. A Vampire.

"Shame we don't have more time together," she said. "You could do with my help running some peroxide through that hair of yours—you look like a badger. I suggest you find some time to visit a salon; slices went out in the nineties, along with the Spice Girls." She snorted.

I scowled at her. I hadn't given much thought to my appearance since I had woken. Only now with Brooke's sarcasm punching at me did I stop to think about it. I grabbed my long curls and glanced at the ends. They were jet black, with stripes of white blond seared through.

The way I looked had never changed before. What else had morphed into something different? I needed a mirror, and I needed one *now*.

I didn't have to search far—there was a large, rectangular, bronze-paned mirror hanging in the entranceway to the château fort.

I sped along the marble floor and clung to the edges of a small table that stood beneath the mirror, simply to stop myself from hurtling straight past.

My body was hardly my own, a mere thought became an action, and one I could barely control. I had awoken having accepted all that I was, and now I had the abilities of Angels and Vampires. But I was in new skin, and though it was disconcerting, maybe it just needed wearing in.

I stretched out, arching my back, and parted my legs to keep myself balanced. I mustered my courage. Gripping the edges of the small table, I dared myself to look up.

I stifled a breath. I could see now why Gabriel hadn't held my gaze when he had searched my eyes. Their once sapphire color was now overwhelmed with flecks of black. It was as though my eyes had become liquid oxygen and someone had ground a piece of coal and sprinkled in the debris before the substance had finally reached its freezing point and solidified into this state. If your eyes are supposed to be windows into your soul, I feared what color mine had now taken.

My hair was different, and I knew without even trying that all the bleach in the world wouldn't remove the darkness. I was grateful that at least my face, though paler than before, was unchanged. My crystal gem, hanging low on a chain, glinted. I placed my palm over the top, thankful that this, the source of comfort to me for as long as I could remember, was still with me. Then I noticed the trace of a new scar running up from the V-neck of my dress across my chest. As I explored it, something in the reflection of the mirror caught my attention.

It was Ruadhan, and he was extending his arm out as he approached me from behind. Only my mind tumbled, playing tricks on me. It was as though I were back on the mountaintop and I couldn't tell if it was his hand reaching for me or if it was a sword. I reeled around, half-expecting a blade to have broken through my bones.

The memory of Ruadhan's face flashed across my vision, pausing on the expression he had worn as he gaped at me, confused and horrified. His voice calling my false name swirled around my head.

I tripped, trying to find my balance as I attempted to move away from him. "No!" I shrieked, my heart pounding.

"It's okay, sweetheart." He surged forward and my eyes—wide with dread—begged him to stay back.

I glanced at my chest, and the memory of that weapon flickered in and out. I backed away and the table crumbled under my weight, collapsing in chunks behind me. It didn't stop my continuing slide across the marble floor and so I crashed right into the mirror, which shattered against my back. I took half the shards with me and the rest poured down as I sank to the floor, pinned in place by fear.

I curled into a ball, wrapping my arms around my knees, and I screamed an ungodly sound—so loud that I thought my lungs might burst.

Everything around me had spiraled, and the only safety I could find was welding my eyes tightly shut. I knew I was hallucinating; Ruadhan was extending his hand, not a sword. I was not on the mountaintop; I was safe. I tried to calm myself down.

I blanked all thought from my mind, and then Gabriel was singing to me. The sweetness of his voice resounded from somewhere locked away.

My gentle harp, once more I waken
The sweetness of thy slumb'ring strain

My eyes welled up, and I opened them to find Gabriel knelt over me. He tilted his head, his lips forming a tight line, but the hum of a song he once sang played in my mind. I was sure he heard it, too.

"*In tears our last farewell was taken, and now in tears we meet again*," I sang slowly to him.

Gabriel was staring, trying to rediscover that innocent, unspoiled girl whom he had met nearly two hundred years ago, straining to see beyond the damaged and broken being that sat before him now.

I let his feelings wash over me, and I was hit with a sense of great loss—of regret. But he didn't let his sadness win for long. He placed his palms to my cheeks and brought his forehead to mine. He was so close I could taste him, like lemon and lime. It might have been winter outside, but Gabriel was my very own summertime.

Brushing the tip of his nose against mine, he inhaled a deep breath and then placed the softest of kisses on my top lip. It was so gentle that I shouldn't have felt it, but it was as though there was an upsurge of ecstasy bursting inside me. As he withdrew, the rapture subsided, and I was left feeling empty.

I couldn't keep it together; I couldn't pretend that everything was okay, as though death's grasp hadn't left a mark on my wrist as it had pulled me far away from him, from everything.

I was nowhere. I was nothing. I was so lost.

I was suffocating.

"Lailah. Take a deep breath." Gabriel tried to gain my attention.

I couldn't reply. My throat was tight and sore.

What's wrong? Tell me what's wrong. He projected his thoughts to me.

As I struggled to focus, I sensed that there were now other bodies in the room. I thought they were watching me, as muffled noises bounced off the walls of the entranceway.

Then, clear as crystal: "Cessie."

His voice.

My vision sharpened, and I looked past Gabriel's shoulder to where *he* stood. My eyes zeroed in on two pinpricks on the side of his neck where the remnants of drying blood clotted on his skin.

Suddenly it was as though I was sucking in every last bit of air from the room. Every muscle became taut, and my gums ached as once again my sharp canines cracked. The room became a neutral backdrop with nothing else in it—only him. A black smudge against a blank canvas. Tall, with messy dark hair and glowing hazel eyes.

He was a Vampire. And I was going to kill him.

I launched myself toward him, but the Vampire didn't move. I hurtled into his body, and he slammed to the ground beneath my weight. I hadn't meant to remodel the marble with a Vampire-shaped hole. The scent of cinnamon was too tempting, and I was overcome with a sense of hunger.

I had no regard for who he was or why he was here. All I knew was that, for whatever reason, I wanted to feast on his blood and then rip him apart.

I straddled the Vampire, my mouth an inch from the throbbing vein in his throat, when Gabriel's arms locked under mine, and he pulled me away. Gabriel turned me into his chest and made soothing sounds in my ear, and as I relaxed, the fury began to subside.

"That's not who you are, Lailah," Gabriel said.

The room moved around me, like an earthquake only I could feel. When my vision stopped blurring and my fangs receded, I withdrew from Gabriel and surveyed what I'd done.

Shattered glass and chunks of wood littered the hallway. The front door squeaked, swinging back and forth, attached to the only hinge I had left intact. Outside, snow had begun to fall, beating down and becoming lost in the thick fog spilling into the entranceway. Ruadhan stood still, shocked, and Brooke helped the Vampire dislodge himself from the caved-in floor.

I knew what I was now.

I not only knew what I was, but I also accepted that I existed as a hybrid of Angel and Vampire in an immortal body. The Purebloods, the Arch Angels—both sides wanted me because I was supposedly the most dangerous threat to both.

The Vampire I had nearly just ended arched an eyebrow in response to Gabriel's comment as he dusted himself off.

"You need to leave." I snarled.

Though his broken skin had healed, the scent of his blood still lingered all around me, and I didn't know if I would be able to prevent myself from attacking him again. I wasn't sure why he evoked such a reaction. Brooke, Ruadhan—they were both Vampires, but I didn't want to hurt them. But then, they hadn't spilled their blood around me, either.

"What's wrong with you?" the Vampire said. "It's me, Cess—"

"Lailah. My name is *Lailah*," I said sharply. It took every last bit of my self-control to remain calm. I wanted to obey my urge. I wanted to kill him.

I ran my tongue over my gums, checking that my fangs weren't about to reappear. A frustrated tear ran down my cheek, and the Vampire misinterpreted it as some sort of sadness.

"Lailah," he said. "It's me."

Bravely, or stupidly, he leaned down and stood nose to nose with me. Licking his thumb, he grazed my cheek as he wiped away my bloodied tear. He took a sharp intake of breath as my scent hit him. Microfibers of red wove through the fabric of his hazel eyes, and I was amazed at the detail I could see now with these heightened senses.

"Gabriel . . ." I gritted my teeth.

Responding immediately, Gabriel hooked his arm under the Vampire's, and with help from Ruadhan, he led him backward down the hallway. The Vampire didn't resist them, but all the while his gaze never left mine.

The Vampire's escorts stopped when they reached the front door, and Gabriel said something quietly to him. I was about to walk away, when the Vampire shouted, "I'm coming back for you."

A sense of déjà vu crept up my neck. He saw the flash of recognition with the widening of my eyes and, even though Gabriel was talking in his ear, his stare—steadfast—remained fixed on me.

My shoulders slumped as I became lost, searching for an answer.

The left side of his lip curved up, and he winked.

Then, just like that, he was gone.

THREE

"GREAT, NOW THAT YOU'VE finished trying to end Jonah, I think we'd better go," Brooke said, wiping her mouth with the back of her arm. I had only a moment to realize it was the Vampire's drying blood that was smeared around her lips before the name she offered grabbed my attention.

Jonah.

I tried to put his face and his name together, and instantly my skin began to simmer, and my mind filled with white noise.

Brooke was already at the doorway, searching outside.

"Brooke—" I said at the same moment as Gabriel said, "Time to go."

Brooke became a blur, departing before I could question her.

I turned to Gabriel, seeking an explanation from him instead. "That Vampire's name is *Jonah*?"

Gabriel flinched when Jonah's name left my lips, and he didn't offer me any confirmation.

"You said his name, outside—"

Gabriel cut me off. "It doesn't matter right now. *He* doesn't matter right now. We need to go. Neither the Purebloods nor the Arch Angels know you're alive, but it might not stay that way if Hanora finds me, finds *you*, here. I need to deal with her, alone." He paused. "She betrayed us once; I don't trust her not to do so a second time."

I understood his urgency for us to depart then. Hanora was Gabriel's oldest companion; he had considered her a friend. Hanora's feelings, however, ran far deeper but were unreciprocated. She assumed Gabriel couldn't be with her romantically because her soul was dark. When Azrael announced that I was harboring some form of Vampire lineage, in a jealous rage, Hanora had told the Purebloods where I was; she must have fled shortly afterward.

I balanced my weight from one foot to the other, caught in my own confusion. I remembered that happening as clearly as everything else, so why could I not recall Jonah?

Gabriel placed his hands over my bare arms; his light swept over me and I faltered.

"Please, Lai. We need to leave," he said.

Gabriel had always tried to protect me. Calmed by his warmth, I didn't think on it any further and simply said, "Okay."

Gabriel collected my backpack from the bottom of the stairs. I followed him quickly, and then he, Ruadhan, and I piled into a rented truck and headed for the airport. There was no sign of Brooke or Jonah; we were all leaving in very different directions and going on very different journeys.

I sat in the back, and Gabriel passed me my backpack from the front seat.

"I'm sorry I startled you," Ruadhan said softly, as Gabriel reversed off the grassy verge.

I coughed uncomfortably. "Sorry. I just—I don't know. I panicked. That's all."

Ruadhan didn't know it was you. On the mountain, Azrael tricked him. . . . Gabriel's words reached me by thought.

I know, I replied.

The truck struggled in the snow, but once on an actual road, it glided along the concrete with ease and Gabriel wasted no time obliterating the speed limit.

"Why are we going back to England?" I asked.

"I have some business I have to tie up, back in London," Gabriel said.

I raised my eyebrows. "I'm coming with you."

"No, it's too dangerous."

"You said, you and me, on the run, hiding—just us. I don't understand—you're leaving me already?"

Gabriel's hands clenched tightly around the steering wheel and I felt his anxiety.

"There are some things I must, *must* do, and I have to do them alone. That's why Ruadhan's joining us." Gabriel took his eyes off the road, briefly, to look at his friend sitting in the passenger seat. "I won't be gone more than a day, and he will keep you safe. Then you and I will leave together."

Ruadhan didn't acknowledge Gabriel; he was hunched forward, constantly checking the mirrors, clearly back on daddy duty.

I need you to trust me and I need you to do as I ask, and then we will be together.

I was already regretting how easily I had agreed to follow Gabriel's lead without question. Now was not the time to be petulant, so instead I eyed the backpack next to me. I rummaged around inside and found some of my clothes and my passport.

"I need to change. My toes are freezing." My bare feet were purple-red with cold; I wasn't dressed for winter or a plane.

"Go ahead. Ruadhan will avert his eyes," Gabriel said.

I pulled out a pair of light-blue skinny jeans, a sleeveless shirt, and a cream-colored cardigan. Toward the bottom of the bag, I found a pair of wool-lined ankle boots and a pair of thick socks.

I slid the jeans on under the dress I was wearing, and then slowly lifted it over my head. I clutched my chest as I tried to wriggle into the shirt.

I flicked my eyes up as I struggled, meeting Gabriel's in the rear-view mirror. He looked away and I felt my cheeks flush.

I loved Gabriel; I felt it in every part of my being, and I wondered if our relationship had ever made it to the ultimate level of intimacy. No. He was too much of a gentleman for anything to have happened. As I thought about Gabriel, to my surprise, my skin started to glow.

What are you thinking about? Gabriel asked me privately.
You.

The snow outside the window was falling thick and heavy, blanketing the landscape in a layer of pure white, as though it were wrapping up the evidence of recent events and covering our tracks as we left.

I was more than happy to leave this place. I wanted a fresh start, to leave my demons behind me—literally.

AFTER AN UNEVENTFUL PLANE journey and yet another long drive, I was relieved when Gabriel finally pulled the rented car to the curb and turned the engine off.

"Lailah, we're here," Gabriel said.

"Where's here, exactly?" I asked, unbuckling my seat belt. I ran the back of my cardigan sleeve over the condensation on the window, attempting to clear it. Splatters of rain pelted down, leaving mini droplets against the outside of the glass.

"Henley-on-Thames. About half an hour or so from the Hedgerley house."

"Little close, no?" I asked.

"Look out the rear window, Lai." Gabriel gestured behind me, where tall streetlamps lit the edges of a riverbank. "That's the Thames."

"Right. And that's helpful?"

"Water, sweetheart," Ruadhan said. "Makes it difficult for rifts to open near it."

I unbuckled the nylon belt and reached for my backpack. "Don't recall that stopping Zherneboh on the mountain; there was a lake right there."

Gabriel placed his hand on the door handle. "It makes it difficult, not impossible. Takes a lot longer to open a rift near water. That lake gave us time. Enough time to reach you. The Purebloods don't know you're alive, and that's the way it needs to stay. We're leaving tomorrow night. Regardless, now that we know they are able to command the rifts, the river makes me happier."

I looked at Ruadhan. "And where will you go?"

He turned in the passenger seat to face me. "Not sure yet, love, but it's nothing for you to concern yourself with." He smiled and his bushy eyebrows lifted.

Gabriel stepped out of the car and then opened the backdoor for me. I followed them to the entrance of a B&B. Rushing in from the rain, we were greeted by a friendly woman hovering by the front desk.

"Two rooms, please," Gabriel said.

"Well, of course! How long will you be staying?" The woman reached for the pen that was pushed through the whitening bun on the back of her head.

"Tonight, and all day tomorrow."

"Well, checkout time is one p.m., so if you want the rooms for the afternoon, you'll need to book for two nights." She smiled, flipping open a large, rectangular leather book and scanning the page.

"That's fine," he replied. Rustling around in his pocket, Gabriel produced a heap of cash and handed over more than I thought he probably needed to.

"Fantastic. Ah, now we have only one room available. There's a beer festival going on not far from here, so we're pretty full. But the two beds are both queen-size, and you have your own bathroom."

"It will do; we're not staying long," Gabriel said.

Taking some fresh towels off a shelf behind her, she handed them to Ruadhan, along with just one key. "Follow me."

Before she walked us up the winding staircase, she pointed out the dining room, a living area, and a ground-floor toilet. I trailed behind as we climbed three flights of stairs—the old floorboards squeaking underfoot—to the top of the Edwardian house. Walking past several doors, we finally arrived at Room 16.

After she'd opened the door for us, she left. As Ruadhan hit the light switch, the bulb flickered, shedding little light on the room. But with these new abilities, I could see everything clearly.

The room was decorated with murky green carpets and floral bed linen, coupled with mismatched curtains. There were two queen-size beds, as promised; an old plastic kettle; some milk on a small table; and a couple of newspapers, thrown messily over the end of one of the beds.

I eyed the door to the shower. Gabriel put his hand to the small of my back and said, "Feel free. I'll put the kettle on for you in the meantime."

Ruadhan handed me a towel from on top of the pile.

"I won't be long," I said.

The door wouldn't shut properly, having warped long ago, so I wedged it closed the best I could. I undressed, checked the water, and then stepped into the shower cubicle.

I took a moment to place my palm over my crystal before turning the knob to increase the heat.

As the water drenched my skin, I scrubbed hard, with a desperate need to wash away the stale odor of death. I recalled the existence I'd had before my life was thrown into chaos. I flitted from job to job, town to town, never putting down roots. I was so alone, except for the visions of Gabriel. He was the only person who had brought me any real happiness, even if it had been in a life gone by.

And Gabriel's words about choice ultimately had helped to bring me back from what should have been my final end. I realized that what I wanted now was no different from what I had sought before I'd found Gabriel again. To *live*, not just exist, and to not be alone. And just like before, I was placing my hope of finding happiness in him.

A knock on the door was followed by Ruadhan's booming voice. "Lailah, love, are you okay in there?"

"Yeah. I'm getting out now," I replied.

I turned off the shower, and as I wrapped the towel around myself, I looked at the new scar running across my chest. Yet another mark acting as a reminder, a warning, and a truth. My scars would never fade away, and I feared that just like them, neither would my knowledge of what was really going on in the world. But if I wanted to be happy, I had to look forward now, not back.

I collected my clothes from the floor and wriggled the door free. When I stepped back into the room, Gabriel had a cup of tea waiting for me, along with a killer smile.

"Thanks," I whispered.

Throwing the clothes to the end of a bed, I sipped the tea, but it didn't warm my insides as it would have once done. Drinking seemed like a pointless exercise, and so I set the cup down. "I don't think I need food and water like I used to."

"Perhaps now the sun will fuel you, as it does me," Gabriel said. The hope in his voice was unmistakable.

Ruadhan, perched on the end of the bed nearest the door, lowered his newspaper. "She has the abilities of both Angels and Vampires, Gabriel. So, perhaps she will need to feed as we do."

Gabriel's body stiffened.

I walked to the bed and sat staring out at the cloak of darkness behind the window, considering what Ruadhan had said. It was not the thought of drinking blood that upset me most; it was Gabriel's reaction to it.

Gabriel joined me, the mattress dipping as his weight met it. "Lailah, it's okay." He paused, sensing my unease. "What you are doesn't define *who* you are; that's still your choice." Gabriel nudged me into his body. My brow dipped. I could refrain from using my Vampire abilities if I wanted to, but earlier today my fangs had cracked and I'd been overcome with fury. That had not been my choice.

As his breath skimmed my neck, I relaxed. "Can you sleep?" I asked.

"I don't have to, but I can. You can, too, if you want. In fact, why don't you curl up now and get some rest? In the morning, I will take you to meet with the sunrise, and if it fuels you the way it does me, then we have nothing to worry about." His pitch rose, and once again I detected hope.

While Gabriel was prepared to acknowledge the darkness within me, he was also keen to tamp that part down. And in a way, he was trying to make me feel better. He assumed I wanted to meet his sunrise. It was what he wanted. But what would happen to us if it wasn't the choice I wanted to make after all?

I fingered the clothes at the end of the bed, and without me having to ask, Gabriel got up, allowing me space to change into my sleeveless shirt and panties. Pulling back the duvet, I nestled myself within its warmth. I watched Gabriel quizzically as he set out for the other bed.

"You'd rather share with Ruadhan tonight?" I asked.

Ruadhan—who was once again reading the newspaper but clearly eavesdropping—laughed jovially, and Gabriel turned back to face me.

"Ruadhan will be going out on patrol actually, so I was just going to take this bed."

"Speaking of which," Ruadhan said, standing to attention, "I better get on duty. I'll be back before sunrise." He slammed the door closed as he left, leaving me alone with my Angel.

Gabriel switched on the lamp that was on the bedside table before turning off the main light switch. The glow was dull at best, but Gabriel's bright eyes glinted and glimmered. He sat next to me and stroked my cheek with the back of his fingers. I didn't say anything; I couldn't. I was too entranced by his eyes as they reached into my soul, spreading his light around my whole being. The lamp behind him created a halo-type effect around his face. How could someone be so divine? I was his Pair; we were two halves of one whole. But he was totally unspoiled, and I was, well, entirely inadequate. By his side, my defects were so much plainer to see.

"What are you thinking about?" he asked.

"You. Me. Us . . ." Gabriel and I might be able to communicate through thought, but we couldn't read each other's minds, which was sometimes a blessing. Although, if we were both open to it, we could show each other what we were seeing or recalling. We could also block each other.

"Specifically?" he probed.

"I'm not good enough for you," I murmured.

"Never think that." He frowned and traced his fingertip down my neck. "You are my everything. Period." Gabriel hesitated and then grinned cheekily. "Room for one more?"

I couldn't help but return the smile. When I was with him, my worries about the world—all the big stuff—just melted away.

Gabriel removed his sweater to reveal a plain white T-shirt. Masterfully, he removed his shoes and socks, using only his toes to wriggle out of them. My insides knotted as I waited to see if he would take off his khaki trousers, and I think he considered it but left them on and hopped in under the duvet next to me.

I was lying on my back, and he put his sturdy arm behind me as he positioned himself on his side. He began tickling my bare arms, and every nerve ending in my body electrified. I grew nervous, anticipating what he might do next. He ran his hand down past my belly button and pushed up the hem of my shirt. Finally, he placed his palm flat on my tummy, pressing his skin to mine.

A current of excitement whizzed through me and something deep down coiled in expectation. I lunged a little too eagerly toward him and he drew back, leaving a gap between his lips and my own.

"Gabriel," I murmured.

He tilted his head from side to side, as though he was deep in thought, and finally lowered himself so that there was virtually no space between us. But instead of kissing me, he brought the tip of his nose to mine and gently grazed my skin. His long lashes brushed my cheek as he moved just below my earlobe, where he placed the lightest of kisses, and trailed down to my collarbone. Moving his hand up my shirt, my whole body rippled with excitement as he grazed my breast, but he surprised me by placing his hand on my scar.

He stayed entirely still for an age when suddenly, hand still across my heart, his lips found mine. His kiss was ferocious as he crushed his lips hard against mine. I replied with the same need, shaping my mouth around his. Gabriel's fingernails grazed the scar, and my eyes fluttered as he stopped.

He bit his bottom lip.

"It's okay; it's just a mark," I said, embarrassed.

He exhaled heavily. "It's not that."

I sat up and he moved away from me.

Why had he stopped kissing me? I stumbled quickly upon the obvious. "Do I feel different now?" I hoped that wasn't what it was.

"No, Lai. No." He sighed and leaned in, gracing me with a sweet peck. "I want to be with you, but I need you to want the same and to decide that for yourself."

I had no idea what he was talking about. Of course, I wanted him. He was all I wanted. I shook my head. "I don't understand what you mean. I do want you."

He cleared the disobedient strands of my bangs that had fallen down in front of my eyes. Placing his hand back over my scar, he pressed down. "Your heart. I need all of your heart, and before you . . . fell . . . I'm quite certain it was torn in two."

His hand was spread wide across my chest, and I placed both of mine on top of his.

"It's all yours. Truly."

His body tensed, the muscles flexing in his shoulders. He started to say something, but then stopped abruptly. "You need to rest. We're up at sunrise. We can talk more about this when we're gone from here, for good."

Knowing better than ever that tomorrow might never come, I tried again. "Gabriel, please. It's only ever been you."

I reached for him, but he snatched my wrist, and his face hardened in a way I had never seen before. He caught himself quickly and brought my hand closer, pressing my palm to his cheek.

His action unnerved me. I didn't know what to say and rolled onto my side. After a few minutes, he snuggled up behind me, moving his strong arm under my waist.

His breath tickled my neck. "I love you, Lai."

"And I love you," I whispered.

I was warmed all the way through as he glowed behind me. I closed my eyes tight and fell into a light sleep.

As my mind emptied of conscious thought, the haze was like a dream as an image appeared, welcoming me to watch.

There I was with Gabriel, under that old oak tree I had seen in my visions—my memories—before. The crisp autumn leaves lifted, swirling with the wind. Gabriel lay on the grass, his head resting in his hand, peering up at me as his elbow dug into the ground. I noticed the chessboard past his feet, the pieces scattered. And I was cross-legged on the grass with a small chromatic, willow harp resting between my legs. I watched as I plucked the strings. I hadn't known I had once been able to play such an instrument.

Yet even then, while peace was singing, her halcyon song o'er land and sea.

Gabriel's words were almost whispered as he sang the song that had belonged to him and me some time ago—in some distant place and time.

Gabriel's face was bright, and his eyes beamed as if he were singing the song through them instead of his lips. Although Gabriel did not age, somehow he looked younger then.

As the wind dropped, the leaves gently scattered. As they did, I realized I could hear everything—from the sound of his voice to the ethereal notes cascading from the harp. The previous memories and visions of my past lives had always revealed themselves to me as though they were in mute. And the scene around me was so very vibrant. It had appeared in pastel shades before, and yet now it was as though the entire memory was in high definition.

Gabriel sat up, smoothing away the long, golden curls that had fallen in front of my eyes; he continued to sing, and then I watched my past self join in.

Though joy and hope to others bringing, she only brought new tears to thee.

We sang in unison, and I marveled at my voice. It was lighter, more delicate than it was now.

But then something odd happened. It was as though I was watching a movie and the DVD had scratched, as that moment repeated on a loop—the same line of the song occurring over and over again.

My voice became lost, a low warble, and Gabriel's became louder, harder, until it felt as though he was screaming the line. The scene in front of me stopped repeating and became a still frame, and silence fell.

The memory had become broken somehow; perhaps the disruption was me waking. But then, from nowhere, Gabriel—just Gabriel— seemed to come to life in the still image in front of me.

He turned his head as everything else around him remained frozen. I was asleep, dreaming, remembering. I was looking in on an old memory and now he was looking out, at me.

He closed his eyes shut and his eyelids seemed to bubble and bulge. When they shot open, his pupils had spilled their black contents into his sapphire-blue irises, mirroring the way my own eyes now appeared. Extending his hand, it looked bonier—like he'd suddenly lost muscle in his arms and shoulders.

And as he reached for me, his voice bled the lyrics.

She only brought new tears to thee.

As the last word vibrated from his lips in a plaintive cry, his eyes flashed a prodigious flaming red.

I sat straight up in bed, beads of sweat falling from my forehead. My shirt was sticking to my skin, drenched in my fear.

"Lailah?" Gabriel shuffled behind me and placed his hands on the tops of my shoulders.

I was too scared to turn to him, in case what I had seen in my dream was somehow real. I might have been perspiring, but my entire body was shivering and my teeth were chattering uncontrollably.

"Are you okay?" I asked, but my words came out half-jumbled.

"Yes. You're not, though. What's wrong?" Gabriel tried to turn my body toward him, but I refused to move an inch. I was too afraid to look at him.

Breathless, I couldn't shake the image of Gabriel's eyes and the words with which it felt like he was threatening me. I had to release the thought as I felt Gabriel trying to connect his mind with mine; I didn't want him to see what I had.

"I'm all right," I said finally. "Just a bad dream."

"Then why won't you look at me?" Gabriel switched on the side lamp and jumped off the bed. He rushed to his bag in the corner of the room and pulled something out before entering the bathroom and turning on the tap. I heard his footsteps returning to me but kept my gaze fixed on the buttercups and their stems on the duvet cover.

He crouched behind me, scraping my damp hair away from my neck and untangling the chain from some errant strands. Placing the mass of curls over my shoulder, he dabbed the bare skin on my neck with a cold flannel. He stopped after a minute and gently wrapped his arms around my chest. He then began to release my shirt, one button at a time. When he'd reached the bottom, he grazed my arms as he glided his hands back to my shoulders and peeled off my shirt. Pressing the wet cotton to my spine, he patted my bare skin, cooling me.

I realized after a few minutes of repetition that he was now tracing the scar left by Frederic.

Gabriel must have started to tremble. His hand twitched, and the flannel became unsteady. Now calmer, I reached behind me to his wrist and guided him to the top of my shoulders, encouraging him to brush the last of the damp cloth down the length of my arms. He obliged, leaning his chin into the crevice of my neck, where his cool breath caused goose bumps to ride down my entire body.

Only then did I become aware that I was naked except for my panties. But I didn't care. Suddenly I didn't feel embarrassed or ashamed. A cold splash hit the curve of my right breast and ran down, trailing toward my belly button as Gabriel squeezed out the last of the water.

I brought my knees up to my chest and wrapped my hands around them. Gabriel mirrored me and curled himself around my body, rubbing my legs with his toes and nuzzling into me.

"Feel better?" he asked.

"I'd be lying if I said no." I paused and tilted my head back so I could see his face.

His eyes bloomed with a watery sparkle—like dew droplets on a blue rose—as though they were crying for me. For the first time, I noticed the tiny filaments reaching from the corners of his eyes, blemishing his porcelain skin.

I turned around so that I was facing him and sat on my knees. I rubbed my thumbs over the marks as if my touch might erase them. "I don't remember you having lines," I said quietly.

He cupped my hands in his and brought them down, parting them at his hip bones.

"You're immortal. You don't age," I said.

"As are you. You have your scars; I have mine."

I thought on that for a moment. The creases in his skin were not scars; he hadn't been injured. I didn't understand, and I highly doubted that Gabriel was going to elaborate—not if he thought the reason for them would upset me.

He changed the subject. "What was it like, Lai?"

"What was *what* like?" I played with the hem of his T-shirt.

"When you were gone. I couldn't hear you anymore. I couldn't sense you. Where did you go?"

"I was trapped. I don't want to go back. Anywhere, in any world, would be better than where I was," I said.

"Which was where, Lai?"

"It was . . . nowhere. I used to fear death because I would wake up again, lost. I fear it now for the opposite reason—" I gulped. "Because now I won't wake up, and nowhere can't be found."

Gabriel took my face in his palms and kissed me. He tasted a little like strawberries from a summer garden.

He leaned into my ear and whispered, "I would tear down everywhere until all that was left was nowhere, and I would save you. I will always save you."

I gripped the hem of his T-shirt and he parted from me, allowing me space to pull it over his head. I ruffled his blond hair before running my fingers down his chest and his stomach.

He followed the movement of my fingers. His love for me exuded from his being to mine. I reached behind his shoulders and squeezed. Bringing him in to me, my chest became flush with his. All I wanted was just for him to hold me, skin to skin.

He reciprocated and laid me back down on the bed. Entwined, I wished that I would never have to let him go, and I fell back to sleep.

FOUR

IT WAS STILL DARK outside when Gabriel woke me. Yawning, I rolled onto my side and dangled my legs off the side of the bed. I was about to reach for my discarded clothes that were strewn across the carpet, but I hesitated; I felt Gabriel's eyes boring through me. I twisted around, covering my bare chest with my arm, and smiled.

He lay across the bed, the duvet covering only his legs. I couldn't help but notice the definition in the muscles along his torso as he reached for my hand and grazed my knuckles delicately.

"Sunrise can't be far away," I mused. We both fumbled to dress as I said, "You know, when I woke up yesterday morning, in the sun's presence, I did sparkle, like you. In fact, I'm sure the light that left my skin met yours."

"I know. We're bonded through light, Lai; our connection is fused together by it. When your light and mine reconnected, it intertwined us back to each other. Could you even remember my name before it did?"

"Yes, it was echoing in my head as I woke up, but I can't say that

I knew you were the owner when I saw you again for the first time. Not until that happened."

Gabriel took my hand. "Come on."

We were at the door when he raised his finger to his lips, signaling for me to remain quiet.

Gabriel shuffled me behind his back and began to faintly glow. The doorknob turned and then the door opened swiftly. Whoever was trying to get in fell backward in surprise, and the floorboards underfoot bounced with his heavy weight.

"It's me!" came a deep bellow, belonging to Ruadhan.

Gabriel stopped glowing immediately and rushed toward his friend, who was slumped against the wall.

"I told you I'd be back before sunrise, lad." Ruadhan snorted as Gabriel helped him to his feet.

"Sorry, did my light catch you?" Gabriel asked.

"Just a tad," he replied, patting down the arms of his sweater. "Make sure that when you do finish me off, you do it more quickly and more effectively than that." He laughed.

His words hit me hard in the chest, and I moved in front of Gabriel to stand between my soul mate and my friend.

"Excuse me? When *he finishes you*?"

Ruadhan scanned the hallway, making sure no one had been disturbed by his fall, and ushered me inside. "I didn't see you there, love." He looked to Gabriel for guidance.

Gabriel hovered in the doorway. "Lai, we need to go, or we'll miss sunrise."

"Not until you tell me what Ruadhan meant." I crossed my arms and shifted my weight.

"Nothing. He didn't mean anything by it," Gabriel said.

I huffed and pushed past Gabriel. "I'm not buying it, but I have all day to chat with Ruadhan once you're running your errands."

Ruadhan and Gabriel exchanged a dubious glance before Gabriel led me down the hallway.

Outside the B&B, the Thames wore a dull gray coat, perhaps reflecting the murky color of the clouds above it. Gabriel unlocked the car and opened the passenger door for me.

"We're traveling by car?"

"It's not far by car. Let's get today done, and then we have all the time in the world to safely test some theories. If you want to, that is."

We set off with Gabriel behind the wheel. I wiped the window with my cardigan sleeve and watched the town disappear as we veered off onto a country lane. The terraced cottages that we passed were sleeping. The end of nighttime was still and quiet, and it reminded me of death.

We hadn't traveled far when Gabriel brought the car to a stop alongside a series of endlessly rolling hilltops.

"We need to hurry." He smiled at me as he began to squeeze the door handle, but an uncertainty brewed within him, passing through to me.

I reached to my chest to check that my ring with my crystal was still sitting in its rightful place, and Gabriel glanced at it.

I fingered the crystal. "Azrael said it was my mother's. She left it, after she gave birth to me. He said he might never find her without it." Guilt twinged in the pit of my stomach. "You said the crystal belonged to my family, the family I had when I was growing up in my first life, and that they gave it to Ethan to seal the deal on our engagement. You said he had it put into a ring—this ring."

"I didn't know it had come from your Angel mother, Lai," he replied coldly.

I fidgeted in my seat. "You must have a crystal of your own; you said Angel Descendants had them placed in their necks so that they could pass through the rifts and bring back the light souls to Styclar-Plena. Did you not recognize it?" I twisted my hair nervously, not sure what he might say.

"No. I didn't. The crystals given to Angel Descendants were carved from the crystal that sits at the center of Styclar-Plena. They are all different shapes and sizes, and they are embedded into our necks; they become part of us. I didn't know who you were then, Lai. And how your mother took it from her neck is beyond me. Only Arch Angels can remove the crystals." Gabriel's brow was dipping and he shook his head, as if doing so might let the answer fall into the center of his thoughts. He didn't consider it for much longer. "We're going to miss sunrise. Come on."

If only the Arch Angels were able to remove the crystals, then how had my mother taken it from her neck? Why had she left it for me, and what had she been thinking when she did? Would I ever know?

I forced the stiff car door open, following Gabriel to a large fence. I think he expected me to go through the gap in between the wood, but instead, I leaped over the top and landed in the grass in a crouching position. I'd jumped automatically, without even thinking, and I felt excited. The cramp that came in my calf after caused a momentary spike of worry, but within a few seconds it had gone.

Gabriel scanned to make sure no one had seen.

"Sorry," I said.

"We need to get to the hill, and we don't have long."

It didn't look like far. I wasn't sure what was behind Gabriel's urgency. "We could stroll, and we'd still be there in ten minutes," I said.

"No, not that hill; it's in view of the road. We need to get to the one farthest away. See that one up there?" Gabriel pointed into the distance. Initially, I couldn't see where he meant, but as I followed his finger, it was as though the whole landscape parted. Like I was wearing some sort of superbinoculars as my sight finally arrived at that distant point.

"I can run, very fast," I said.

"No." Gabriel's voice growled, and several birds in the trees took flight. He snatched my hand up in his.

I stalled, taken aback by Gabriel's tone.

He collected himself and scooped me up in his arms before I had a chance to react. "I'll take you. The way Angels, the way *we*, travel. Clear your mind," he instructed.

I did as he asked, but I kept my eyes open. It was as though the world had suddenly become a painting and we were spilled water, running through the landscape, transforming it into a blur of bleak color. The hilltop was the one solid image that remained through the wash of grays and greens on either side of me.

We arrived just as the sun was rising.

The grass underfoot was slippery from an overnight rain and so Gabriel placed me down carefully.

"How'd you do that?" I said, gasping.

"An Angel's abilities come from the power of thought. It might have just felt like you were somehow teleporting because the action is faster than the speed of light on this plane, but you're still traversing the land," he said, and to make sure I understood added, "I was *running*."

"Vampires—"

He cut me off. "They're different—most of their abilities have a more physical, instinctual sense. Just so you know, that little trick wouldn't work with a mortal; I was able to bring you because *you're like me*." I didn't miss the emphasis he placed on his last three words.

I stood evenly with my feet apart; fully balanced, I waited for the sun. "So do you have to do something, think of something specific, to travel by thought?" I wanted to know how it worked. I had done it outside the château fort, but if I understood the mechanics, maybe it would help me to control my abilities.

Gabriel tipped his chin toward the waking sun and answered softly, "I shouldn't need to tell you how, Lai. It should just . . . come. But there are restrictions: you can't travel by thought across water."

"Why?" I interjected.

"In the same way you can't walk on water, you can't run across it, either, no matter how fast you are."

The sun distracted me from asking any further questions. The vibrant orange glow hummed as it rose. I tensed as it gradually climbed higher, and Gabriel sparkled. I looked to my own skin; my hands were less pale and warmth radiated from my palms.

As it eventually reached its peak, Gabriel was awash with shining white crystals seeping from his skin and surrounding him. A burst of silver and gold shone from behind his ears, as if the source of the energy were originating from the nape of his neck.

A halo of microscopic crystals wrapped itself around me. Sparks flared from the crystal gem on my ring. I unclasped the chain and dangled it away from my body. I placed it on the grass. Parted from my touch, still it sparkled.

I took a step backward and quickly scanned my body. I was still glittering. As I swayed my hands, a million tiny star shapes moved with me.

And then, just like that, it was over.

Tears streamed down my cheeks as a surreal awe flowed through me. My knees buckled, and I dropped to the wet grass.

Gabriel sat himself down ahead of me and crossed his legs, waiting. "You look a little surprised."

"I kinda thought . . ." I stopped, feeling silly.

He pursed his lips. "Thought what?"

"That maybe you'd have wings or something." I half-laughed as I said it.

Gabriel's left eyebrow arched. "No, I'm afraid us Angel Descendants don't have wings. Only the Arch Angels do." Stretching his arm behind him, he picked up my ring and threaded the chain through his fingers, tilting his head curiously. "How do you feel?"

"I don't quite know. It was like someone had bottled up all the days of summer and then let me drink it in one go. Does that make sense?"

"Yes." His smile widened, stretching high on his cheeks, and his eyes sparkled. He played with my ring. "You don't need this. I don't think you ever did."

"I know. Why would I need a key to a door I never plan on opening?"

"That's not what I meant. The crystals may open and close the rifts for Angel Descendants, but they also keep the Angel Descendants in possession of their gifts on this plane."

I shook my head. "I don't understand."

"The crystals were placed in our necks not just to command the rifts, Lai. They keep the Angel Descendants immortal on Earth and our special talents working here, too. The crystals act as a conductor for the sun. The light meets the crystal, is churned over, and then spreads and seeps through our veins. It works in reverse, too: As long as our energy remains clear and light, it feeds back into the crystal, keeping it working."

"Your very own renewable energy," I said.

"Do you remember I told you that there was a time, before Angel Descendants were paired, that many of them became unhappy with their existence and chose to fall?" He paused and I nodded. "The Arch Angel who accepted their request removed the crystal from their neck, and when they passed through to Earth, they became mortal."

"But my mother left me her crystal. That was nearly two hundred years ago, so she's . . ." I panicked at the implication that she might be dead. Because of me.

"No. Not necessarily. Time passes at a different speed in Styclar-Plena. It takes Angel Descendants an awfully long time to age and die here, naturally. Once mortal, those that wanted a true end, well . . . they found ways to die." Gabriel's lips turned down in sadness. "I doubt your mother would have wanted that. If she is still alive, it would seem as though she has maintained a distance from you, and long may it stay that way," he said.

"Why? She's my mother. . . ."

"And Azrael is your father. It didn't stop him striking a deal with the Arch Angels to bring about your final end for his own gain. No. We take no chances. *We trust no one.*" Gabriel's tone oozed authority. There was no point trying to argue; this topic was clearly nonnegotiable.

I looked to my chain, dangling from Gabriel's fingers contemplatively. "Why do you think she left me her crystal?"

"I don't know. You'd been infected by a Pureblood; she wouldn't have known what the result of that would be. Perhaps she was trying to give you every possible chance at survival." He paused and to further iterate his point added, "That was a long time ago, Lai."

"I know it was. I don't understand—your crystal is embedded into your neck. Mine is attached to a ring; it's not part of my body." I ran my fingers over the blades of wet grass.

"Orifiel, when he first passed through the rifts, was holding a piece in his hand. But he and the other Arch Angels were created organically from the crystal itself. They don't need them to pass through the rifts or to keep their gifts here; they only need them to command the rifts." He paused. "It's not the same for us Angel Descendants; we need the crystal gems. I would suspect that they were placed into the neck so as to be fully integrated with our physical form. That crystal wouldn't give a mortal any talents, Lai. It's not a transferable deal. You have to have the light within you, from the crystal in Styclar-Plena, for it to work, and you always had plenty of that. You still do."

"Let's not forget I also have the venom of a Pureblood, and they certainly have a lot of similar traits."

"That's true," he said. "Only perhaps, given your Angel lineage, the Pureblood's traits were heightened or stronger within you."

"Can Vampires become invisible, too?"

"Nope, that's reserved for us Angels. Why'd you ask?"

"Because I'm pretty sure I have masked myself before. So I guess I need this crystal to keep my 'Angelic' powers, right?"

"I'd have agreed, if I hadn't just watched you place it down away from you. Even without the crystal, you still absorbed the sun, the same way an Arch Angel would."

"That's . . . strange."

"Yes. But that's good news. If you were parted from the crystal, you wouldn't lose your gifts."

"Or my immortality," I said at the same time as I realized this.

"Your immortality could stem from either your Angel heritage, or, well, you know."

Despite his history of saving Vampires, Gabriel had a real issue with using the word *Vampire* with any reference to me. But it was hardly as though I could just disown my Vampire lineage any sooner than I could my Angel side. The second I rejected either, I didn't know—nor did I want to try and guess—what might happen to me.

"I think I'll hold on to it anyway." I looked to my ring once again, hanging below Gabriel's palm. It was the only possession I had that was as old as I was. The one thing I had held on to throughout my entire existence.

Gabriel took my hand in his and lightly kissed my ring finger. "Yes. But if you don't mind, I'd prefer to have it taken out of this band. I'd *prefer* it if you weren't wearing something that symbolized your promise to someone else."

"Ethan is gone, Gabriel. He's gone because of me. If anything, I think the ring represents the friendship he and I had, long ago."

He didn't say anything, but his gaze remained fixed on the bottom of my chain, where my mother's devotion and my best friend's commitment to me hung low.

At my strained expression, finally he said, "We'll work something out." Gabriel blew out a steady stream of air, and I noticed I could see it clearly even in the daylight.

Placing my chain back around my neck, he did up the clasp and positioned the ring centrally below my collarbones. "I gave you the chain. At least you carried around a small part of me all these years."

I met his gaze with my own. "Forget about the chain; forget about the ring and what sits at its center. It has *nothing* to do with us. You carried my heart around all these years, that's what I know, and it means *everything*."

As I kissed him, I whispered to his thoughts: *Everything*.

FIVE

BACK IN THE SMALL room of the B&B, Gabriel and Ruadhan not so subtly suggested I have a shower. I knew it was so they could talk without me present. This had to stop—them treating me like glass that could shatter with the lightest touch. But I knew I had to lead up to that with Gabriel. A confrontation now was not the way to get him to open up to me.

When I reemerged in a pair of jeans and a white T-shirt, Gabriel stopped conspiring long enough to turn and greet me. "You look . . . well."

I knew what he meant—my skin was still shimmering from the effects of the waking sun.

The beep from Gabriel's iPhone turned his attention away from me. He exchanged a knowing glance with Ruadhan before sliding the phone from his pocket.

"It's time I was leaving," Gabriel said to both of us.

"Where are you going?" I asked. A sense of unease swelled in my belly, and I couldn't be sure if the feeling belonged to Gabriel or to me.

"I told you I had a couple of things to sort out before we could leave. This is one of them. I won't be long, I promise," Gabriel replied, striding over to me.

He clutched my waist, drawing me into his body, and I closed my eyes as I inhaled his citrus scent. "Why won't you tell me?"

"Sometimes, ignorance is bliss."

He pulled me into a drawn-out hug, and as I tried to find him in my mind, I realized that he had blocked me, hiding his thoughts and feelings from me. I wasn't going to get my answers this way after all. As he pulled away, he hesitated, gripping my elbows. Wherever he was planning to go, whatever it was he was planning to do, he was uncertain. I felt it as strong as I felt my own heart beating.

Gabriel gripped my elbows tighter, his fingers pressing almost painfully into my skin. "I told you—it ends here. Here is today, and today is the beginning of that end."

He snatched his jacket from the bed and was gone before I could argue.

As the door banged shut, I forced a smile for Ruadhan's benefit and made my way over to the kettle. I might not need caffeine anymore, but I suddenly wanted something familiar, something *normal*, to do.

Ruadhan eyed me quizzically. He waited for the kettle to whistle before placing his hand over the top of mine on the handle. "Get your coat, love. We're going for a walk."

"I doubt Gabriel would approve of you letting me out of this room," I said, scooping up my cardigan.

Ruadhan's brow creased, and he merely nodded in agreement.

He opened the bedroom door and gestured for me to step through first.

We traipsed across the landing and down the winding staircase— the old banister wobbling as I skimmed my hand down it. Ruadhan eyed the foyer as he clicked the latch on the heavy front door and then placed his hand in front of my chest, preventing me from taking another step.

I stood behind Ruadhan, glancing from left to right.

"Let me check outside, make sure it's safe. Just stay here a moment, sweetheart."

I loitered in the chilly entranceway and crossed my arms, waiting patiently. Gabriel could control his temperature; I needed to learn that trick. I hated being cold. I looked at the rustic flagstone floor, tracing the outline of the slabs. There was a small crack over by the coat stand, and as I focused on it, I realized that I could distinguish every speck of dirt and dust trapped inside it.

"It's all clear. I didn't mean to worry you. Better to be safe than sorry," Ruadhan said, locking his arm into mine as he escorted me down the driveway.

It was still very frosty, and the subzero temperature had caused the rain from the night before to form a skating rink across the pavement. I followed the outline of the riverbank and a large bridge appeared in the distance. It reminded me of something from a travel guide, and I took a second to breathe in the freshness of the morning once again. I looked up toward the sky, but the sun was hidden behind light gray clouds.

"Where are we going?" I inquired as we began making our way down the lane, passing the last of the local stores.

Ruadhan pawed at the stubble on his chin. "I'm not sure."

We strolled alongside the riverbank for a while. Ruadhan seemed consumed in private thought. We walked past a sign that read "Mill Meadows," and Ruadhan nudged me toward the gate of the park, eyeing a bench next to the pathway.

"Are you all right?" I asked.

Ruadhan uncoiled a scarf from around his neck, placing it down for me to sit on, and I smiled at his chivalry. I took a seat next to him. The park was tranquil as the trees that bordered it swayed gently in the soft breeze.

"I'm so sorry about what happened on the mountain, Lailah," Ruadhan finally began.

I shifted uncomfortably. "It's okay. You didn't know. I hadn't known. I'm sorry I didn't tell you who I was before Azrael did." I had just as much to apologize for—perhaps more. When Ruadhan had pushed Ethan's sword through my chest, he thought he was ending a Pureblood; he hadn't a clue that the girl in shadow was me. I had deliberately kept my past from him—everything, including my real name. Gabriel had thought it was safer to keep the little we did know about me a secret while he searched for the answers to what we didn't.

"I care about you, love. I only want you to be happy," Ruadhan said, scratching the tops of his legs.

"I know that." I was so lucky to have someone like Ruadhan in my life. I couldn't lose him. "Ruadhan, what did you mean about Gabriel finishing you properly?"

"Oh, little love. I told you once before, I had a debt to repay to Gabriel for saving me. But now he has found what he was looking for, he doesn't need me anymore. And so, I have asked him to end

64

me before you leave together." Ruadhan didn't look at me, instead choosing to stare out over the Thames.

I stifled a gasp. "No, Ruadhan, just because we're leaving doesn't mean you shouldn't go on. I don't care what you say, you don't deserve to die; there's nothing for you in death."

"I don't fear death, Lailah." His words were smooth as he continued to stare out at the river.

"You should," I shot back.

Ruadhan finally turned to face me, taking my hands in his. He squeezed them as he attempted to reassure me.

But I wasn't reassured. He needed to understand. "Before you tell me your life has already been taken, let me be clear. You are *not* dead. You should cling to the existence you have, because there is nothing for you *after* this. . . ."

"You're right, love, and I know I cannot change the color of my soul. But Gabriel will afford me one final moment of light." His voice dropped into a low whisper. "And even though it will be but a single moment, it's one in which the Devil will no longer own me. I will know my God again. I will find peace." He cleared his throat. "With no purpose left here, why would I cling to what I have become— to *this?*"

I snatched my hands away. "Because today you exist. And because tomorrow, if you choose it, you can *live*." I halted for a moment as a couple passed us by, but Ruadhan interjected before I had a chance to further my argument.

"I have fulfilled my duty, sweetheart. There's nothing left for me to live for."

"If you don't want to live for yourself, then live for me. I still need you," I pleaded. "I want to be happy, Ruadhan. And I want that for you, too." As I said the words, I exerted as much conviction into them as I could muster.

"God knows, you *deserve* to be happy, Lailah, but . . ." Ruadhan said, his gaze falling to his feet.

"But what?"

"You know that Purebloods walk the Earth, infecting human beings to build their armies. I know you, and I don't think you can simply turn away from that."

I hesitated, a shiver running up my spine as I tried to pretend that what he said wasn't true. "You don't know me, Ruadhan. I *will* go away; I will run and I will hide."

"Maybe." He fidgeted where he sat. "But you won't be able to turn a blind eye for long. You'll stop running."

"That's a very large assumption."

"No, it's not. You knew Zherneboh was coming, and you ran toward him not away from him. Why did you do that?"

"I didn't want him to end you all. He was after me, not you. If I were killed, then the weapon he had created would be gone, and there could be no war."

"You were prepared to sacrifice your life for us. For everyone." He cleared his throat, choked up at the memory. "Zherneboh may have intended to produce a weapon in order to wage a war between the worlds, but what if, instead of creating an enemy for Heaven, he created a savior for Earth?"

I edged away from him. I didn't want to hear this. "I am no savior. You have me confused with someone else." I found my feet and stood up abruptly.

Ruadhan joined me and placed his hand on my arm, stopping

me from walking away. "Gabriel is prepared to grant me my last request, and I ask it of him because I have no reason to go on. I no longer have a purpose to serve. Give me a reason . . . give me a purpose, Lailah. If there is even a glimmer inside you that you will fight, that you will deliver freedom to the world . . . then I shall wait for you, and I will be right beside you while you try."

I crossed my arms and rubbed them, trying to rid myself of the chill. But I knew it wasn't coming from the cold breeze nipping at my skin. I peeked up. Ruadhan's eyes were expectant as he waited for my reply, and I began to crumble a little inside. "If I try, I will fail."

Ruadhan pinched the top of my shoulders with his fingers and sighed. "Little love, you will only fail if you don't try."

I took a deep breath, absorbing Ruadhan's message. How could I take on an army of Pureblood Masters and their Second Generation Vampires? I couldn't even control my abilities yet. And it wasn't just my life I was affecting; it was also Gabriel's. After all that had happened, all that he had been through to find me, to save me, to still love me—I didn't want to be the cause of his unhappiness.

"It's not just me, Ruadhan. It's Gabriel, too. He knows . . . he understands the dimensions, the beings that inhabit them, the risks, and he wants to run." There was a part of me that felt as though I was being a coward, as though I was hiding behind Gabriel, but it was true.

"Lailah, you must search your soul and pick your own path. You must trust in yourself to make and own those decisions. If you don't, any freedom, any happiness you might find, will only be short lived."

"And what if the path I choose leads me away from everything I have been searching for," I said.

"You mean *Gabriel*?"

At the mention of Gabriel's name my mind stretched, trying to connect to him. There was nothing; he was still blocking me.

"What, Ruadhan? Why'd you say his name like that?" I said, pushing.

Ruadhan frowned, and he rubbed his chin vigorously. "Since he came back from the States, he's different."

"Different how?" I asked.

"Never mind. Let's walk back. You look uncomfortably cold." For once, Ruadhan didn't usher me ahead of him, instead striding away and leaving me to trail behind.

But I wasn't to be put off so easily. I was sick and tired of being treated like a child. I caught up with the six-foot-tall Ruadhan's pace. "Ruadhan, how is Gabriel different?"

He didn't look at me as he continued on briskly. "Gabriel's trying to protect you the best way he can. I understand that. He knows what he's doing, but he hasn't exactly been forthright with me about what that is. And I have a feeling, for the first time in a hundred years, that I wouldn't agree with his methods."

"Ruadhan, is he in danger?" I was jogging now.

Finally, Ruadhan's pace let up, and he gazed down to meet my eyes. "Yes, as are you. As you both always will be, if you run."

We continued on, and I found myself quietly flapping about Gabriel. Where was he? What was he doing? Had the Purebloods or the Arch Angels found him?

I stretched my mind wide and thought of him, but a sheet of light filled it—blinding me and preventing me from seeing past it. I had become well-practiced at building a wall in my head to keep Gabriel out, but it seemed as though his preferred method was a blanket of untraversable light.

But then, as I followed Ruadhan up the sloping driveway back to the front door of the B&B, something changed. I shut my eyes and concentrated on the light, and a small hairline fissure seemed to branch across the white sheet. I immediately felt a sensation of rising emotion—of panic—as if Gabriel's emotions were seeping through. I reached for the door frame to steady myself as Ruadhan stepped inside, and I focused on the tear in Gabriel's white cloak. And then I saw it: the shape of a sun set within a marble floor.

I knew where he was.

He was in the cottage on the grounds of the Hedgerley house. Nausea stewed within me, and I thought then that Gabriel was in some sort of trouble. I tried to reconnect but the crack had already been restitched by the light, and I was left stuck on the outside of Gabriel's sheet once more.

Adrenaline surged, and I shot out onto the road and made for the woods so fast that all I left in my wake was a whip of air that skimmed Ruadhan's back.

SIX

MY FIRST INSTINCT WAS to run, and so I dashed with a super-speed along the pavement, knocking into a stranger as he made his way into a convenience store.

It was risky to let anyone see me, so I ran into the woods. I ground to a halt. As I did, the muscles in my legs contracted with a stab of pain. I shook it off.

I didn't know my way from Henley to Hedgerley. Eyeing the thick trunk of a tall hawthorn tree, I placed my hands on the bark and sprang up its side. The ridges and uneven surface dug into my palms as I clawed my way to the top.

I scoured the vast land spread out all around me. But it was useless. I might be able to run faster, but it made no difference if I didn't know where it was I was trying to run to.

There was nothing elegant about the way I scrambled down the tree's side. As I neared the bottom, my ankle buckled, and I lost my footing and plummeted toward the iced dirt. Just as I was about to hit the ground, my feet arched, and I landed on my tiptoes as though I were a ballerina, balancing *en pointe*. But it didn't last long, the heels of my feet suddenly smacking back down to the iced mud.

I might possess some supernatural gifts—the same as a Vampire and an Angel Descendant—but I had no idea how to control them, and for some reason my Vampire abilities were starting to bring with them a dull ache.

Gabriel and I had traveled to the hill by the power of thought, but he said I should just know how, as though it were not something that required some form of tutorial. If I wanted to get to him, I was going to have to try.

I took a deep, calming breath and closed my eyes, imagining the cottage in the garden of the Hedgerley house.

Nothing happened.

I screwed my face up, closing my eyes tightly once more, desperately wanting to open my eyes to find it in front of me.

This time, it was instant.

It felt like my body rocked backward before catapulting forward, as if the world had stopped spinning for the briefest of moments. I was staring at the cottage ahead of me in the distance.

I'd done it. I had traveled here by thought.

Standing at the edge of the forest, I heard a woman's voice. I slunk behind the deciduous shrubs and hid.

I focused on the cottage. The door was slightly ajar, and the voice came again from outside the entranceway.

Hanora.

The air was damp with dew, but I caught a trace of citrus as Gabriel walked up beside her.

Hanora inclined her head in my direction, then looked away as Gabriel placed his hands on her arms.

She balanced her weight from one high-heeled boot to the other. She clutched her long, extravagant wool coat around herself, holding her elbows with her slender fingers. A silk scarf was wrapped around her head, the burn marks still scarring her skin—the same as the last time I had seen her. I still didn't know how she, a Vampire, had come by such damaging marks.

I focused, using my Vampire abilities to tune into their conversation.

". . . come inside with me, Mary," Gabriel said.

Hanora's eyes flashed red, and she jolted backward. "*Mary?* In *her* death, hope is now gone?" Her every word was laced with sadness. "With *her* end, I no longer own the name you gave me?"

Gabriel's expression was unreadable, even for me, and still blocked from him, I had no idea what he was thinking or feeling.

"You're free," Gabriel said. "You're not mine anymore. You are your own person." He paused. Reaching for her again, he stroked the edge of her downturned lips. "You now belong to yourself again, which is why I'll no longer call you by the name I gave you the night we met."

Hanora didn't seem to like what he had said, and she edged back from him.

"No, it's okay. Please, come inside with me; it's dangerous out here, for both of us."

Still she seemed unsure. "You've forgiven me?" she whispered.

Gabriel nodded firmly. Stepping toward her, he pushed down the scarf with his thumbs and carefully brushed the back of his hand over her eyebrow. "Have you *me?*"

What was he talking about? What was he even doing here with her?

"Come. Let us talk inside." He took her hand in his own.

I bit the inside of my cheek.

He turned around, willing her to follow him inside, and this time she did as he asked.

As the door to the cottage closed, a million thoughts whirled through my mind. Gabriel had business to tie up; perhaps she was on the agenda. He had spoken softly and touched her tenderly, despite her betrayal. But then Gabriel was an Angel, created in light; of course he would forgive her for betraying him, me, all of us. He had saved her, spent nearly a hundred years with her, and somehow, despite what she was, she had loved him. Perhaps, this was his way of saying good-bye before he took me away.

But then, a jealous thought struck me as I considered what that good-bye might look like. So despite the stupidity of it, I began to stride toward the cottage.

I was nearing the entrance when the sound of brambles snapping behind me caught my attention.

I reeled around. From across the field, his hazel eyes bore through me. I recognized him from the château fort—he was dressed in vintage chinos, a deep V-neck T-shirt, and a dark leather jacket. It was the Vampire I had nearly ended. It was Jonah.

Panic rose inside me, and I darted fast from the cottage, grinding to a wobbly halt in a clearing.

"Charming." His voice traveled on the icy breeze as he suddenly appeared in front of me.

I threw up my hand. "Stay back! You need to leave." I stepped backward.

"We need to talk." Without warning, he jumped high into the air, landing just a few feet away from me.

I closed my eyes and took a deep breath. I waited for my fangs to crack, but they didn't. I tensed my body, anticipating that surge of inescapable rage, but it didn't come.

"Feeling all right there, beautiful?" As he purred the words, my mind tumbled over itself, and I felt that same sense of déjà vu creep over me once more.

I shuffled backward. "I don't know you. But I do know that, if you get too close, I might not be able to stop myself."

"You know me very well, actually. Are you not the tiniest bit curious?"

I met his stare. "I believe that's the very thing that gets the cat killed in the end."

His eyes grew bigger, his gaze reaching for me. He took another step closer and I grew anxious. Not because I feared him, but because I feared who I might become around him. My instinct was to once again run, and I sped into the woods. My legs stretched and my body glided, but seconds later I slammed into Jonah, who had raced ahead of me.

I flew backward, smashing into a tree, and I wrapped my arms around the trunk behind me to stop myself from falling.

"I said, *we need to talk*." His jaw was rigid and his stance unmoving. "You remember Gabriel, you remember the others, but you don't remember me." He scowled, as though he were offended.

"Have you forgotten what happened just yesterday? You're playing a very dangerous game, Vampire," I sneered.

"The name's Jonah. But you know that, don't you?"

It made no difference whether I knew his name; I didn't know who he was underneath it. Reluctantly, I nodded my head.

"Then please use it instead of referring to me by what I am, especially with that tone. And, for the record, you're a *Vampire*, too," he said, injecting the same scorn into his voice.

I turned my back on him. My skin was starting to tingle, but it was a very mild sensation—my body simply acknowledging his presence.

"You're going to run with Gabriel, right? That's the grand plan?" he shouted from behind me.

I paused. *Why was I pausing?* "Yes. If that was what you wanted to talk about, the question you needed an answer to, you have it. Now leave me alone." I jumped and then clambered up the side of the large tree. Once at the top, I focused on the branches of its neighbors and began springing from one to the other.

I'd made it across only two of them when a firm hand clutched my ankle, and with one swift tug I was plummeting to the ground. Jonah's arms were outstretched, ready to catch me, but instead I swung my body away from him and landed in a crouching position.

"You're really starting to get on my nerves," I barked.

"Good," he replied. "I'm glad I'm having some effect on you. Just like old times." His lips curved into an arrogant grin.

I glared at him.

Sighing, he said, "You're a Vampire, Lailah, as much as you are an Angel. I doubt Gabriel will ever be able to accept that. He will stifle you, and worse still, he will make you vulnerable."

I hesitated, Jonah's words about Gabriel struggling to accept my darker nature echoing my own, private concerns. But I trusted Gabriel. I realized there was even a reasonable explanation for his meeting with Hanora: It was business; that's all, business.

Disregarding Jonah, I turned on my heel and ran back the way I had come through the forest. Just before I reached the opening to the clearing, the sound of knuckles cracking caused me to stop. Jonah sat perched on a fallen tree ahead of me, flexing his hands.

"By rights, you should probably be faster than me, but you're not. . . . That's a problem." He rose to his feet and strode over to me. "I didn't come here to talk to you about Gabriel."

As impertinent as he was being—showing no regard for what I asked of him, senselessly attempting to get a rise out of me, and essentially all-out vexing me—something about him prevented me from trying to run again.

I didn't try to stop him as he reached out to me. He glided his hand underneath my hair and tipped my face to one side, stroking my cheek with his thumb.

It took me a moment to find my voice. "What did you come here for?"

He grinned deviously. "Ahhh . . . five minutes ago, the fate of Puss in Boots was more important to you than answers."

I raised my hand to bat him away, but he snatched it, wrapping his fingers around my own.

He leaned down so that our eyes were level, rendering me unable to escape his stare. "I came back for you, to talk about your future. You won't be able to outrun *them* forever."

My gaze fell to his feet, but he nudged my chin up until I met his eyes once more.

He squeezed my fingers and offered me a gentle, reassuring smile. "I only came back to make sure that you embraced all of yourself." He paused thoughtfully. "Embrace everything and all of what you are—the most deadly force to walk this world."

"Why? You believe I can free this world, too? You think I am some sort of savior?" I challenged, Ruadhan's call to arms reverberating in my ears.

"Who said anything about that? I only care about *your* freedom, *your* life. I can't watch you . . . fall." He hesitated. "Not again. Never again." Jonah's grasp around my hand tightened.

Who I had been to Jonah was a mystery to me. Why was he the only thing, the only person, I couldn't remember?

"I know why you've forgotten," Jonah whispered. "I know you." He brushed the tip of his nose against my ear. "And without me, you won't wind up a savior, but a martyr." Moving his eyes back to mine, he stared at me. "You will meet your end."

Within an instant, Jonah's fangs cracked. In one swift movement, he had his hand spread in the small of my back, crushing me into his body, while he hooked his sharp fangs into the skin of his wrist. He dragged them down, creating a bloodied laceration.

He spat out a clot of blood. "Time to remember me, beautiful."

I opened my mouth to protest, clenching my fists into balls, ready to free myself from his grasp, but his scent of cinnamon met me first. Lashes of a burning whip assaulted my body. The red haze returned, clouding my vision.

Jonah's presence had caused me to yearn inside, but in that split second I realized that it was his blood that pushed me over the edge.

He knew it, too. And, more important, he knew why.

My fangs broke through my gums, and I whined as they painfully cracked into place against my will. I lunged forward, straight toward his exposed throat, only this time I desperately tried to fight my instincts—my overwhelming urge to consume him. I clutched his wrist, trying to stop his blood from spilling out of his skin. As he fought me, I became aware of how dry my throat was. I knew that I could relieve the feeling if I helped myself to him, but still I tried to restrain my body's reaction.

"It's okay, beautiful; drink from me," he goaded, grasping for the back of my head so that his wrist was inches away from my desperate lips.

I knocked him to the ground, straddling him, and the air around me seemed to warp. Unable to hold off my desire any longer, I snatched his arm and ran my nose along the cut, breathing him in. As I verged on granting his wish, a sarcastic bout of laughter escaped Jonah's lips, and as he pressed his thumb to my cheek, it grew louder.

The world stopped.

I heard his laughter again—only more gleeful, more honest—but it wasn't coming from below me; it was resurfacing from somewhere inside me. I knew that sound. No longer did the fragrance of cinnamon overrun my senses; instead, I could smell warm mince pies and mulled wine. I could only taste Christmas. As though a bucket of cold water had been thrown over me, it flooded the febrile fire that had ignited and my rage ebbed away. I became numb.

I lifted myself from off his lap and fell away from him. My fangs receded, and the red fog began to slowly lift.

He looked at me with bemusement.

I may not have known who he was, but I could never, and would never, forget that laugh that had left his lips once upon a dream.

I ambled away from him back into the clearing, holding myself steady as I went. He didn't immediately follow me. I hoped he would have the good sense to leave me be.

I was halfway across the field, slipping as I hurried, when a single bloodied tear fell down my cheek—the last flicker of my inner flames. But before I had the opportunity to wipe it away, Jonah had bolted from the forest, diving on top of me.

He pinned me to the frosty ground, his eyes a dangerous whirlpool of swirling incarnadine eating up his hazel. Locking my arms above my head, he growled. He clutched my thigh around his waist but, restraining himself, he simply blotted my bloodied tear away.

Still the sound of his laughter was echoing insanely around my head.

"You need to drink from me," he pleaded.

I could have thrown him off but I was lost, focusing on his smile that was flashing from my memory back into my conscious thoughts.

"I think it's only improved your section of the tree," I mumbled.

He held my waist firmly and brought the tip of his nose to mine, where he hovered.

I was so captivated by the sweet sound of his laughter that I didn't hear the gunfire.

Jonah's body became looser, and he was no longer lingering over my lips. I met his swollen, bloodshot eyes as he fell away from me.

"Lailah . . ." He winced. "Run!"

SEVEN

I WAS SLOW TO react. Too slow.

Jonah was being hauled away from me, dragged across the clearing by his ankles. He thrashed around, coughing up blood and trying to stand. A young boy was trying unsuccessfully to fetter Jonah with chains. Before the fire inside me had time to reignite at the sight of his blood, I was being pulled across the damp grass in the opposite direction. A dull throb came over my entire body, and my limbs felt disjointed.

I should have been able to move, to fight, but my body had become weak. In my kidnapper's free hand, silver chains clattered noisily as the length of them skimmed the ground next to my body. I was like lead.

"Let me go!" I shouted, trying to tip my weight forward. I could see Jonah in the distance, gripping his calf, and trying to stem the flow of blood that was bubbling through a rip in his chinos.

"Use the silver! Tie it up!" A voice bellowed from behind me as the young boy nervously teetered around Jonah, circling him as though he didn't know what to do. "Cameron!" The voice shouted again.

I pulled away from the arm that was tugging me backward. My abductor released me, and finally my palms met with the ground. The person behind me surged forward, toward Jonah and the young boy. Jonah was now on his feet, but he was stumbling. The low growl and shrill hiss that left him were sinister and menacing. I hoped that they were warning enough to keep his attackers back.

A pair of sturdier, heavier arms yanked me to my feet. There were silver chains twisted between his fingers and wrapped around his arms, and they grazed my cardigan. I yelped as a searing heat began to melt my skin underneath the layers I was wearing. The guy didn't seem to notice, and he wasn't trying to attack me the way his companions were attacking Jonah.

They must think I'm human. . . .

My thoughts jumbled. It was as though the silver acted as a magnet, drawing me away from my very self so that my mind was pulled in two different directions, leaving an expanse of darkness in between. And the nearer my body came to the chains, the worse it became until I was plunged into darkness.

MY EYELIDS WERE HEAVY. Muffled voices came from somewhere nearby. I forced my eyes open. I was surrounded by an odor of stale cigarette smoke. My face was resting on aging polyester, but my body was too heavy for me to sit up.

I blinked frantically, and I realized I was in a vehicle. The bumps of the road underneath me made my body bounce. In my peripheral vision, right beside my face there was a mass of silver chains, bundled lazily together.

I possessed the traits of both Vampires and Angels, and that silver was too close.

There was no one with me. I was alone in wherever—whatever—this was, but there were others, somewhere. The silver made my head spin; the waves in my mind warped and as long as those chains were so close, I didn't think I would be able to get up.

I bided my time, waiting for the next bump to come. When it did, my body jolted, and I tried to push myself farther from the chains. It didn't work; the chains only bobbed closer. A link met my cheek, and immediately my skin sizzled.

Another jolt from the road came, and this time, more out of instinct than collected thought, I threw my body backward, away from the silver.

I managed to catch my breath. Though still foggy, my mind began to regain control, and the second my legs responded, I was on my feet.

I scurried to the far corner, as far away from the bindings as I could get. I was in the back of a small Winnebago. I had been lying on a sofa beneath burnt-orange suede curtains that were drawn but falling away from the rail. A small table and chairs were at the end of the space, together with an ashtray overflowing with cigarette butts, a deck of cards, and several boxes of matchsticks. What was once a garish blue carpet adorned with swirling patterns ran the length of the floor, but it was hard to see through the trodden-in mud and filth.

The only thing between me and the next room was a beaded curtain in the doorway. Through the moving strips, I could make out a driver, with his companions seated next to him, at the front of the vehicle. Nothing but a darkened road, lit only by the headlights, stretched out ahead.

I didn't know why they had taken me from the field or what had become of Jonah. And though I still didn't know who he had been to me, the very fact that the memory of his laughter, *that* laughter, had stopped me from ripping him apart told me that he had been someone important. Someone I wouldn't want dead.

I considered tearing through the curtains, letting my fangs crack, and forcing them to tell me what the hell they were doing and what had happened to Jonah.

"I said I was sorry, Fergal." A small, nervous voice sounded, and I detected the thick Irish accent immediately.

"No, not all right. You let it get away." The passenger next to him, whom the small boy had referred to as Fergal, snapped in reply.

Were they talking about Jonah? I hoped that they were.

A tense silence fell, and I automatically reached for the wall of the Winnebago to steady myself as we rounded a bend.

The driver said nothing but began winding down his window; it squeaked, only making it halfway before jamming. As the air blew into the van, the scent of my kidnappers hit me hard.

Humans.

They weren't Vampires or Angels. They were ordinary human beings. And they had taken me against my will. Along the side of the vehicle there was a door. I could just open it and jump out. It would be easy. I could even try to just think myself away . . . Or, I could confront them before taking my leave and teach them some manners.

The driver lit a cigarette. "Cameron, you said that demon

belonged to the same group that took the girl, which means we've gotten lucky. They've come back and she might be with them, if they haven't killed her already."

My interest was piqued just as I was easing myself toward the door. They knew what Jonah was and they had been spying on us in Hedgerley, waiting for us to return, waiting for me. But why?

"I wouldn't be so jammy, Phelan. Thanks to this eejit, that demon is a walking wounded, and it's gonna be none too happy about it. You should have bound its legs in silver—you let it escape!" Fergal shouted at Cameron.

"I didn't mean to," Cameron said. "Doesn't matter; took it down long enough to rescue the *bure* back there."

Bure? I gritted my teeth. Who was he to call me "girl"? And I didn't need to be rescued.

Phelan took another pull on his cigarette. Blowing the smoke from his lungs, he said, "Why did you tell Cameron to shoot it in the leg? Why not the chest? Why injure the thing instead of killing it?"

"I don't have to answer to you," Fergal retorted. "I'm in charge, remember?"

"Aye. Humor me, then," Phelan replied.

"I wanted to interrogate it so that we could find the girl quicker," Fergal said. "You're forgetting what the Angel Aingeal said. . . . You know, we gotta find the girl and all that."

My heart stopped.

The Angel Aingeal.

My mother.

"What's your hurry, Fergal?" Phelan piped up in a confident, controlled voice. When no reply came, Phelan carried on, "If your father was still alive, he'd be reminding you of the tortoise and the hare."

Fergal punched Phelan in the shoulder, causing him to swerve the vehicle, and shouted, "Feck off with you, that's a child's story."

"Exactly," Phelan muttered.

I had no idea who these hardy boys were, but they knew about Vampires and they were searching for a girl who, unbeknownst to them, was in the back of their Winnebago. Nothing about their conversation suggested that they knew I was the girl they had been tracking, and they hadn't noticed the effect the silver had on me. For once, I had the upper hand.

With my mother's name ringing in my ears, any thoughts I had about leaving diminished. If these lads knew where she was, then perhaps I could find out.

I had no idea how these travelers had come to be in the presence of my mother, and regardless, who knew what their motives truly were? Not long ago, Michael had taught me just how easy it was to be deceived. I hadn't paid enough attention to my gut, and that nearly got us all killed. No, I wouldn't be fooled again. I would play it smart.

Just that second, the Winnebago veered off, turning a sharp right. Then the engine shut off.

I sat myself down at the table, far away from the silver, and waited. The boys jumped out of their seats and, still arguing, made their way around the side of the Winnebago. I pushed my hair behind my ears and wondered for a moment if, on closer inspection, they would recognize me.

The handle of the door shook as someone tried to push it down from the outside, and then it creaked open.

The main light switched on, and the guy who had been driving, whom they had called Phelan, stood in the doorway. He looked straight at the empty sofa, and then his eyes quickly darted to where I was perched in the far corner.

"Ah, you're awake."

"Who are you?" I shot back.

Phelan sauntered over, scratching the back of his neck. The material of his long-sleeved shirt clung to his biceps. The tendrils of a black tattoo glided up his neck, stopping just below his square jaw. He wore a beanie hat and had shaved sideburns that still left a gray shadow, giving him an almost military appearance.

Eyeing me closely, he pulled out a chair and swung it around so that he was resting his arms on the back of it with his legs straddling either side. "No one important. My friends and I were passing by and saw you being attacked. So we helped." He gave a nonchalant shrug, but he was staring at me intently, running his hard eyes over my every feature.

"It's a little hazy," I lied. "Attacked by whom?"

"Just some guy."

"Right." I folded my arms and crossed my right leg over my left.

"What were you doing out by the forest, all by yourself?"

"Taking a morning stroll."

"To where? Or rather, from where, exactly?" He pushed, scraping the feet of his chair as he balanced his weight on the front two legs.

"From the hotel I was staying in, out to the local shop, for milk."

"Really?"

"Really." Why was he so interested?

He shifted uncomfortably, and we continued to stare each other down. He opened his mouth to say something, when another one of the boys jumped through the doorway.

"You're up. You all right?" he asked cheerily, bouncing through the messy room. He stood next to the would-be soldier who was questioning me.

"I hear you rescued me from some creep, so I guess a thank-you is in order?" I smiled coyly and moved out from behind the table.

"Aye, the name's Fergal." He extended his hand for me to shake.

He was much shorter and slighter than my interrogator, who was still watching me carefully. Fergal wore baggy gray tracksuit bottoms, with the tongue of his Converse sneakers sticking out over the top. He had on a warm-looking, cream-colored vest over the top of a long-sleeved shirt, but it was the gold cross hanging low around his neck that caught my attention. I thought for a moment that it pulsed with a white glow as it shimmered under the lighting. I returned Fergal's wide smile as he played with his mass of blond hair, teasing it forward. He looked like a member of a boy band—not a gun-wielding Vampire slayer.

I edged in closer to him, taking his hand, and a weird sense of calm flowed through me, but it only lasted as long as his handshake.

"Don't suppose my brother here has bothered to introduce himself?" Fergal jovially nudged the other guy in the shoulder.

"It's Phelan. And what may we call you?" he retorted, standing up.

I wasn't sure what name to give. Circling my palm with my fingertips, I considered Fergal a little longer than I should have before replying. "Brooke." It was the first name that popped into my head. Okay, the second name, but I wasn't about to give Hanora's.

"Right, well, we're setting up camp here tonight. We can drop you home tomorrow if you want. Or can you call your daddy—ask him to come fetch you?" Fergal offered sweetly.

I had been gone some time, and I knew Gabriel would be worrying about where I was. Well, if he had returned from his meeting by now. I could easily open my mind and call to him, but I knew the second I did that, he would arrive and take me away. And if he thought these lads knew where my mother was, he'd be even quicker to remove me from their company, to ensure I couldn't find out. I needed . . . time; time to crack these travelers and find out what they knew; and time to think things through.

"Actually, I'm kind of a loner. Could I crash with you for a couple of days?" I asked.

"Might be a bit difficult, that, like." Fergal dropped his gaze to the floor.

"No," Phelan chimed in fast, all the while continuing to stare at me.

Fergal tilted his chin back up and glared at Phelan. Then, turning his attention back to me, his right eyebrow arched, he said, "Can you cook?"

"I worked in a bed-and-breakfast once. I make a mean fry-up." I tried my best to sell myself.

"Grand, you can help Iona in the kitchen," Fergal said.

Phelan's mouth opened, ready to protest, but Fergal had already placed his hand on my back and was shimmying me out of the doorway before Phelan's protest could meet the air.

EIGHT

I TRAIPSED ACROSS YET another empty field. I glanced up at the sky as the winter's night drew in. This far from the city, no layer of pollution hid the stars, which had come to life—gleaming brightly.

I scanned the immediate area and could make out a motorbike, a large motor home, and a caravan, which was rigged up to the back of a truck. Looking back, the Winnebago I had just left was well worn, with large sections of the garish blue paint having long chipped away.

The door of the adjacent motor home swung open and music blared, spoiling the tranquil setting and cutting my observations short.

Several bodies dashed toward Phelan and Fergal, greeting them with slaps on the back. I hung behind, taking in the scene in front of me.

"Cam said he shot one in the leg!" A voice belonging to a burly young lad sounded and, before he had finished his sentence, Phelan had knocked him onto the ground.

"Hey!"

"We got company," Phelan said. Peering at me over his shoulder, he studied my expression. I nudged my shoulders up and down, to reassure him that I was oblivious to anything that had been said. A fake half-smile tugged at the corners of his lips.

A small figure weaved through the boys, launching herself into Fergal's arms. She bear-hugged him, and he rubbed her back reassuringly.

"Thank the Lord you're okay," she whimpered.

Brooke wasn't lying when she'd once told me that Vampires could see in the dark. Though I had to focus, I could see the girl's features. By her reaction, my initial thought was that she was Fergal's girlfriend. But the bend in her nose, the curve of her plump lips, and her washed-out gray-blue eyes told me that the two of them were in fact related.

"I made chicken casserole. They wanted to eat before you got back, but I said no, we eat together. Always together." She beamed triumphantly.

Fergal fluffed her long, white-blond hair affectionately.

"Come on, everyone, I'm starving. Let's eat," he instructed, and the bodies piled back into the motor home.

I hung back, wondering if I was doing the right thing. It would be easier just to do as they had intended with Jonah: pick one off and interrogate him about my mother and about their intentions. But there were other ways of getting answers—better ways; ones that, through deception, rewarded you with the absolute truth.

"You coming?" Phelan hustled me forward through the door.

Unlike the beaten-up blue Winnebago we had arrived here in, this motor home was huge. Phelan directed me to a large round table in the middle of an open-plan sitting room and kitchen. Down the hall, there were many doors; bedrooms, I guessed.

I was ushered into a seat by Phelan, who wasn't about to let me out of his sight, and I thanked him as I pulled in my chair.

The living area was contemporary, with veneer blinds, a flat-screen TV, and a leather corner sofa that wrapped around the walls. This van didn't smell of smoke; instead, the inviting smell of cooked chicken and stock warmed me through.

The table had been set for eight people; the young girl hurriedly positioned another place mat and set of cutlery under my nose before switching off the stereo and scurrying back into the kitchen.

She returned speedily with a large casserole dish, which she placed at the center of the white tablecloth next to a stack of freshly cut bread, a jug of extra gravy, and a few cans of beer.

Taking her seat opposite me, she called out, "Dinnertime!"

Phelan and Fergal were already seated, with me stuck in between the two of them. Once I sat, they bowed their heads, and Fergal said, "Lord, we thank you for this food and this drink that will keep us strong. Lord, we ask you to bestow upon us your blessing, while we continue with your work. Lord, we ask you to protect the congregation back in Lucan. Lord, we thank you for keeping those who have fallen, alongside you in paradise, for they died in your name. Amen."

I was the only person at the table who was not bowing their head in grace. But I repeated the "amen" under my breath, just before eager hands grabbed and tore at the bread and can tabs clicked backward, spraying fizz.

"Hey, guys, manners. We have a guest," Phelan instructed, and the group quieted.

Fergal flashed him a quick glance, and Phelan responded with the lightest nod of his head. If I weren't supernatural, I think I would have missed it.

Fergal passed me a tall beer can, and I took it out of politeness.

"This is Brooke." Fergal gestured to me. "We, er, helped her out today. She's gonna stay with us for a day or two, help Iona out in the kitchen, like."

"She's staying?" the girl said.

A smug smirk creased Phelan's cheek, as though he were pleased that even she seemed to think the idea was ridiculous.

"Yes, well." Fergal glared at Phelan. "Doesn't the Lord's work extend to helping others, like?"

I suspected it wasn't the Lord's work that had been the reason for the offer. I thought instead that it had everything to do with Fergal disliking Phelan trying to take charge.

"It is our duty to help lost souls." One of the lads at the table piped up in agreement.

The girl bobbed her head enthusiastically, as the guys at the table exchanged whispers.

"Yes, of course." She beamed. "I'm Fergal's sister, Iona. This here is Cameron."

"'Lo," the boy sitting next to Iona said, barely looking up as he waited patiently for his turn to take a piece of bread. I recognized his name—and more so his not-yet-broken voice—from the Winnebago. He was small and mousy, definitely the youngest of the group; he couldn't have been more than fourteen, fifteen tops. He had a podgy face, a small freckled nose, and messy red hair.

"You've met Phelan. This is Dylan and Jack." She held her hand out, gesturing at the two twentysomethings to the left of me. "And this here is Riley and Claire; they're newlyweds." Her eyes settled on the teenage couple in between Cameron and Phelan. I could tell without looking that they were playing footsie under the table. "Riley is also Dylan's cousin."

"Chug some of your black stuff—it might make you feel better after what happened to you today," Fergal encouraged, referring to the can of Guinness in my hand.

"So, Brooke, Cam said the boys found you in a meadow, and that you were attacked by . . ."

"Huh-hum." Phelan cleared his throat, shooting Iona a stern stare.

"That's right, some weirdo," I answered, taking a sip of the bitter stout. "It all happened so fast, and the next thing I knew, I was being rescued by your fellas here." My eyes slanted to Phelan, and testing for a reaction, I said, "Not sure why you bundled me into the back of your Winnebago, though. . . ."

"Oh, you should know we call the Winnebago 'Little Blue.'" Iona smiled. "Blue is a heavenly color you see. And well, she's little, like—"

"You blacked out. We thought it best to take you from harm's way." Phelan ignored Iona's tidbit, stopping short of taking a bite of his chicken to interject. "Plus, you didn't have a purse on you. No phone, no ID, not even enough money to buy milk with . . ." His eyes narrowed as he watched for my reaction.

As I had already gathered from his earlier Q&A session, Phelan was, unlike the others, suspicious of me, but he was keeping his reservations to himself—for now, at least. By all accounts, it seemed as though he wanted to play a secret game of Battleship over dinner. Fine by me.

"So, what brings you to Hedgerley Village? Are we still in Hedgerley?" I asked.

"We're here on vacation," Phelan answered swiftly.

Miss.

"We're a few miles out of the village. We won't be going any farther for a while. . . ." Iona added, looking to her brother for confirmation. Fergal nodded.

"How old are you?" Phelan fired his question quickly.

"Phelan!" Claire said. "Ignore him. A girl shouldn't have to answer questions like that. Besides, age ain't nothing but a number, baby." Claire's tight curls bobbed above her delicate shoulders as she shook her head. Riley stopped chewing long enough to plant a soppy kiss on her cheek, and she grinned happily.

"I don't mind. Seventeen." I turned the can of beer, pretending to read the label.

"Very young to have worked in a bed-and-breakfast, isn't it?" Phelan said.

Trying to buy time, I reached for a piece of bread and tore off the crust above my plate. "Here in Royal Britannia you're allowed to work once you turn sixteen."

Miss.

But good shot, Phelan. I continued, "You mentioned Lucan—"

"Nobody mentioned Lucan." Phelan jumped on me before I had a chance to finish my sentence.

"Fergal did, when he said grace. Is that where you're all from?" I took another sip of the disgusting black liquid.

"Oh, yes," Iona said, "we all hail from Lucan. Well, except for Dylan; he's a southerner. Well, by comparison. There weren't enough of us left, so he came when Riley . . ." Iona's white cheeks flushed a rosy color as she trailed off.

Direct hit.

An awkward atmosphere descended upon the table. My game with Phelan was over before it had even really started. With Iona, I would sink his battleship.

Turning toward Fergal and deliberately positioning my back to Phelan, I said, "It's been a long day. Is there somewhere I can put my head down?"

"You've not touched your food," Phelan said.

I wasn't sure if he was trying to make some sort of point or if he just wasn't finished playing with me yet.

"Fergal?" I smiled.

"Aye, come with me."

I followed Fergal through the long corridor of the motor home, right to the very end, where he opened up a small room for me. Inside were two sets of bunk beds, but he assured me that I was the only occupant this evening.

"Until more of the family join us, it's all yours. You're welcome to stay awhile. It'd be nice for there to be another girl to keep Iona company. Claire's not much of a listener and Iona's had a tough time, like."

"Oh?" Fergal was quick to trust me. As his expression softened at the use of his sister's name, I considered Fergal wasn't just letting me stay to wind up Phelan. No. He loved Iona and thought I could help with whatever issue she was struggling with.

"Our daddy recently passed. Sounds like you lost your folks, too?" he continued.

I didn't enjoy lying to Fergal. For some reason, in his presence I was calm and content. Maybe it was my new abilities; perhaps I could detect the light souls now. "Yes. You could definitely say I was orphaned." Not a complete lie. "Have you been here on vacation very long?" I asked. Hopping onto the top bunk, I noticed the window next to me at the end of the galley. I began taking off my cardigan, but I thought it best to leave my jeans and shirt on.

"Some of us longer than others." Fergal didn't give much away.

I snuggled under the blanket and put my head down on the lumpy pillow.

"I'll ask Iona to wake you at seven thirty; the rest of us are up and ready to eat at eight thirty. Night, Brooke." Fergal winked at me as he closed the door.

I took a breath. I was in the presence of people who claimed to have spoken with my mother. Where was she? Was she safe? I reached for my crystal and cupped it in my palm, squeezing it. She was a mother I had never known but who had sacrificed everything to give me the best chance of survival. I had to find out why she had revealed herself to this group—when she had spoken to them and what she had said.

My mind whirled, remembering how Jonah had winked at me in the same way Fergal just had, right before he was wrenched from the château fort. My thoughts wandered away from the task at hand to Jonah instead.

I hoped that he had managed to get that bullet out of his leg and that he was somewhere safe. He said he knew why I had forgotten him, and he thought that endangering his existence would make me remember somehow. My memories of him were now splintered cracks in the glass of a broken mirror, hiding his full reflection from me.

I wouldn't be able to just think him back into my head, but part of me wondered if I'd had more time to concentrate on that laughter if he would have been freed from the mirror.

I guess I would never know.

His words about me not being able to outrun my enemies echoed in my consciousness, and I didn't have to search my soul to know that he was exactly right.

I considered the life I would lead—no, we would lead, Gabriel and I—if I ran.

Ruadhan hadn't known me all that long, but he was right about one thing: I wasn't sure I could ignore everything that I knew was going on in the world. But then I had no idea what Ruadhan thought I could do about it. I was but one person. The Arch Angels, the Purebloods and their clans were many; the odds were stacked against me.

Before I could give any real thought as to how I could possibly help, I needed to decide if I was going to fight or flee, and with Gabriel ready to whisk me away, I needed to work that out fast.

NINE

I TOSSED AND TURNED. I had no urge to sleep, and I didn't trust Phelan to stay put, even if Fergal had confirmed that the group was not planning on traveling any farther. The two lads seemed to be engaged in some sort of power play. Everything about Phelan was unsettling. He was closely guarding this crew's secrets, but he wasn't in charge; Fergal was. That didn't sit right, either. Whatever Fergal was in charge of, he hardly seemed the best man for the job. Phelan— from his soldierlike appearance, and the way he held himself, to his reluctance to trust a single word I said—pointed to "leader." Or maybe "terrorist." I wasn't sure yet.

I looked to the small window. The dark veil of night had faded to a light gray; the sun wasn't far from rising. What felt a little like heartburn sat on my chest, and I wasn't sure if it was from being parted from Gabriel or if I needed the sun's rays to refuel. As quietly as I could, I hooked my fingers underneath the plastic seal of the window frame and tilted up the pane of glass. It was a tiny gap, but with some clever bending, I might be able to just squeeze through.

Latching my arms around the outside of the frame, I hoisted my body up and out. It was a fair drop. For a human. It posed no trouble for me.

Once my feet hit the grass, I took off in a sprint, hoping no one was watching. There was no breeze, but the crisp, cold morning hit my face as I charged across the field. A rumble from the motorway up ahead made me grind my heels into the mud, taking half of the earth with me as I skidded to a clumsy stop. I bent down and felt the soil beneath my hands, taking a moment to be grateful that I was alive, here on Earth.

But how long would that last? The abilities to run fast and travel by thought might aid me in escaping my enemies, but they certainly wouldn't help me defeat them.

The Vampires who stormed the Hedgerley house were incredibly strong. I should be strong, too. Searching the empty land, I found the tree line that separated the fields from the motorway.

I traced the outline of the biggest tree and closed my eyes, imagining myself beside it. I attempted to travel by thought. But when I opened my eyes, I was still in the same spot. The sun was not far from rising, so not wanting to waste any time, I sprinted over instead. I ground to a halt, bending over and clutching my knees as shooting pains rode up the back of my legs. Why was using my abilities causing me pain? I shook the worry from my head. Still, I would ask Gabriel.

As I thought his name, I had to actively stop my mind from stretching to his. If he was waiting for me to reach out to him, the second I let him in, he would have a direct line. I wouldn't be able to lie to him about my whereabouts. While I wasn't ready for him to know where I was, I did want him to know I was okay. I'd have to find another way to get a message to him.

The sun was only just waking. I still had time. I approached the yew tree, stretched my arms around its trunk, and I tugged. It moved a little, but as I pushed my weight backward the tree didn't break the ground. My shirt rode up over my midriff, and the cool dew dampened my skin. I huffed and tried again. Still nothing.

"Nice try," said a now-familiar voice.

I let go and tripped. "Jonah?"

He leaned lazily against a nearby tree stump. "One and the same."

The very sight of him made my body contract; like a built-in alarm, it sounded, telling me that he was nearing the walls of my fort.

His gallant stroll toward me was marred by a limp. His chinos bulged over the top of a tightly wrapped bandage around his calf.

"Are you all right?" I said. "They shot you in the leg?"

He scraped his hand through his dark, disheveled hair. "Your Angel patched me up, but it's not altogether healed."

I yanked my shirt back down over my jeans. "Gabriel? He knows you're here, in England?"

Jonah moved next to me, and I automatically shifted back in response.

He rolled his eyes. "You're still worried you're going to react to me?"

I bowed my head. "Yes."

"Hey, nothing to be ashamed of, I have that effect on women."

I glared at him.

He bit his bottom lip and circled me. "How do you feel? When I'm . . . near?"

"Does it matter?"

He wet his lips. "I'd like to know."

He knew full well the response he was trying to get from me. I cursed that my body reacted to his manipulation. I sighed and told the truth. "Every muscle in my body contracts."

"Every muscle, hey?"

I reached for a fallen branch and hurled it at his head, but he ducked before it could wallop him in the face.

"Now, now, no need to get touchy. I can explain why you feel the way you do, but all you need to know right this second is that, as long as I'm not bleeding, you're safe."

"It's not my life I'm worried about."

"Well, considering you claim to have completely forgotten me, it's nice to know you care." Jonah put weight on his injured leg and flinched.

"Are you—"

Jonah shook his head, cutting off my concern, so I continued with protest instead.

"I don't claim anything. I *have* forgotten you. Clearly you make less of an impression than you think."

Jonah shifted his weight, trying to ease his pain. "Didn't seem that way in the forest. And there I was, ready to take a shortcut, but I wonder if you'll eventually remember me without my help."

"You mean without your blood?"

"Yes. Your mind may have forgotten me, but your body certainly hasn't. I was hoping that, before you drank me to an end, your mind would catch up and you'd find it in yourself to stop." He paused.

"Do you plan on telling me why you think my drinking your blood would somehow inspire me to remember you?" I challenged.

"No. This isn't the time or place to have that conversation. Right now, Gabriel has us out searching for you. Apparently he can't sense you. I'm going to assume that's some sort of special ooey-gooey Angel thing," he added sarcastically. "I caught the scent of the kid who shot me so it wasn't too hard for me to find you. Not sure why you're still with them, though . . ."

"They have something I need."

"Such as?"

"Information. I need a few days with them." I wasn't sure whether Jonah would agree, but I had no choice, so I continued, "You think you could tell Gabriel not to worry and that I will be back soon?"

"In case you hadn't figured it out yet, *those guys* are Vampire slayers, demon hunters, or, more accurately, kid farmers with silver pitchforks. You're in dangerous territory. If Gabriel knew you were with them, he wouldn't let you stay, and I'm kinda with him on this one. I gotta take you back." Jonah hunched his shoulders and strode toward me.

"You do that and Gabriel will take me away for good. I need some time. Just a few days. Please, Jonah." I didn't want to ask a favor, but I would if I had to. "Don't tell him where I am."

He stopped in his tracks and rummaged around in his jacket pocket, producing a packet of cigarettes and a lighter. "You think my desire for you to not run off with him would outweigh the need to keep you safe?"

"But I am safe. They don't know who or what I am. Besides, according to you I am the most deadly force walking the Earth. I don't think I'm in any kind of trouble." I hoped my statement had more confidence than I did.

He pulled a cigarette out of the box with his lips and lit up. "The most deadly force walking the Earth, who can't even uproot a measly yew tree? Yeah, I was watching."

So much for trying to sound confident. And yet, suddenly I did feel confident. His words were like a challenge. One I accepted. I returned to the aging tree and wrapped my arms around its base. I stooped down and yanked with all my might but not even a pebble bounced at the tree's roots.

About to try again, a plume of smoke infiltrated my vision. A pungent taste of burning ash stung my tongue, and I coughed. Jonah was right behind me. He slid his hand underneath my shirt and spread his palm wide across my navel. Everything tingled at his touch.

Pushing the inside of my thigh with his knee, he spread my legs wider apart. He took his cigarette from the corner of his lip and held it between his fingers, still clutching the packet in the palm of his hand. He edged back and brushed his hand against my bottom. I was about to smack him, when I realized that he was sliding his cigarette box into the back pocket of my jeans.

"What are you doing?" I said in a huff.

"Positioning you correctly."

Moving his body around mine, he tucked my bangs behind my ear. Finally, he rested his chin in the crevice of my neck. "Pull."

I gulped hard as a nervous, excited knot twisted inside me. But knowing that this very action would make the difference between Jonah ratting me out or not, I ignored it and instead threw my weight into my bottom and desperately tried to pry the tree from the ground. Jonah exerted force onto my belly with his palm, pulling me closer into his frame so that my body was flush against his. I thought, perhaps, he was trying to help. That he'd yank with me.

The tree barely shifted.

Apparently his help stopped with showing me proper form.

I slapped Jonah's fingertips from my midriff, and he released me. "Sorry, beautiful. Looks like you're coming with me. You might have to face the awkward conversation with Gabriel sooner than you'd like."

I reeled around. "What awkward conversation is that exactly?"

"The one where you confess that you're not ready to ride off into the sunset with him." Jonah took one more tug on his cigarette, blowing the smoke from his nose, before flicking the stub over his shoulder.

"That's not why I want to stay. I told you, they have something I need."

"Sure thing, beautiful. You keep telling yourself that." He stared at me, his hazel eyes shining with sarcasm. "A deal's a deal. Come on—time to return you to the 'lost and found.'"

Annoyed with myself, I kicked the bark of the tree that had defeated me.

The sun had begun to rise, and I felt its warmth on the back of my arms. My Vampire abilities might be failing me, but what if . . .

I scanned from the top of the tree's branches down to its roots before closing my eyes. I had to make this damn piece of wood move. If I could travel by thought, surely I could exert strength in the same way? I imagined the ground cracking beneath my feet; I imagined the wind picking up and assaulting its base; I imagined it falling.

It was as though the world were rocking: As I flashed my eyes open, to my surprise the whole tree was at a 90-degree angle, half-uprooted. The air swelled and I stretched out my hand, lining it up with the tree.

"Fall," I begged, allowing my arm to sway limply at my side.

Jonah sucked in a breath as the whole tree crashed down, smashing into its neighbor. A row of six trees tumbled like dominoes, rhythmically colliding, one after the other. The last one went down with an almighty thud, and a cloud of dust smothered the two of us.

Jonah's eyes were wide and his expression perplexed. For once, nothing came out of his mouth.

I wiped dirt off my hands. "Right, well, I think I've made my point."

Jonah didn't protest. Instead he became no more than a blur of color as he sped a few feet away from me and then reappeared. I tilted my head in confusion before realizing why he raced from me.

I was starting to glow in the presence of the rising sun.

I breathed in the magical rays, and my whole body prickled with heat. A halo of crystals surrounded me, and I raised my palms to my face and smiled in wonder as bulbs of light bloomed in my hands.

I cupped the brilliant white jewels and blew at the center. The light flowed forward, splitting itself in two and twisting around the trees that I had just uprooted.

"Rise," I whispered.

The trees vibrated, and then they bounced on the ground, the glow wrapping around their bases.

"Rise," I said, louder this time.

As if by magic, one by one they climbed back toward the sky, the roots replanting themselves in the dirt.

All the energy I had just absorbed had left me and was floating over the trees. Once I was no longer glowing, Jonah returned.

I had no idea how I had commanded the light, and I didn't know how to control it. The sparkles merged together at the top, becoming a single ball of pulsing light. I rolled my fingers nervously in my palm. As if the effervescing ball was responding to me, it split into branches that coiled around the trunks.

From nowhere, a silver tear sliced vertically beside the trees. As if the air were a piece of fabric being cut in two and pulled open, strobes of golden rays cascaded through the gap.

A rift was opening from the first dimension, right in front of us, and it wasn't one that I had created.

I panicked and flexed my hands, and the jeweled spirals of my making stopped.

One by one, they plummeted to the ground. The light gathered and spilled out like a waterfall, flooding where Jonah and I stood.

Jonah cursed, and before I had a chance to blink, I was swept onto his back and we were hurtling through the field.

JONAH STOPPED AND SET me down beside a well, far away from where we had been.

We were miles away, but I concentrated on where we had run from and I was able to focus in on the trees were once again stood tall, appearing untouched by my actions.

The distance made it difficult, and the scenery wobbled and rocked back and forth, in and out of focus. But then, the silver glimmer of the rift came into view, prominently displayed against the bleak landscape. And next to it now, a towering figure draped in white robes floated in the air. There were great white feathers on his back, stemming from between his shoulder blades. They fluttered, and his form shook until his very being became microscopic particles. As he reentered the rift, it closed behind him.

Like an elastic band, the scene snapped back.

I turned to Jonah, who winced as he tried to balance his weight.

"Are you in pain?" I asked.

"The kid farmers you're so keen to spend time with shot me with a silver bullet, Lailah. Gabriel removed it, but not before it had caused some damage."

I shook my head. "You're a Vampire. It should have healed by now."

"Silver reflects light. And that light began traveling through my blood before I found Gabriel."

"What will heal it?" I asked, scanning the land around us, ensuring no other rifts were opening.

He looked at me as if I should have known the answer and then shook his head. "Doesn't matter. It's not important. That was a nice show you put on back there. You drew the attention of the Arch Angels, though—that wasn't clever."

"It's okay; he didn't see us. I just watched him go back through the rift and it closed behind him." I paused. "Not too much wrong with my Angel side, it seems, other than some control, of course."

"You gotta stop doing that."

"Doing what?"

"Referring to yourself as if you're split in two, or as if somehow your soul is half and half."

"It is: half light, half dark."

Jonah pressed his lips into a tight line. "No. You weren't conscious when that guy carried you off, and he was laden with silver. Silver affects Vampires."

"What's your point?"

"You weren't sporting your fangs when that happened, beautiful. You were just you. Not glowing like an Angel and not lit up like a starving Vampire." Jonah collected his thoughts. "Do you remember me offering you my blood, on the mountain, before you . . . died? Do you remember any of that clearly?"

I vaguely recalled a pair of big black eyes staring down at me. That was the moment that I saw my light, reflecting back at me from the darkness. Had those eyes belonged to Jonah? "I've told you, I don't remember you. I'm sorry."

"You accepted everything you were before your body gave up. You must have, because you came back. Do you remember what that felt like, right before?"

I looked toward the horizon. I did remember. "It was like an explosion, as if there were an upsurge of light and dark all at the same time—as if they collided and merged together."

Jonah placed his hand on my shoulder. "You aren't half light and half dark; you're one whole. And that whole is all kinds of shades of gray."

My lower lip twitched nervously. "So what does that mean?"

"I dunno. I'm hardly an expert on the subject. It makes you *different*. It makes you *capable*. And if you've got the abilities of both, then it's likely you have the vulnerabilities of both, too."

"Yeah, I figured. . . . Good news for me, right? Get me near a Pureblood or an Arch Angel, and I won't last five seconds."

"No. Embrace all that you are, and you will be untouchable." Jonah's tone softened. "Forget your new friends. Let's leave, and you can tell Gabriel you want to stay awhile, that you want me to stay awhile with you." He hesitated as I crinkled my forehead. "Look, you need me. If you want to run off into the night with your Angel, fine. But if you at least let me help you first, you'll stand a chance when they catch up with you." When I still didn't answer, he tried again. "You can't run as fast as I can, you couldn't uproot that tree using force, and you couldn't control whatever it was you just did back there. You're struggling when it should be easy. Let me try to help you."

"I'll think about it. . . . But first, I have a question, and the answer to it is back the way I came." I listened for the noise from the motorway and tried to get my bearings.

Before I could leave, Jonah seized my arm and yanked me in toward him. "You have two hours."

Our sudden closeness made my heart thud in my chest. "What? No. At least give me a day!"

"Half a day. And I will be back to get you. Understand?"

I wrinkled my nose but finally conceded. "Fine, but not a word to Gabriel about where I am, *do you understand*?" I shrugged him off, annoyed that his touch affected me and that my body betrayed me so easily.

Jonah's cheeks creased as he let out a half-laugh and ruffled my hair. "You're still pretty stubborn. I guess some things never change."

His words stung me. I didn't appreciate the closeness he seemed to find habitual, or the way he spoke to me as though he knew me better than I knew myself. It unnerved me.

I didn't want to be unkind, so I spoke softly. "No. Some things don't. I love Gabriel." I paused. "In my nearly two hundred years of walking this Earth, no matter how many times I died and woke up, I never forgot *his* face."

Jonah wore a blank expression but his body had hardened and his right hand was clenched into a fist.

"I know I'm asking you to keep Gabriel in the dark about where I am, but please don't let that cloud your opinion of my feelings for him." I thought that was all I needed to say, but that arrogant grin was already edging up his cheek. "Remind me, what name did you call me?"

Running his tongue along his teeth and then grinding them together, eventually he replied, "Cessie. I knew you as Cessie."

"I'm sorry, Jonah, but in case you hadn't gathered, Cessie was a mask—one I have taken off. Just to be clear, whatever happens from here, I'm Lailah, and my intention is to spend the rest of forever with Gabriel."

His face fell. I turned, gearing up to run, when he tugged at my shirt and spun me back around to face him.

"Cessie, Lailah, Cinderella, Sleeping Beauty . . . You've had, and I gave you, plenty of names. What is it that dude said? 'A rose by any other name would smell as sweet.' Call yourself whatever the hell you like; it doesn't change who you are. Not then and not now."

We stared each other out for some time before I finally conceded. "All right. Point made. And that *dude's* name is Shakespeare, by the way."

He loosened his grasp, freeing me. "Great, him you remember."

I walked away, rolling my eyes. "You've gotta have the last word, don't you? Why do I get the feeling that that's something else that hasn't changed?"

Jonah seemed to relax, and then he winked at me. "Go on. Go infiltrate your camp of pitchfork-wielding kid farmers. But be careful."

I mouthed a quick "thank you" before I fled back toward the motor home.

TEN

I RAN UNTIL THE oversize motor home was in view. Day had woken, and I worried for a moment that I had spent too long with Jonah. I didn't think it was seven thirty yet, but with no watch and no phone I couldn't be sure. I slid around to the back of the motor home, just in time to see my window snap shut.

Crap.

I hovered, debating my options, and eventually made my way to the side of the van, hoping I could reenter through the door.

Phelan stood in the doorway with his hands placed on either side of the frame. When I approached he said, "Right, you, time to leave."

"What? Why?" I asked as innocently as I could.

I moseyed toward him, but he jumped to the ground and met me midway. "Because I don't trust folk who sneak out of their windows, that's why," he said. "What exactly were you doing out here?"

The wifebeater he wore with his loose pajama bottoms allowed me to see the many tattoos that ran the length of his arms and across his chest. They made me even more wary of him.

I had to think fast. "I didn't want to wake anyone, that's why. I've only been out here two minutes. I just needed to, you know, step out."

"To do what?" He placed his hand around my forearm to keep me rooted to the spot.

"Erm, I needed to . . ." I shifted my weight from one foot to the other, and I felt the bulge of Jonah's cigarette box in my back pocket. "Smoke. I needed a smoke."

Phelan's eyes narrowed; it was as if he were a human lie detector, inspecting my features, as if they would somehow reveal the truth. Putting my finger up in the air to warn him of my movements, I reached in my back pocket and produced the box. I held it out for him to see.

He took his hand off me and grudgingly gestured for me to sit on the cold grass. He sat across from me and held his hand out for the box. He removed two sticks and gave one to me as he dug inside his pajama pocket for a lighter.

Placing the filter to my lips, I pulled as he lit it. I had to stifle a cough as I inhaled the smoke. Phelan tilted his head and gave me that "I don't trust you" look he was getting so good at, before sparking up his own.

He rolled the cardboard box over and over in his fingers. "You get around, don't you? This here packet is in French."

I wasn't expecting him to say that, and I mentally cursed Jonah for not having stocked up on duty free this side of the Channel.

Ignoring him, I took another puff on the disgusting cancer stick. Trying not to take it in, I blew out the smoke before it found its way to my lungs. Not wanting to meet his eyes, I studied the black pattern and the many crosses that rode up his neck. They were covering an elongated scar that stretched right up to his chin.

Batting my eyelashes and refocusing on his big brown eyes, I said, "Did it hurt?"

Phelan looked cautiously to his chest while holding the cigarette in between the tip of his thumb and his index finger. The ash had burnt halfway down, yet he still didn't flick it away. Exhaling a cloud of smoke, he scratched the back of his beanie hat. "No, just ink work."

I squeezed a tight smile. "I didn't mean that."

Phelan looked a little taken aback, but his expression quickly returned to hard and unemotional.

"Phelan, is that Brooke out there with you?" Iona's sweet voice chirped from inside the motor home.

"'Tis," he answered, still focused intently on me. He didn't shift an inch.

"May I have her help in the kitchen?" she asked, raising her voice slightly.

Stubbing out his cigarette and wetting his lips, Phelan stood up. After dusting down the back of his bottoms, he took my hand and, in one swift tug, yanked me up to my feet.

As I stood, he drew his arm in and pulled me in close. "You didn't have a pack of cigarettes yesterday. I know, because I checked you for ID. They didn't just magically appear in your pocket. Where'd you get them?"

I cleared my throat. "I did. I haven't left this place since I got here." Despite my best efforts, my voice cracked.

Phelan tucked my hair behind my ears before bending down so that he was cheek-to-cheek with me and whispered, "Then I guess all that dirt on your clothes magically appeared overnight, too?"

I opened my mouth, but nothing came out.

He tutted as he pushed my chin up. He then stared at me for a moment before finally releasing my hand and striding back toward the motor home, disappearing inside.

It took me a few seconds to gather myself. I hadn't considered the thick layer of dust and mud that smothered my clothes.

The smile on Iona's face when she poked her head out of the motor home fell away when she saw the mess I was in. "Oh dear, I didn't realize you'd gotten so dirty yesterday. Come on, you can borrow some clothes and then we have to get breakfast on. It's nearly nine, and the boys will be hungry, like."

Iona was already fully dressed, wearing a cream-colored winter dress made of wool. A matching cardigan and thick tights finished her look. Well, nearly finished her look. As I judged her conservative outfit, her oversize Scooby-Doo slipper-boots suddenly transformed her from "elegant young lady" to "adorable kid sister."

Iona led me down the hall to her bedroom. It was a bigger space than the room I was staying in; her queen-size bed was made up with a pretty pink duvet, and fresh flowers sat on her bedside table.

"Tulips? Do you have an admirer, Iona?" I closed the door behind me.

She giggled, embarrassed at my suggestion, and said, "Naw, Fergal bought them for me. My daddy used to make sure I always had fresh flowers in my room. He did it for my ma, too, before she passed. . . ."

"I'm sorry," I said.

"Fergal got me a necklace, too, as an early birthday present. I'm seventeen soon." From her pillowcase, she pulled out a silver locket. "So I could have them near my heart, always."

She played with the chain before holding it out for me to take.

I lurched backward. "No, I couldn't. . . . Why don't you show me?"

Keeping my distance, I peered at the large silver oval resting in Iona's palm. I read the word *Petal* engraved on the outside.

"Daddy used to call me Petal," she said. "He used to call my ma Petal, too."

"Something to do with the flowers?" I asked politely.

"Aye. He always said that we were his angels, and that we deserved them freshly picked every day."

I hesitated. "Another pet name for you both, his angels?"

"Um-hum." She nodded, wearing a happy smile.

She carefully undid the clasp and opened the locket. There were two photos, one on each side: an older gentleman—Iona's father—staring back at me on the right, and on the left, a handsome, dark-haired lad.

"That there's my daddy," she said proudly.

"They are lovely pictures. I thought you said you had one of your mother and father. Who's that?"

"That's Padraig, my other brother. He also passed, just before my daddy." Iona's dejected expression made me sad. Her eyes glistened in a watery coating and she coughed, trying to choke back her brewing tears.

My heart went out to Iona; her family had suffered so much loss. It didn't take long for me to hit on the reason behind it: They hunted Vampires. Chances were, the Vampires fought back.

"Your brother looks a lot like your father," I said.

"Padraig had a different ma; my daddy's first wife died giving birth to him. Then, a couple of years later, when Daddy was twenty, he met my ma and had me and Fergal," she explained.

"I thought you said Fergal got you the locket so that you could have your parents with you."

Iona closed the locket and tucked it back into the pillowcase. "Naw, so I could have *them* with me—my daddy and my brother. I asked my daddy for one of my ma once, but he said she never liked having her photo taken. That if I ever wanted to see her face, I only needed to look in the mirror." That memory caused her plump lips to stretch wide.

Iona was so gentle, so childlike. If you could put her in your tea, she'd remove all the bitterness and would be the most deliciously sweet honey you'd ever tasted.

She opened up a chest of drawers and started rummaging around, finally taking out a very long and frilly skirt.

"Is there any chance of a pair of jeans?" I asked quickly.

She looked at me over her shoulder, and pursed her lips. "Are you sure? I've got some lovely skirts and, well, *lads* wear jeans you know...."

"Yeah, I'm sure. If you have a pair, that is." I was beginning to realize how traditional this group was.

Iona nodded, and pulled out another drawer, searching for what I assumed were likely her only pair. I took the opportunity to scan her bedroom walls, which were full of posters perfectly tacked side by side. The right-hand corner was covered with multiple boy bands, and in the left it was Scooby-Doo, *The Wizard of Oz*, and Harry Potter.

"You like Harry Potter?" I asked.

"Aye, I love magic! My daddy wouldn't let me read past the third book, though; he said it got a bit too dark." She handed me a small pile of clothes.

"You're nearly seventeen, right?" *And you hunt Vampires. . . .*

She bobbed her head, her pale skin flushing pink. "I get frightened. I like happy things, like music. All different sorts. And I like to dance and sing. I listen to lots of songs while I cook, which I always think is funny, 'cause they say music is food for the soul, like."

"That's very true." I held up the clothes. "Thank you for these."

Iona grabbed my arm lightly as I pushed down the door handle. "Wait! It gets a bit cold." She opened the bottom drawer of her bedside table and reached inside.

As she did, a ray of sunlight, which was streaming in through the window, reflected off an object in the drawer. I rose to my tiptoes to peek over her shoulder. In the drawer was a silver dagger in a leather holster.

It was bizarre to think that this most innocent and kind-hearted of girls was involved in demon-slaying. Could she be a real-life Buffy Summers?

"Here!" she exclaimed with glee, springing up and placing a pair of cartoon slippers on top of the clothes in my arms.

Maybe not.

"Thank you," I said, making my way out of her room to get changed.

Once inside my tiny room, I began unbuttoning my muddied shirt, trying not to bang my elbows on the sides of the two bunks. Slipping it off and unbuttoning my jeans, I was down to my underwear. Shame there was no time for a shower, though I wasn't even sure if there was one in the motor home. I pulled apart the parcel of clothing and wriggled the jeans on over my hips, zipping them up. Luckily for me, Iona and I were a similar size. I slid the cami top over my head and tucked it into the waistband.

The scar on my chest, which ran over my heart, was visible above the neckline. I frowned. A rose by any other name, huh? I wondered if Jonah thought of me that way—like a rose. If I were one, you'd never be able to tell; most of my petals had been plucked a long time ago, leaving only a stem covered in thorns.

In the absence of a hairbrush, I tipped my hair over my head and fluffed it up from underneath, before running my fingers through my bangs.

Just as I was reaching for my cardigan at the end of the bed, the door opened. I spun around, expecting to see Iona. Instead, Fergal was leaning against the door frame.

"Oh, sorry, Iona asked me to pass you this, thought you might need it," he said, handing me a fitted cashmere sweater.

I took it and smiled politely. "Thanks."

Fergal's eyes swooped up and down, and when they found mine again they twinkled. "You look much fresher for a change of clothes."

The sweater was thicker than my cardigan so I pulled it over my head, ruffling my hair once again in the process.

"Ah, you're a pretty doll, aren't you?" Fergal said, and to my surprise he came in close to me. "But you're missing one thing."

He took off his beanie hat and his long blond strands cascaded across his temples and covered his ears. He positioned the hat on the back of my head. Then, he collected all of my waist-length curls and pushed them behind my shoulder.

"There." He smiled, but then hesitated. His eyes locked with mine as though they were imprisoned by them. "Huh."

"What?" I asked.

"Your eyes. They're like a coccinella septempunctata. Well, if they came in blue, like."

Coccinella septempunctata? A ladybug? Perhaps these guys weren't quite the pitchfork-wielding kid farmers Jonah had assumed them to be.

My eyelashes automatically fluttered out of embarrassment. I wasn't pleased with how my eyes now appeared; it was as though they branded me, warning the world that I was different—that I was dangerous.

"Some sort of mutation . . ."

"Aye, it's pretty cool," Fergal said. "You can keep my hat. It suits you better."

Fergal strolled out of the room, closing the door behind him. I popped the slippers on my feet. Given I had already squashed Iona's attempt to dress me in a "respectable housewife" outfit with the jeans, they couldn't hurt. Plus, they made me smile, and that was not something I did a lot of, and something I didn't expect to be doing anytime soon.

ELEVEN

Iona and I set about creating an enormous breakfast buffet for the lads. I was in charge of frying the eggs and bacon, while Iona grilled sausages and cooked hash browns in the oven. Iona was a well-oiled machine in the kitchen, and I was reminded of the time I had worked in the B&B in Scotland.

"Do the lads ever cook for themselves? Or at least help out in the kitchen?" I asked.

Iona giggled. "Naw, not really, we're a bit more traditional. They have their duties and, well, I have mine." She paused, perhaps realizing that to an outsider this setup appeared very outdated. "Anyway, I like cooking for them; it makes me feel *useful*. Claire helps me sometimes, when she's not busy with Riley, like!" She giggled.

I turned the eggs over in the pan and laughed along with her. I wasn't about to challenge Iona; I needed her to think of me as a friend, to trust me enough to reveal the things I wanted to know.

Several teapots were on the go, and jugs of coffee, fresh juice, and water were spread onto the table and continually replenished. While the lads waited for their food they drank their morning kick-starters outside with rolled-up cigarettes. Phelan, however, remained perched on the sofa, watching my every move and inadvertently reminding me of the caution I needed to exercise.

The motor home smelled like a café as the odor of sizzling bacon swept through the living area. We served up breakfast, and the lads clambered around the table, hungrily snatching all our hard work onto their plates before traipsing back out of the motor home. Only Riley stalled, taking a moment to glance down the hallway before he left. I noticed that Cameron wasn't present.

"Where are they going?" I asked Iona.

"They're eating in Little Blue this morning," she said.

Phelan hovered before leaving last. He clearly didn't want me to overhear their conversation. It wasn't a problem; I was glad he had left me alone with Iona.

Nothing that we had cooked remotely interested me. I had never seen Gabriel eat anything, and I knew what Vampires survived on and it certainly wasn't bacon. As I thought about blood, my throat began to tingle and a hot flush rode up my neck. At first I thought it was because of the oven and the stove in the kitchen. "Is it just me, or is it really warm in here?" I asked Iona, tugging the sweater over my head.

"Naw, it's cold with the windows open. You feeling okay? You're not coming down with something are you?"

"No, I don't think so. Is there a bathroom in here?"

Iona pottered over to the table, cloth in hand, and gestured to the hall. "It's the fourth door down."

I folded the sweater neatly and repositioned the beanie, making sure my long hair was covering the worst of my scars, the one that ran the length of my back. Even wearing a cami, the mark was visible, branching out just below the nape of my neck. I headed for the bathroom. Once inside, I ran the cold tap and splashed my face. It didn't do much. Drying my cheeks on a towel, I looked up at the mirror to see that my skin was indeed flushed. My vision was blurring. I was trying to refocus when that all-too-familiar red mist clouded my sight. My eyes flashed red and I panicked. I ran my finger over my teeth, but there was no sign of my fangs. I ran the tap again, this time rinsing my eyes, and after a few moments, the black smudges reappeared over my sapphire blue. This morning I had felt hollow, and despite absorbing the sun, I knew my body was still craving something. I worried that it was a craving for blood.

I returned to the kitchen to see Iona filling the sink with water and dirty dishes.

Claire stepped into the room, scrunching the last of her mousse into her curls. "All right, girls?"

Claire was truly stunning: She had a tiny frame, which she dressed well; her caramel skin was flawless; and her makeup was simple but effective.

"Morning! They're next door." Iona opened the fridge and took out a bowl of freshly sliced fruit and a bottle of water. "Here."

"Thanks." Claire took her breakfast from Iona and stole a fork from a drawer before making her way outside.

"Claire eats with the lads?" I asked as I removed the foil from the grill plate.

"Aye. She goes with them to—" Iona stopped abruptly. "She's different from me. She's a married woman, so she accompanies Riley, makes sure he's got everything he needs."

"Right." I threw the foil into the trash. "She's very young to be married, isn't she?"

Iona slipped her fingers into yellow rubber gloves and stood over the sink. "Claire's sixteen, and she loves Riley. When all this is over, they'll probably make some babies." She giggled.

"When all what's over, Iona?" I had to be careful, but after my conversation with Phelan this morning, I feared I was going to be booted out before I could gather more information about my mother.

Iona stopped scrubbing the frying pan and thought carefully before answering. "Nothing. I just meant the holiday is all. When we go home, they will set up house back in Lucan."

"You don't live on the road?" I asked.

"Oh, no, we're not travelers. Back home we all have houses and family and the church. We don't normally leave Lucan; the lads have their hands full doing our Lord's work there." The frying pan reclaimed her attention, and she whispered under her breath. "I hope we can go back soon."

Before I had the chance to delve any further, the motor home shook as Fergal came charging through the door. "Iona! We're leaving. Cam called."

Iona swung around from the sink, and she gripped the work surface. "Oh," she said quietly.

Chains and other objects clattered against one another as they were gathered and tossed into Little Blue, accompanied by the double click of guns being loaded.

"Brooke, you'll stay with Iona and keep her company," Fergal told me.

I nodded, and he rushed back the way he had come. Something was going on, and I wanted to know what, but if the lads were leaving I could talk to Iona, do some digging, and then get away. This was the opportunity I had been waiting for.

"Wait!" Iona cried, tripping over her feet to reach Fergal outside.

Phelan suddenly appeared from nowhere. Grabbing my hair, he jerked me backward into his chest. "I don't know who you are, and I don't trust you." He tugged my hair down and my neck made a cracking noise.

I gulped hard and tried to pull away. "What the—"

He pulled me in and brought his lips to my ear. "When I get back, that girl better be in one piece, or you won't be." His words were like flames, licking up the air around me so that I felt suffocated.

He shoved me forward as a crestfallen Iona reappeared.

"Be careful. I mean, have fun," Iona whimpered to Phelan, caught between the truth and the lie of what was going on, of who they really were. I could sympathize with that.

As Iona scurried off to the bathroom, I wished I didn't have such sensitive hearing; my heart broke on her behalf as her tears gushed. Clearly, she didn't want Fergal to leave. How many people had left her, never to come back?

I turned back to Phelan, my skin simmering as I prepared to retaliate—when I stopped. He looked stunned: His eyes were huge, and his chest had stopped rising and falling as he held his breath. His smooth skin became creased as his forehead crinkled, and his eyebrows dipped. My first thought was that my eyes were shining red warning lights, but then he wasn't reaching for a stake or a gun.

His Adam's apple bulged as he swallowed and edged toward me. "I'm sorry—was it painful?"

"Well, I don't appreciate being manhandled, but no," I replied, unsure of him.

He stood precariously in front of me—a cold, silent exchange of confusion passing from him to me.

"I didn't mean that," he said finally, repeating my earlier words, and I realized then that he was referring to the horrific scar running down my back—Frederic's last mark on the world, on me.

He stepped forward. "Your scar, when did you get it?"

I scuttled back and he stopped, allowing me my space.

"A few years ago," I replied honestly.

Phelan eyed me, turning on his human lie detector once more. The motor home outside grumbled as the engine started and the band of slayers set off. His eyes slanted, and he hesitated. "Your ma is gone, right?"

"Yes," I whispered.

"Do you swear on your ma's memory that you got that scar a few years ago, as you say?"

Why was he asking me this? What did it even matter to him?

"Brooke?"

"Yes. I swear on the memory of my mother."

Phelan exhaled noisily, almost as if my response had disappointed him. Striding toward the door, he looked back over his shoulder. "Don't forget what I said: One piece, or you will be many." His jaw locked, and then he was gone.

His motorcycle growled as it started up and then screeched as he set off in pursuit of the motor home. I wasn't going to last here a few more hours. I needed answers, and I needed them now—before Phelan came back.

Iona was still in the bathroom so I wandered outside, my eyes resting on the truck-pulled caravan. I had a feeling I knew where the weapons I had heard them gathering had come from.

The door was secured with a silver padlock. I couldn't place my hands on either side and use force to break it because I could seriously damage my skin, which I would not be able to explain. If I was going to get in, I needed another way.

I remembered that Gabriel had once started a car by touching his index finger to the ignition; perhaps that trick worked for locks, too. I closed my eyes and imagined it unlocking. When I opened them, nothing had happened. Perhaps I needed to touch it? I didn't want to, but I didn't have a better idea.

I took a sharp breath and moved my fingertip over the key-shaped hole, thinking about the mechanism turning. A spark of light left my finger, followed by a click, but my skin sizzled and I yelped as I leaped backward.

I bolted back into the motor home and retrieved a small wooden spoon from the kitchen drawer, taking a moment to make sure Iona was still in the bathroom.

Back at the caravan, the lock turned; now I just needed to get the padlock from the door. I leveraged the spoon and used it to lift the padlock up. It hit the ground with a thud as it fell.

I was in.

I yanked the door open and beheld Aladdin's cave. Well, if Aladdin cared for a vault full of silver, instead of gold, crafted to create Vampire-exterminating weapons instead of jewels.

I didn't dare go in, but from where I stood I could see sharpened wooden stakes, silver spears, and what looked like some sort of flame-throwers chained across the back wall. A variety of guns positioned in holders were strewn over a ledge, and next to them—hanging from hooks and dangling from the roof—were single silver maces and handheld crossbows. A multitude of mismatched buckets sat side-by-side; one was full of bullets, another consisted of jagged-edged throwing stars, and the last contained bundles of chains cast entirely from silver. It dawned on me quickly that perhaps these guys actually knew what they were doing; maybe they were experts at killing Vampires. Clearly they were well funded and scarily good at amassing a horde of very accurately crafted weaponry to take down the enemy.

"Brooke?" Iona's sweet voice tweeted in my ear.

So engrossed in my own thoughts, I had failed to notice that she was standing beside me. "Iona. I'm sorry. I, well, I just popped out, and the door was ajar," I lied, edging back from the caravan—from her.

"We hunt demons," she said, her voice cool and smooth.

I was surprised by her admission. "I see that."

"You don't seem surprised?"

"Not much surprises me these days," I answered, keeping check of her movements.

She shrugged. "Phelan will be angry with me if I talk to you, but come inside. I'll fix you a cup of tea and we can chat, like."

Maybe she was lying—perhaps trying to lure me inside the motor home and then she would try to kill me. But her expression was sincere, as though she just simply needed a friend. And so I followed her back indoors and sat down while she prepared a teapot.

At first, we sat in silence, sugaring our tea and stirring incessantly, until she eventually spoke.

"Demons walk the Earth, Brooke. My family, Phelan's family,

and the others protect our community—the congregation back in Lucan—from the Devil's creatures. It's been this way for generations, but something terrible happened." As Iona spoke, her gaze never left her mug. Finally she placed her spoon down and looked up at me from across the table.

"What happened?" I encouraged.

"You believe me? *About the demons?*" she whispered.

"Yes, if that treasure trove out there is anything to go by."

"Oh yes. Demons invade our town, stealing and murdering our people. Daddy never knew what they did with the ones they took, the ones whose bodies we never found." Her words were rushed. "My daddy was a reverend, and he said that the mouth of Hell sits on the outskirts of Lucan. And the Vampires we hunt come through Hell's gates, disguised to look like us."

Iona thought that Second Generation Vampires came from Hell. Clearly, she didn't understand that they were human once, turned by a greater evil—the Purebloods.

I wrapped my hands around the mug and placed it to my lips, as though I were sipping the warm tea. "Iona, I think Vampires who look human were human once. They became Vampires; they were not born that way, no?"

"That's just what you see on the television, like. Daddy said they came straight from Hell's mouth, and that the Devil's own would never reveal their horns."

I nodded.

"But then, we got a new task. My daddy was in charge; he said an Angel came and gave us a new purpose. We left Lucan, but something went wrong, and my daddy . . ." Her voice squeaked. "Nearly all of them were killed by the demons. Hardly any were left. So now Fergal's in charge," she explained.

"You said an Angel came, Iona. What *exactly* did the Angel say?" This was it, the answer I had been waiting for.

"She appeared to my daddy and my uncle, and asked them to find the girl. She said we must find her before they did."

"Before who did?" I demanded.

"I'm not sure. D-daddy only told me that she came and asked us to seek out the girl, said she needed saving, like," she stuttered, taken aback by my outburst.

"Saving from *what*? Saving from *who*, Iona?" My hands clenched tightly around the mug and my cheeks burned.

Who had she wanted to protect me from? The Purebloods? The Arch Angels?

Iona fidgeted uncomfortably where she sat. "Saving from herself, I think."

What? My thoughts tumbled. Had my mother wanted me saved from what I had now become?

"Where is this Angel, Iona? Where can I find her?" The question left my lips so fast that I couldn't be sure she'd heard me.

"I dunno."

"I need to, I *have* to know. Did your father tell Fergal? He's in charge now, right? He knows where she is?"

"Brooke! Your hands!" Iona leaped up from her chair and ran into the kitchen. She rushed back over, thrusting a tea towel over my hands. I'd crushed the porcelain and the scalding-hot water was drenching my skin. I hadn't even noticed.

Prying the broken pieces from my clutch, she grazed her finger against a serrated edge, causing her thin skin to split. The faintest trickle of blood dropped onto the table as she withdrew.

My eyes darted to the tear in her skin, and before I knew it, I had her by the scruff of her cardigan.

Iona yelped and my fangs cracked as I touched her soft skin against my lips, inhaling her scent. But, for whatever reason, she didn't appeal to me.

"Erm, sorry to interrupt, I need a word." A shrill voice found me through the haze of crimson clouding my vision. I paused, and I loosened my grasp on Iona.

I took a deep breath, coming back to myself. I placed my hand over my mouth and, as I peered up, Iona did a double take. I worried that she had caught sight of my red bulbs burning out.

The scream that escaped Iona's lips told me that she'd seen too much.

Iona looked from me to the pale stranger who stood outside the door frame, eventually resting her vigilant stare back on me. I didn't say anything, allowing time for my fangs to recede and my eyes to soften.

Iona darted backward. Reaching behind the sofa, she pulled out a silver blade. Unsure of whom to feel more threatened by: the girl she had befriended who, moments ago, had her by the scruff; or the random visitor who had appeared from thin air and was now lingering in the doorway of her makeshift home.

"Brooke, who is that?" Iona bumbled. She kept her eyes glued to the entranceway but pointed and waved the dagger in my direction.

"It's okay. I know her." I collected myself, trying to pacify Iona.

"Brooke, huh?" the girl said, arching an eyebrow. "I guess that makes me Lailah."

TWELVE

Iona didn't react to the mention of my name, so I said, "It's okay. Everything's fine. I can explain—but first, I need to speak with . . . her. Please, just stay here."

I cautiously stepped around Iona and followed Brooke outside. Taking her arm, I shuffled her farther from the motor home.

"What are you doing here?" I said. "How'd you even know where I was?"

Brooke swept her newly long and darkened hair out of her eye line before placing her hand on her hip. "I followed Jonah this morning. You need to come back with me. Now." She gave me the once-over and snorted as she pointed to my feet. "Did I not teach you anything? Cartoon slippers? *Really?*"

"Hair extensions? Really?"

"Frozen in time, remember. I can't grow it myself," she replied with sarcasm, twirling the wavy curls that hung just above her hip.

"Whatever, I don't care. You need to leave. Do you have any idea who these people are and what they spend their time doing?" I spun her around and shoved her away from me.

She immediately reeled back around to face me and brushed the tops of her arms where I had just touched her, as though she were flicking off dirt. "Okay, first, don't push me. There's no need to push. And second, I know who they are; Jonah told me. They're spying on the Hedgerley house, you know. They've got this little guy hiding in the garden. It's hilarious! I was smashing doors, slamming windows shut, you should have seen him—too funny!" She grinned.

"Did he see you?" I asked, feeling bad for poor Cameron.

"No." She adjusted the sunglasses perched on top of her head. "I just made enough noise to draw them out. Meanwhile, I came to get you. In case that chick has clocked that I'm a Vamp, I'd rather explain the whys en route." She reached for my arm and tugged for me to follow her.

I listened for Iona, and as I focused, I could hear her talking on the phone. "I dunno, she just turned up. All she said was that her name was Lailah. But Brooke . . . Oh Fergal, I . . . I think she might be one of them, I'm not sure. . . ."

Fergal shouted so loudly that I could hear his end of the conversation, too. "You're kidding me!" he said. "Are you sure that's her name? Never mind. Listen, just stay away from Brooke and keep Lailah safe."

Fergal hung up, so I turned my attention back to the real Brooke and dug my heels into the grass.

"Why'd you go and use my name? Are you completely insane?" I had to hold myself back from giving her a good slap.

"Why'd you use mine?"

"Oh, I don't know, something to do with the fact that these guys are searching for a girl—a girl who happens to be called Lailah. I thought, in case they knew it, it might be best not to give *that* name. Yours was the first one that popped into my head." I threw my hands up in the air in disdain. "And now, thanks to you, Iona is on the phone telling her brother, who happens to be the leader of this little band of Vampire slayers, that a girl called Lailah just rocked up—and guess what? He seemed to know my name. And, to make matters worse, she now thinks I might be some sort of demon."

"So, let's leave." Brooke tugged her jacket down before pointing two thumbs over her shoulder.

Hesitating, I said, "I can't. Not yet."

I needed to know where my mother was. Even though she hadn't been in my life for a very long time, I believed that if anyone could help me figure out which path was the right one, it'd be her. Gabriel said he didn't trust anyone, and that extended to my mother, but she had sent these people to find and save me. Why would she do that if she meant me harm? I wanted to find her, but I would have to do it without Gabriel's help.

Iona's father may have wrapped her up in cotton wool and not told her about his Angel encounter, but based on Fergal's reaction to my name, that was not the case with him.

He had to know where my mother was.

Brooke shook her head. "If they think you're a demon, you're in trouble. Why would you want to stay here?"

"I have my reasons. I came for an answer, and I'm not leaving until I have it."

"What question could be so important—"

"My . . . my mother. My Angel mother . . . I think they might know where she is." I considered the situation we were now faced with. "Look, they came here to seek out the girl to save her. To save *Lailah*. So, whatever happens from this moment on, you need to keep my name. They won't harm you if they think you're me. Do you understand?"

"Jeez, if they are here to save the girl—not to, you know, kill the girl—then why don't you just tell them you're that girl? Ask your frickin' question and be done with it."

"Have you forgotten the Purebloods and the Arch Angels? If they find out I'm alive, they will come for me. I have to be clever about this." Brooke's attitude of indifference irritated me.

"Getting pretty cynical in your old age, aren't you? Right now, I couldn't care less about your stupid question. If you want to risk your ass, then come back for it, but only after . . ."

"After what?"

Brooke took my elbows, her lips pulling in a tight line as she stared at me. "Apparently you don't remember Jonah. So let me take a moment to remind you that you were friends, once before." She stopped briefly and tapped my forehead. "And while it may have escaped your memory, on more than one occasion, he saved you. And when you went running off up that mountain to meet Zherneboh, the deadliest and most heinous Pureblood of them all, guess who came chasing after you?"

"Jonah," I said quietly. He'd said he'd been there, but I couldn't place him in the picture of what happened that night.

Brooke's eyes narrowed, and she pursed her lips.

"Why are you telling me this? What does any of it have to do with me going back with you right this very moment?" I demanded, aware that Iona was long off her cell and I could hear her shuffling about in a drawer.

Nudging her mouth toward my ear, she said, "Because Jonah's dying, and only you can help him."

As she stepped back from me, I saw how strained her expression was.

I thought back to this morning, how Jonah seemed to be hobbling. "The bullet?"

Brooke nodded. "Took him a while to reach Gabriel. The silver had melted, some of it worked its way into his bloodstream, and the light is slowly making its way around his system. Once it has . . ."

I shook my head, confused. "What can I do?"

"He needs to feed from you. When you first met, he was hurt, real bad. He drank your blood, and it healed him."

I healed Jonah? How can I not remember that? *Him?* I wanted to help, but I realized something. "I'm different now," I said. "I don't know if that would even work."

"You have to try. Please. I don't know how long he has." Brooke took my hand and began to gently pull me away.

I conceded. As I prepared to follow, Iona called after me. "Brooke, wait . . ."

She had begun to run toward us, but I said, "I have to go."

I didn't get a chance to explain myself. The rumble of Phelan's motorbike announced his approach.

Brooke cursed as Iona threw her weight into Brooke's chest. Iona was trying to put some distance between the two of us. The second I saw Phelan jump from his motorcycle and crouch down, crossbow in hand, I knew why.

Brooke's jaw cracked. She was about to reveal her fangs and attack Iona. I had to keep Brooke's true identity concealed for her own safety—not to mention save Iona's life.

"Lailah!" I shouted. "Whatever happens—please!"

Brooke met my urgent stare, and her fangs stayed hidden. But a silver net was thrown over me. Boulderlike silver weights held it in place down at my feet, so there was nothing I could do to remove it.

I fell to the ground, screaming. My eyes blazed red and my skin simmered as the threads etched their way through the fabric of my borrowed clothes, sizzling through my skin. Everything fuzzed, and my vision blurred as static crashed through my mind in waves, curling and bouncing off the corners.

I scrambled to raise my hands to my eyes, where a barbed piece was burning through my eyelid, and I screeched as the silver seared my fingers.

Everything went black.

A melody sounded through my thoughts: Gabriel's voice singing to me.

My gentle harp, once more I waken,
The sweetness of thy slumb'ring strain.

A light appeared at the edge of the darkness and a hairline crack formed, through which the words sifted. I listened as the verse repeated over and over. I focused intently, and, as the next lines followed, I heard my voice singing:

> *In tears our last farewell was taken,*
> *And now in tears we meet again.*

Gabriel's voice came through again, so gentle, as though somehow the mere vibration of his voice created the same sensation inside me as his skin meeting mine. The fissure widened and expanded, responding to my quickening heartbeat as his words touched me.

Over and over, the shared verse of our song repeated. The light pulsated, growing, until the glow of the luminous sheet flashed, blinding me, and then there we were, under that old oak tree. The same memory that had resurfaced through my dream only two nights ago presented itself once again. I was playing the harp, and lying beside me Gabriel sang the next lines of the song:

> *Yet even then, while peace was singing,*
> *Her halcyon song o'er land and sea.*

I smiled at him and sang him the next part:

> *Though joy and hope to others bringing,*
> *She only brought new tears to thee.*

I waited to see if the same terrible sight would emerge, the way it had before, but the image distorted, splitting into two pieces. The fractured image flipped across my vision, leaving a new scene to emerge.

It was Gabriel and I riding on top of Uri, my beautiful white mare. Gabriel's arms were wrapped around my waist as we rode bare-back along the footpath of a forest. The ground was littered with leaves, and the trees on either side seemed to meet overhead as the thick branches interwove themselves, forming a heart-shaped claw above us.

My once innocent face flushed pink as Gabriel gripped my hips, moving with the rhythm of Uri's stride. It was so still—eerily so. The vivid color of autumn's burnt oranges and dull yellows contrasted against Gabriel's emerald-green velvet jacket. As we rode on, the path seemed endless; nothing up ahead that we were trying to reach, just a stretch of forever that we were traveling on together.

I heard myself then, continuing with the song I had left behind under the old oak tree:

> *Then who can ask for notes of pleasure,*
> *My drooping harp, from chords like thine?*

I watched Gabriel lift my long blond hair over my shoulder and rest his chin in the crevice of my neck. Then I heard him begin. I heard him start the next lines of the song that had meant something to us then:

> *Alas, the—*

It stopped. The image froze. Gabriel's voice reached me, but it wasn't his voice back then; it was his voice now—hard and blunt.

"Lailah. Lailah."

I was with Gabriel. I didn't know where, and I didn't know how, but I could feel his breath skimming my neck. I couldn't open my eyes; it was as though they had been welded shut.

I started to slip back. The image was there but still held on pause, and I tried to think away the frozen seal, melt it somehow with my will so I could continue to watch, but there were voices again—swirling around, distracting me.

"She's not ready to wake. It makes no difference, anyway. You should say your good-byes."

I let the sounds fade out; I wanted to be here, in this image. I drifted back into my dream.

The frame unstuck and continued to play. I watched as I giggled nervously, happily, as he sang to me:

> . . . *lark's gay morning measure,*
> *As ill would suit the swan's decline.*

"Please, Gabriel. It's been two days. Please wake her up; it's nearly too late." Brooke's urgent and jagged words scratched the record, causing it to bounce and stop once again.

"I told you yesterday, she's not helping him."

"Please!" she wailed.

This time I tried to figure out what they were talking about. What was so important that they would interrupt me in this magical moment?

As I strained to remember, the image of Gabriel and me riding Uri appeared—now just a still image, as though it was only a glossy photo floating in midair against a black sheet. The bottom edge seemed to catch fire. The more I tried to recall what was going on out there, in here, the photograph slowly but surely became devoured by the flames that lapped up its side.

As his name shaped in my consciousness, the entire picture melted and then dripped away. The image of me and Gabriel was now replaced with his name, emblazoned across the black space, flaming with embers of amber.

JONAH

THIRTEEN

I SQUEEZED MY SWOLLEN eyes and forced them open. Everything was blurred, as though I were staring down a camera lens that was out of focus.

"Lailah. It's okay; you're safe. Can you sit up?" Gabriel's anxious voice reached me and then I found him through the cloud.

"Yes, I think so," I murmured, my voice cracking. I coughed, clearing my throat.

"Get up—you need to come with me!" Brooke barked from somewhere in the room.

"Leave us," Gabriel demanded.

"No, she has to come right now," she insisted.

"Just give us a minute, please," I asked weakly.

I found the strength in my back to sit up and was met with the dwindling hue of a setting winter sun outside an open sash window next to me. A freezing breeze hit my skin, and a chill ran the length of my bare arms and legs. I looked down through the haze and realized that I had been dressed in tiny pajama shorts and a T-shirt.

I was momentarily thankful that there was so little material touching my skin. Though my eyes were open, I had to concentrate to keep my left lid from shutting—I could feel the ridges seared across it.

"You're not fully healed yet," Gabriel said. "Some of the netting caught your lashes and burned through. But it's okay; it will be all right."

I was on a bed, and Gabriel sat beside me. "Silver," I choked out.

"Silver," Gabriel confirmed.

"How long . . . how many days?" I whispered.

"A couple. Not long. The same it would take any Vam—Brooke or Ruadhan to recover from something like that."

Still he found it difficult to use the V word in reference to me.

"How did I get back here?" I began.

"Me. I saved your ass, now get the hell up!" Brooke wailed.

"You need to rest. Another day and you'll be good as new." Gabriel ignored Brooke. He stroked my cheek with the back of his fingers, and I followed them as he rested his palm across my chest.

I took a sharp intake of breath. "Gabriel, your hand!" I grabbed it too quickly and became dizzy, but I rolled his sweater's sleeve up to his elbow. His skin was dotted with blemishes—like moles or dark freckles—and where his veins sat below his skin, they were darker—almost gray.

He snatched his hand from mine and pulled down his sleeve, not meeting my eyes.

"How has your skin changed?" I said. "What happened while I was gone?"

"Only what had to happen," he replied somberly.

The mattress sprung as Gabriel's weight left it. He turned away from me and made his way to the door in the far corner of the room.

He took Brooke by the shoulders and began hustling her out. He forced her through the door, and when she tried to knock him out of the way she screamed my name. Gabriel fought her, and she yelped at his grip, which was clearly too tight.

"Gabriel, stop!" I swung my legs over the bed and balanced myself precariously. Straightening up, I stood and took a step forward, but my legs buckled beneath me.

Gabriel charged over and caught me, helping me to my feet. As he supported my weight, I whispered into his ear, "Tell me what happened to you, please."

Propping me upright, he finally met my eyes. His jaw locked and his stare was resolute. "I told you before. You have your scars; these belong to me."

"Lailah, please, Jonah needs you!" Brooke raced back over to my side, taking my hand in hers. This time Gabriel allowed her to pull me away, and she marched me to the door.

"Even if Lailah wanted to help him, Jonah won't allow it," Gabriel said.

"Why?" Brooke said. "He helped her enough. She's here—in part, at least—because of him."

Gabriel wore a blank expression. His blond hair was tucked behind his ears, and I noticed then that his face looked a little gaunt. It was probably my fault—the worry I must have caused him while I had been gone, only to return injured. Although I still felt a little like I was not completely compos mentis yet, Brooke's reason for seeking me out suddenly sparked in my memory.

"It's okay, Gabriel," I said. "If you stand by, it will be safe. If Jonah doesn't let go, you can intervene. But Brooke, I can't make any promises."

"I know." She squeezed my hand, as though I were an old friend.

I nodded in agreement, gulping hard and hoping for her sake and his that I could save him. As we marched down the landing, I stopped dead in my tracks.

"What?" Brooke asked.

I spun and nearly fell over my own legs, making my way back to Gabriel. He was lingering at the end of the bed, staring out the window with his back to me.

"You really don't want him to drink my blood, do you?" I asked, the reason behind it creeping around me like a ghost.

"No, I don't," Gabriel said, "and there's not a chance in hell I would allow it. But it doesn't matter, as I said; he won't do it anyway." His words were empty, as though none of this mattered and Jonah's end was now a foregone conclusion.

I searched my mind, my eyes rolling up toward the ceiling and down the sides of the white walls, trying to place Jonah, but the memory of him refused to come. But then something dawned on me; I knew at least one reason why Gabriel wouldn't agree to it. "Because if Jonah drinks my blood, his Pureblood Master will become aware of me. Because they are connected and they always will be." I stifled a gasp. "They will know I'm alive."

I glanced to Brooke, who looked downward.

Silence drifted through the bare room. Gabriel bowed his head, convinced that there was nothing that could be done for Jonah. And even though it went against every fiber of my being, I couldn't help but wonder for a moment if Gabriel even cared.

I wasn't ready to face my adversaries—I wasn't nearly prepared—but then there was no way I would just let Jonah roll over and die. I might not remember how, but he was in some way part of this family, and since when did we give up on one another so easily? And if I couldn't even save him, here in safe confines, what chance did I stand of saving myself out there?

No. I wouldn't let my fear of them stop me from trying.

"Take me to him," I told Brooke in a firm voice.

"Lai, wait." Gabriel was suddenly in front of me, blocking us from finding the stairway. He rubbed the tops of my arms, and a strained and sorrowful smile stretched across his lips, pitying me. "You don't remember him, but I need for you to say good-bye *properly*—"

"What do you mean *properly*? What are you talking about?"

"Look, just listen to me. I don't know why he doesn't exist in your memories anymore, but for your sake, just in case one day you do remember . . . you might regret not having said good-bye, the right way." His lips twitched as he finished.

I had no idea what Gabriel meant. What right way? I pushed past him, gesturing for Brooke to take me to Jonah.

I realized we were no longer in a B&B; instead, we were in yet another house. Brooke rushed down the stairs and along the long stretch of hallway to a study at the very back.

Outside the door, I gripped the handle, but Brooke placed her palm on top. "He doesn't look very well. I don't think he'd like it if you seemed surprised or upset. And Lailah, he's a little confused."

"Confused how?" I asked.

"He doesn't seem to know who I am anymore. He keeps reminding me of conversations we've never had, and for the last two days he's been calling me Sleeping Beauty."

Oh no. Unbeknownst to Brooke, Jonah had given me that nickname; he had told me as much before I returned to the motor home. He had mistaken her for me. This was becoming an all-too-regular misunderstanding.

I gave her a quick reassuring smile and noticed that, for once, Brooke had no makeup on. Her stupidly thick hair was pinned back, away from her face—messy and unkempt—her sunglasses on top of her head. And she was wearing a black tracksuit, as though she was already in mourning. It occurred to me then that she clearly hadn't wanted to waste a second away from him. Despite her hope placed in me, she thought it was the end, too.

"I need you to stay out here and guard this door," I told her. "No one comes in. If anyone tries—Gabriel or Ruadhan—then bang hard and fast, understand?" I said, pushing the handle down.

Jonah sat in a large leather chair; his feet were resting on a matching ottoman and a blanket was draped over his legs. He was positioned so that he could look out a large window onto the gardens of the property, and he was clutching a sheath that housed a deadly knife. All the lights were off, except for a lamp that stood a few feet behind him, so I could only just make him out as night spilled into the study.

I cautiously made my way over, passing the wall-to-ceiling bookshelves as I went, trying to keep my legs steady. I didn't want him to see that I was hurt.

He didn't acknowledge me as I pulled up a stool next to him. I joined him quietly in the shadows.

"Jonah."

"Busy," he said.

"Doing what?" I asked.

He pointed at the window, keeping his focus. "I'm on watch . . . making myself useful," he said, though his words were fatigued.

"Jonah, I need to talk to you." I placed my hand on his.

He caught me off guard, the blanket falling to the floor as he spun his body around so that he was facing me. He grabbed my hand, clenching his fist around the top of mine, and grazed the sheath against my knuckles as he contemplated me.

I gasped. His skin was pinched and ashen. His floppy, disheveled hair was drenched with sweat, which dripped down his forehead. His hand was bony, as though his skin were wearing away.

"Jonah, it's me. It's Lailah."

He released his grasp and ran his hand down my long hair, then broke into a smile. "Sorry, beautiful. My sight"—he took a second to catch his breath—"my senses are, well, they seem to have left me. Pass me the vodka, would you?"

I searched the room.

"Down there." He nudged his head in the direction of his feet.

I shifted my stool back, scratching the hardwood with a squeak. I lifted the bottle—together with the tumbler that sat next to it—and poured a neat drink.

"I'm on death row here. Fill her up." He winked at me, and oddly I felt my heart falter.

I did as I was told, and he dropped the blade to the floor before taking the glass from me. His hand wobbled as he struggled to raise it to his lips, and I thought for a moment he might drop it. He only just managed to tip the clear substance to the back of his throat.

Brooke was right; he had no time, no time at all.

He needed to take my blood. I had to make him, right now. "Jonah, I'm going to sit on your lap now, okay?"

A surprised look overcame his face. "While you're always most welcome, beautiful, I should probably ask why?"

"Because I need you to take my wrist, and I need you to drink from me. I can make all this go away." I got up and positioned my legs on either side of his waist. I wedged my knees into the worn crevices of the chair and gripped the leather arms.

He responded slowly, straightening his back and sitting up higher in the chair. He reached for my hands, but he missed.

"Seeing double?" I asked.

"Yup. Two of you, ordinarily, would be quite the treat. But both of you are a blur." He found my hips instead and placed his head to my navel, his skin meeting mine. His cheek was stone cold. He used me to stop himself from swaying, but then, after a heavy breath, he pushed me away. "I know you are going to argue with me. But I'd rather not waste our last meeting like that." He cleared his throat and struggled on. "I'm not going to drink from you. If I do, they will know, and you won't stand a chance." He raised his palm across my bare midriff, and it took all my will not to moan as he grazed a laceration from the net that was not quite healed.

He bent down, reaching for the bottle on the floor and discarding his glass. Sitting back straight, he moved his hand from my waist and unscrewed the bottle cap before taking a swig, half of it missing his mouth.

"They'll find out anyway. It's only a matter of time," I insisted.

"And you need all the time you can get. I'm not going to take that from you."

He took another gulp, but his body rejected the vodka and he spat it out. The bottle fell from between his fingers and bounced noisily, spilling its contents across the floor as Jonah struggled to find any air.

"Jonah!"

Panicked, I took my wrist, and for the first time in this new body of mine I willed my fangs to appear. I tore a strip down my wrist and, pushing the skin together, I helped my blood to bubble to the surface. I hoped his senses were not so far gone that the smell of my blood wouldn't cause a reaction. I needed it to overpower his desire to protect me.

Still straddling him, I felt his brittle bones strain under my weight as I thrust my hand to his mouth. At first he didn't react; he remained perfectly still and I thought for a moment that he was already gone.

But then his hand slapped over my wrist and he clutched it tightly. Finding some strength, he drew me close so that I was nose-to-nose with him. I nodded encouragingly as he held my arm suspended in the air.

"I can't risk you. I would never risk you." Slowly, one by one, he uncurled his fingers, and moved my palm against his cheek. He nuzzled it, straining to breathe in my fragrance. "There is only one thing I want you to do for me, Lailah. . . ."

I suddenly couldn't speak; a huge lump had formed in my throat.

"Let me die on your lips."

He molded his mouth to mine.

It was the sweetest form of torture: an impossible kiss, born brilliant but doomed to die.

Who was I to Jonah that he would ask this of me? Trying to join the dots in my mind with this line of thought only caused more creases, but then they seemed to iron out as his trembling body held mine.

Finally, I just stopped thinking altogether and began feeling instead.

I was overcome with emotion as my lips pressed to his, my breath rasping in the back of my throat. I felt that if I parted with my own breath, it might replace his last and keep him alive.

Every tear that now gushed rained the forgotten memories of his touch. As though he had been a melody playing in the back of my mind, his lips against mine now shaped the words that I hadn't been able to remember.

His laughter surfaced through my mind. The way his kiss had once tasted sweet. And, though he wasn't wearing it, I could almost smell his sultry fragrance of woods in summertime. And then an image of his face; his bad-boy exterior crumbling away as his lips curved into a seldom-seen sincere smile; the glimmer in his eyes offering me a light in which to see him through the darkness, revealing who he really was to me.

And just as I recognized him, he was preparing to once again become only a distant memory.

I wasn't going to let that happen.

I broke away. "No. You're not going to die. Just this one day, nobody dies."

FOURTEEN

I LAUNCHED MYSELF OFF Jonah's lap and flicked on a lamp next to the window. I had to persuade him now.

"Jonah, just breathe," I begged.

"I always get the last word in the end. Stop fighting me." He argued through gritted teeth. He grabbed me by the elastic in my shorts and tried to use my lips as the white flag of his surrender to death. And then he stopped.

He tilted his head, letting the glow of the lamp illuminate the side of my face. "W-w-what happened to your eye?" he said, panting.

Struggling to sit up, he gently stroked his thumb over my lashes before placing his index finger under my chin and nudging my face back up.

"When?" He was practically whispering, and I knew that every word he used on me was a wasted breath.

I didn't want to answer him; my mind was reeling, knowing that there was nothing I could say that would make him take my blood willingly. I was lost, caught in my own rising desperation, when the door started banging angrily.

Brooke.

Jonah jerked forward in alarm and reached for his knife. I got to it first.

Then I knew what I had to do.

"There was something outside the house; it attacked me," I lied, gesturing toward my eye. "I think it got in. I'm going out there. I'm going to protect you."

I made my way to the door and I heard him fall to the floor.

"N-n-no," he stuttered, clawing his way across the hardwood as I raced away from him.

I flew through the door, slamming it firmly behind me. Brooke stood alone; there was no one else in sight.

"Who's here?" I whispered.

"No one. It felt like he was slipping away and I had to know what was happening."

I remembered then that Jonah had created Brooke; she was connected to him through his blood and fed on him to survive.

"Where's Gabriel?" The words left my lips so fast that no human being could have understood. I whipped Brooke's sunglasses from off her head, chucking them across the room.

"What are you doing?" she asked.

Speedily, I pulled out her hair clips, which were pinning back her bangs, and parted the curls over her shoulders. "I said, where's Gabriel?"

"He left, went to join Ruadhan on patrol. He said he wanted you to say your good-byes in private. Seriously, what are you doing, he's dying in there!"

"Shhhh . . ." I put my finger on her lips and signaled for her to remove her top.

I reached out for Gabriel in my mind, but sure enough he'd put up his sheet of light. I decided it was probably best if I took a leaf out of his book. With what was about to unfold, it would be better if he couldn't sense me if he did try to tune in.

"I need you to swap your clothes with mine and, in a minute, I need you to run into that room. I'm going to chase and then attack you. Do you understand?"

"No. Explain."

"No time. Do you want him to live?"

She didn't ask any more questions.

We changed clothes at lightning speed.

"Hair. Cut it off above my neck. Now," I instructed, sliding the blade from its holder.

Brooke bounced back a little, realizing that it was cast in silver. I passed it to her so that she was touching only the steel base, feeling a little woozy from its proximity now that it was free from the sheath.

She did as I asked, tugging it through my thick hair. As my long, confused waves cascaded down to the marble floor, I frowned. I didn't have time to feel upset over such a stupid thing; it was just hair. Yet I knew, in that moment, that I was taking yet another step away from being able to recognize the reflection in the mirror.

Ready, I tucked my crystal gem inside Brooke's hooded top, now on me, and nodded to her.

She stood in front of me in the skimpy pajama set, her jet-black curls bobbing down nearly as far as her belly button.

If she ran fast, he wouldn't know it was her; he would think it was me.

"Don't let him see your face."

Brooke did as I asked. Taking a run-up to the door, she burst through it, lumps of wood crashing down to the floor. I bolted after her and careened around the room in pursuit, deliberately knocking over the bookcases and creating chaos.

It was only then, as I slammed into an antique writing bureau and broke it clean in half, that I saw my chess set on a table in the corner of the room. The heavy ivory pieces stood poised, ready for a new battle on the checked board. I felt breathless as the unthinkable occurred to me: Only ever for the briefest of moments could Gabriel and I be in the same space, at the same time; and only ever when one of us was taking something from the other.

My attention refocused as Jonah whimpered my name. He was now halfway across the room, struggling to stand. He tried to push himself up off the floor, only to fall back down to his knees.

I growled and hissed and allowed a sharp shriek to escape my lungs.

I hoped I had done enough to convince him that I was a Vampire intruder, wishing that his impaired senses would aid me in my deception.

I needed him to believe that I was about to end Lailah.

I grabbed Brooke by the back of her hair and threw her out of the doorway, Jonah's blade falling from her grip and plinking off the floor. The sight of it falling from her hands provided yet more assurance to Jonah that she was me.

I stepped over the strips of the caved-in door. Bending down slowly, I reached for a sharp piece of wood and knelt with my back to him. I made it appear as though I were about to spring up and rush after her, ready to stab her in the chest.

I took my time scooping the piece of wood from the floor, trying to listen to see if I could hear him breathing—praying that he still was.

Relief washed over me as I felt Jonah's arm wrap around me from behind, pulling my back into his chest. Thinking that it would be his last stand, he found one final bout of energy.

I hadn't accounted for him picking up the silver blade, and I wished for a moment that I'd had more time to consider it as he plunged it into my side.

His arm over my shoulder, he used me in part to hold himself up, thrusting the knife repeatedly through my skin. My body convulsed, jolting forward each time it left me, bile rising up my throat. But with each strike he kept me held firmly against him, and it felt like acid was coursing through my body. I didn't dare scream or shout; I couldn't afford to give him any indication that I was me.

It felt like I had become the outlet for the last of his unspent wrath as he assaulted me with lashings of loathing, perhaps for what he was. He was hissing with hatred, presumably meant for the Pureblood that had made him this way, and he was raging at the recklessness of his inner demons that perhaps, through his existence, he had struggled to silence.

But no matter what he did, he couldn't cause me any greater pain than making me witness his end.

I think that was the moment I truly knew it.

I wasn't just trying to save a member of this family, a protector, or even my best friend.

No. Only love hurt like this.

I held on to that very thought while my insides burned, my skin blackened, and my body writhed against his chest.

155

Finally he stopped. No more indignation left, he was ready to end me.

He dropped the blade, grappling now for the sharpened piece of wood that I was still barely clinging to. He grazed my skin as he wrenched it from my grasp, and automatically I reached for his hand, my own quivering as he knocked it back.

He raised the stake in the air, high above my chest, and at the same moment he bit into my throat, his fangs splitting and tearing the skin of my neck. I coughed and spluttered, my blood bubbling over my lips and dribbling down my chin. But, just then, I heard the most wonderful sound in the world: Jonah swallowing my blood.

I wasn't sure whether he had recognized my taste or whether, as he glanced up, ready to ram the stake through my heart, he'd caught sight of my damaged eyelid. Either way, his straining fingers released the piece of wood and it fell, clattering to the floor.

His fangs started to loosen, as though he was trying to let go, and so I reached for the back of his head and summoned any remaining strength to rise up. I tilted my face so that my free-flowing blood would continue to meet the back of his throat.

He became a passing tide, lapping up the sands of my shore, taking part of me with him. Forming a cherry opal gem, he would wear me, a dead weight around his neck, for the rest of his existence—or mine.

He wouldn't be able to stop now; it was too late for that. And I was glad.

I allowed a small scream to escape my lungs, shrill and agonized. Crimson tears stained my cheeks.

My blood had already merged with his and entered his system. He moaned next to my ear, and I was sure it wasn't out of fulfillment;

it was pain, realizing that it was me who sat in his lap. Anguish sounded in his sobs as he registered what he'd done—aware now that I had fooled him into doing the one thing he would have died to avoid doing.

My legs went numb, my chest was tight, and the world around me was dark. Then, what felt like an upsurge of electricity suddenly sparked through me to Jonah. A short, sharp shock of white light passed between us, and he released me.

This wasn't the first time I had experienced that sensation. Jonah needed to feed off the dark energy in my blood to be able to heal himself, and somehow he was able to take only what he needed from me. The spike of white light had stopped him from drinking me to an end the first time we'd met, and it had stopped him now. I didn't know how or why it came, but I was grateful for it. But this time I was different. And the price of saving Jonah would end up costing me far more than I had imagined.

My face met the floor, and I saw, though at an odd angle, Brooke, cross-legged at the end of the hall. She was frozen to the spot like a beautiful little Buddha.

Everything was quiet. No one shouted for help, no one moved, and I listened now only to the rise and fall of Jonah's chest somewhere behind where I lay.

I was oddly serene. Only I could have saved him, and I had. He couldn't fight, so I had done it for him. I had to tell death, "Not today; never today."

And, for once, death had obeyed.

I DIDN'T KNOW HOW long Gabriel had been with me, but I found myself now enveloped in his arms.

I could see why images of Angels were depicted with perfect porcelain faces surrounded by bright light, guiding the souls of humans in death; we could have been a painting. His glow raced around me, gliding over every inch of my aching body.

It didn't heal me completely.

He couldn't take away the fiery affliction riding up and down my torso. It had been caused by silver; his light couldn't repair it. And so he carried me as my arms fell limp and my fingers drifted toward the floor.

I left the pain and the nausea as everything spun, and I became lost to the darkness.

Utter stillness, my mind painted black.

This sleep was dreamless.

A SHEET OF BLACK cloaked my mind, but then something formed at the center of the nothingness: a dark, textured swirl.

A white dove flew through the center, and it fluttered before me, staring with its perfect crystal-blue eyes. It searched deep down inside, seeking to discover me.

The dove hovered, as though it were trying to entrance me with its beauty. Then it began beating its quilled feathers more rapidly and, without warning, wrapped them around its front, covering itself entirely.

A quaking, inhuman cry echoed, and the sound of death rushed toward me. Black keratin inked the dove's white wings until their purity was painted over and all that remained were two wide eyes peering out at me over the now-indistinguishable feathers of night. The ink seeped into the bird's eyes, making its orbs swirl like blue and black dye dropped into water. They closed slowly and then re-awakened a ravenous red.

The dove was gone, and in its place was a toxic raven that soared high in the air, and when it finally stopped, a raised sore formed above its left eye.

The raven swooped and darted toward me.

It seemed to hit an invisible force, which threw it backward; it was then that I saw a frosted gray sheet, trapping the bird and protecting my mind.

The raven squawked as its wings transformed into a cloak and its claws morphed into bladed talons.

The Pureblood revealed his true form to me.

An uneven, grotesque grin curled over deadly fangs, and his jaw snapped low, emitting an ultrasonic squall from his throat.

Straightening his index finger, he raised his arm very slowly and then stopped at the center of my vision.

His eyes flashed as he pointed menacingly at me.

Zherneboh.

FIFTEEN

I BOLTED UPRIGHT, GASPING as the skin across my belly smarted.

Gabriel sat beside me on a wooden chair. He grabbed my clammy hands in his own.

I panted shallow breaths, and eventually whispered, "He knows. They know."

Gabriel's hand clenched into a fist and fear fluttered across his eyes. The silence between us spoke more than any words. We both knew what this meant. We also both knew how very much I had defied Gabriel.

A wave of resentment rushed through him and then over me.

"Lai, how could you?" He shot out of the chair and kicked it against the fireplace across the room.

Gabriel's action caught me off guard. I scanned the room and saw Ruadhan, who was now standing at attention behind Gabriel, very much like a soldier. And why not? We all knew a fight was coming.

Because of me.

"I'm sorry." And I was. Truly sorry, that what I had done caused him great upset. I didn't want to be the cause of Gabriel's unhappiness, but I would never apologize for choosing to save Jonah.

"You couldn't even remember him, Lai," Gabriel said with frustration. "And he won't thank you for it."

But I did know Jonah. And I knew that I'd had feelings for him before I fell on the mountaintop. A realization that I had no desire to explore, let alone confess to. It would be far better, far *simpler*, if no one knew that I remembered Jonah at all.

"Whether he thanks me or not, I couldn't let him die," I said.

Gabriel scraped his hands through his hair and returned to my side. "Your inability to walk away from trouble will be your undoing, Lai." He pursed his lips. "I'm afraid that if you can't understand that your life is worth more, I won't be able to protect you."

Ruadhan hovered behind Gabriel but remained silent.

I was getting sick of Gabriel's attitude. "Who am I—who are you—to decide that my existence is worth more than anyone else's? We're not the same as the Arch Angels, and we're not like the Purebloods. Zherneboh knows now, but he would've found me sooner or later. He will chase me down for the rest of my existence."

"What are you saying?" Gabriel returned quickly.

I tilted my chin up to Gabriel. He sat down and allowed me to plant a small kiss on his sumptuous lips.

"I love you with everything I am," I said. "But I won't run."

Gabriel inhaled sharply, staring at me as though I had just ordered my own execution.

"No, Lai. I can't, *I won't* let you go to war with them."

Ruadhan placed his hand on Gabriel's shoulder. "The little love is right, Gabriel. Let her stand and be counted."

Gabriel shrugged Ruadhan away and stood up. "I don't believe I'm hearing this. This is supposed to be your beginning, yet your actions can only lead to one thing—your end. And you!" He swung himself toward Ruadhan. "Is that what you want for her?"

"I don't intend to start a war," I said, trying to sound as composed as possible. "But I can't live my life on the run. We have to figure something out. Until Zherneboh's gone, we won't be free."

"Free? Free to do what exactly, Lai?" Gabriel turned, his eyes wide.

"To be together, forever," I replied quickly. "I need to learn how to use my abilities and control them, fully." I remembered that there was a group of people not far from here that might know where my mother was. "I want to stay here, at least a little while longer. Will you help me?" I asked softly.

Gabriel considered what I was asking of him. "You asked for this. You knew if you let Jonah drink from you that Zherneboh would find you, but you did it anyway." He paused, his forehead crowding with lines. "You left Ruadhan's care; you put yourself in danger. You talk about spending forever with me." He paused and then his voice dropped low. "Yet you run away from me at every opportunity you get."

His whole body trembled with rage and fear. He marched out of the room, passing Ruadhan as if he weren't there.

"Gabriel . . ." My insides knotted.

He hesitated in the doorway, his arms outstretched, gripping either side of the frame. He didn't look back, but said, "Every day that goes by, I recognize you less."

And he was gone.

I sat dumbfounded by his sharp words. To Gabriel, my act of saving Jonah was the same as throwing myself to the wolves. He loved me, and so I'd thrown him to the wolves, too.

Ruadhan sat by my side and rubbed my back. "It's okay, love."

"I need to speak to him."

"No, sweetheart, leave him be. He's trying to protect you, and you're making that difficult for him, but you're right in what you say. And what you did for Jonah was an act of kindness; it's part of who you are. There's no shame in that."

I knew exactly what Ruadhan was thinking. "I can't save them all, Ruadhan. But I need to face Zherneboh if I want to save myself, to save Gabriel."

Ruadhan's eyes shone, and he squeezed my hand. "One day at a time, love. And defeating that demon is as good a place as any to start."

Though my mind spun with thoughts, it was my body that needed immediate attention. My throat was dry. I was hollow and empty inside. But I feared the thing that would fortify me.

"I think I need, you know . . ." I bowed my head.

"Aye. Gabriel still has business to tie up—his arrangements had to be changed—so we'll be here a few more days, but then he will want to take you away. In the meantime, you need to feed." Ruadhan's bushy eyebrows lifted; he knew that was not something I wanted to do.

"Jonah offered me his help, before—"

Ruadhan flinched as he took in the vicious scars left behind from Jonah's retaliation.

"I doubt Jonah will help now, love. He's barely uttered a word since . . ."

"I'll talk to him," I said.

"You can try, but I'm not sure how much good it will do. How are you feeling?"

"Not great. But I can see properly out of my eye again."

Ruadhan nodded. "That's healed. You've been unconscious for over a week now, but your skin, where the blade—" Ruadhan stopped, considering his words carefully. "It's repaired, but I'm afraid the marks will likely remain."

I stared down again, and while they were unpleasant to look at, strangely I didn't feel embarrassed by the bruised lumps around my navel. These scars were different from my others. They were marks born out of love. How could that be ugly?

I swung my legs off the sofa, and Ruadhan helped me to stand. I pushed my newly short hair behind my ears. "I had to cut it off, so he wouldn't know it was me."

"It suits you, love. You look like a proper little warrior."

His smile was reassuring, and once again I was grateful this family, such as it was, included Ruadhan.

My skimpy pajamas were stained with my blood. "Are there any clothes I can borrow?" I asked.

"Up in Brooke's room. Come on, I'll take you."

He offered me his arm, but I shook my head. "No, I'd rather you find Gabriel, please. Try to make him see. I do love him, Ruadhan."

"Aye. As I said, he's not been the same since he came back from the States. He seems more, well, he's acting more *human*."

Ruadhan was right. Gabriel's reactions, his mood, were far more changeable and different than before. But I wasn't making his life an easy one.

"I'll speak with him, but then we need to find you . . . something to drink. You need to be fully fueled, and I'm betting Jonah drained away a lot of your dark energy," Ruadhan said.

My throat tightened as Ruadhan's words crept up my neck like a pair of hands, ready to strangle me.

I hobbled out of the living room and found the stairway. I wrapped my arms around my waist, above my wounds, as I stepped carefully. I found Brooke's room and flicked on the tall lamp.

Jonah was sitting on the end of the bed. He snapped his head around as my breath caught in the back of my throat.

He bounced up from the mattress. "What are you doing in here?" His words were flat as his eyes scanned my body—and my scars.

I was relieved that he looked the way I remembered him—he was no longer knocking on death's door and seemed completely fine.

"You look brilliant," I said. "I mean, you're all better." I started to walk toward him, but he put his hand in the air. "What's wrong?"

"What's wrong?" He glared at me with contempt. "*What's wrong?*" he snarled. "Look at you." His nostrils seemed to flare and wicked flames lapped the corners of his irises.

I ran my hand through my short hair. "I came to get some clothes." I hobbled toward the wardrobe in the corner of the room, opened the doors, and pretended to rummage through a neat pile of jeans. They dropped to the floor as Jonah spun me around and dragged me back across the room by my arm, positioning me next to a large lamp.

"Look at yourself," he said.

"Look at *yourself*," I repeated, referring to the way he was rough-housing me. Still he didn't release me. I didn't need to examine my skin. I wasn't ashamed. "I did what was necessary," I said.

His top lip quivered angrily, revealing his fangs. His grasp around my arm tightened, his toned arms flexed, and his chest rose as though he were restraining himself.

"And I'd do it again," I said, cracking my own jaw.

That did it.

He grabbed me and launched me across the room and onto the bed. I propped myself up by my elbows, but Jonah was fast, straddling me and pushing me back down to the duvet. Pushing his thumbs onto my hip bones, he pinned me in place underneath him. His eyes blazed ruby red as he watched my face, waiting for me to show remorse.

When I didn't, he finally said, "I despise you for what you did, for what you let me do to you."

He grazed his hand across my tender, newly formed scars, and I let out a small moan as he touched one of the worst.

"I'm not sorry," I whispered.

He bowed down so that his cheek was against my bare waist, and he closed his eyes. "You're not sorry for letting me . . . inflict these *marks* on you?" He breathed against my skin.

"No," I choked out. My throat was so dry.

He remained there for a few more moments before stretching back up. Using his knees, he nudged my legs apart and wrapped them around his waist.

"You're not sorry for bonding me back to you with your blood?" His fingers trailed down the outside of my thigh.

"No."

He lowered himself so that his lips were next to my ear. "They know you're alive now, don't they?"

I swallowed hard and nodded softly.

He hovered, and as he began to lift himself up, I found myself instinctively squeezing my thighs around his hips, holding him there. His dark hair fell over his temples, and he looked at me with uncertainty. "You're not sorry for the decision you stole from me? For what this means for you now?"

"No."

"Then tell me, *do you remember me?*"

I looked everywhere except at him, but my thighs squeezed the truth tightly as I let the lie leave my lips. "No."

He lingered for a moment, but then grabbed my legs firmly and pushed me away. He stood up, tugging the back of his hair. "So, you decided to risk yourself out of what exactly? Guilt? Debt? Pity?" He didn't let me respond. "I hate you," he hissed.

Hesitantly, I sat up. "No, you don't." I coughed. "You're just upset."

"I am not upset. I. Am. Desolate."

I crept off the side of the bed and reached for the top of his shoulder. "There's a fine line between love and hate, or so they say. I do understand."

Jonah's body became rigid. Eventually he turned around and began ruffling his fingers through my short, messy hair. Bringing me in close, he trailed his fingers over the scar running down my back. I winced and he pulled away. "It might well be a fine line," Jonah said, "but it's not one I'm treading, and I never really did. It was your blood before, only ever your blood. And now, connected to you or not, how could I want you? Look at the state of you."

His words were cold, uncaring, and they cut through me. I

trembled and wrapped my arms around myself, listening to the pure revulsion spill from his lips with such arrogance.

He added, "You're damaged, beyond repair. Inside and out."

"You don't mean that." The words poured from me in disbelief.

"You may have been beautiful once, but not anymore."

I felt for the elongated scar across my back. It was hideous, but it always had been; that hadn't changed. "I, I don't believe you. You were ready to meet your end to keep me from harm. You asked to *die on my lips*, Jonah."

He silenced me, placing his index finger firmly over my mouth. "That was then. Things change. You changed."

I shook my head, refusing to accept it.

Then he placed his palms over my cheeks, looping his fingers through my hair, and kissed me. His touch was gentle at first, barely even there, as he grazed my top lip. But then, as he squeezed my skin against his own, it became harder, and it felt cruel.

He parted from me, his eyes tightly closed, caught in his own darkness. Perhaps if he couldn't see me, I didn't exist to him anymore. He shook his head before he opened his eyes. I stood frozen, anticipating what he was about to say.

"You used to taste like apples, you know. Sort of sweet and sour mingled together. You were delicious. You felt impossible on my lips."

"And now?"

I watched a large lump forming in his throat as he swallowed. "You *taste* like . . . you *feel* like death."

Truths—real truths, like that—were nearly unbearable to hear. But he was right, of course.

I was marred, muddied, maimed.

His brutal words knocked the wind out of me. I let the tears spill silently from my eyes.

Before he left the room he said somberly, "Gabriel will protect you, Lailah. You should go with him. And when you go, I will forget you, the way you have me."

SIXTEEN

I WAS STILL LOST in thought when Brooke came into her room.

"It's okay," she said. "What happened?"

My throat was so parched that my voice cracked. "Jonah."

She looped her arms around my back and let me cry. I wept for both Gabriel and Jonah, and oddly, for the same reason. Neither of them seemed to recognize the girl they had once cared for. Instead, they now saw a stranger before them. And I cried for myself. Just when I needed to become strong, I felt so weak.

"That's enough now," Brooke demanded, parting from me.

"He hates me. They both hate me," I whispered.

"I don't," she said. "Jonah's still here because of you. That was the bravest thing—the worst thing—I have ever seen. You didn't even cry out, when he—" She stopped. "Thank you, Lailah."

Brooke's sincerity was unexpected but welcome. I nodded, accepting her gratitude.

"I came to borrow some jeans," I said. "What was he even doing in your room?"

Brooke made her way over to the wardrobe and began pulling out various piles of clothing.

"I snuck out. He was probably waiting for me to get back. I've been sneaking out a lot lately; it was easier when you were unconscious. As usual it was all about you where Gabriel and Ruadhan were concerned. And Jonah. Well, mentally he seems to have checked out."

Brooke placed a pile of clothes on the bed and riffled through it. She handed me a pair of black skinny jeans and a plain, black top.

"Ruadhan said you'd need to feed when you were awake. I'm betting you're hungry, and trust me, your first attempt is going to be messy." She paused before continuing. "Better if you blend into the night. No distinguishing features should anyone happen to see you."

I didn't want to even consider what she was implying. I pulled the jeans over my hips and lifted the top over my head. She helped me pull it down; it was a little tight and the material made the lacerations that were not quite done healing itch and sting.

She fluffed my hair and wrinkled her nose with discontent. "I'll fix your hair for you tomorrow."

Ignoring her, I asked, "Where've you been sneaking off to, Brooke?" I squeezed a pair of boots over my calves.

"Don't get mad, okay? But I've been hanging out with Fergal and the others."

"What?"

Brooke shrugged her shoulders at me, an innocent expression plastered over her face. "Only have yourself to blame. . . . After what you did for Jonah, I wanted to repay you somehow, and so I thought, if I got to know them, you know, they might tell me where your mother is." She smiled sheepishly.

"You really are all kinds of crazy. You're a Vampire; they could have killed you." My voice cracked and my stomach lurched.

I didn't have the energy for this.

"They think I'm you, remember? How do you think you got back here, after Phelan launched a silver net over your ass, huh? I told them I was the girl they had been searching for, and that while you were, well, a demon of sorts, you'd helped me." Brooke began refolding the leftover clothing.

"And they bought that, did they?"

"Not at first. But they removed the net, and then I put on a bit of a show. You know, a bit of running and jumping and all that, make them see that I was . . . special. That's what they were expecting, so that's what I gave them. Luckily for you, they believed me." She tottered to the wardrobe, depositing the disused tops in a heap. "Fergal let you go if I promised to return. I wasn't planning to, but after what you did for Jonah—for me—I thought I might be able to get your answer."

"And did you?"

"Not yet, but I will."

Disappointment squashed the tiniest bit of hope that had been rising inside me. "No, you're not going back. It's too dangerous."

"They're all right, Lailah. Really. I think they're all on the level, and besides, don't you want—"

"Not if it means risking you," I protested, and I meant it. I would find a way to get the information on my own. "You didn't tell Gabriel . . . about my mother, I mean."

"No. I figured there was a reason you hadn't already informed him."

I was slightly surprised that Brooke had given any thought at all to the situation, let alone about what I may or may not have wanted shared.

"Besides, as I said, it was all about you. Nobody seemed to care about anything I had to say," she said.

That was more like it. There was no thought; she had chosen to exercise her childlike petulance, rather than her emotional intelligence.

"And BTW, I didn't know you cared about me so much," she said sarcastically, marrying her hands at her chest.

"Well, I do. Besides, Gabriel and I are only staying here a little while longer. When we leave, you and I will say good-bye, and I'd rather you were in one piece for Jonah. I don't want to give him any more reasons to hate me."

Just then there was a knock on the door and Ruadhan stepped through. "Are you decent, love?"

I nodded, and he gestured for me to meet him.

"Good luck! You're gonna need it, newbs," Brooke shouted after me.

We walked down the darkened hallway and stairs; nighttime had fallen, and I was grateful that it might provide us with some cover. Terrible things went on in the dark because they went unseen. Perhaps after, I could just pretend it hadn't happened. Perhaps I could convince myself that my actions were all just part of an elaborate nightmare and that I wasn't one of the horrors hidden under this night's black cloak.

I was turning the steel handle of the front door when Gabriel appeared, taking my hand and pulling me into him.

"I'm so sorry," he muttered, and my whole being filled with his light.

He placed his forehead to mine, breathing in and out steadily, but his heart was thudding fast. "Lailah, don't block me. Okay? I need to know you're not in trouble, and you won't be able to call to me if you build your wall."

Gabriel wasn't coming with us.

My heart fell, as I realized quickly that Gabriel did not want to see what came next. It would never be something he could truly be comfortable with. I knew then that, if I fed on blood, I was taking yet another leap away from the person Gabriel was already struggling to recognize.

"I promise," I said.

RUADHAN AND I WALKED away from the house, and glancing back, I wasn't surprised that the property we were now staying in was yet another ridiculously large estate, positioned at the front of its many acres of land. Ruadhan suggested we run to the village of Henley, but I didn't have it in me. It was as if Jonah had taken most of my energy when he drank from me. I was left tired and empty.

"Come on, love." Ruadhan swung me onto his back, and we sped through the tree line. Within minutes, we were outside the back of a restaurant, hidden by the thick, bare trees of its garden.

"Thank you," I said, hopping down to the ground. "Are we waiting for a dark soul?" I asked quietly.

"Yes, love. You need to be energized by the sun to keep your Angelic powers strong, but you also need the dark matter transferred through the blood of a dark soul to keep your Vampire abilities working properly."

Ruadhan had confirmed what I'd already come to suspect. His

answer to my next question would likely do the same. "Gabriel really isn't comfortable with this, is he?"

"No, love. But he understands that, above everything else, you need to be able to protect yourself. Now more than ever. It's for the greater good."

There were those words again—always for the greater good. Orifiel thought as much, sacrificing mortals to keep Styclar-Plena and its inhabitants alive. Gabriel was prepared to let Jonah die to keep me safe because he thought I was worth more. And now Ruadhan was quite willing to allow me to feed, under some delusion that, in the end, the many I might free would outweigh the few people I might kill.

"Ruadhan, I can't—"

"Shhhhh!"

A drunken girl stumbled out of the back door, flinging her clutch onto a circular table. She rummaged inside it, producing a packet of cigarettes and a lighter. Her high heels bent beneath her unbalanced weight as she plonked herself down on a bench.

Ruadhan was concentrating on her movements. Finally, he looked at me and shook his head. She wasn't the one.

"How can you tell?"

Before he could answer, a young guy dressed in jeans, sweater, and a scarf slammed the back door and grabbed for the girl.

"Get up! We're leaving." He tried to hustle her away, but she refused.

"No! You leave."

The two entered into a heated argument. Eventually, the girl allowed the guy to drag her to the door and he pushed her through it, slapping her bottom as he did. She let out an angry yelp as she fell back inside.

Without warning, Ruadhan seized the guy, placed a hand over his mouth, and hauled him through the patio and into the gardens.

The girl swore over her shoulder, unsure of where her gentleman friend was, but I listened closely to her footsteps—she took the opportunity to leave the restaurant.

I drew my attention back to Ruadhan, who was holding the guy captive in his arms. Ruadhan was making hushing sounds, locking his eyes with his prey, and the guy stopped struggling.

"Love, are you ready?" he asked, rolling up the guy's sleeve.

I edged forward, contemplating what I knew I had to do.

"Take his wrist; it will be easier for you."

Ruadhan held the guy's arm up for me, and reluctantly, I took it.

"It's okay. He's a dark soul, I promise," Ruadhan said reassuringly.

I was so empty inside, in dire need to fill the void. But, as I looked at the young man's face, it wasn't his I saw. It was Gabriel's.

If I did this—if I ever did this—I feared it might be the beginning of the end for us.

Ruadhan's eyes narrowed as I shook my head and turned away.

The next thing I knew was the smell—only the smell. My fangs burst through my gums, and I moaned as the scent of fresh, warm blood met me. I spun around. Ruadhan had torn the guy's skin and was once again offering me his wrist.

A smoky haze was surrounding me—all the color draining from my vision. All but one: the color of blood.

"Take it." Ruadhan tore another strip of skin from his hapless victim.

Although the scent made my mouth water, it was in no way as enticing as Jonah's.

And as the thought of Jonah entered my mind, the thought of Gabriel quickly superseded it.

No.

My fangs receded into my gums and I bobbed backward, shielding myself from the sight in front of me.

"Lailah?" Ruadhan called.

"I can't. I'm sorry. I won't. Please, let him leave," I begged through gritted teeth.

"Love, you must, if you are to stand any chance—"

"I said no."

RUADHAN INFLUENCED THE GUY once again before letting him leave; he wouldn't remember anything. Unwilling to part from my side, Ruadhan had taken me into the restaurant and bought a large bottle of vodka from the bar. The server wrapped it up in a paper bag for us before we left.

Once we were back outside, Ruadhan unscrewed the lid and offered it to me. Standing outside the restaurant, I shook my head and wandered over to the side of the Thames. The small rippling waves were only scarcely illuminated by the tall streetlamps.

Ruadhan joined me, once again holding out the bottle. "Drink some. . . . It takes the edge off."

My throat was beyond feeling dry; there was now a severe scratching sensation, which made it painful for me to speak or swallow.

I reached for the paper bag and took a long, hard swig from the bottle. Ruadhan was right; for the few moments it trickled past my tonsils, I didn't hurt as badly.

"Now don't go telling Gabriel I'm encouraging you to drink. It has a much greater effect on our kind, remember. Just a few drops here and there, until you're ready."

I took another swig. "How can you tell who has a dark soul, Ruadhan?"

"You can sense it. For us, for Vampires, light souls show themselves in a very subtle aura; there's almost a glow around a human's figure. Mortals with a dark soul have nothing. We look for the glimmer. If there is none then—"

"Dinner," I finished.

"Aye. And before, when we were slaves to our Pureblood Master, if we were stealing light souls for them to change, the glimmer was what we looked for. We took them, Lailah. They still take them, and they infect them with their venom, and they change them forever."

I took another gulp of the vodka, but too much, and I coughed some of it up. "I know what they do, Ruadhan." I screwed the cap back on and clutched the bottle tightly. "I'll hang on to this, if you don't mind."

I paced up the road, mustering some strength in my legs. Ruadhan was at my side, linking an arm with mine. "Mortals need food and water to live. You need the dark energy transferred in the blood as much as you need the sun's light, Lailah. To survive, you are going to have to take both. I think you know that. And time is against you." Ruadhan clenched my arm more tightly. "You need to overcome your inner demon before you're able to conquer the one that exists out here."

"Didn't you know? He's one and the same." I tapped my forehead. "He's in here and he's out there. I can't drink blood, Ruadhan. You heard Gabriel—every day he recognizes me less."

We didn't talk any further, and I insisted on walking, using my own two legs, back to the house. My decisions would burden only me, no one else. I wouldn't let anyone carry my weight on their shoulders.

Not anymore.

SEVENTEEN

I WANTED TO GO straight to my room when we returned to the house, but Gabriel called to us from the kitchen as we removed our shoes at the door.

Ruadhan ushered me down the long hall, and when we walked into the room Gabriel looked nervously at me; I returned a weary smile. Jonah stood in the corner, a cigarette in one hand and a tumbler in the other. He didn't even acknowledge me, instead reaching for his bottle, and I was reminded of my own. I placed it down on the kitchen table.

Gabriel approached me, but I was so exhausted that I found it hard to even wrap my hands around his neck as I collapsed into his chest. He rubbed my back, and from the corner of my eye I saw Ruadhan shake his head, letting Gabriel know that the events of the evening had been unsuccessful.

A flash of light from inside Gabriel passed through to me. I knew by his reaction that I had done the right thing.

Jonah paused as he withdrew his cigarette from his lips, taking longer than he should to exhale the smoke from his lungs.

"What happened? Was there trouble? Lai, I didn't sense anything was wrong. . . ." Gabriel's bright blue eyes flickered.

"Uh-huh," I said, gulping.

"We will try again tomorrow night, after she has met the sunrise," Ruadhan ventured.

Gabriel's chest fell with disappointment.

"N-no." I struggled to speak. "We won't. I w-won't do it."

Jonah, who had remained silent throughout this exchange, stubbed out his cigarette, and I was faintly aware of him sliding his tumbler across the work surface. I peered up at him, but he failed to meet my eyes.

"Lai, you look very pale," Gabriel said, placing the back of his hand against my forehead, as though I were coming down with some sort of fever. Little did I know how right he was.

"I'm always . . ." I stopped, catching my breath. "Pale."

All three of them watched me quietly as I reached for the bottle of vodka and excused myself. They didn't stop me from going outside. Ruadhan even twisted the knob of the French doors opening up onto the garden and switched on the outside lights.

The yellow flash stung my eyes, and I flapped my hand at Ruadhan. "Off, please." I closed the doors behind me and chose to slide my back down the brick wall instead of taking a seat at the table and chairs. I sat on the cold paving slabs, fingering the paper bag. The stinging sensation in my throat was only getting worse.

As I chugged back the vodka, I welcomed the warm coating that seemed to seal the slices, but for every shot the relief lasted only a few seconds.

Ruadhan and Gabriel were talking heatedly inside the kitchen.

"I opened up his wrists for her, tried to make it easier on the poor love, but still she resisted," Ruadhan said.

"Why did she resist?" Jonah asked.

"Stubbornness, I'd say. It's not good for her, Gabriel," Ruadhan said. "She must feed. You saw her face; she's not well. And she never will be if she doesn't get what she needs."

"You're assuming that she needs it; she might not. Perhaps the sun will be enough. And we can't force her to do what she doesn't want to," Gabriel's smooth voice reasoned.

I swirled the bottle around in front of me. I absolutely wanted to drink blood. It wasn't something I could reason with; it was a need, a compulsion. But Gabriel clearly found it difficult to cope with the idea, and so for him, for us, I wouldn't.

I was giddy, but I wasn't drunk—just light-headed. I could only hope that Gabriel might be right, that the sun would be enough and that I didn't need anything else. But I knew, deep down, that wasn't the case.

I stopped listening in to the conversation and focused instead on the sky. It was navy blue now, and though the full moon shone, a formation of dark clouds was looming, ready to cover its luminosity.

"It won't work," Ruadhan shouted, forcing me to listen again. "You know that. It has to come from the vein; it has to be fresh, or she won't get the dark matter."

My eyelids grew heavy, and I allowed them to close as I placed the bottle beside me on the ground. I was drifting off, but I shook myself back to reality as Gabriel appeared beside me. He moved the bottle and stretched his arm around my shoulders. "You should sleep. Come on, let me take you inside."

His warmth felt good against my skin. "No. I don't want to sleep." I nuzzled into his chest.

"I think your body disagrees."

"I'm afraid if I fall asleep . . ."

Gabriel didn't have to ask why; he knew what I was afraid of, and that I always would be until Zherneboh was gone.

"You can't stay out here; it's freezing. Let me take you to your room."

I reached for the bottle of vodka. Gabriel blocked me. "You don't need that, Lai. It's not long till sunrise." I wondered for a moment if Gabriel even knew pain like this. I didn't have the energy to look up as we made our way through the kitchen, but I knew Jonah was still present by the pungent scent of burning tobacco.

"Are you coming with me?" I asked Gabriel at the foot of the stairs.

"I need to speak some more with Ruadhan. I think Brooke is in her room, and I believe she's keen to give you a haircut—that is, if you're sure you don't want to sleep."

"No. No sleep." I sighed and dragged myself up each stair.

"Lai," Gabriel called after me. "I—well, I think you did the right thing. Tomorrow's another day, another sunrise, let's see what happens."

I managed a smile in reply.

Any other moment in my life, my knees would have buckled at the expression he was wearing for me; it was one that oozed pride. And although my knees felt like they might do just that, for once it wasn't due to Gabriel.

As I climbed each tall step, I called out Brooke's name, but she didn't appear. She must have taken the opportunity to slip out once more, and I mentally cursed her for being so stupid.

In the absence of my stylist, I made for the first door directly in front of the stairs. I found a bed but had no idea to whom it belonged. As I hauled myself onto the sheets, I decided it belonged to Ruadhan.

I lay on my back. It must've been at least 2:00 a.m.—only four more hours till sunrise. All I had to do was lie here and bear it.

And then I heard Gabriel's voice:

Alas, the lark's gay morning measure
As ill would suit the swan's decline

And then there he was; there we were. His hands were gripping my waist as our journey atop Uri replayed.

The autumn leaves rustled and crunched under Uri's hooves, springing back to life as she strode onward.

But this time, as I listened, I was distracted. And then I knew why.

Blood.

Even here, in my dream, I ached for it. The sequence parted, forming two large bubbles and reflecting in both, but then the colors of autumn swirled and became more concentrated. The bubbles now filled with red.

The two spheres moved away from me, and then, at the center of each, swollen black spots formed, enlarging in size. It took a moment, but a new shape formed around the outside of the orbs.

Jonah's face.

A new scene. I stared into Jonah's eyes, standing beside a frozen stream. I desperately grasped his bloodied wrist, bringing it to my mouth. But then I found his lips instead.

The moment played back: Jonah, gripping me in his arms, and my thighs wrapped tightly around his hips as I continued to kiss him forcefully, until cherry liquid spilled from his lips. I watched myself drowning in him, as he pushed me to the ground, lapping me up in return.

Blood.

My lips at Jonah's neck, I guzzled his essence.

Blood.

I WOKE STARTLED.

The door slammed against the plastered wall, and Jonah strode through the room, positioning himself to the right of the bed. His expression was blank as he glared at me.

I propped myself up. The memory explained why Jonah had tried to goad me into drinking from him. We had been bonded by blood; and then I had died. Even though forces of both dark and light had brought me back, our connection to one another had ceased. He must have thought that if I drank from him now, our bond would be renewed and I would remember . . . everything.

Yet, I had recalled Jonah, without his blood. What we were before I had fallen on the mountain . . .

No. I couldn't let that train of thought continue. The road it led down was dangerous and destructive.

Still Jonah just stood there, rooted to the spot.

I looked past him out the window and sighed with relief when I realized sunrise was near.

"You don't belong in my bed," he said finally. His stance was rigid, defensive, and downright uninviting. Struggling to shift my legs off the side of the bed, I wobbled as I found my feet, sinking into the deep carpet beneath me.

I struggled to find my voice. "The sheets smelled of vanilla, not of you."

Jonah arched his left eyebrow as I stumbled out of the room.

Gabriel was waiting at the bottom of the staircase, as though he knew to expect me. His lips formed a hopeful smile, and his eyes shone brightly as he held out his hand.

I could do this.

I could ignore my cravings and survive on the sun's energy alone.

I took his hand and he paused for a moment, running his fingers through my tangled, messy hair. He kissed my temple gently and led me through the house, out of the kitchen doors, and into the garden.

"It's nearly sunrise," he said.

The dawn smelled of freshly cut grass, and the air sang with a shrill chill. We walked slowly down the garden path, and eventually Gabriel came to a stop. I looked over my shoulder, wondering if Ruadhan would be observing from the window.

The clouds seemed to part, almost as though they were anticipating my arrival. The sunrise was beautiful.

I felt for my crystal around my neck and positioned it over my top. Gabriel had said that he didn't think I needed it like he did, that the way I sparkled without it indicated I should possess my abilities without needing a conductor. But it was my comforter, and today I would need all the comfort I could get.

The strobes of light overcame the gray and cascaded onto my

skin, making my face, neck, and arms tingle. I was filled with a newfound energy. But Gabriel's glow barely shimmered against his frame.

A whip of white light beamed down to his neck, struggled, and then just stopped. The veins under his skin seemed to pop; the lines that I had noticed around his eyes seemed to stretch nearer to his ears, only covered by the loose waves of his blond hair.

What was going on?

My skin glistened, absorbing every last bit of the sunlight that spread over me, twinkling like crystals refracting and bursting—expelling stars back into the sky.

Then a pulse of light surged from my body and my knees buckled.

I looked up at Gabriel. His veins had reverted back to a gentler color now, and his lines were nearly unnoticeable; they were more like soft, aging fissures. But he had stopped absorbing the sun's rays long before me, and I didn't know why.

Gabriel pulled me up from the ground, and as I steadied my frame against his, I took a deep breath. The sting in my throat was diminishing, and I felt something in that moment that I hadn't for a very long time. Hope.

Gabriel brought me into him. He breathed in my fragrance and I tried to do the same, but his scent of citrus only lingered for a second, as though it had been diluted somehow.

"How do you feel?" he asked slowly.

I stepped back from Gabriel, searching for some sign of pain inside my body. But there was none. "I feel . . . fine. The sun is enough," I answered with a huge sense of relief.

Gabriel wrapped his arms around me once more, and I rested

my cheek against his chest. "Do you *promise me* that's how you really feel? You don't need . . . blood."

"Yes, I promise, Gabriel." I paused and then asked quietly, "Where did your light go?"

His grip around me tightened. "It's complicated, but nothing to worry about."

"Please don't keep things from me." I paused. "Tell me, and while you're at it, explain to me why you met with Hanora."

He peered down, studying my face; he rubbed his thumb over my cheekbone. Satisfied, perhaps, that I was looking well, he finally released me and answered my question. "That's why you were in the field, where Jonah found you? You didn't trust me? You followed me to the cottage?"

"I didn't follow you. I sensed something was wrong, and I got to you."

He took a moment, but then answered me. "Lai, the reason my light is less strong than it was has to do with my meeting with Hanora."

"I don't understand. . . ."

Gabriel tucked my straggly hair behind my ear and shifted uncomfortably. "Hanora traveled with me for a very long time, Lai. I met with her and we spoke at length. We reminisced over our journey together, and I said good-bye, in a way that she understood was a final good-bye. I needed for her to stop following me to ensure your safety." His expression was pained as he finished. "I guess you could say I lost a little bit of my light when that happened."

Silence drifted between us as he waited for my response.

"Tell me the truth. Did you . . . I mean . . ." I gulped and Gabriel's eyes grew large, anticipating what I was about to say. "Were you *with* her?"

Gabriel looked surprised, stunned even, and he shook his head. "No, Lailah."

He wasn't shining as brightly now, because he was sad that he had lost a close friend. One he'd had to give up, for me.

"I'm so sorry," I said.

Gabriel nudged his nose against my own. Leaning in, he kissed me softly, and I thought he was shaking as he did. "Come on," he said, once again entwining his fingers with mine and leading me away.

At the same second that Gabriel tugged my hand, a flame inside my chest seemed to ignite. Something was brewing inside me, the beginning of an electric storm. Striking against dry sand, the splinters of lightning bounced off my insides, unable to conduct the waves without any moisture.

I was suddenly hollow. I felt worse than I did before.

Gabriel noticed my hesitation. "What's wrong?"

Looking into his wide eyes, I couldn't tell him. "Nothing."

He tilted his head, tracing every twinge in my expression, searching. And, for a second, as he stifled a breath, I thought that he knew. He opened his mouth to speak, but nothing came out. Instead, his gaze fell to the ground, and he blinked rapidly before meeting my eyes again.

"Gabriel, I *promise you* nothing is wrong."

He stalled but then squeezed his fingers between mine. "I love you, Lailah." His words were uttered almost in a whisper.

I was confident then that he believed me. If I was wrong, if he knew the state of my soul, he didn't say. I wanted honesty from him, but perhaps that was not what he wanted from me. Perhaps, it was easier for him to live with the lies than to accept the truth. And if living the lie would mean he would live it with me, then I wouldn't say a word.

Never a word.

EIGHTEEN

WE HADN'T EVEN MADE it through the back door when a rumble disturbed the tranquillity of the new morning.

Ruadhan and Jonah both appeared within a blink of an eye as Gabriel and I watched the large motor home along with Little Blue and the truck-drawn caravan drive down the side of the property, breaking part of the fence as they swerved onto the grass, leaving deep, muddied tracks.

"It's okay," I said calmly. "It's Fergal."

Jonah stepped forward. "The Vampire Hunters." His fangs cracked and a shrill hiss escaped him.

I realized that while I had been recovering, Brooke had likely enlightened Gabriel and Ruadhan as to where I had been, which meant that they probably knew these were the same people who had shot Jonah in the leg with a silver bullet and then thrown a silver net over me.

What they didn't know was that Brooke had been paying the group regular visits, pretending to be me. The door of the motor home swung open, and Brooke appeared. I tried to focus on her face—and was sure I could see a sheepish look splashed across it.

She flitted over. "Hey," she said, sweeping her bangs out of her eyes.

"What the hell?" Jonah began, grabbing her by the shoulders. Prying herself from Jonah's clutches, she stepped around him. "So, erm, the Sealgaire—"

"The who?" Jonah snapped.

"The Sealgaire." She shrugged. "That's what they call themselves."

Gabriel's jaw dropped, as though this were not the first time he had heard of this group. After a moment, he looked to the others and translated, "The Hunters."

"Yes, well, as I said, the Sealgaire—the guys—well, they came here to save the girl." She glanced to me. "And when I told them we would be leaving quite soon, they insisted on coming here to help. You know, to protect me." She fiddled with the buttons on her jacket.

I didn't think what she'd said could have possibly sounded any more ridiculous.

"Why would they want to protect a Vampire?" Gabriel's tone was dark, bordering on frightening.

I sighed. "They think she's me. They think Brooke is the girl they came here for."

Everyone was staring at me now, and I wasn't sure what else to add.

"One of you, fill in the gaps and quick," Ruadhan said, peering over my shoulder to the band of teenagers that were now filtering out of the vehicles.

"They tracked us to the Hedgerley house, before we left for Neylis.

They shot Jonah, not far from there, when they saw him with me. They assumed he was a Vampire attacking a random girl, and they took me with them." I paused, collecting my thoughts. "When they asked my name, I gave Brooke's. And then when Brooke—the real Brooke—turned up out of the blue the next morning, she called herself Lailah."

"Love, why—" Ruadhan began.

"I didn't think," Brooke said hastily.

"Point is," I said, "shortly after her arrival, they started to think I was a demon. They don't believe that Vampires were human before. Iona—one of the girls—said they believed that they came straight from the mouth of Hell. And apparently that's near to where they live, in Lucan." A whip of air brushed my skin as Phelan sped up the side of the garden on his Yamaha.

Brooke tipped her sunglasses to the top of her head. "I know I said I rescued Lailah from them but truth is, they released her because I convinced them that I was the girl they were looking for."

"I knew you were lying," Jonah said.

"You knew nothing. And you two were so concerned with Lailah's well-being that you didn't bother to question me." Brooke snorted, looking from Gabriel to Ruadhan.

"Look, it doesn't matter. They only came here to find and save the girl." I tried to reassure Gabriel, but my words were becoming weak.

Brooke interjected again. "I've been spending some time with them lately. . . ."

"You gotta be kidding me." Jonah was angry. He looked as though he was struggling to restrain himself from having a full meltdown.

Brooke ignored him and turned to Gabriel. "Gabriel, they are okay; trust me. All light souls, they only want to help. And they can—please let them. Just until you leave."

Gabriel ignored Brooke. His focus was on something behind her.

I followed his gaze and found it fixed on Phelan, who was leaning on his motorcycle, embroiled in a heated debate with Fergal. Phelan stopped, distracted by the sight of our stares, and he began to march over to us. From here, it looked as though his hand was clenched around the barrel of a gun.

Gabriel was gone, reappearing in a blur directly in front of Phelan. He snatched the revolver from his hand and flung it far away. They stood nose to nose, regarding each other.

Without hesitating, I tried to run over, but soon realized that I was not as fast as I had been before—nowhere near. As though my body were stalling, I stopped several feet behind the two of them and bent over, grabbing my legs.

Jonah was suddenly next to me. "The sun wasn't enough for you, was it?"

I ignored him, and after a moment he strode forward to stand beside Gabriel.

Fergal—not one to let Phelan take charge—also made his way over, and the four of them took defensive stances as they eyed one another in silence.

"Fergal!" Iona's voice chirped.

She didn't look at me as she met her brother by his side, taking his hand in her own. Gabriel's chin tilted in surprise, and a small, delicate pulse of light exuded from his aura.

Iona's eyes were like two moons wrapped in blue cellophane, unable to disguise their prominent glow. Her mouth fell agape as she said, "You."

I strode forward to stand next to Gabriel, who, studying Iona, said nothing.

"Do you know each other?" I asked awkwardly.

"I remember you; you were there that night," Iona ventured, gawking at Gabriel.

Gabriel tickled my shoulder and, after hesitating a moment, turned to me and said, "I'd like for you to go to the house and wait inside."

"But—"

"No buts," Gabriel said. "Jonah, take *Brooke* back to the house. I'll speak with him." Gabriel gestured to Phelan.

Fergal puffed out his chest. "Naw, I'm in charge. You speak with me."

Gabriel nodded as Jonah took me by the arm and proceeded to escort me back down the garden. I tried to protest, but I couldn't shake him off; his hand was clamped down too tightly.

Jonah noticed, and without looking at me, said, "What? Don't have the strength to get rid of me? That's a problem."

Sliding along the slippery grass, I replied, "I could. I'm choosing not to. I'm fine. Anyway, what do you care?"

"I don't." He steered me toward Ruadhan, who was holding Brooke by the wrist while she shouted at him. Brooke tugged herself away from Ruadhan and immediately began firing questions at Jonah, but he ignored her. Striding to the back door with Brooke in pursuit, he left me alone with Ruadhan in the garden.

I strained to hear what was happening inside. Jonah unzipped his jacket and threw it over the work surface as he moved through the kitchen. The clip-clop of Brooke's heels told me she was trailing Jonah as he strode through the house. I tried to focus on what she was saying, but it hurt. I needed blood; I needed the dark energy that it gave. My abilities, all of them, were fading, and that horrible dry feeling was creeping up my throat once more.

"Love, I'm going to join Gabriel. You'll wait inside?" Ruadhan asked, breaking my concentration.

I nodded and began to walk away. "Be careful, Ruadhan," I said before closing the back door behind me.

Neither Brooke nor Jonah was anywhere to be seen, so I sat myself down at the kitchen table. Frustrated questions whirled around my mind. Iona recognized Gabriel, but she was sixteen; he wouldn't have known her long ago. Which night was she referring to? I didn't have any answers, and right this second I was in too much pain to think any harder.

My gaze fell on the bottle of vodka on the countertop. A quick drink might help. After checking to make sure I was alone, I wandered over.

I unscrewed the cap, clutched the glass with both hands, and drank. The spirit trickled to the back of my throat like wet cement filling in holes. I took another shot and wiped my mouth with the back of my arm.

I crouched down and drained away every last drop of alcohol, which brought some relief as it swilled around my system. I refilled the bottle with water from the tap and screwed the cap back on, set the bottle back on the counter.

"Hey."

I spun around.

"Didn't hear me coming?" Jonah said.

"Of course I did." I tried to keep the slur from my voice as I stepped forward.

"Where are you off to, exactly?" he said.

"Dunno," I replied tipsily. Ruadhan hadn't exaggerated—alcohol really did have a greater effect on Vampires. Already I could barely see straight, but Jonah's bright-orange sweatshirt was proving helpful. I found myself grinning as I remembered making fun of it the day we took a trip out to the market in Mirepoix.

"What's so funny?"

I coughed, clearing my throat, and said, "Your sweater."

"You said it suited me, once," he replied coldly.

I bobbed my head and hiccuped. "I'm sure I was being sarcastic. You look like a pumpkin." As I covered my mouth, I lost my balance and tipped forward into Jonah's chest. He automatically placed his hands on my waist to steady me.

"You've said that before, too, but you don't remember, do you?"

Was he challenging me? No . . . he couldn't possibly know my secret. "No," I lied.

His eyes narrowed. I thought he was about to argue with me, but instead he peered over my shoulder. "Vodka might hit you harder than if you were human, but it wears off much faster, too. You'll be all right soon enough."

"I don't know what you mean," I warbled, but he had already lifted the glass bottle and was eyeing it suspiciously. In a flash, he was at the sink, and then back at the counter again so speedily that I barely caught it.

Tightening the lid, he peered over his shoulder at me and said in a hushed voice, "It was half-empty this morning. You filled it back up too high."

"Oh." Okay, so what? I reassured myself that there was no problem; no one knew that the sun hadn't worked, other than me and, perhaps, Jonah. And that was the way it was going to stay.

"When are you going to tell him?" Jonah said. But by the time I gathered my voice, he'd already left.

NINETEEN

I fidgeted about in the chair Brooke had sat me in while she brushed through my wet, matted mop of hair. She dragged the comb through the tangled ends, finally setting it down to pick up a pair of scissors.

"They've been talking for ages!" she whined. We were positioned in front of the window overlooking the garden, and there was still no sign of movement from the motor home.

"It's fine; nothing's wrong. I'd know if there was," I said. Jonah had been right—it had been only an hour and the vodka had already worn off.

"I just want to know what's happening. Fergal wants to stay here, until we leave." She tipped my head forward and began separating my hair, twisting it and shoving a clip through the top layer. "I'm thinking pixie cut. Let's go über short, with some volume on the top."

"No. Keep as much length as you can."

I would never be able to grow my hair back down to my waist.

As Brooke had pointed out, the whole frozen-in-time thing apparently didn't allow for regrowth.

"Really? I think a pixie cut makes more of a statement. Plus it's really in right now—all the celebs are wearing it." She relaxed her body, waiting for my reply.

"No thanks. Just tidy it up."

Brooke huffed and began trimming. When she started chuckling to herself for no apparent reason, I asked, "Something funny?"

"Oh, no, no, I just remembered something Fergal said the other day. It's nothing—an in-joke—you wouldn't get it."

"Fergal, right . . . Did you not bother to get to know any of the others while you were there? Iona is really sweet," I said, playing with a loose thread in my top while trying not to move about too much.

"Iona? Jeez, you're kidding me, right? She's a wet fish. She's worse than you were when we met! Total loser." She stopped chopping and released the hairclip, making a start on the top. "No, I spent most of my time with Fergal. You said he might know where your mother was, so, you know." She didn't elaborate, taking a second to think before continuing. "Can't say I minded much—he's pretty easy on the eyes."

Brooke finally began fluffing my now-damp hair and then went to get some mousse from her bag. I started to wonder if my mother's whereabouts were the only reason she had been frequenting the Irish group.

"Right. And how are things . . . you know, between you and Jonah?" I posed the question, dangerous as it was.

Squirting the white foam into her palm, she rubbed her hands together and began massaging it into my scalp. "Okay, I guess. I feel, well, I feel less of a pull to him these days. I've been learning to drink from mortals. When you were, you know, dead, he was unavailable, so Ruadhan helped me. Since then, Jonah's been taking me out, teaching me how to control my thirst so that I don't kill anyone. When Jonah was sick, Ruadhan took over again. It's been going really well." She sounded pleased.

"But I thought that, because you weren't changed by a Pureblood, you needed to drink from Jonah to get what you need?"

Moving in front of me, Brooke placed her thumbs over my forehead before brushing my bangs across my eye. "Sit still," she instructed, as she reached for her scissors and started snipping again. "The Purebloods change light souls and feed off dark ones; Jonah says it's for the dark energy that's carried in the blood. Second Generation Vampires feed off dark souls, too, but unlike the Purebloods they were human once, so they need the blood to keep their bodies functioning, as well as for the dark matter." She angled my chin up and combed through my bangs once more. "Jonah thought, because he was my maker and he's not a Pureblood, that I couldn't survive on mortal blood alone, that it wouldn't be enough—and he had no faith that I wouldn't be able to take it without killing." She paused, scraping my bangs back, and wiggled her eyebrows. "He was wrong on both counts."

"Okay, but you are bonded to Jonah through blood. You've spent your entire existence feeding off another Vampire. I didn't think anyone or anything else would ever compare?" This was at least what Gabriel had led me to believe.

Brooke shuffled past me in search of her hair dryer and flat iron. "True. Until the day he no longer exists, I will be bonded to him, but if you want to label me, I'm Third Generation. I think perhaps the connection isn't as strong as it would be if I were a Second

Generation, like him." She stopped and sighed. "Maybe I've just lost interest. I mean, the physical connection will always be there, but I guess, emotionally speaking, I've left the building." Scratching the back of her head, she marched over, uncoiled the wire, and proceeded to blow-dry my hair.

Huh. That was the last thing I had expected Brooke to say, but then I couldn't help but suspect that perhaps Fergal might have something to do with it.

The heat blowing on my bare neck was a new sensation. When Brooke finished, she unplugged the dryer and switched on the irons, twirling her own waves into a large bun on the top of her head to keep it from falling into her eyes, grunting as she did. "Jeez, be grateful that your hair's short."

Why she had bothered to get dark hair extensions was a mystery to me. But then, in doing so, she had inadvertently helped to save Jonah's life by resembling me. Had she decided to go long in some weird attempt to look a little more like me in the first place? The girl Jonah had taken a liking to in the nightclub also had long dark hair. Had Brooke been trying to conform to what she thought was Jonah's "type"? While the idea seemed ludicrous, Brooke's next statement made me think that maybe I was on to something.

"I'm taking them out, first chance I get. I don't want them anymore." She stopped for a moment, craning her neck over my shoulder and scanning outside. "I wish they'd hurry up. I want to see—" Brooke caught herself quickly. "Well, I need to go see them. Who knows how long you have before you gotta leave, and that question of yours still needs answering. Clock's ticking," she mused.

"Sounds like you want to see your new buddy." It didn't really make any sense. Fergal had a light soul.

"I wouldn't say that." She now set her irons on my newly cut hair. "Fergal is hot, though. Did I mention that?"

"Yeah, you mentioned . . . and you said all of them are light souls. That would include Fergal, right?"

"Yup. I don't feel the urge to drink him—any of them—dry." Curling the ends of my hair in her palm, she encouraged them to sit neatly as she further mused, "It's weird. When I'm close to Fergal, I feel, I dunno, kinda calm, sort of chill."

Funny, that was how I had felt when Fergal had come close to me, too.

She didn't continue with the conversation. Plumping a little more mousse into my two-toned layers, she unplugged the irons but was distracted by a sight outside. "Gabriel and Ruadhan are coming out. Let's go see what's happening!" she practically squealed.

Brooke rushed out of the room, but I stopped briefly to check the haircut in the mirror sitting on top of the dresser. Although I should have been assessing my new sweeping bob, I was drawn instantly to my own eyes: They were still muddied—the sapphire-blue irises looked drained.

I attempted to tuck my new bangs behind my ear. I was sluggish at best as I descended the stairs. I had no idea whether my abilities were still working, but I knew without them, something terrible could happen.

Gabriel called us into the kitchen, and I took a seat at the table, glancing at him and then at Ruadhan. Jonah was perched on top of the island in the middle of the kitchen, but I didn't meet his eye.

"So, can they stay?" Brooke piped up, unable to contain herself.

"Lailah and I will be leaving here in two days," Gabriel began. "They can stay until then."

If I wanted to find out where my mother was, I was running out of time. And now I had a whole new problem: trying to survive without blood and the dark energy that came with it.

"The day after tomorrow? But that's so soon," Brooke argued.

"What do you know about them?" I asked softly.

Gabriel hesitated, but finally slid out a chair and took a seat. Ruadhan strode toward the back door, keeping a watch outside.

"The fixed gateways to the first and third dimensions both sit on the outskirts of Lucan, from whence the group hails." Gabriel directed his answer only to me, not looking to Brooke or Jonah. "It seems that, for generations, the O'Sileabhin family has served the town as both the reverends of the church and protectors of the congregation—guarding them from, well, demons. They formed a band of men known as the Sealgaire—Vampire Hunters."

I shook my head. "Fixed gateways?"

"Yes, in Styclar-Plena there is a gateway that remains open at all times. It was the first rift that Orifiel passed through; it never closed. The gateway out opens on Earth in Lucan, and not far from it there is another gateway—a dark one—that is fixed, leading to the third dimension."

"Then why do the Angels need the crystals to command the rifts?"

"For exactly that: to command them. So the rifts open where a light soul is leaving a mortal's body, wherever in the world that may be."

Gabriel smiled, and I was sure it was at the thought, the memory of his home, of Styclar-Plena. Inadvertently reminding me that he and I didn't share the same views on Orifiel's solution to keeping the crystal in Styclar-Plena fueled. When he had told me the story of Styclar-Plena—the solution devised of fueling the crystal with the light energy released from mortals—he didn't seem conflicted by the fact that for every rift the Angels opened to claim the light souls, further rifts had also opened from the third dimension as well. The Angels coming here was the very reason the Purebloods had been able to come, too, and they took the lives of humans. A sacrifice the Arch Angels deemed worthy to keep their world alive, and one that in my opinion was not the Arch Angels' to make.

"I met one of the reverends myself in Lucan, nearly a hundred years ago, when I was passing through. The O'Sileabhin family has been around for a long, long while." He paused. "They told me that they now travel in search of a girl they were instructed to seek out and protect. That would be you." Gabriel gripped his hands together in a prayerlike shape, and I could almost hear his thoughts turning over.

"And what do you think? Are they okay? They don't mean me any harm?" I asked, playing once again with my wayward bangs.

Gabriel observed my action, and his dimples dipped. "Your work, Brooke?" He looked to her.

"Sadly," Brooke huffed. "She wouldn't let me cut it any shorter."

Gabriel's eyes flitted back to me, and they glowed as he smiled.

Jonah jumped down from the island, snorting as he did and pulling a packet of cigarettes from his back pocket. As he patted the bottom of the box, drawing one free, he said, "Haircuts? Seriously? Gabriel, there's a bunch of trigger-happy kids out there who are in the business of maiming Vampires. Might not concern you, but the rest of us are exactly what they like to shoot at." He lit the end of his smoke.

"Not everyone else here is a Vampire," Gabriel replied with a scowl.

"Oh, I'm sorry—I forgot for a moment. S-silver doesn't have any effect on her whatsoever, does it?" As he stuttered, the same angry expression that he'd shared with me in the bedroom found its way over his face—the one he'd had as he recalled the silver blade with which he had scarred me. He collected himself quickly. "She has fangs; she drinks blood. So, in case you hadn't noticed, yeah, she's a Vampire, too." Jonah blew out a stream of smoke from his nose, and his knuckles ground into the wooden work top.

Gabriel rose from his chair, knocking it over as he did, and glared at Jonah. "No. Unlike you, she doesn't have to drink blood. Lailah's different from you—she's like me. Don't you forget that," he growled.

Ruadhan swiftly sped over and stood between the two, placing a hand on both of their chests. "Okay, lads, come on, we're on the same team here."

Jonah continued to tug on his cigarette, but after a moment Gabriel relented and turned back around to Brooke and me. "I've told you before, I trust no one, Lai, not where you're concerned. But I'd rather have them here, with us, where I can keep an eye on them." He paused. "They were sent to *save the girl*. I've now given them per- mission to help *protect the girl* instead."

"What do you mean?" I said.

"They came armed and ready to fight. Forty-eight hours and we're gone from here. In the meantime, should the Purebloods or the

Arch Angels get even a whiff of where you are and come looking, the lads out there will be waiting," Gabriel said.

Jonah snarled. "You're giving the kid farmers permission to stalk around this house with guns loaded with silver bullets and god knows what else? You have got to be kidding me."

"It's all right, lad. Gabriel's made it clear they're not to come in the house with any silver or any weapons. They'll be guarding the property from the grounds," Ruadhan added.

Gabriel didn't even acknowledge Jonah; instead, he pointed at Brooke and then at me. "They think that Brooke is you, and that you're Brooke. That's the way it's going to stay, for your safety. Okay?"

Brooke seemed to breathe a sigh of relief; I could only assume that she didn't want to have to tell her new friends that she'd been lying to them all this time.

"And what about Brooke's safety?" I said.

Brooke didn't give Gabriel a chance to respond, cutting in quickly. "No, no, I'm fine with that. They're on our side. I'm not worried. You keep being me and I'll keep being you."

"Very honorable of you, Gabriel. Never mind about Brooke, hey?" Jonah piped up, echoing my thoughts.

Again Gabriel ignored him. "Lai, you were right. They don't believe that Vampires were ever human. They know me to be an Angel, and their family has had encounters with our kind before, so they trust that what I am telling them is the truth. I've explained that I granted redemption on behalf of the Lord to Ruadhan, Jonah, and yourself, and that you work for me now."

"The Lord?" I interrupted.

"We're only here two more days. I'm not going to start educating them now. You'll all just go along with their beliefs and tell them nothing, understand?" Gabriel scanned the room. Jonah was the only person shaking his head in contempt.

"Iona recognized you," I said. "Have you met her before?"

"They were there in Creigiau the night you found Jonah. I saw her, that's all," he answered.

I scratched behind my ears. "I don't remember seeing them." I stopped midsentence, as the reason for their presence suddenly dawned on me. "They were there, seeking me out, weren't they?"

Gabriel paced over to me, placing his hand on my shoulder. "Yes. Most of them were killed by Eligio's clan that evening—including Fergal's, Iona's, and Phelan's fathers, who were both reverends of the church. Fergal has assumed leadership by all accounts."

I bowed my head. Nearly all their family and friends had met their ends as a result of their mission to find and save me. Their deaths spilled yet more blood on my hands.

Ruadhan coughed, gesturing out the glass French doors. "The small blond one's on his way over."

Brooke bounced up, speeding to the door. "Fergal. He'll be wanting to see me," she said, a little too happily.

Jonah seemed perplexed by Brooke's enthusiasm. Stubbing out his cigarette, he marched after her. "You're not spending any more time with them. I don't care who they think you are—it's dangerous."

Brooke's eyes flashed red in reply. "I'll do what I like."

"They won't harm us, and they wouldn't dare harm Brooke, Jonah," Ruadhan said. "They are doing the Lord's work, so let them be helpful and feel that they have at least in part fulfilled the task they were given."

"They're all light souls. That's good." I tried to add a positive note to the conversation.

"Aye, love. But mortals' souls shift, from light to dark and vice versa. It can take time for a light soul to become tainted and turn dark, but just one ill action—one bad decision—can be the catalyst for an instant change. All the more reason for people to live their lives as gracefully as possible, every single day." Ruadhan never missed an opportunity to inject his moral teachings into a conversation.

Brooke brushed past Ruadhan, opened the door, and ran over to meet Fergal as he approached.

"What the hell is she doing?" Jonah roared, striding through the doors and watching Brooke's movements from the patio.

I followed him. "Leave her be, Jonah." I tried to pull him back by his arm, but he shrugged me off easily. I lost my balance and I landed on my backside, grazing my arm on the paving slabs. Jonah looked down on the ground and shook his head in surprise.

Gabriel was beside me within a split second, helping me to my feet, and then he turned to Jonah.

"Leave it, please. Give me a minute with him," I said.

Gabriel remained still, his hands curling into balls, and I was startled as a darkness stretched from his mind to mine.

Please, Gabriel.

I spoke my thoughts to him but it caused a pang of pain in my temple. He turned back to me and took a moment to consider my request. He placed the lightest of kisses on my forehead and left me alone with Jonah, but not before flashing him a look of warning.

I marched over to Jonah, but he wouldn't meet my gaze. He was now staring intently at the Irish lads who were rattling around in the caravan, removing crossbows and rifles.

"Jonah." He wet his lips and cracked his jaw from side to side, but said nothing. I tried again. "Jonah, I wish—" I stopped.

Finally he peered down at me, and as the cold morning breeze chilled me, his vanilla aroma tickled my senses. I much preferred the way he used to smell. "You wish for what?" His voice was hard.

"It doesn't matter."

"I didn't mean to knock you down. I'm sorry," he murmured. He leaned down and whispered in my ear, "I shouldn't be able to knock *you* down, and Gabriel knows that, too."

I was quick to argue back. "It was my fault. I tripped. I'm still getting used to, well, being this way." I was aware that Gabriel might well be able to hear what I was saying, and I wasn't about to admit anything to Jonah.

He rolled his eyes and took my wrist. Carefully, he elevated my arm in the air and bent it in toward me, drawing my attention to my elbow. My skin was cut and a trickle of blood was clotting across the scrape. At first I was shocked; there was no way I should be injured so easily, and the damage should not have stayed on my skin for more than a few seconds even if I were.

Jonah made no attempt to say anything, and I swiftly conceded that he no longer cared. Perhaps he was beyond wasting any words—or breath—on me.

But then, finding my eyes and capturing my gaze, he said quietly, "If you're all kinds of shades of gray, then you need the dark as much as you need the light. You have to stop fighting it."

I didn't just listen. I heard him, and I knew he was right. I was a finely balanced mixture of light and dark. Without both, I could not exist.

TWENTY

GABRIEL WAS ON HIS phone making arrangements for the next evening when I reentered the house. He'd been staring at me intently through the glass doors, watching my every move. I started to head for my bedroom, then tiptoed down the hallway, checking over my shoulder to make sure he was no longer spying on me, and made for the front door. Before I had a chance to leave, Ruadhan's hand was on my back.

"Where are you off to, love?" he asked.

I sighed but held my hand firmly on the doorknob. "I'm only popping out. I want to test my abilities, but I'd prefer to do it alone. You understand."

Ruadhan's palm flattened against the door. "You know you can't be by yourself."

I was running on fumes. Perhaps it wasn't safe to go out alone. Still, I wanted my privacy so I said, "They don't know where I am."

Ruadhan frowned. "No, they don't. But still, it's not safe. Gabriel said the sun did what it needed to do; he said you don't need to drink blood." He eyed me speculatively. "Is that correct?"

Ruadhan wasn't convinced that Gabriel was right. He was accurate, of course, but I needed to figure this out in private—free from anyone with an agenda of any kind. I was wasting time fighting with myself when I should have been working out how to fight my enemies.

I nodded and gave an encouraging smile. "Yes, it is. I'm fine."

"There's plenty of land around the back of the property. Perhaps we can go together?"

Past experience had taught me how hard it was to win a fight with any of these beings, so I tried a different tactic. "No. Actually, I think I might go and check that Brooke is okay. I can practice later."

As I made my way back down the marble hallway, I was cut off at the pass—this time by Gabriel.

Hurrying off his phone, he stuffed it into his back pocket. "Lai, I don't want you down there by the Irish on your own."

Could a girl not get some alone time?

"Then come with me," I suggested.

Gabriel hesitated, thinking carefully before he spoke. "The Sealgaire were sent to find and save the girl, Lailah. They were tasked by an Angel. An Angel called Aingeal."

I froze. Of course, Fergal would have told Gabriel, and now he was searching my expression seeking some form of confirmation to his rising suspicions.

"I know," I said finally.

"That's why you didn't return immediately? You were seeking answers?"

I didn't reply but bowed my head.

"If they know where she is, they aren't saying. And Lailah, even if they did, it would be too dangerous."

"I understand." There was no point arguing with Gabriel, so I didn't try. "I'm sorry for causing you worry."

I reached for Gabriel's hand, and he cleared his throat. "They can't know we're *together*. They wouldn't understand an Angel and a demon, reformed or otherwise. And your name is Brooke."

"Right," I said. As my arm fell back down to my side, Gabriel gave my hand a small, apologetic squeeze. "Gabriel?"

"Yes," he said, following me.

"Phelan, the older lad, I don't trust him. Light soul or not, he's not the friendliest. If you're watching them, I would suggest that he's the one to keep an eye on." I wasn't keen on Phelan; he made me uncomfortable, plus he had recently thrown a silver net over me and I hadn't quite forgiven that, regardless of his misguided reasons for doing so.

"Fergal told me that Phelan was the one who attacked you. He's lucky he's still breathing. He won't get near you, I promise."

As Gabriel's words left his lips, they were laced with a jagged edge, and the hairs on my arm stood on end. I put it down to Gabriel being overly protective. Later I would come to wish that I had paid more attention.

Outside the door to the motor home, the smell of cooked food floated through the air from the open windows. Riley and Dylan were strolling across the grass toward the house, silver chains in one hand, guns in the other, and they nodded at Gabriel as they passed us by.

Gabriel knocked twice, and the door swung open. Phelan stood on the other side, leaning his elbow against the wall, his hand behind his head.

"May we come in?" Gabriel asked politely.

Phelan's vest rode up his torso as he stretched, revealing jeans that hit below his cut lines. As usual his beanie hat covered his head. Funny how he seemed to think it was cold enough to wear a wool hat but not a sweater. His brown eyes narrowed as he considered me, but finally he stepped back and invited us both inside.

Always chivalrous, Gabriel guided me in first, and I sidestepped Phelan as I entered the motor home.

Iona was in the kitchen. Her long blond hair swished about as she juggled multiple frying pans and toasted bread, stopping only to fill up jugs with orange juice. Some of the lads were strewn across the sofas, with plates full of food balanced in their greedy hands, and Brooke and Fergal were snuggled up in the corner. I raised my eyebrows, and Brooke—startled by our arrival—gently shifted from under Fergal's arm.

"Gabriel!" Iona skipped from the kitchen, her flouncy shift skirt swaying around her legs as she fell over herself to greet him.

Gabriel smiled. "Iona."

It was hard to miss Iona's blush. Her gaze finally fell on me, and she strained a cautious smile. "Brooke. I'm . . . we're very sorry about what happened. We didn't know who you were, that the Lord had granted you redemption."

This wasn't an easy situation, and all eyes were on me. Yes, I was standing next to an Angel, but this group was used to exterminating demons, and that's exactly what they thought I was. To be fair, they weren't completely misinformed.

"No, I'm sorry. I should have explained myself sooner. I wasn't entirely sure you would understand."

"As I've said to you all," Gabriel began, addressing the room, "the few Vampires I travel with are not the same as the rest. They have rejected the Devil and now revere the Lord. I'd appreciate it if, for the short time we are in one another's company, you respect that fact."

Fergal nodded, less interested in what Gabriel was saying and far more rapt with Brooke, whom he was now sneakily tickling underneath her top.

But Iona was hanging on Gabriel's every word with a look of pure wonder.

Phelan said, "Never known a Vampire who could speak before. But then, we're used to slaughtering you before you get the chance, like."

I exchanged an I-told-you-so glance with Gabriel just as the smoke alarm began to screech.

"Oh no!" Iona ran back into the kitchen, where smoke was billowing from the toaster as the bread burned. Iona tried to release the toast while jumping up and down in the air to clear the smoke below the alarm. The lads in the living room didn't move an inch.

Iona was struggling to stop the siren, and Gabriel stepped in to assist her. He took the tea towel from her fingers and Iona stared up at him as he stretched, waving it in the air and finally pressing his finger to the small red button.

Overheating grease from the sausage pan drew Iona's attention, and she took the frying pan off the stove. A sizzle of oil splattered on her skin and she recoiled, clutching her hand.

Without a second thought, Gabriel wrapped the tea towel around the small burn and led her to the sink, where he ran the faucet.

A streak of jealousy shot through me like an electric shock as he held her hand, but I let it go. This was Iona. She hadn't deliberately meant to hurt herself. Still, she faltered at his touch and collected herself less quickly than I would have liked.

"You all right in there, sis?" Fergal shouted.

Iona merely squeaked as she peered up at my Angel. Gabriel took her wrist and, where she'd been mildly scalded, pressed his thumb over the burn. The fact that Iona's breathing hitched a little as he bore over her did not go unnoticed by me, flailing senses or not.

I didn't make a polite exit. Instead I shuffled backward, tripping slightly over the plastic surround of the door frame. I knew Iona meant no harm—if anything she was likely embarrassed—but nonetheless I didn't have the stomach for this, not today. Not any day.

I wondered if, when Gabriel saw Jonah and me together, he got that same nauseating sensation that I was feeling now.

I ambled around the side of the motor home before striding off into the depths of the grounds as briskly as my legs would allow.

The darkened clouds swirled above me, covering the sun, before releasing a pelting rain. I ran but not for long. My muscles felt tight and worn. Doubled over, I gasped for fresh air.

A few scant bushes, some shrubbery, and an odd cluster of trees here and there dotted the unlandscaped acres. I couldn't quite make out the main road in the distance, but the whoosh of cars let me know it was there. It was the only thing giving life to this dreary, lonesome spot.

But right here, it was just me, myself, and I.

I thought about Zherneboh and the fact that he now knew I was alive, but as yet there was no sign of any Pureblood Masters or their Second Generation Vampires. I wondered what was taking them so long. Maybe we were close to water—which helped to prevent rifts opening—but if they believed that I could keep my form in all the dimensions, and therefore destroy Styclar-Plena, or even the third, wouldn't they be doing all they could to find me? And fast?

Maybe I should stop worrying about why they hadn't found me yet and concentrate instead on being ready for them when they did.

To truly be the most powerful being to walk this world, surely I should be physically stronger or be able to do something that, perhaps, they were unable to do? But I wasn't, and I couldn't. Even before Jonah had drunk my blood, I was struggling to summon and control my Angel abilities, and when I used my Vampire abilities they came with a dull ache—in fact, thinking about the tree, they hadn't come at all.

I had to try.

I skimmed the scenery, finding a fence and gate separating some of the land ahead. I closed my eyes and envisioned standing next to it. When I opened my eyes, I was nowhere near the fence. I was elevated. I flapped, unable to travel forward and unable to drop back to the ground. I desperately squeezed my eyelids and tried to imagine weights around my feet; I tried to imagine something—anything—to help me meet the grass. Then I plummeted, falling to the ground too hard, and my ankle caught beneath my leg. I stifled a squeal, plucking my leather boot out from underneath me.

I was in trouble.

From the outside in, I was not the way I should have been. My body was failing me. I knew what I needed, but I also knew what that meant. If I drank blood, I would survive, but the likelihood was that my relationship with Gabriel would not.

Disgruntled, I rose to my feet, deliberately exerting pressure on my ankle. I didn't care if it buckled; I didn't care if it broke clean in half. I was going to stand, and I was going to walk over to the tree in the distance, and I was going to find the strength to uproot it.

Mind over matter.

I lugged myself down the lawn, hell-bent on making it to the willow tree. I walked under its drooping branches and pressed my palms against the worn bark. I wiped the sweat from my brow and squatted at its base, gripping the trunk with my arms.

I counted to three and reached deep within myself, calling upon any strength I possessed to flow through me.

I pulled long and hard. I lost track of for how long and how many tears had streamed down my cheeks while I did, but by the time I wailed in defeat, blood was inking the lines of my palms, trickling down my wrists.

My head spun and I passed out.

At least, I thought I'd passed out.

I was sitting under the tree's spindly branches, staring out between them into the land. There was no color; it was as though the gray clouds had run with the rain and turned the scenery monochromatic.

Except for one thing.

A beautiful blue butterfly danced across my drained vision. It flew past, slowly, and then returned.

Where had it come from?

Was I dreaming?

A sense of panic rose in my chest as I realized if I was, Zherneboh could find my mind. As the fear overcame me, the butterfly responded. With an unnatural speed, it zoomed in front of my nose, twisting and spinning up and down, left and right.

But then it just stopped.

I searched the backdrop, but it was still. I calmed. No smell of burning ash, no harrowing screech. Zherneboh wasn't here.

And then the butterfly came back to life. It hovered above my shoulder, brushing my earlobe.

The clap of the butterfly's wings met me, and then a voice—one that belonged to a young girl. "*El efecto mariposa*," she whispered.

I struggled to crane my neck to the right, and at the base of the tree beside me sat a fresh-faced child, dressed in a long sapphire-blue dress with a black cardigan covering her arms. I was immediately drawn to her eyes, which were like marbles—opaque glass surrounding hazel star-shaped swirls that gazed up toward the sky, startling me.

I would have thought her imaginary if I hadn't felt the press of her iced skin on mine as she took my hand. "You are the why," she said. "He is meant to save you. Let him save you, Lailah."

And then her figure dissolved and the Morpho butterfly returned, taking her place. It ascended into the air, stopping at arm's length from my chin and beating its wings together as though it were waving good-bye.

My eyes illuminated at the sight. The butterfly's iridescent blue wings seemed to absorb and then reflect the light shining from my eyes, until they became so brilliant, and so bright, that they transformed into white flame. Like a piece of paper too close to a bonfire, the black outline of the wings caught fire. The butterfly burned before me, and white-hot embers scattered across my vision.

When I came to, Gabriel was kneeling beside me, cradling me into his chest. As my sight refocused, the first things I saw were his eyes of sapphire gems gleaming back at me.

I recalled how they had reminded me of a Morpho butterfly once before, and how they reminded me still of the same. He had said he would save me—he would always save me—and I thought then that the girl was a sign, reinforcing the things I already knew and was battling to hold on to. Maybe she was my mind's way of telling me that I must continue to fight for Gabriel so that he could continue to fight for me.

I would hold on. I would find a way. I would not give in.

TWENTY-ONE

Gabriel accepted my explanation that I had over-exerted myself while using my abilities. It was the truth; I just failed to mention that they weren't exactly working properly.

I knew I was running out of time; every move I made only caused my body to slowly drain away what little energy I had left. I searched for clues in the strange vision that had crept over me while I was unconscious—seeking out *how* I could let Gabriel save me—but I was coming up short.

I sat on the end of Brooke's bed, having showered long ago, pretending to show an interest in her many outfit combinations while secretly letting my mind wander. Finally, she thrust a pile of clothes into my hands.

"Come on, get dressed," she said. "The marshmallows won't toast themselves, you know."

Gabriel was with our new "friends," and Brooke, who was now wearing the tightest pair of leather pants I had ever seen, and I were to join.

She explained that our garden guests had insisted on hosting a bonfire—an olive branch, extended by Fergal. It was an opportunity for all of us to chat and get to know one another better, although I knew the only beings from this house that any of them really desired to converse with were the Angel and "the girl." The rest of us, I figured, would likely not stay too long and I was glad. That scratching sensation in my throat had returned with a vengeance, and I had to resist the urge to claw my skin with my unkempt fingernails. It was a strain to find my voice let alone hold up any decent conversation.

"In a minute," I said. "Bathroom break first." I barely had the energy to dress myself. I needed time.

My feet might as well have been severed for all the use they were as I tried to make it to my own en suite. I had to concentrate on every wiggle of my toes and every forward motion of my thighs.

Too tired to make it as far as my own bedroom, I fell into the main bathroom just off the landing. My head swam with dizziness. The sink, though only inches from me, blurred into the eggshell white of the wall.

I collapsed onto the ceramic tiles, and as I sat, legs sprawled out, my towel fell below my chest. The scar running across my heart was red and purple. The streak was so prominent—so obvious—against my pale, chalky-white skin.

Every breath hurt.

The thought of Jonah's blood—the memory of me drinking from him once before—branded my vision. I was so engrossed that, for a second, I could taste him. But then I realized I had actually bitten my tongue and my own blood was spreading across my taste buds. It didn't taste bad; it tasted sweet. It tasted good.

Blood pooled in my mouth, and then automatically my fangs cracked, stabbing my tongue a second time.

I swallowed.

My blood was in no way the same as a Vampire's—full of dark matter—but I had been told that blood itself was still a fueling substance and helped to keep a Vampire's form functioning. That didn't, however, apparently stretch to drinking one's own blood. Although for a few minutes I stopped aching inside, all too quickly my chest began to jerk.

I was going to be sick.

I didn't have time to get to the toilet; instead, I reeled around and gripped the edge of the bathtub behind me, violently throwing the blood back up. I tried to keep it down, knowing that it had done something good before my body rejected it.

My efforts were desperate, the sound of heaving impossible to stifle, but I refused to let it all escape.

The creak from the landing told me that someone was approaching.

A knock on the door came three times in quick succession.

"Who is it?" I choked out as I wiped my mouth with the inside of my towel.

The door swung open, and Jonah towered over me.

I grappled for the shower curtain hanging from the rail above the tub, and in one clean movement slid it across, before propping myself up again.

"Why can I smell your blood?" he demanded.

Jonah stooped to my knees. He knocked the hood of his sweatshirt down and scraped his hand through his dark, disheveled hair. His hard, marblelike hazel eyes stripped me bare. "I asked you a question."

Squeezing his lips together, his look of irritation and discontent filled me with a great sadness. I wished I could unburden myself to his waiting ears, like I would have done once before. But it was a selfish wish; he didn't want that. I had bonded him back to me against his will. I was nothing more to him than a prison sentence, trapping him inside my walls and persecuting him for a crime he was tricked into committing.

The sudden rising of bile, mixed with blood in my throat, overcame all other thoughts. I lurched forward as my belly contracted, but, trapped by Jonah, all I could do was grab his arm. Somehow I managed to choke it all back down.

My towel slipped, and I instinctively grabbed for my chest, covering myself. When I found Jonah's eyes they locked onto mine, as though he were probing for the truth, as though he cared. But then his gaze flitted down to my hands clutching my chest, and he traced the outline of the scar running underneath them, across my heart. Without saying a thing, he cupped his hands over mine, nudging them lower down, only just allowing me to keep my modesty.

He ran his fingertips over the ridge of the scar before pushing down on my white skin as though he were testing to see if it would leave a mark. And though his action was clinical, I couldn't help my insides fluttering at the touch of his skin on mine.

I hadn't realized I was holding my breath until he said softly, "Breathe, Lailah."

I did as I was told and sucked in a bout of air. As I exhaled, I found myself breaking into a light and dizzy laugh, knowing how ridiculous and how terrible it was that he could literally cause me to stop breathing.

His frosty exterior melted away for a moment, and I thought a smile of his own appeared on his lips in return.

But as my stomach churned, I moved a hand to my belly, pushing away the cotton, and his eyes followed. I thought for a second that perhaps he had seen the smear of my blood inside the towel. I was wrong. His smile faded fast and finally died as he took in the sight of my skin, showing itself between my widespread fingers. I met his stare then, as the marks left by the damage he had inflicted on me revealed themselves in distinct dark lashings against my milky skin.

He sprung off the floor, flicking his hood back up, and his body tensed. Again he asked, "Why can I smell your blood?"

When I didn't reply, he reached forward and, taking my wrist, yanked me off the tiles. He brought me in close, refusing to release me, silently demanding an answer to his question.

I coughed awkwardly, struggling to keep myself covered by my towel, and pulled my hand back to my chest. "I don't know why. Excuse me." Shutting the door on him as I left, I was relieved that I had managed to escape without having to explain myself.

I was stepping inside Brooke's bedroom when I heard the rings attached to the top of the shower curtain skim backward, followed by Jonah cursing loudly.

Crap.

Now comfortably dressed in jeans, T-shirt, and a sweater, I joined the others in the kitchen as Gabriel proceeded to advise us on how we were to conduct ourselves with our Irish guests.

Brooke hovered at the back door. "Yeah, yeah, can we go now? They've already got the fire going!"

"Yes, I suppose we should," Gabriel said. "But remember: No details, no storytelling; just be polite and listen to what they have to say."

Everyone had freshened up for the occasion, though it was only

Brooke, in her skimpy top, who was ignoring the fact that it was bitterly cold outside. Ruadhan was as smartly dressed as ever in a long tweed jacket, trousers, and leather shoes. I appreciated that he appeared older than the rest of us even though he wasn't actually as ancient as Gabriel or me, technically speaking; yet his lines and graying hair caused me to feel safer, in wiser company.

Jonah had left the house—I assumed to feed. I didn't know if he was planning on making an appearance at this little gathering. I hoped he wouldn't. His cruel and cutting words circled in my head.

"After you." Gabriel held open the doors, ushering Brooke and then Ruadhan through.

He waited for them to leave and then strode over to me in the corner of the kitchen. Taking my hands in his, he kissed my curled fingers and gazed down at me. "Lai, are you sure you're feeling okay? It's just, I know what you said, but you look a little—"

"I'm just tired from earlier. I overdid it outside—that's all." I cut off Gabriel's concerns, and he paused and then nodded lightly. I was well aware that my physical appearance was already starting to conflict with the promise I had made; yet still he seemed to believe me.

"I don't like that we aren't moving, on the river, the Sealgaire, or otherwise. While we are here, if at any time you sense danger, from whomever, no matter what, you mustn't hesitate to think yourself away, okay?" Gabriel said.

"Okay," I answered, though I didn't think I could simply think myself away right at this moment.

"Tomorrow evening I have to go out of town—the last of the business I need to tie up. We'll leave the next day," he said matter-of-factly.

I couldn't face arguing with him, not right now at least. "I'd like to come with you, if you don't mind." I wasn't so willing to let him leave me behind this time around.

"I think it's best if you stay here. But I will have to take someone with me." He paused, and his muscles knotted in his broad shoulders, anticipating that I wouldn't like what he was about to say.

"What do you mean *someone?*"

Releasing my hands, he scratched his temple and moved a few stray hairs from his vision. "The gentleman I do business with always knew that one day, when I was ready to cash in the last of my chips, it would come only because I had decided to stop."

"What chips? You don't need money, Gabriel. You have your abilities. Can't you just influence people to get what you need?"

"Influencing, if it's done in such a way that is wrongful, can be *damaging*, Lai." He seemed uncomfortable with the question.

"Damaging how?" I pushed.

"It's not important." His body stiffened and a dark looming sensation stretched from his being to mine—one that felt like fear.

Wanting the feeling to subside for him, I moved on. "What does he think you are stopping exactly?"

"He knows I am an Angel, and he knows about Vampires, but that's all he knows. I'm not the only Angel he does business with. He always assumed the day would come when I would want to fall, and he, like most men would, thought that decision would come from the influence of a woman." He raised his eyebrows. "I had to cancel my meeting with him when you went missing. And so, instead, he's invited me to a soiree he's hosting at his home in Chelsea to finalize our arrangements and bid me farewell."

"And what—you need to take a woman with you to do that?" I said, sensing where this was going.

"I think it's best if I live up to his expectations. I don't want him to become suspicious of the reasons why. I want him to believe that I have now chosen to fall and live a mortal life with a human. Because that is the story I would want him to tell, if he were ever in a position of having to confess what he knew."

My eyes swept across the floor, finally resting back on his. "Doesn't he know that you can't fall, not without the Arch Angels' agreement?"

"He doesn't know any of that, Lai." He straightened my sweater and stroked the tops of my arms. "I've kept his understanding of things as minimal as possible. It's safer that way."

I wanted to ask exactly what kind of business it was that he was involved in with this gentleman, but the only question that came from my lips was a jealous one. "Who were you planning on taking with you?"

"He's expecting a human." He paused. "I was thinking of asking Iona."

I pushed down the nervous feeling rising inside me. I already feared I had hurt him. By asking the details of his meeting with Hanora, I had shown distrust in him, but I hoped he recognized that it wasn't that. My question, my worry had stemmed from my own insecurities.

"Speak to her. And if she wants to go, then I suggest, in the absence of her father, you ask Fergal's permission. They are traditional like that." I turned on my heel.

Gabriel reached for my waist, pulling me back in toward him. "Lailah, are you okay with that?"

"Yes," I said too slowly.

He peered over my shoulder and then planted a sweet kiss on my lips.

I parted from Gabriel. "You're worried they might see?"

"We have to be careful," he said, "but you make it very difficult for me. All I want to do is kiss you."

I smiled softly, and standing on tiptoes, I pecked his cheek. I sighed and walked to the doors. "Let's get this over with. You okay to follow behind?"

"Following you is easy, Lailah. It's the watching you leave that's hard."

TWENTY-TWO

THE CHOKING FUMES WAFTING from the roaring bonfire hit me square in the face. I approached the group with caution. The Seal-gaire, as they preferred to be collectively called, were sitting on fold-out chairs, ramming marshmallows onto long skewers and toasting them against the yellow and orange flames that danced against a darkening sky.

It didn't take me long to find Brooke, giggling like a giddy school-girl next to Fergal on the grass, slightly parted from the rest of the group. She barely acknowledged my arrival, giving me only the faint-est glance as I assessed the seating arrangements.

Ruadhan was engrossed in a conversation with Riley and Claire, while Cameron stood quietly beside them. Dylan and Jack were miss-ing, but Gabriel had told me the lads were taking shifts, patrolling the perimeters of the property. Iona was nowhere to be seen, but I could hear her singing in the kitchen of the motor home. I smiled, one because she had a beautiful voice, and two, and more important, because I could just make it out from here. My abilities had not yet left me completely.

I sensed I was being watched as I moved around the fire. Phelan was staring at me, gesturing for me to take up the seat next to him. I had no desire to converse with Phelan, but then there weren't a lot of options.

Reluctantly, I headed over, moving the plastic chair slightly farther away from him before sitting down on the torn fabric.

Lifting a white marshmallow from a bag beside his feet, he pierced it with a metal spike and handed it to me. "Here," he said with an almost taunting voice.

I shook my head in reply.

"Fluffy 'mallows don't interest you, like?" he said sarcastically.

My eyebrows arched. "No, they don't. But to be honest, I'm more concerned that you wouldn't be able to refrain from pushing me into the fire while I toast it."

Phelan's broad shoulders fell a little as he relaxed, a genuine laugh falling from his lips. "Touché."

"So," I said.

"So," he repeated. "You're a demon." It wasn't a statement or a question; the elevated pitch in his words made it sound more like . . . wondering.

Hot from being so close to the fire, I tugged at the neckline of my sweater. "I'm many things."

Phelan got up to retrieve two cans of beer. As he offered me one, I recoiled at the sight of the silver dagger clipped to the waistband of his sweatpants.

He tapped it and said, "Protection—you understand."

I shook my head as he waved the beer can at me.

"Just blood then?" he asked.

"Not quite. You got anything stronger in there?" I peered over.

"Aye." After rummaging, he handed me a miniature bottle of gin, and I gripped it somewhat gratefully. We exchanged a "cheers," and I unscrewed the cap and knocked it back.

I searched for Gabriel. He had been making the rounds but was now walking toward the motor home—I could only assume to speak to Iona about the soiree. Before he stepped through the entrance, he turned around and his eyes, brought out by the royal-blue button-down parka he was wearing, met mine.

Are you okay?

I didn't answer his thoughts, but nodded instead.

I returned my attention to Phelan. "Fergal seems to be getting on nicely with—Lailah."

"Surprises me a bit. He only just lost his brother. He's perked up since he met her." Phelan hunched over, parting his legs as he continued to slurp his beer. Despite the winter's early evening, he had dressed in his usual wifebeater, with only his hat and a dull green scarf wrapped around his neck for warmth.

"He was very close with Padraig, I take it?" I ventured, trying to tease back my new bangs from my vision.

Phelan's eyes found mine quickly, and he looked at me with a sense of confusion. The flames from the fire seemed to warm his gaze. Contradicting what I knew about him, they somehow made him seem softer.

"Iona?"

"We had a little time to chat. I'm sorry for your family's loss. I understand you were in Creigiau seeking out Lailah, the night they . . . perished."

Phelan withdrew a roll-up from behind his ear and fiddled with it in his fingers before finally lighting it. "We were looking for the girl, and we found her. Might have taken us a while to track her down again, but here we are, so it wasn't in vain." He took a long drag of his cigarette. "We lost Padraig before that night. Fergal, well, he's still a child, and he cries like one, too. That will be my pa's influence; he got on better with him than his own, like, so is no surprise." Phelan's tone was filled with disdain. "She, however, is not quite what I was expecting. I assumed we were seeking out someone a little more . . . divine." He paused. "We're *friends* now, right?" His voice was laced in sarcasm. "So, between *friends*, she doesn't strike me as being any sort of celestial being, Brooke." The cherry at the end of his smoke brightened as he pulled on it while making his point. Turning his body in toward me, he said, "I don't like being deceived. I knew you weren't who you said you were the second I met you."

"I didn't think I'd fooled you even for a moment, Phelan," I offered uncomfortably, sloshing around the last few drops of gin in the miniature bottle.

"And from one *friend* to another, I don't think you are who you say you are now," he said.

Despite his—correct—intuition, he didn't know anything for sure, and I highly doubted that he genuinely believed I was "the girl." So I ignored his comment.

Setting the bottle down on the ground, I crossed my arms and gripped the hem of my sweater. I hadn't expected it to be so hot that I would need to remove layers, so I was only wearing a small cami underneath, which allowed for the scar running across my chest to be visible.

As I pulled the sweater over my head, my top rode up with it, exposing my skin. But Phelan had already seen the worst of my scars—the one left by Frederic. It made no difference what he saw now.

Holding the cigarette between his lips, Phelan studied the one across my heart, but then his gaze found the far more damaging scars left by Jonah's knife. "Your marks came to you by the hands of humans?"

I found myself kneading my fingers through the back of my hair, feeling for the bump on the back of my skull left by Ethan when he had inadvertently killed me in my first life. "Some," I replied, unable to remove the quiver from my voice. "But most of them came from Vampires."

Phelan hooked his thumb under the collar of his shirt, pulling it away slightly from his skin, so I might see his better. "And what, you don't like yours?" he asked, releasing his shirt and flicking the ash from his cigarette instead.

"Not especially. Do you?"

"I'm proud of mine. They brand me a righteous warrior, fighting in the Lord's name. Every single one I am left with is a reminder of a battle—a warning to others that I won."

"Then why have you got crosses tattooed over the one on your neck?" I asked.

"Each cross is a symbol of every demon that I've killed. You may notice that I wear more tattoos than I do scars." He paused for a moment. "If you came by yours by the hands of the demons you fought, you shouldn't be ashamed of them, like. They stand for something." He blew out a stream of smoke from his nose.

"Unlike yours, mine represent stupidity and ignorance. They only show me to be a victim." I thought for a moment, finding myself clutching my waist. "Well, nearly all of them."

Phelan dropped his cigarette to the ground, stubbing it out with his sneaker, and handed me another miniature. I thanked him and took the bottle, only sipping the spirit this time.

"What about the one on your shoulder?" His voice was a little softer now, more sincere. "You told me when you got it, but you didn't tell me how."

I screwed up my face, confused. In the motor home, I had thought he was asking after the horrific, jagged scar running up my spine, the one Frederic had inflicted on me—not the one from the night I found Jonah.

"What?" he said, responding to my bewildered expression.

"I'm sorry. I thought, before, that you were asking about the one down my back, not that one."

Phelan's pupils dilated a little, but I didn't know why. "Then how'd you come by the one on your shoulder?"

My bangs fell into my eye line as I tipped my chin. Irritated, I tried to shake them away as I shrugged nonchalantly.

Phelan removed his beanie hat and leaned over to me. I instinctively shuffled back.

He frowned. "It's made of wool."

Pushing my bum to the back of the chair, I nodded at Phelan, and now, with permission, he stood in front of me. Squatting down, he inclined his upper body toward me. I regarded him warily as he slowly lifted the beanie up and over my head and awkwardly tucked my bangs inside.

As he leaned back on his haunches, he placed his hands on top of mine, which were resting on the metal arms, and tipped his body in toward me. "That should stop your fussing." His hands clenched and he pulled me to my feet, the bottle of gin dropping from my lap and rolling on the ground. I took a sharp intake of breath, and—despite the ashy, melting smell coming from the fire—he was so close that all I could taste was his mint aftershave.

He scanned the area, and then moved his solid arm across my back roughly and pulled me into his body. "Tell me," he whispered, "how'd you get the scar on your shoulder?"

I didn't answer, yelping instead as the silver of his blade met my torso and simmered against my skin. At the same moment, Phelan seemed to dive backward.

Jonah was behind him, grabbing him by the back of his shirt and growling with his fangs on full display. Jonah placed a hand around Phelan's throat. I thought he'd been out feeding; perhaps that's why I expected his fingers to be coated in blood. But instead they were dusted in charcoal.

Fergal sprang off the ground, reached for a revolver, and darted over, pointing it at Jonah's back. "Let him go, demon."

Cameron remained where he stood, but Riley was already pulling a blade and a gun from his waistband and circling us.

Ruadhan zoomed over to Fergal. "Put the gun down, lad."

I found my footing and rubbed my skin, trying to cool the scalding sensation, but it was already fading. I didn't know if Gabriel had heard the commotion or had felt my pain; either way, he appeared next to me.

He skimmed over my body with worried eyes and placed his hands across my tummy.

Are you okay?

I didn't answer him. Instead, I held up my hands to assure Fergal that I meant no harm. "Jonah," I said assertively.

He didn't divert his attention away from Phelan, whom he held captive by pressing his elbow to Phelan's chest. "You shouldn't have touched her—" Jonah spat angrily, his eyes lighting up ruby red.

"There's no harm done. Let him go," I said.

When he still didn't release Phelan, I stepped in. Standing on tiptoes, I cupped Jonah's cheek and nudged his face toward mine. But my action caused him to snatch my wrist with his free hand, and he pushed me away. A simple action, but one that caused me great pain.

I moved back in, and without thinking, I wedged my arm underneath Jonah's, creating a gap between his forearm and Phelan's neck. Exerting as much strength as I could, I pried him away from Phelan, who managed to slip out from Jonah's grasp, sucking in air as he did. I knew Jonah had let me free Phelan, because right now, Jonah was far stronger than me.

Fergal stood next to his cousin, and Brooke rushed over to Fergal's side, glaring at Jonah.

Jonah's body was rigid, but the fire behind him roared, as though what was going on underneath his skin was reflected in the crackling flames. Everyone was gawking at us.

"We need a minute, please," I said.

No one moved. Then Iona's bracelets jingled through the still silence as she trod cautiously across the grass to see what was going on.

"Please," I insisted.

The group dispersed. Ruadhan squeezed my shoulder to remind me that he would not be far away, and Phelan shot me a "this isn't over" glare before finally leaving with Fergal and Brooke.

You too, I spoke to Gabriel.

Lailah—

You too, I repeated.

Hesitantly, Gabriel departed, back in the direction of the motor home—back toward where Iona now stood.

I placed my hands on Jonah's chest, but still he did not look at me. He stared out at the stretch of land ahead, unwilling to give in to my unspoken request.

Back on tiptoes, I rose higher and placed my thumb and index finger to his chin, forcing him to meet my eye. "Phelan touching me—any guy touching me—shouldn't matter to you. *Does* it matter to you, Jonah?" I had to know. He had told me with conviction that I meant nothing to him, yet here he was, appearing from nowhere, ready to do terrible things to a person who had come too close. Why?

His lips pulled into a thin line. "No," he said.

His reaction was precisely that: a reaction. He was bonded to me through blood, nothing more.

I sighed. "Everything you said about me was right, and I don't doubt you meant every word. I know what I am; who I am right now is a mess. I'm not going to stand here and argue otherwise."

Jonah placed his hands to my elbows. Though his lip rose, it seemed he managed to hold back what I assumed would only be more unpleasant character assassinations.

So I said, "And I am sorry that you are bound to me by my blood, but don't risk yourself on account of that. If I were to die, you would be free again, so let the chips fall where they may."

Jonah's grip tightened and a resentful flash of red ignited his irises. The butterfly girl's words came to me, and I repeated them to reiterate my point. "*El efecto mariposa*, Jonah—the butterfly effect.

Stay away from the typhoon—stay away from me—or it will sweep you away as well."

Jonah's eyes cooled, and I swept my hands over his, skimming his soft skin before turning away. But within a blink, he was blocking my path. "What made you say that?" he barked.

Never would he let me have the last word. "Say what exactly?"

"*El efecto mariposa.*" He dragged his hand through his messy hair.

"Forget it. I'm not going to give you more ammunition to degrade me further." I didn't want him adding "insane" to his long list of my defective qualities.

"I'm not messing around. Tell me what made you say that—" Jonah's heartbeat had suddenly become loud and quick. It felt like the fire had erupted, melting the entire world around us, and the drum of his heart was being beaten by a lone soldier marching through the darkened wasteland, crying out.

"I had a dream. I dunno, a hallucination probably. It's not important."

Jonah looked as though I had slapped him in the face, and his heart skipped a beat, as though the soldier had found someone in the nothingness.

"It is important. Those words mean something to me. Tell me about this dream," he demanded.

I crinkled my brow. I thought that perhaps the words spoken by the girl—my subconscious—were reminding me to stay true to my cause; that one way or another, Gabriel would save me, and I him. It was a little odd that they meant something to Jonah.

"Jonah," Gabriel interrupted, returning to my side, unwilling to stay away any longer.

"I'll leave you to it," I grumbled. I took my opportunity; I had no inclination to delve into the peculiarities of what might well have been simply a delusion.

I wandered back toward the house, but as I found myself inside the kitchen, I stopped. They may have been forty feet away from me and now arguing in hushed voices, but the mention of my name caught my attention and so I zoned in, straining to pick up what was being said.

". . . I was wrong." Jonah's words flared.

"No, you were exactly right. She's safest with me. Look what you did to her—" Gabriel retaliated. The conversation dipped in and out, and I peered over my shoulder, trying to find them again and attempting to squash the other sounds so that all that existed was their voices.

". . . you were so busy making eyes at that girl that you left her alone with him. You put her in danger. Your attention isn't where it should be."

Jonah was talking about Iona. The problem with tuning in to private conversations was that there was no filter. Using my ability hurt, and not just physically. What Jonah was implying of Gabriel literally caused what little color I had left to drain from my cheeks.

TWENTY-THREE

By late afternoon the following day, the sun was hiding behind thick clouds. The sky stretched in a murky-colored fog. I was glad. I feared absorbing any more of the sun would only do me damage, and I wouldn't have been able to explain to Gabriel why I didn't want to meet it.

Fergal had agreed to Iona escorting Gabriel to the soiree that evening but only if he could join. And Gabriel, short of any other choice, had conceded.

I was upstairs with Ruadhan, putting off meeting with Iona, who had asked for Brooke and me to help her get ready for the occasion. I was already half an hour late, but still, I didn't rush. After what I had overheard Jonah saying, my insecurities were once again resurfacing and I was regretting the time Gabriel had already spent with her.

"She'll be waiting for you, love," Ruadhan said as I continued to chuck the few possessions I still had into a backpack.

"Hmmm," I mumbled. "Have you packed your case yet?" I changed the subject.

He barely lifted his nose from his book. "Aye."

Gabriel was keener than ever that we leave the next day. The Sealgaire knew I was alive and where I was, even if they did think that Brooke was me, and Zherneboh had already reached into my mind once. Understandably, Gabriel was unwavering in his decision for us to move on. I had made my feelings clear; I wasn't going to run from them, and that hadn't changed. But knowing I was physically far from being ready to take any sort of stand, we had reached a compromise: We would cut all ties and go, but Ruadhan would come with us and help me to harness and learn to use my abilities.

What they both didn't know was that those abilities were fading fast and that I was in constant pain. A sort of flulike sickness had taken hold of me. My temperature switched frequently from searing hot to freezing and that stabbing itch had moved down my throat to the center of my chest. But that was a problem I was going to have to solve by myself.

I tucked my crystal ring inside my T-shirt. There was nothing else to do but meet Iona. It might at least distract me from my illness.

Leaving Ruadhan in my room, I ran my hand down the exposed brickwork as I walked down the stairs. I was halfway down the hall, traveling toward the back exit, when I heard Iona's voice.

I followed her gleeful giggle to the grand dining room. The aging hinges creaked as I pushed the door open.

Iona was at the varnished dinner table, opposite Gabriel, with my chessboard placed centrally between them. Gabriel's huge smile disappeared as he saw my dejected expression, and the soft aura of light around his figure dulled.

Iona twisted around excitedly in her chair. "Brooke! Guess what? Gabriel's teaching me to play chess!"

I tried to collect myself, shaking the resentful thoughts from my head before they could fully form. "I see that."

"I was giving Iona a tour while she waited for you, and she saw the set," Gabriel explained, but he could see that I was not pleased.

I closed my eyes, taking a breath, and quickly threw the wall up in my mind. I wanted my privacy.

"The pieces are so pretty. Look at the pony, like!" Iona lifted the white knight in the air, replacing my fingerprints with hers. "Do you play?"

I glanced at Gabriel and then back at Iona. "I used to. Once."

Gabriel stood up swiftly, but in this room, with its double-vaulted ceilings, even with his six-foot height he looked small.

I searched past him, not quite ready to meet his eye, and the face of the grandfather clock screwed to the wall told me we were running out of time.

"We had better get you ready," I said to Iona.

"Aye." She scampered to her feet. "It's a proper birthday treat, like."

"Oh, I'm sorry. Happy birthday, Iona," I said in a smooth, ex-pressionless tone.

"Naw, it's not today; it's tomorrow. Sort of an early present!" She beamed and played with her long, loose curls.

My gaze was drawn to the white-blond, silky waves, and I found myself envying her looks. Her innocent milky skin and soul of the same was untouched, unmarked, and unmatched by me.

"We'd better get you ready then, hadn't we?" I said.

She bounded joyfully over to me, taking my hand and forgetting, perhaps, that I was a demon. But then she was childlike in so many ways. I didn't give Gabriel any of my attention, but I couldn't help casting one last fleeting glance at the chess set. A remarkable piece of craftsmanship that had once belonged to me. But, along with Gabriel, it now seemed to have been gifted to Iona.

IN BROOKE'S BEDROOM, I combed out Iona's gorgeous thick hair with a paddle brush, waiting for Brooke to show up.

"Do you have something elegant to wear?" I asked in a bid to make conversation.

"Aye." Iona pointed to an ornate chair where she had draped a gown over the arm. I couldn't see it properly, but a pair of what looked like very ugly shoes sat beneath it. I laughed to myself; I wouldn't have even noticed before Brooke.

Thankfully Brooke didn't take too long to surface. She'd been in the motor home, no doubt spending yet more time with Fergal, but at least she was here now. Dumping down a multitude of make-over gear on the carpet, she shuffled me out of the way.

"It's okay, ladies. I have arrived," she announced.

Forty-five minutes later, a whole heap of powder dusted the dresser, and hair clips, rollers, and other paraphernalia were scattered messily around our feet, but Iona was ready. I partially wished that Brooke wasn't as talented at this type of thing; Iona lit up the room.

"You look lovely," I said sincerely.

Iona stood in a pair of Brooke's Louboutin nude pumps instead of her own shoes. But Brooke was fully on board with Iona's gorgeous dress: A sequined taupe boatneck bodice with a fully flowing chiffon skirt glided lovingly over Iona's curves. Brooke had placed rollers in the ends of Iona's hair, and her angelic locks floated down to her bottom.

"Do you really think so?" Iona asked, half rubbing away the pink blush from her cheeks.

"Don't touch my masterpiece!" Brooke cried as she reached for the angled brush and swept it back across Iona's skin.

"Yes, I do," I replied.

Iona couldn't help breaking into a glorious grin, her plump lips shining with clear lip gloss. "Do you think Gabriel will think so?" she said sheepishly.

My heart dipped. Brooke stopped fussing with Iona and shot me a quick glance—more of a warning to keep quiet, I surmised, than out of any real concern for my feelings.

I didn't answer. Instead, I began tidying up.

"How could he not?" Brooke beamed, making up for my bullet dodging.

"He's really something. Very handsome, like. And he's so gentle and sweet, and—"

"Yes, well, he's an Angel. *Has to go back to Heaven sometime*," I interjected, bearing false witness.

Iona's shoulders slumped, and she said, "Yes, I know. I wish I had more time with him. He asked me to sing for him yesterday."

I stopped what I was doing. "He what? Why?"

"I told him I only used to sing, properly like, for my daddy. I don't feel very comfortable singing for anyone else. And he said I should try. That it might help."

"Oh." Okay, maybe Gabriel was just being kind to her. I tried to push down the sickening feeling that was stewing in my stomach, and

I wasn't quite sure if it was because I felt so unwell or because of what Iona had said. I had a feeling it was a little of both.

"You're going to be late." Brooke broke the conversation and ushered Iona through the bedroom door.

Iona hobbled out. She coped about as well as I did in high heels, but she made it to the landing and to the top of the stairs. I didn't have to look to know that Gabriel was waiting for her at the bottom. She teetered down each step, hoisting the length of her skirt up as she did, and I waited until she'd made it to the hallway before I dared to look down.

If Gabriel had faltered at the sight of her, I had missed it, because he was now searching the landing for me. Fergal, looking incredibly dapper, raised his eyebrows at Brooke, who was leaning on the banister.

"There's a car outside. I'll join you in a moment." Gabriel opened the front door, and Fergal stepped through, and the second he was gone, Brooke zoomed back into her bedroom.

Iona hesitated at the front door and asked, "May I use the toilet before we leave?" Gabriel gestured down the hallway.

Once Iona was out of sight, Gabriel appeared on the landing and took my hands in his own. Despite how I felt, I couldn't help but glow a little as my eyes swept over his smart attire. He was wearing a three-piece navy suit, complete with a matching double-breasted waistcoat, but his crisp white shirt was unbuttoned at the collar, teasing me with a show of his smooth chest. His usual shaggy blond curls were gelled back, giving him a definite gentlemanly appearance. But no matter what he wore, or how he wore it, Gabriel sucked you in with those huge sapphires of his, making him the most exquisite being in any room.

You don't look well, Lailah. I'm worried about you. He spoke his thoughts to me.

I wasn't expecting him to say that.

I know, because of the clouds, you weren't able to meet the sunrise, and you're exhausted from practicing yesterday, but . . . He glanced at the floor before finally meeting my eyes again. *Tell me, Lailah, is the sunrise truly enough or do you need blood?*

I wavered. My body ached terribly. I contemplated my answer, wondering for a moment if he might understand. Perhaps, the way I thought he felt about it was all in my head? But there was no way of knowing for sure, and I wasn't prepared to take the risk. "I—"

"Gabriel?" Iona's voice chirped, stopping me dead in my tracks.

Gabriel released my hands and peered over his shoulder to where Iona stood at the foot of the stairs. "I'm coming. I'll meet you in the car."

Iona's heels clipped the marble floor unevenly as she tottered to the front door. When Gabriel's gaze returned to me, his worried frown had briefly transitioned into a gentle smile, one that had been caused by Iona. And it niggled at me.

Lailah—

Just . . . go, I said, turning myself away from him.

Gabriel took a deep breath as he reached for my arm and pulled me back to face him.

I love you. I will do what needs to be done, and I'll be straight back. Stay indoors with Ruadhan and keep your mind open in case you need me. I can be back here in a blink of an eye, remember?

I noticed Gabriel tapping his trouser pocket, and I wondered what he was taking with him. As I moved my stray bangs from my eyes, he leaned down and planted a sumptuous kiss on my lips. I returned only a blank stare in reply.

I don't want to leave when you're upset.

"Then don't," I said aloud.

I have to. I'm securing our future.

I didn't reply and reluctantly he left. When I was sure that they were gone, I shuffled into Brooke's bedroom and shut the door behind me.

"When are you planning on leaving?" I asked quietly.

"Whatever do you mean?" she replied with a devious curve of her lips as she scooped up the many dresses from off the chair.

"As if you're going to let Fergal go to a party without you."

"I didn't say I was with Fergal," Brooke protested.

I shot her a knowing look and said, "You didn't have to. And if you're going there, masquerading as me in god knows what company, I'm coming with you."

"I'm pretty sure I'll be safe on the arm of a demon slayer. . . . You're so holier than thou sometimes. If you want to spy on Gabriel and Iona, just say it. Jeez!"

Brooke sifted through the dresses. Finally, with a wicked grin, she launched one at me. "Okay, come. It's your funeral. Put that on." She arched her eyebrow. "Dare to bare?"

Regarding the see-through fabric, I hesitated, but only for a moment and then nodded. "Fine. You can dress me. And Brooke—do we have time for you to cut my hair?"

MY COMPLEXION APPEARED EVEN more ashen than last night, so I encouraged Brooke to paint me in as many layers of white foundation as necessary.

She cut my hair in the pixie style she had initially envisioned, slicking back my new choppy look. She dressed me in a vintage, floor-sweeping gown that clung to every nook and cranny. The back was made of a thick nude material that covered my scars; the ones along my waist, however, were visible. Phelan believed that our scars branded us, and he was right. But just the same as a secret tattoo, my wounds marked the symbol that only I knew the meaning behind—the words that I would not utter aloud, and the feelings I didn't want to admit that I had, for Jonah.

I spun a tiny thong around my fingers, deliberating, and Brooke waited to see what I would do. I placed it down.

"What's happened to you, Lailah?" she asked, and it was hard to miss the pride in her voice.

"I'm not Iona," I said quietly.

"Er, yeah, I know that," she replied, handing me a pair of pointy, blood-red stilettos.

"It's time I stopped trying to be." Everything about the way Iona looked reminded me of how I once did, all those years ago, when Gabriel met me. And I sensed her traditional, softly spoken ways were much the same.

The person I was back then still existed inside me somewhere, and I would hold on to that part of who I was by not allowing myself to feed on the blood of mortals. But I had changed; I had grown into new skin. This skin.

It was time to show it.

Brooke handed me a stunning dress coat, and I carefully slid my arms into the long silk sleeves, fastening the delicate buttons with my frail fingers.

Brooke eyed me. "Lailah, are you *okay*?"

"Yes."

"Only . . . and don't get me wrong, you look hot as hell, kudos to my efforts . . . but it took a whole bottle of foundation to make you look like you're not, well, decomposing." Her words were awkward as she pulled a piece of fluff from her conservative floor-length gown. She looked alluringly demure, which meant she had dressed for Fergal this evening.

I ignored her. Brooke's iPhone buzzed, and she picked it up from off the bed. "Right, that's Fergal with an address. So, you do your whole traveling-by-thought thing, and I'll meet you at the bottom of the road. We can catch a cab; I'm not pelting to London in these heels."

I shook my head.

Brooke chewed her bottom lip, and with a fractured voice, she asked, "You can't, can you?"

At this point I highly doubted I would be able to get to the end of the road without freezing midthought. "No," I answered.

Brooke strode to my side and squeezed my arm, like we were actually friends or something. "When I said *your funeral*, I was speaking figuratively, you know that, right?" She hesitated as my vacant, muddied eyes contradicted the nod of my head. For the second time, here in this very room, she surprised me. Leaning in, she wrapped her arms around my back and whispered, "So why do I get the feeling that you're dressing for your deathbed?"

When I didn't reply immediately, she choked a little, her breath catching in the back of her throat.

I patted her back reassuringly and, overcome by her gesture, I said, "I had a choice, and I chose to live, Brooke. And I'm trying my best to, I promise I am, but—"

"But what?" Jonah's voice smacked me like a baseball bat from behind, and I wobbled in the stiletto pumps.

Brooke pulled away. Her cheeks flushed scarlet.

"Call a cab; we're leaving," I told Brooke, digging my heels into the carpet.

"Erm, I don't think Ruadhan's gonna just let you go to the party," she added quietly. "You know, *stranger danger*?"

"We're leaving through the front door," I said. "I'll meet you downstairs."

Brooke hovered nervously before finally making her way to the door.

"Neither of you are going anywhere," Jonah ordered, and Brooke grunted as he held her back.

"Brooke," I said, "you don't belong to anyone. You can leave if you want to. And so can I. Call that cab."

She retreated to my side, looking caught in a tangled web between Jonah and me. Fingering her iPhone, she scooped her clutch from the bed and her false eyelashes fluttered as she blinked. "Well then, I'll wait for you in the hall." And she was gone.

I turned slowly and purposefully, my eyes sweeping the floor to Jonah's dirty boots and then up his lean, muscular body. Finally, I rested my determined gaze on his.

He seemed to sway, perhaps surprised by my new pixie crop; perhaps by my no-nonsense stare. I didn't realize that it was because of my hands.

He marched over, snatched my fingers, and pushed back the soft scarlet silk of the coat sleeve, uncoiling the expensive ribbon to reveal the worthless package it was wrapping. I could coat my face in as much paint as I liked, but there wasn't much I could do about my sallow, bony hands.

"You're dying," he said like a doctor with a terrible bedside manner.

"I know."

His expression was unreadable, but the way his body shook— with his hands on mine, his vibrations traveling through me—told me plenty. I wondered if his connection to me through my blood caused him to feel my torturous decline, and if the minute my life truly ended, wherever he was, he would somehow know.

"He will save me, Jonah. I just have to let him," I said, clinging to the words of the butterfly girl.

"How about you start trying to save yourself for once? You need to drink blood!" he shouted.

"I can't do that to Gabriel. There's another way; there must be." Shaking the sleeve back down, I peered up at Jonah's moody expression. "I won't apologize for what I did, but I am sorry for what that means for you now. You said when we left here that you would forget me, the way I had you. I hope tomorrow will bring about the end of your suffering—you will never see me again." I wished that, when we left here, he would find some happiness.

The edges of his fierce lips turned down and his eyes narrowed, yet he said nothing. Concluding that the conversation was now over, I straightened myself and limped away.

"But you haven't forgotten, have you?" His words billowed up into the air, surrounding me like stifling smoke.

I gripped the wooden door frame, suffocated by his words.

"You do remember me," he said.

A cool bout of air skimmed the nape of my naked neck as he

met me at the door. He molded his body around me from behind, exerting pressure on my hip bones with his fingers and nudging his chin into the crevice above my collarbone. "You didn't recognize my aftershave. . . . What did I smell like to you before?"

I wavered, unable to stop the single unruly tear falling from my eye as I remembered him all over again. I whispered, "Like woods in summer."

He stroked his thumb across my cheek, mopping up the thought of him, and said, "I stopped wearing that aftershave after you died."

There was no lie I could give, no excuse that made any sense, and so I didn't try.

"When did I come back to you?" he asked softly, in a deceiving tone that suggested no punishment in exchange for my confession.

"It doesn't matter," I swallowed. "Because as quickly as you came back, you left me again." I may have remembered him, but the second I fooled him into drinking my blood, I had become a stranger and he had turned his back on me.

He spun me around suddenly, clutching me by the small of my back. He hoisted me off the floor, closing the gap between us. Now at eye level with me, he rubbed the tip of his nose against my cheek, and with a frustrated, impatient force, met his lips with mine.

I refused him, pressing my palms into his hard chest and replanting my feet on the floor. "It was my blood before, only ever my blood. That's what you said. That's all it is now."

His hazel eyes darted around my face, settling on my lip, which was twitching. Bringing his hands to the back of his neck, he looked trapped. "I, it's—"

I cut him off. "That's all it is now, Jonah." I tried to steady my warbling voice. "There is no other reason you would feel compelled to kiss someone that . . . that tastes like death."

I marched out of the room, but he came after me. "If you don't drink, and soon, you are going to *die*."

This time I would not let him have the last word. I carefully descended the stairs and peered back over my shoulder before his resentful, perfect face could disappear out of view. "It's my decision, my choice. You will respect it."

TWENTY-FOUR

THE BENTLEY PULLED UP outside a four-story whitewashed villa on Egerton Crescent, the most expensive and exclusive road in all of Chelsea, or so the chauffeur told us. The driver opened up the passenger door, and Brooke and I, as elegantly as possible, stepped out.

"Wow," Brooke gushed.

I wasn't as surprised as Brooke. Every property Gabriel owned, every piece of clothing he wore reeked of wealth, and he was here this evening to meet with some sort of business partner. I expected that business partner would reside somewhere that was nothing short of lavish.

The gentleman at the door smiled at us, and I was pleased he had seen us arrive in a Bentley; it made us look like one of them. Aware that Gabriel was not too far away, I threw up the wall in my mind to ensure that he would have no sense of me. Courtesy of the car service, I tipped the last drops of champagne to the back of my throat and gestured for Brooke to go on ahead. If there was a guest list, she would need to influence the doorman. The sight of us might not be sufficient enough.

Ruadhan hadn't argued too hard with my choice to come here, agreeing that I was capable of making my own decisions. But I wasn't completely trusting that he hadn't tipped Gabriel off. But I suspected that, even if Jonah had accepted what I'd said, he might follow anyway to keep tabs on Brooke, which to my mind might not be a bad thing.

I walked with Brooke up the diamond-shaped slabs that covered the steps leading to the wide black-and-gold door.

Brooke had worked her magic, and the doorman held out his arms for our coats. I took a nervous breath as the gentleman did a double take at the sight of me in my see-through red-and-white-rose-covered dress.

Ordinarily, Brooke would be beaming at me being so daring, but instead she looked sorrowful.

Her sadness made me feel closer to her, and I took her arm as we entered the grand, granite-floored hallway before us. A crystal chandelier hung high above at the center, catching the light and causing me to squint. At the very far end, an archway presented beautiful gardens that continued out the back. The hallway had two staircases—one at each side of the room—with cast iron railings. If fairy tales were set in the twenty-first century, this would have been the king and queen's castle, and I would be the witch infiltrating the stately home.

Waiters and waitresses wearing smart shirts and black trousers sashayed around the huge space, their brass trays holding champagne flutes that were being lifted by the many guests engrossed in conversation. The plinking of piano keys drifted into the hall, bouncing and echoing off the exposed brickwork. The notes were low and despondent, as though they were bored.

I automatically did a sweep of the floor, making sure Gabriel, Iona, and Fergal were not in the room.

"I'm going to find Fergal," Brooke said.

"Okay, but Brooke—"

She glared at me. "It's Lailah, remember."

In a hushed voice, I said, "Fine, but you remember, I'm not here, if Gabriel or anyone else asks, okay? And *Lailah*—don't be stupid enough to give out *your* name," I reminded her sternly.

She rushed away from me, weaving and bobbing through the aristocrats in search of her new Irish beau. Cricking my neck from side to side, I tried to find some strength in my legs, but I knew from how heavy they felt that Jonah was right: My body was giving up.

I roamed through the huge entranceway, swiping a glass of champagne off a tray as a waiter went by. Though I kept to the edges of the room, every person I passed seemed to stop and stare at me. Perhaps wearing such a revealing dress wasn't the best idea when I needed to blend in. Still, for the first time, I didn't feel shy or embarrassed; I wore it as though it were part of my own skin. Let them stare.

Hovering outside one of the reception rooms, I caught sight of Brooke standing by an antique Victorian fireplace. Beside her, Fergal was gripping her hand. Iona stood near, already looking like the third wheel. Gabriel wasn't with her. I tried to zone out the chatter, listening intently for his voice, but my abilities were failing and it hurt to try to use them.

Another waiter marched past me, and I grabbed his shirt. "Excuse me, is the gentleman of the house here?" If Gabriel wasn't with Iona, he was doing business.

"Yes, I believe Sir Montmorency is in his study. He will be down soon enough; you may speak with him then." He followed the trail of roses down my dress and, with a chivalrous smile, he left, but not before I replaced my empty flute with a full one.

My chest was sore and my throat was scratching, but at least the alcohol provided some form of light relief. So Gabriel was likely to be in the study, wherever that was, but the waiter had said that the owner would be down soon, which meant it was upstairs somewhere. Lifting my dress so it wouldn't catch under my heels, I ascended the stairs as inconspicuously as possible. I peered cautiously over my shoulder to check that no one was following me and continued to climb the steps.

The landing was, like the rest of the house, steeped in history and extravagance, with a double-vaulted ceiling and numerous pieces of artwork hanging across the main wall.

I listened for Gabriel's voice again, and this time, ever so faintly, I heard it. I slid my feet from the stilettos, knowing that even the slightest sound might give me away. I tiptoed down the varnished hardwood, right to the far end of the corridor.

I snuck over to a door that was slightly ajar, and I peered in through the small gap. Gabriel was seated in front of a huge desk facing an older gentleman who held a pipe in his hand; the smoke wafted, filling the room with a strong and sweet aroma. The man was leaning back in his chair. His gray checked jacket was buttoned smartly, and a chain draped below his top pocket. My gaze was drawn to the shine of an ornate silver pocket watch peeping out over the top, which warned me away.

Behind the man was a lit roof terrace with dark-green, London-style lamps and plants, accessed through double doors that were surrounded by thick, chocolate-brown velvet drapes. The many bookcases filled with leather-bound tomes lining the walls made me think of Ruadhan. He probably could spend a year in here and never get through them all.

Gabriel placed his hand inside his pocket and then stretched his arm out across the table, placing down some shiny wrappings. The gentleman removed his pipe from the corner of his lips and fingered the silk before glancing once more at Gabriel. When he opened them, he didn't hide his pleased expression. He laughed and glided his fingertips over what appeared to be a handful of crystal spheres.

"Well, I have to say, you haven't disappointed."

I found myself spreading my palm across my own gem, which hung low on my chain. Like mine, the ones Gabriel had given the man were no ordinary crystals.

Gabriel tilted his head as though he were somehow bidding farewell to the gems.

"The money will be in your account by tomorrow morning," the man said matter-of-factly.

So this was where Gabriel's wealth came from. Selling off crystals from Styclar-Plena to men like Sir Montmorency.

"You have buyers for all of them so soon?" Gabriel returned quickly.

Flipping the wrappings and re-covering the gems, Sir Montmorency drew his pipe back to his mouth and made puffing sounds as he inhaled the tobacco. "Yes, one buyer actually."

I couldn't see Gabriel's face, but his body tensing told me that answer caused him concern.

"One?" Gabriel said.

"Yes, one. He's been doing business with the Montmorency men longer than you have, in fact. First time he's buying, not selling, though. When I told him I was expecting a bounty this evening, he insisted on coming in person. I believe he has a silent partner."

Gabriel rubbed his fingers inside his palms, perplexed. I thought then he might take the crystals back—tell his business partner that the deal was off. Gabriel surely wouldn't take risks, just to make money? But he didn't say anything.

"In fact, I have several otherworldly acquaintances—yourself included—here this evening. I believe you know Malachi? I expect you have much to discuss, now you have chosen to fall."

Malachi—a fallen Angel. The same one that Gabriel had sought out in search of answers and the being I had watched in a vision.

Sir Montmorency collected the silk wrappings and strode to a safe in the wall. "This is the last of them, yes?"

He tapped in a security code. The locking mechanism turned over twice before releasing.

Gabriel didn't reply. Clearing his throat, he said instead, "I have been doing business with your family for the best part of a century, Sir Montmorency. I trust that when I tell you I have nothing left to part with, you will not seek me out."

The gentleman did not hesitate as he tucked his prizes into the vault. "Yes. I am glad for you, Angel, that you have found your purpose. Your existence here with her will certainly be an extravagant one. She is a very beautiful girl; I trust you will now begin your own family?"

I took a quick breath, but Gabriel's reply came instantly. "Yes, she is, and I hope we shall."

Gabriel had said he would tell this man what he expected to hear, not the truth, but I wondered if he was thinking of me. I drained the champagne glass still clutched in my hand, only this time to steady my nerves.

"Good man. Have many sons, and you shall remain immortal through them," he said with a sense of pride.

"Your wife tells me your youngest is missing?"

I leaned back, concerned that as Sir Montmorency turned he might catch sight of me.

"Yes. We haven't been able to find him for several weeks now, but it's not the first time he has disappeared only to return with a heavy head. My daughter-in-law is troubled, though. *Women*," he mocked.

My attention switched from the conversation in the study to the sound of footsteps coming up the staircase. Fearing I had outstayed my welcome, as quietly as I could, I backed away from the room.

Just as I turned around, I collided with a figure, and he grabbed my arms quickly, keeping me from falling. The champagne flute in my hand dropped to the floor, and the guy bent down to retrieve it. "Are you lost?" he asked, and as he returned to a standing position, one hand still clutching my arm, his gaze traveled up the length of my dress until his eyes finally rested on mine.

I was taken aback. I knew him, and automatically a huge grin spread over my face, accompanied by a nervous laugh. "Yes, a little. I'm sorry," I whispered, unsure whether he would recognize me.

"Darwin, what's going on out there?" Sir Montmorency's voice traveled from the doorway, and I was relieved that it wasn't Gabriel who had come to investigate the commotion.

Darwin's smooth lips stretched as he smiled at me. "I was just giving my friend here a tour of the upstairs."

I didn't dare look over my shoulder in case Gabriel had been drawn out, and I was thankful to hear the heavy steel handle push down as Sir Montmorency clanked the door firmly shut.

"Well, you've certainly blossomed in a short time. . . . Still dropping glasses, though, I see." Darwin's jade-green eyes slanted from behind his retro tortoiseshell glasses, which highlighted the small bump just below the arch of his nose, giving him a welcome human imperfection.

"You remember me?" I asked quietly.

"Well, you look *different*, but I never forget a face, especially one with a smile as lovely as yours. You might want to rethink your contacts, though—bit too X-Men even for my liking."

"Well, look who's talking. This, I believe, is a very upmarket occasion, and yet you're wearing a T-shirt with the number forty-two and a little planet on it."

It was true, Darwin was every inch the gentleman—his smart suit and brogues certainly gave that impression—but his dark-blond hair, gelled back at the top into a hair tie, with his short back and sides combed neatly underneath, and that T-shirt . . . Well, a debonair gentleman he might be, but that shirt branded him as nothing short of a geek. But then he knew as much; he'd told me so when we'd met.

"It's my father's party, but given I live here, I can walk around wearing what I like. And forty-two, just so you know, is the answer to the ultimate question of life, the universe, and everything. Well, according to *The Hitchhiker's Guide to the Galaxy*, of course."

"Of course . . ." I said. I was excited to see Darwin again—he had been kind to me when we'd met—but he was the son of Sir Montmorency. And Sir Montmorency did business with Angels. That was enough to make me wary.

Releasing them from my left hand, I let my stilettos clatter to the floor, and I slipped the soles of my feet back into the stiff patent material. Darwin pursed his lips, taking both my hands in his, and stepped back from me, giving my outfit the full once-over with an arched eyebrow. "I'd ask you what you're doing here. . . . I'd even demand to know why, when I came back to the pub to see you, you had disappeared. But all I want to do right this moment is tell you that you look stunning."

I blushed. "Thank you, that's very generous of you to say."

"Nothing generous about it. I am a fella with very discerning taste. Come, let's catch up." He released my hands, gesturing for me to follow him down the landing.

I hesitated. "It's lovely to see you, but I should really get back to the party."

Darwin opened his mouth, but didn't say anything. Instead, his attention found its way to my crystal gem.

I had a feeling Darwin wanted a closer inspection of my crystal. He'd been interested in it the night we met in the pub where I was working in Creigiau, a few nights before I came across Jonah. His car, carrying himself and his friends, had broken down outside, en route to Holyhead, and he had made an effort to befriend me that evening. He'd even tried to persuade me to travel to Chelsea with him, on his way back from his business trip, but I met Jonah the night before he returned.

Clearly the crystals were worth something to his father, and I was curious to know what Darwin did. He had no idea what or who I was, other than a girl he'd made an acquaintanceship with one evening. I might be able to get some information out of him.

"Actually, I could spare five minutes." I smiled.

"Wonderful." Darwin was pleased, and he encouraged me to walk with him. As we passed the paintings on the wall, a particular portrait caught my attention.

Bodies lay strewn across a grassy verge, which was saturated in a thick red paste. In the background, a figure—entirely antithetical to the rest of the painting—looked onto the scene with bright-green, upside-down triangles for eyes. The figure's frame was boxy, and its head was too large for its body, painted as just a large white circle. The being's hands were dressed in black gloves, which were placed forward in front of its chest, palms spread wide. It was some sort of strange-looking robot, set among images of mankind, in what looked like a depiction of the apocalypse.

Most harrowing of all was the image at the center of the portrait, where a beam of white light shot up high into the sky, expelled from an indistinguishable blazing ball. The heinous painting made me halt.

"Awful, isn't it?" Darwin said. "It's been in the family for centuries. Despite the garishness of it, my father won't have it taken down. Story has it that a seer had a vision so disturbing it brought him to his knees. He said it foretold the end. He gouged pokers into his own eyes and then painted that blind."

It took me a moment to find my voice. "Does your father think this depicts the end of all days? Is he particularly religious?"

Darwin shrugged. "More so than I am. He sees signs in things, hidden messages, or so he says. He believes in Heaven and Hell."

"And you don't?" I couldn't remove my attention from the canvas.

"I think everyone is so busy looking at fluffy clouds, they ignore the stars," he answered mysteriously.

"So no, then. No Heaven, no Hell—"

"In a way . . ." He cut me off, placing his hand to the dip in my back. "I'm a physicist, so what you call Heaven and Hell I like to think of as different worlds—dimensions, perhaps." He paused, exerting a little pressure where his palm rested, encouraging me forward.

I wasn't expecting Darwin to say that. Did he actually know about the dimensions or was his suggestion just the theorist in him?

He continued, "Either way, something is going on out there on a far bigger scale."

We drifted away from the painting.

Was he suggesting that beyond the dimensions, there was something *more*?

I asked slowly, "What do you mean?"

"The universe is infinite. Worlds, and the existence within them, simply reside in a small pocket of it. But even if the universe—in all its infinity—is the jacket, say, to which the pocket belongs, there is still something bigger walking around wearing that jacket." He hesitated for a moment to check his phone, which had beeped twice, before continuing, "The universe itself is a logical enough place. It doesn't give without taking; all things within it must be equal. I could go on and on. . . . It's mankind who are illogical and unable to comprehend infinity in the first place, lacking the ability to process the very nature of it, let alone the meaning of it all."

I found myself captured by Darwin's theory. "Do you think it's that impossible to comprehend? Do you think we will ever know the meaning?"

"I believe there is one perfect moment of clarity, when our minds become truly free. Where we see, hear, and know *everything* we were blind, deaf, and ignorant to. Where we find order in the entropy of infinity."

Darwin stopped. "My office." He pulled a key out of his pocket.

Stepping inside, there was an L-shaped desk that wrapped around the right-hand corner, only breaking to allow access to the terrace. A single bed was at the other end, perhaps for when he got too tired to make it to his actual room, assuming there was one; I couldn't imagine him entertaining women of his own creed in here. Beside it was what looked like a laboratory table, covered in cutting equipment, clamps, pliers, and a large microscope. The tiles around a log-burning fireplace were littered with books with titles referencing theoretical and experimental physics and string theory. Yet, despite the room having such a grown-up feel to it, there were framed posters of *The Hitchhiker's Guide to the Galaxy* dominating the wall space, making the diploma and degree certificates barely noticeable amid all the sci-fi pictures.

"Have a seat. I'll fetch us a drink," he said with a smile. "Don't you go anywhere."

"I'll be here," I replied, tottering into the middle of the room.

He leaned in over my shoulder and said, "I've heard that before." And then he left, leaving me to amuse myself.

I noticed Darwin's certificate was crooked, and so I pottered over, straightening the frame. It read "Massachusetts Institute of Technology" in a large elaborate font across the top, conferring "Darwin B. B. Montmorency" a master of science in physics below, accompanied by a red stamp and various signatures on either side.

He was certainly a smart cookie.

I swept my gaze over the mahogany desk, where papers were strewn over every available inch. I pawed my neck, as an irritation rode over my skin. Curious, I walked over. Most of the documents were on letterhead displaying the CERN logo. I had heard of CERN;

I remembered seeing something about it in a newspaper once—something to do with particles, underground caves, or some such. I hadn't understood it so had paid little attention.

I scanned the letter on the top, addressed to Darwin, and rather impolitely began reading the text. It talked about the Higgs boson and something called a singlet particle. None of it meant anything to me—it was über genius stuff—but what I did understand was the "thank-you" at the bottom of the letter: a thank-you for providing yet another crystal sphere for the collider, and a password made up of numbers 1.008/4.003—an access code to some sort of report. Was Darwin giving them crystals from Styclar-Plena? And if so, why?

"Here we go!" Darwin called out. With two champagne glasses in his hand, he kicked the door shut.

I took one and he tapped the top of my glass lightly with his, saying "Cheers!" and I necked the bubbles in one go, desperately needing something to coat my throat. As long as I had only one or two glasses at a time, and then left a sufficient gap, I could ease the pain without getting tipsy.

"You're eager. I should have perhaps brought the tray," Darwin said, gripping the stem of his flute with his thumb and index finger.

"Perhaps you should have. What's all this? It looks terribly official."

"Have you heard of the Hadron Collider in Switzerland?" he asked, sipping champagne. "You must have seen it on the news a few years ago. You know, lots of boring scientists smashing together particles in search of the elusive Higgs boson?"

I shook my head.

Darwin drew a breath. "The Higgs boson is a particle; it gives mass to matter. For years and years, the best minds in the world have been trying to prove its existence. The press that was released explained that they thought they had in fact now found it using the collider."

"Oh, okay, very good." My mind whizzed, trying to connect what he was telling me with the mention of the crystals Darwin had donated to CERN.

"No, not very good—phenomenal!" He threw his hands in the air. "Okay, what if I told you that, in all these years no one could find it, prove it, let alone harness it? What if I told you that I have *helped* by providing CERN with, well, objects that they wouldn't otherwise have known about?"

"Right . . ." Crystals. *You gave them crystals from another world, another dimension, but why?*

Darwin pulled out his desk chair and gestured for me to sit. Thinking that perhaps I was completely inept and wanting to impress me with his cleverness, he continued, "They tested them in the collider, and they found the Higgs boson."

His gaze once again drifted down to my chest, eyeing my own crystal.

My mind spun as he finished with a dramatic flair, "They found Higgs boson—or the God particle, if you will—within the object."

The God particle? In the crystals?

"You want to know something even more special?"

"Yes," I said.

Darwin pulled around an additional chair from behind his laboratory table and stalled for dramatic tension. "They found the singlet particle."

I didn't know what the singlet particle was or how it related to the gems from Styclar-Plena.

He pushed his glasses to the top of his nose. "The singlet particle, if harnessed, can allow an object, perhaps even a person, to travel through space and time. We're not ready to go public yet, not until we can stabilize the particles."

I tried to make sense of what Darwin was telling me. The Arch Angels were born organically from the crystal's light; they could travel through the dimensions and retain their abilities on Earth without the need for a crystal. The crystals only aided them in commanding the rifts to form. But the Descendants needed the crystals, and I was created as a Descendant. Yet I glowed just as the Arch Angels would in the sun's presence, without the gem around my neck. Did that mean that these particles Darwin was referring to existed within them, and for some reason within me? Was that why we could pass between the dimensions—the worlds—that existed at a different rate of time and in a different state altogether?

"So what exactly are you saying?" I asked carefully.

Darwin tipped back the last of his bubbles, and raising the glass in the air, he said, "It means we have found a way to travel through time, through different dimensions. The possibilities are endless, Cessie." He clinked his glass with mine, and I remembered that he knew me by that name—the one I thought was mine when I met him.

"And that's what they're doing, experimenting?" I wondered aloud.

"No. The—" He hesitated. "The objects I've provided them with only had residue elements. They were able to identify the particles, but they were not strong enough to remain in an active state for more than a fraction of a second. I'm looking for more of them and hoping to find one that has more active elements present. If I could find one that was fully charged, there's no telling what we could do."

No telling what we could do indeed . . . Take a fully loaded working crystal, extract the particles, and we could potentially open the rifts to the first dimension and then disappear into white light as we walked through. Worse still, we could cause some huge explosion in caves under the earth and what—have the dimensions overlap and wipe out humanity?

My mind continued to reel, swirling with these dangerous thoughts. Azrael had said that I could keep my form in all three dimensions—the Arch Angels couldn't; neither could the Purebloods. I was a one-off commodity. So, how long would it be before these humans found out and made me their guinea pig? How long before they plonked me in the middle of this Hadron Collider and tried to split me open to see what might spill out?

I smiled. "Well, I wish you lots of luck. Would you mind if we went back down to the party? I'm here with a friend, and I'd like to check on her."

Darwin looked a little crestfallen, as though I was nowhere near as excited as I should have been to hear such information, such a secret. It was best for him to think I hadn't understood or didn't care—safer, even.

"Of course, but we must come back. I'd love to have a look at your necklace, if I may?"

"Sure," I lied, now having no intention of letting him near it.

As we trundled down the winding staircase, there was a loud clapping of hands, and the hum of voices died away as footsteps made their way into the drawing room. Darwin grimaced, and I hovered midstep. "What's wrong?"

"Speech time. My father's opportunity to be ostentatious about his sons—something he never misses." His expression showed boredom.

"Sounds like he's proud of you; that's a really nice thing," I offered. I had on countless occasions wished I had a family who cared about me enriching my life.

"Yes, well. He's proud of the family name. One thing he and I can agree upon at least: the importance of family." Placing his luxurious specs on the top of his head, Darwin's bright-green eyes shimmered against the lighting from the chandelier as he took my hand and helped me hop down the last step.

The entranceway was now cleared, and I shooed Darwin on. "I'll follow you; I just need to use the ladies' room," I lied again.

TWENTY-FIVE

THE MOMENT DARWIN WAS out of sight, I rushed over to a table outside on the patio, where plenty of wine sat poured out and additional bottles rested in buckets of ice.

I reached for a glass of red wine, and though it matched the color of blood, it might as well have been water.

"Hurts like hell, doesn't it?" Jonah's prickly voice jabbed me from behind.

I ignored him.

Jonah tugged my arm gently, turning me to face him, and I squirmed as my Play-Doh-like skin absorbed his fingertips. He did a double take, his eyes swiftly sweeping the length of my dress. He trailed the lace red and white roses growing up between the middle of my legs, blooming across my breasts. But his gaze fell back down to my midriff, where the scars he had left me showed through the transparent material.

He'd also come dressed for the occasion, wearing smart trousers and a dress shirt, which he hadn't managed to do up all the way. But,

Jonah being Jonah, he had thrown on a black jacket over the top and had pulled the hood only halfway over his head. I didn't need Brooke to tell me that every inch of his outfit was couture—even down to the hoodie.

"Why?" he asked bitterly.

"I think I missed the question?" I replied, placing the wine glass on the table behind me.

"Why do you do it? You go out of your way to cover the scar on your back, but not those. You insist on continually brandishing them. Are you *trying* to provoke me?" He ground his teeth.

"No," I answered. "Just so happens that this dress shows them."

Tilting his head and running his gaze up and down once more for good measure, he arched an eyebrow and said, "Speaking of which, that dress hardly leaves anything to the imagination." He winked at me, and my heart fluttered. I'd missed the way he did that. Pushing his hood down, he cricked his neck from side to side.

Then his palm was suddenly spread out across my tummy, and he stroked his thumb over the thin material carefully. I could smell him now, but only barely; he was wearing his old aftershave. I breathed in his familiar scent of woods as he stood within an inch of me. I peeked up and found his marblelike hazel eyes, which strangely made me think of the butterfly girl's.

He lowered himself and placed the tip of his nose just above my earlobe. "I inflicted these on you, and they are ugly. Why don't you cover them?"

I felt my chest tighten. "The real mark you left on me doesn't sit on my skin, Jonah." I placed my palm over the top of his hand still resting on my midriff. "These scars don't mean what you think they do. They don't show hate, or horror, only . . . heart."

He lingered, his hot breath against the skin of my neck, and I felt that same hungry feeling I had felt for him before.

Finally, he extracted himself and blinked heavily, staring down at my worn eyes. "What you did that night . . ." He wavered. "You made me a better person once. Hell, you made me think of myself as a *person*. And then you tricked me, and you made me a monster all over again. And I thought you did it out of pity, or perhaps some vain attempt to cling on to who you think you were, who you think you should be still." He paused, and his hazel irises flashed crimson, but then they cooled. "But I was wrong, wasn't I? You didn't do it for either of those reasons, did you?"

I couldn't meet his eyes. I hadn't even wanted to admit the reason to myself. I was afraid that if I spoke my secret aloud, it would become real. And what good could come from confessing that I had loved him? What good would it do to tell him that despite his cruel words, I still loved him now? None. Because I loved Gabriel first.

He found my chin and tilted my face up, forcing me to look at him. "When did you remember me?"

My breath ricocheted off my throat as I inhaled.

"Tell me, *when*—"

I gave in and answered honestly. "In the study, when I felt your lips press onto mine; that was the moment you came back to me. And twenty minutes later, you left."

Jonah wrapped his arms around my back, but he held me too tightly. A weak moan escaped my lips as my body contracted; I found no pleasure within his touch.

He responded immediately, and I wondered again if he somehow felt my pain, if it passed through him. It was the only explanation I could match to the urgent alarm ringing in his voice as he said, "Please, feed."

I had to consider it this time. The throbbing under my skin was becoming too painful, and I allowed myself to break down for just a moment. I nuzzled myself into Jonah's chest and started to sob, but my body wouldn't even grace me with tears; instead my chest heaved in dry, shallow movements. He didn't push me away; instead he lightly stroked the back of my hair.

I gathered myself, angry that the thought of giving up had even dared to enter my head. I loved Gabriel, and I wasn't ready to let go. He was meant to save me; even if I didn't know how yet.

I reached for yet another glass of wine, but as I urgently raised it to my lips, from over Jonah's shoulder I could see a glow in the window of the drawing room.

I hurried back inside, working my way along the elegantly dressed crowd that had clustered in the drawing room, but I found myself unable to see past the raised glasses. One face in the crowd, though, I did recognize: Ruadhan. So, he didn't trust me to be here after all.

Stooping to avoid being seen by him, I managed to catch sight of the golden glow through the many bodies. In front of a bay window, overlooking the landscaped gardens, the light illuminated what I never expected to witness: Gabriel kissing Iona.

I felt myself tear in two. Sir Montmorency had Darwin to his left and the happy couple to his right. The room became distorted; all I could see was Gabriel's lips pressing gently down onto Iona's. His hand caressing the silk of her neck, he further gifted her with his touch. If this was a kiss for some sort of show, it certainly didn't explain why Gabriel's skin was pulsing with luminosity.

Just then a bell sounded midnight. I was fixated on Gabriel and Iona, and as it repeatedly struck, tiny speckles of white crystals seemed to form around Iona's figure. I couldn't understand where they were coming from. Was Gabriel's glow so strong that he was causing her to shimmer against him? I scanned the room, but no one else seemed to notice the light pulsing between the two of them.

A gentleman beside me began patting my shoulder, as though he were able to sense my despair. And then he leaned in and muttered quietly, "I wouldn't be so upset if I were you."

"Excuse me?" I spat out. I twisted around to find Malachi's face. He was just as plain as he had been when I'd seen him in my dream while I slept in the barn in Neylis. Swiftly I recalled what happened in that vision, whose face had appeared next—Hanora's. I'd been jealous of her, and now I was finding myself dissolving into envy once more, but this time for her very opposite. I grew angry with myself; I had no right to feel upset. Knowing that I had told Gabriel my heart, my whole heart was his, when now and in truth there was a part that belonged to Jonah.

The fallen Angel beside me cleared his throat, bringing my attention back to him. "I'm an old friend of Gabriel's. It's a pleasure to finally meet the girl he's been searching out all this time. I wouldn't let that little show over there cause you trouble; he's only trying to protect you." Everything about Malachi was unreadable. It must take a lot of practice to achieve such nonchalance.

"You have me mistaken for someone else" was all I could get out. Gabriel had brought Iona into his chest, clinging to her dearly, and I looked away.

As I willed my legs to stretch, Malachi was once again trying to capture my interest. "You will meet with me tomorrow, alone."

Right now all I wanted was to get out of this room, but he had me by my arm, waiting for some sort of agreement. "Do I have 'idiot' stamped across my forehead? Why would I do that?"

One swift tug and he had me only an inch from him. "If you do not wish to see this world burn, you will meet me. You need to know what I do. I will come to you." Malachi slicked back his ash-blond hair, nodding at me astutely, before disappearing into the now-chattering cluster of guests.

I endured one final fleeting glance in Gabriel's direction. Iona was speaking in his ear, and those divine dimples dipped the way they had for me. I paced down the length of the drawing room, bumping into bodies as I went, until, through my blurring vision, I found an archway at the very end of the room. Leaning my weight against the brickwork, I took a breath.

I caught sight of a grand piano at the far end of some sort of entertaining room. My legs had become jelly, and they managed to hold me up only long enough to get to its stool. I placed my head between my knees and counted to ten. My heartbeat eventually slowed, and my mind stopped twirling and spinning.

Confident I was alone—there was no sign of Jonah or anyone else—I searched for the nearest exit so that I might find my way out of this labyrinth of a house. As I did, my eyes settled on an antique chromatic harp on the adjacent wall.

My mind flashed to the memory of the one I had played with Gabriel under the old oak tree. If I could have, I would've cried to try and rid myself of this troubled sensation in my muddled soul.

I slid my toes out of the stilettos and, placing my bare feet to the cold parquet flooring, I regained my balance and wandered over. It was inviting, as though it were an old friend; as though it were calling for me to free it from its silent sleep. I looked to its two columns, which crossed in the middle, its elegant shape reminding me of a swan.

I hovered tentatively behind it, almost afraid to touch my fingertips to its strings lest they cause them to snap. But there was another fear, a bigger one: I was afraid that if I awoke the harp with our song, when I stopped playing, the dream of Gabriel and me would fade into nothing more than an echo. Like a sunset, it would become lost to the darkness.

I skimmed the thick, varnished wood and gently glided my fingers across the strings. The emotions I had felt the last time I played came rushing back to me. I plucked a string, letting the note reverberate through the space.

I closed my eyes, this time running my fingers across the strings, and it was as though they were willing me along. The melody that came resounded with revered remembrance. I played the first few chords of Gabriel's and my song over and over, and then I let my fingers proceed to the first verse, and I began to sing.

Though initially my voice warbled, the hurt in my throat seemed to fade, finding its way perhaps to my heart instead. *"My gentle harp, once more I waken. The sweetness of thy slumb'ring strain."* I sang Gabriel's part, and then on to my own verse, *"In tears our last farewell was taken. And now in tears we meet again."* The feel of the smooth strings against my skin comforted me, and I began to feel content. *"Yet even then, while peace was singing. Her halcyon song o'er land and sea. Though joy and hope to others bringing. She only brought new tears to thee."* I found my eyelashes fluttering as I repeated that line—the words that had left Gabriel's lips in my haunting vision of him. And as my sight refocused, I saw that some of the guests had gathered in the room, listening to my impromptu performance.

Pushing through the crowd, Gabriel appeared holding Iona's hand. Surprise surfaced in his face, and he seemed unable to liberate a smile. I realized then that either this song caused him pain, or perhaps I did. Maybe it was both.

"*Then who can ask for notes of pleasure. My drooping harp, from chords like thine?*" I sang.

Darwin emerged then. Taking up a stance beside a bookcase, he observed me curiously. Then came Brooke, Fergal, and Ruadhan, along with someone I didn't expect to see: Phelan.

He eyed me quizzically, but there was no disgruntled demeanor to him, not while I sang.

"*Alas, the lark's gay morning measure, as ill would suit the swan's decline.*"

A stranger hovering next to Phelan began to speak. I didn't try to overhear, but I watched the man's lips shape, forming the words "voice of an Angel."

Though the bell's chimes had faded some time ago, a new alarm seemed to strike Phelan. As if his copper eyes were two pennies, they seemed to drop.

He knew who I was.

"*Or how shall I, who love, who bless thee,*" I sang, and Gabriel's fingers, intertwined with Iona's, released. He strode toward me. "*Invoke thy breath for freedom's strains,*" I continued, the trill in my voice beginning to resurface.

Standing in my shadow, Gabriel hid me from the crowd. His downturned lips were worried and woeful. He extended his shaking hand to me, and though he stood but a few feet away, his eyes were so absent, so distant, that he couldn't have felt farther away.

I plucked the strings rhythmically, but as I played the notes to the song, the last verse wasn't forthcoming. The lines had utterly escaped me, buried perhaps too deep under this new skin. I tried to find them, squeezing my eyelids closed once more.

As if the swan had pecked me, I withdrew from the harp, startled. "Why can't I remember the last lines? They were yours; you sang them for me," I said, a quiver in my voice.

The audience remained still and silent, as if I had cast a spell on the room, rendering the guests of the palace frozen. But before Gabriel could answer, a tremendous vibration shook the entire house. Violent, fierce hissing came rushing down the staircase, through the hallway, and spilled over into the room.

And as the heavy chandelier in the hall became unhinged from the cracking plaster of the ceiling, it smashed to the granite flooring, shattering into a million pieces, and the room erupted into hysteria.

"Leave, now!" Gabriel shouted at me.

I stared at him blankly.

"By thought," he instructed. "Think of the house, and will the light to take you there," he said speedily, but still I clutched the wooden back of the harp, unmoving.

Iona clumsily fell toward Gabriel's side. "Gabriel, I don't feel right." Even in my weakened state, I could see she'd become a silhouette of silver. I could only imagine what she would have looked like to me if I weren't nearly drained away.

Gabriel looked back and forth, from Iona to me. Rushing toward us, Fergal and Brooke weaved between the crazed bodies crushing one another to get out of the house.

The clatter of serving trays and glasses breaking against the floors added to the commotion. I could see Phelan through the crowd, removing a gun from his back pocket; I watched him click the catch off the safety. "Get her out of here!" he shouted across the room.

Darwin disappeared from the corner of my eye as he bolted up the staircase.

"I'll go with her," Brooke said to Gabriel. She was saving me from having to confess that I couldn't travel by thought.

"Wait," I said, seeing Ruadhan in the back of the crowd and knowing there was then only one member of our group missing. "Jonah's not here. I left him outside a while ago."

"*Gabriel*—" Iona seemed to beg.

"I will find Jonah," Gabriel said. "Go, now, *please*."

He didn't trust me to leave; he knew me too well. But I didn't get the opportunity to protest as Brooke scooped me up, and the next thing I knew we were on the opposite side of the black iron railings that surrounded the common in front of the house.

"Thank you," I said with a weak breath.

The guests were gathering on the pavement, confused as to why the earthquake they had expected seemed to not exist outside of the house. But, the villa's windows still continued to shatter and cracks ran down the external walls of the property.

Whatever was going on inside, it wasn't good. But I didn't sense Zherneboh; I couldn't feel his presence within me or anywhere nearby. My mind reeled. Why, if Vampires had descended onto the house, were they not out here, trying to steal me away? Perhaps they didn't know I was here, or maybe it wasn't me they were here for.

Brooke stared at the front door. "I need to go back inside. Fergal's in there."

"Fergal? What about Jonah? Are you not at all worried? You're connected to him. I thought . . . I thought that you *loved* him." I rushed, as the thought of returning inside crossed my mind, too.

"Yes, of course I do. I do. But I dunno . . ." she said. "You know, Johnny Depp said that if you love two people at the same time, choose the second one. Because if you truly loved the first one, you wouldn't love another."

Only Brooke could quote Johnny Depp at a time like this. Yet the words loomed over me like a shadow, as though I needed its darkness to see the light in my own choices.

"I'm going back in—" she began. I reached to hold her back, but my attention was drawn away as my gaze fell to a sole figure, marching through the crowd on the road.

He might have been wearing all black, like a thief in the night, but his eyes—although they appeared weaker and duller than the last time I had seen them—were impossible to miss. His hooded jacket hung out of shape around his shoulders and his shirt underneath was torn; he had been involved in whatever it was going on upstairs.

He darted across the road, knocking into a woman in a beautiful, slinky red dress. She yelped, but he continued, undeterred, racing toward the entrance of the common. I watched, unable to take my eyes from him.

Azrael.

TWENTY-SIX

My father, who had tried to kill me in order to return to Styclar-Plena, was here, alive and kicking.

He moved past as though he hadn't noticed Brooke or me standing next to the railing. He was clutching the silk-wrapped packages Gabriel had sold.

Was he the acquaintance Sir Montmorency had spoken about? The one attending in person this evening to collect the crystals on behalf of a silent partner? If that were the case, then clearly the silent partner had no intention of exchanging any form of currency for them. A chill coursed through me and I wasn't sure if it was at the thought of who that silent partner actually was, or the fact that Gabriel had sensed something sinister was afoot but parted with the crystals anyway to ensure our future was nothing short of a wealthy one.

Brooke followed my line of sight and looked to me in confusion. "Is that—?"

"Go and get Gabriel, right now!" I told Brooke as I left to trail my father.

My bare feet stuck in the wet blades of grass as I followed him outside. If he knew I was behind him, he didn't let on. It was only as we reached the lamps bordering the opposite side of the common that he stopped. His back to me, he didn't move.

"What? Can't bring yourself to look at the daughter you made and then tried to murder?"

Stuffing the gems into his pocket, he turned around slowly; finally, he pulled down his hood and settled his washed-out eyes on me. "You are no longer my concern, Lailah." He spoke smoothly, indifferently.

The very sight of his face caused anger to bubble within me. The last time I had seen him, he was towering over me, tauntingly witnessing my demise. *He was my father.* Or at least he had been—once.

"You're working for them now—the demons?" I demanded, stepping a little closer.

He didn't reply.

"Well, I'm guessing it's not the Arch Angels. Seems as much as I am no longer your concern, you are no longer theirs," I goaded.

"No." Azrael's eyes narrowed, his jaw locking as though I had touched a nerve. "Because of you, I am now fallen."

"Yes, and that makes you rather mortal. I could rip you in half." It was a lie, but one he didn't know the truth of. "So, you will tell me who you are working for and what they want with those crystals?"

He sauntered over to me. Looking me square in the eye, he raised his sleeve to my cheek and rubbed my skin. I knocked his hand away, but it was too late. He had seen the pallor beneath my mask.

With an arrogant tut, he said, "You couldn't even rip open a willing victim, not if your life depended on it. And it does depend on it, doesn't it, Lailah?"

He began to stride away.

My body stiffened, and for the first time in a while, I could feel my gums itching, as though my fangs might crack. I ran after him, grappling for his shoulder, but he pushed his weight into me, knocking me to the damp ground. He hovered above, with a defiant, irritated curl of his lips. Reaching down, he fingered my necklace, and in one swift pull he snapped the chain, stealing my crystal from around my neck. He imprisoned it within his palm.

"What? That's all you care about? Crystals? Why aren't you calling out for the demons? Why don't you tell them I'm here?" I demanded.

Why wasn't he trying to take me with him? He could see that at this moment I was no threat. If he were in cahoots now with the Purebloods, why was he walking away from me?

He stooped down. "They *are* coming for you, Lailah, but not this night. But don't you worry; they won't keep you waiting long." He sneered. "Funny, I may be sentenced to an existence of mortality on this vile plane, but you . . ." He laughed. "Ah, Lailah, you will either end up Zherneboh's slave or Orifiel's prisoner. For you, the only true escape now is death. I suggest you find it before they find you."

His tone oozed callousness and cruelty. His task this evening had nothing to do with me and everything to do with those crystals.

Azrael hadn't changed. If anything, my impending doom was the only thing that seemed to cause a smile to form on his hate-filled lips. I thought he was about to leave but instead he shoved me farther into the grass, as though he hadn't hurt me enough already.

Then, from the darkened common, Brooke appeared. I hadn't sensed her coming. She gripped Azrael's jacket and hurled him to the ground beside me; my necklace flew through the air. He moaned, and underneath his jacket he held his arms across his chest, as though he was in severe pain. He struggled to his knees, raising his palm to his eyebrow, where his skin had split from the tumble. Brooke loomed over him, brandishing her deadly fangs.

He gestured pitifully, shouting, "No, please!"

She looked to me for guidance, and Azrael took advantage of her hesitation. He launched his weight into her, searing her skin with a silver pocket watch concealed within his palm. I recognized it as belonging to Sir Montmorency.

Brooke's moan transformed into a scream as the silver met her chest. Azrael straddled her, freeing a silver blade from his back pocket. He might have been a fallen Angel now, but Azrael had come prepared, and neither Brooke nor I had counted on it.

About to strike her, he paused. "Know this, Lailah. When Zherneboh takes you, find no comfort in thinking your friends are safe. I will make sure the demons find them next, and I will make sure it hurts."

His words were like a blow to my face, and my eyes clouded in a dangerous fog. It was one thing to despise, to degrade, and to disparage *me*, but to attack Brooke, to threaten my *family*—that was something else entirely. A rush of energy came over me, the very last of what I had left.

My fangs burst through my gums and my muscles became taut. I sprang to my feet, and Azrael's arrogant grin receded. I careered into him, landing beyond the railings. The blade and the watch were lost to the roadside.

I clutched his jacket and he wriggled free of it, rolling backward. I growled, flinging it far from sight, and circled him. It was only as his gaze fell to my hips that I allowed my attention to veer away.

Inside my palms, ribbons of black smoke floated from my skin, and a terrible darkness stretched over me. Yet as I met his eyes once more, they remained cold; still they did not afford me the regret—the repentance—that I desired and deserved. Even as he stood, an inch from death, he would not waver.

"You're not worthy of a mortal existence." I threw my hands up in the air and willed the smoke to levitate, to wrap itself around his throat. But this was not some dark power within me taking hold. While the threat he made on my family may have ignited my reaction, his death would be entirely for me. I wanted it to be slow. I wanted him to suffer.

He was phlegmatic as he said, "And you, my daughter, are no different from them."

His words hit me, and I hesitated. The smoke stalled as it weaved a noose around his neck. My shoulders slumped, as though he were on trial and had just outed me as a witch—a confession that might save him from his execution. A sly slant of his eyes told me that he thought I wasn't capable.

He was wrong.

But I was too weak to control the smoke, and it evaporated.

Azrael's chest rose as he filled his mortal lungs with oxygen once more. Finally, he stood and bowed his head in some form of smug farewell. But he paused—perhaps waiting for me to break down, to part with some feeble drivel about being better than him, before he took his leave. I was quite certain he wasn't expecting the verdict that I delivered.

Weakly, I curled my fingers over his shoulders. On tiptoes, I brought my nose to his ear and whispered, "You're wrong. I will be different. . . . *I will be worse*." My fingers molded around his throat and I took a moment to savor his gasp of disbelief. He was responsible for my last breath on the mountaintop; now I would take his.

Azrael's bones crunched as, with a sudden inhuman strength, I snapped his neck clean, breaking it as easily as a stick of chalk. I let go, and Azrael's limp body fell, lying motionless at my feet.

The surge of adrenaline fueling my form—the last of my reserve—ran dry. My insides stuttered like a car stalling in the winter, the throttle choking as my body convulsed. I swayed, searching for Brooke. She was already on her feet, staring at me, dumbfounded. Her dress was scorched, but her skin was fast healing underneath the burnt fabric, and I was relieved that she was okay.

I trudged over to her, every muscle in my legs aching as though I had run a marathon, but Brooke's gaze was not on me—it was behind me.

It was agonizing to turn my neck, but I did. My vision was blurring, but in the glow of the streetlamps, next to Azrael's body, a thin stream of black liquid dribbled vertically in the air. And through it, a thin, bony hand stretched out, its skinny fingers clawing as though it were playing the keys of a piano—looking, searching, for the notes it needed.

And then came a second arm, followed by a head and torso, emerging as though being born. The shriveled creature was clothed in translucent gray skin that highlighted its prominent rib cage. Now on all fours and bouncing like a deranged lemur, it prowled around Azrael's flesh, sniffing at his neck.

It was a scavenger—a being that existed in the third dimension and came through the rifts to claim dark souls; the same as the Angel Descendants who came here to claim the light ones.

A cloud of dark smoke billowed up and out of Azrael's form,

gathering into one mass, and it floated until all the plumes had formed into a perfect swirling ball.

The scavenger collected it somehow in its deformed fingers. But it had no eyes with which to see. Only empty eye sockets, covered over by its skin. It sniffed the air once more and then stretched its sunken head.

Where a mouth should have been, the skin seemed to break, and flesh-colored tentacles spat from the hole like a star-nosed mole, jiggling as the breeze passed over them.

The tentacles hovered above the dark energy and guided the smoke into the scavenger's mouth. And when the last of it was secured, the tentacles suddenly popped back in and the skin reformed, locking them away. The scavenger's mandible drooped low.

On all fours, the heinous figure suddenly and dangerously twisted around. Weighed down by Azrael's darkened soul, the creature arched its back. Its hands and face low to the ground, it scuttled back toward the black crease in the air.

I didn't watch it reenter. The scene around me distorted as my vision blurred. The small dark spots of my irises stretched out in front of my sight, and the stinging sensation in my throat stabbed me with a brutal force. Only this time, it was relentless; it might as well have been a knife plunging over and over into the soft tissue of my throat.

I tried to refocus, to concentrate, but the world was tipped. There was no up or down; there was only rocking and a sickness rising within me.

As if the world had become mute, the rumble from the house and the sirens of emerging police cars all just stopped with the click of a finger. Inside my own head, there was only the thrum of harp strings, and every note that played Gabriel's and my song. One by one they snapped, as my memory plucked at them, and my mind drifted to the thought of the old oak tree.

I SAT IN DIRT. I could barely see, but the jab of tree bark against my back told me where I was. I hadn't intended to travel here by thought, but I no longer had any control over my body. I was under the old oak tree. Nearly two centuries since I had last visited, my old friend still stood tall here in the present.

I panicked, knowing I was dying, and knowing Gabriel wasn't here.

With no way to connect to him in my mind, I was alone and out of time.

I tried to squeal but the noise that escaped me was but a strained rasp. I lifted my heavy arm in the air, but it seemed to dip in and out of focus. Existing halfway between life and death, I no longer belonged here.

The fear of what was about to happen hit me, and even though my body felt like it was on fire—my very skin melting into my bones—still I didn't want the end to come. I would rather burn like a thousand suns for all of eternity than simply not exist at all—than be alone, trapped in the nowhere.

The delicate fabric of my dress tore as my head fell between my legs, and unruly, crimson tears streaked down my cheeks. It only furthered my disintegration; I couldn't even cry without losing part of myself.

And as I drained away along with my bloodied tears, the words of Gabriel's and my song became no more than a gentle whisper. The world seemed to fold in on me like a black envelope. My blood formed the melting wax. But before death could impress its mark and seal me away, the rhythmic thump of a drum creased the design. And the sound was getting louder, moving closer, and becoming stronger.

"Lailah."

A thumb and forefinger pressed into my cheek, shaking my face from side to side.

I caught only glimpses of his face as the world tipped upside down. As though I were on a fairground ride, I could only see his features each time the big wheel turned over.

"Look—here." His voice was stern, commanding my obedience. He pointed two fingers at his eyes as I tried to stabilize my sight, and for a moment I saw the hazel stars of the butterfly girl fluttering back at me.

Only they didn't belong to her, they belonged to Jonah.

"Focus, Lailah," he said. His strong arm lifted me from the trunk, and I was leaning back on a firm chest instead. Sitting in his lap didn't stop my head from falling or my body from limply flopping forward.

"Breathe through your nose, not your mouth," Jonah further instructed. He wrapped himself around my chest and positioned my face in the crevice of his shoulder. I could hear the beat of the drum stronger than ever, and I tried to use it as a way of leading me back.

"What d-does *el efecto mariposa* mean to you?" I stuttered, recalling what he had said to me at the bonfire, confused as to why his eyes seemed to match the butterfly girl's.

Although Jonah's attention was fixed on his left wrist, which he was slicing open with his fangs, for a fraction of a second, he stalled. "A sign to me that gives meaning to the chaos." He ripped a second strip down his vein. "You didn't respect the decision I made, so I'm not going to apologize for taking away your choice now." He tipped my chin up, trying to force-feed me the blood he had gathered on his skin.

I spat it out, struggling to breathe, my mind whirling once again.

Furious, his body became rigid beneath me. "Do you think that Gabriel would rather you were dead than have you take my blood?"

I shook my head; he had misinterpreted my reason for refusing him. Either way, Gabriel was about to lose the one he loved—Gabriel was no longer the reason why.

"I didn't know it before, but I do now. I'm the one who is meant to save you," he begged, once again bringing the inside of his wrist to my mouth. In this state, I couldn't even detect his scent, and I was glad. It eased my struggle.

I brought my hand up to where my cheek rested on his chest. It flickered in and out of focus like a weakened candle. I slid my palm underneath his shirt, placing it on top of his heart, feeling the thud of the drum, and I closed my eyes softly. The vision still didn't make sense, but somehow the butterfly girl was connected to Jonah, not Gabriel as I had thought.

I stroked his smooth skin, my bloodied fingers sticking to his flesh. "I believe you."

He pushed his wrist back to my nose. "Then take my blood."

I refused.

"I don't understand," he said.

I stifled a dry tear and whispered, "Who will save you from me?"

If I drank from Jonah, I wouldn't be able to stop.

He pressed his hand to my hair. "I'm not supposed to be. *Not beyond you.*"

If I weren't nearly withered away, I would have hit him. I couldn't trade his life for mine, and I wouldn't.

As my mind became set, the beat of the drum faded, and I tensed, knowing what came next: the nowhere.

"Don't you dare make her death count for nothing!" Jonah shouted, though his voice—just like the thought of him—was becoming distant. I didn't have it in me to ask him whom he was talking about.

"Look at me." Jonah gripped my waist, tightening his arms around me, and I submitted, gazing at the fierce fibers of red glowing through his hazel eyes.

He shook his wrist once again under my nose as he said, "You won't end me."

His words all blurred together as my gaze dipped back to the ground, my eyelids heavy. I was listening, but it was only when he finally murmured, "Please, Lailah, don't leave me in the darkness all alone," that I really heard him.

I rolled my eyes back to his, knowing what I had done to him. I had imprisoned him there, sentenced him to the very thing I myself feared most. He didn't love me, but perhaps any company—even mine—was better than none at all.

I conceded.

And then I succumbed.

TWENTY-SEVEN

I TRIED TO CONSUME Jonah's blood, but as the first droplets spread across my tongue, the part of my brain that controlled the signal—the compulsion—to swallow had gone.

He pressed his wrist harder against my lips and though my mouth filled with blood, I coughed, and none of it remained.

It was hopeless. Azrael might have been dead, but his words to me were very much alive; *not even if your life depended on it* was embodied in my inability to take from Jonah, my willing victim.

Jonah hovered over my ghostlike body, his words sounding like china smashing as he said, "Kiss me."

His lips pressed to my own. A warm liquid trickled across my tongue. He'd cut his lips and he was feeding me his blood, disguised in a last good-bye.

These lips that he once tried to use as a white flag of surrender, he now coated in dangerous red. I was still unable to reach for his neck, but his thumbs pressed down on my cheekbones and his fingers threaded through my short hair.

Darkness descended over his face, and as his blood sat in my mouth he withdrew. "Breathe, Lailah."

I wasn't aware that I was holding my breath. But he knew what he did to me. My automatic reaction was to gasp, and as I did, the air took his blood to the back of my throat.

Jonah's essence seeped through my system. At first I was calm. The stars overhead reappeared, one by one. Then I was back in his lap, and his wrist was once more under my nose. He eased it to my lips, and I nuzzled into his cold skin, cautiously lapping up his offering.

Initially, his blood was bland, but then with every purposeful swallow he became sweet. He was delectable, and I wanted every last drop of him.

I yanked his arm farther into my chest so that there was no gap between us, and I dug my fingernails into his skin, causing contusions that offered me yet more of him.

The sounds around me—the rumble of cars speeding down a highway somewhere in the distance, the rustle of each individual feather of a bird flapping its wings somewhere close, and countless other cracks and taps and whispers—roared in my ears. But, then, the Vampire moaning beneath me cut through all the other noise.

I crashed into his body hard. The oak tree yawned and stretched as it uprooted with the force, cracking in two and falling with an almighty boom.

Still I was guzzling his blood, and all I knew was what he was: a Vampire. Beyond that, I didn't care.

Hungry, hot, and hysterical, I flipped over, tearing his shirt apart, the buttons plinking free as they became detached.

His heart would provide me with so much more.

Splatters of crimson smeared around his lips. His eyes were weak and fading. Still, all I saw was a Vampire.

I ran my tongue down his neck, tasting the beads of sweat dripping down his skin. Around his collarbone, his pores oozed a strange summerlike scent, and I stopped. But then, in an instant, my greed overtook my hesitation.

I pressed my cheek to his firm chest. I scraped my nails over the outline of the muscles running up his torso until I finally brought them over his heart.

"Finish it," the Vampire uttered through pained rasps. His voice sparked no recognition. But just then, the skip of his heartbeat pulsed beneath my hand.

I cricked my neck and listened to its rhythm.

The beat of the drum.

I might not have been able to see him through the darkness, but I could hear him.

Jonah. My salvation.

Horrified, I dragged myself across the grass on my bottom, desperately trying to put some distance between the two of us.

I brought my knees to my chest and curled into a tight ball. I watched silently as his skin began to restitch, and I heard the breaths he struggled to take as he came back to himself. I'd ravaged him; the streak of my clawlike marks trailed his torso where blood still soaked his skin.

I trembled, and my hands shook with violent vibrations. I looked to the night's sky and wailed, sickened by what I'd done to him.

Incoherent, muddled emotions rushed through me. Anguish, disgust, and then a strange sense of lust as his fragrance drifted on the soft breeze.

Jonah stared blankly as he tried to prop himself up against what remained of the fallen tree. I had desecrated it; one of the only things that Gabriel and I had shared that was still left. And I had defiled Jonah in the process. How quickly love had turned to hate, how easy it had been to obliterate. I was consumed with ferocity—everything wiped away by my darkness.

Seeing what I had done to Jonah, I had never felt so small, so weak, so overwhelmed by my impulses. But physically, my body had never felt so strong. The surroundings felt similar to the way they had the morning I'd woken in France. My ability to see in the dark was fully restored. The texture of each blade of grass beneath me, every fragment of dust that hung in the air—everything appeared sharp and detailed.

But I had only been in demo mode before.

It was as though when I had woken in the clearing and absorbed the sun, my body was awaiting the dark energy to finish charging my battery.

And now I was in full play.

Connected to Jonah through his blood, every ache as he healed traveled through me, as though they were my own wounds. This must have been what it was like for him, too, when he was attached to my physical decline.

His presence made my insides burn. I had to fight the urge to rush over and drown in him in order to extinguish the blaze.

Was this what it felt like for him, too?

And if it was, how had he resisted it all this time? It was my love for him that had stopped me, that was stopping me still, but I knew now that he didn't feel the same. So perhaps it was the idea that he had held on to, that he was meant to save me; that "her life" would count for nothing if he didn't, as he had said. Though I had no idea who the *she* was.

As Jonah got to his feet, he cracked his dislocated shoulder back into its socket, and I flinched as the sting passed through me. I bowed my face into my folded arms—hiding from him, from what I had done.

JONAH'S HAND RESTED ON my spine, and his breath skimmed the back of my neck as he crouched beside me. His touch caused a confusing knot to form in the pit of my stomach and the muscles of my inner thighs to contract.

"Lailah," he said calmly.

Still I could not bring myself to look at him.

He slipped his hooded coat over my shoulders and tried to pry open my hands, which were wrapped around my knees.

"It's okay." He pulled me into his arms.

Desperately trying to subdue a rising dizziness, I said, "I'm sorry."

He didn't answer me.

My words were not enough. I unclasped my hands and let my knees fall, frantically bringing my palms to his chest once more and tickling his skin with my fingertips.

Seizing the opportunity, he moved the sleeves of his jacket around my arms, bending my elbows inside, and then played with the zipper that sat below my hips. He brought the material together, grazing my outer thighs as he did. He was deliberately averting his eyes from my near-naked body as he began to slide the zipper up to my collarbone, where for the briefest moment he rested his fingers gently.

A lustful, fiery affliction struck me repeatedly at the smell of his intoxicating fragrance. I was overcome with a sense of want, and I bit down on my bottom lip. I shifted to my knees, clawing the skin of his chest, and I nudged my nose to his and hurriedly found his lips. I kissed him, but he didn't respond. Frustrated, I tried again more urgently this time, but still his lips wouldn't part for me.

I whipped the zipper back down to my belly button and snatched his hand, pressing it underneath what was left of the thin material across my chest. I leaned in once more, encouraging him to meet me.

Jonah flexed his palm over my skin, exerting a tender squeeze before skimming the curve of my breast with the back of his hand, but then he stopped. He broke away, refusing my kiss for a final time.

"Jonah—" I pleaded. I was sure he could feel the compulsion, the need, pulsing down my form; the overwhelming desire to have him—somehow, anyhow.

In a flash, he'd done up the hoodie. He pressed his thumb into the middle of my lower lip. Assertively he said, "The feeling will pass."

Disappointment filled me. I knew I was being selfish, but if he could feel my body yearning for him, why would he yield and offer me a release, when I had never offered him any in all this time—when I had refused him, only hours ago?

I swiftly removed my hands from his chest, embarrassed and hurt. I took a few moments to collect myself. "If you believe that you were meant to save me, know that you did. You should run now; you should never stop running." I paused, watching for something—anything—in his expression that would offer me the final confirmation of what I already understood. He didn't love me, he didn't want me, and now that he had fulfilled whatever purpose he thought he was meant to, he would forget me. "I'm sorry for everything, truly. I will go . . . take some satisfaction in knowing that I will suffer the same agony as you—that my penance is now paid."

Jonah's eyebrows dipped as I rose to my feet, pulling the jacket down firmly, ensuring I was covered.

This was really it, our final farewell; I would never see him again. He stood to meet me, and I reached for his hand to squeeze a last apology, a final thank-you. But the moment I met his skin, that delirious craving gnawed at me again, and unable to stop myself, I forced his mouth to mine once more. He yanked his hand away, withdrawing from my frantic grasp.

"You really don't want me, do you?" I said, breathless.

In the darkness, I waited for his answer.

"No," he said firmly.

The final nail in the coffin. I flipped up the hood of Jonah's jacket as I pictured the house in Henley. In a flash, I was traveling by thought, so his words fell to an empty field when he finished, "Not like this."

I ARRIVED IN THE gardens of the house to raised voices coming from inside.

Once again able to break down the wall in my mind, and with no further need to keep Gabriel out, I let it drop. He was right there on the other side, waiting.

Where are you, Lailah? His thoughts found me immediately.

At the Henley house, I answered swiftly.

Entering the property through the back door, I marched through the kitchen and down the hallway toward the commotion from the living room. Before I had a chance to get inside, a blur of light appeared in front of me and transformed into Gabriel's figure. He didn't waste a second. He flung his arms around me and pulled me in close. "I've been searching everywhere for you. . . ."

He was breathing heavily as his right hand pushed away the hood hiding my face, and he pressed his thumb against my cheekbone. Finally when he released me, he wore a concerned expression.

Rubbing his temple, he simply said, "Go and put on some clothes."

I nodded and then traveled by thought to the landing.

I couldn't sense Jonah's presence, so I unzipped his jacket and threw it to the end of his bed before making my way to Brooke's room.

I yanked on the nearest pair of jeans I could find and a plain T-shirt. I hadn't intended to check myself in the mirror atop the dresser, but as I rushed past it, I glanced quickly at my reflection.

Blood.

Splattered all over my face, staining my neck. The sight of it stirred something within me, but I pushed the flutter down as I realized that Gabriel had seen it—that he must have known I had drunk from Jonah.

I ambled to the bathroom and scrubbed my face over the sink, trying to rid the blood and smeared mascara from my skin. I would have spent longer assessing my efforts if it weren't for the sound of Iona's cries from the living room.

I darted downstairs. My body fully energized, I felt as though I could run forever and my legs would never tire. Inside the living room, Iona sat perched on the edge of a chair in the far corner of the room. Gabriel was kneeling beside her, holding Iona's hand in his. Ruadhan stood a little farther back; I assumed he had been monitoring her while Gabriel had searched for me.

"What's going on?" I asked.

Gabriel shifted, which allowed me to see Iona fully. She was glowing so brightly that even I had to squint at her form.

"Is Fergal back yet?" he asked.

"I didn't see him, or—" I paused, thinking carefully before I finished my sentence. "Lailah. I didn't see either of them." I stepped closer to him and Iona.

"You're burning up," Gabriel said to Iona. "I need to fetch some ice. Ruadhan will stay with you." He then gestured for me to follow him out of the room.

"No, please don't leave," Iona said with a sob. She may have been elegantly dressed, but she sounded like a small child.

Iona wobbled as she tried to stand. Gabriel eased her back and said softly, "I will only be a moment, I promise."

"It's okay, love, I'm here," Ruadhan said, reassuring her.

I followed Gabriel down the hallway and into the kitchen. He unbuttoned the top of his shirt, shrugged off his suit jacket, and hung it over a chair.

"What's going on? What's happening to her?" I asked.

Gabriel balanced his weight against the top of the chair. "I think Iona is Of Elfi," he said, as though I should understand what the hell that meant.

I shook my head.

His eyes met mine. "The Endlrich Of Elfi. Offspring of fallen Angels."

"Children of fallen Angels?" I repeated quietly.

"Yes. Some of the Angel Descendants that fell mated with mortals and their children are known as the Endlrich Of Elfi."

"So what, her father was a fallen Angel?" My mind flipped and whirled, and then I remembered what Iona had said about her father having called her and her mother his Angels. "It was her mother, wasn't it? She was the fallen Angel. Her brother Padraig had a different mum, but not Fergal, which means he is Of Elfi, too. . . ." My thoughts turned to Brooke—yet another complication for her to contend with. Not only was Fergal the leader of the Sealgaire, but he was also a child of a fallen Angel.

And Brooke was a Vampire.

"Fallen Angels exist here without any gifts, in a mortal form. But it takes them hundreds, thousands of years, even, to age and to eventually die. Iona turned seventeen when the clock struck midnight. In Styclar, that is the equivalent to one day. It's the moment when we become fixed in our forms, immortal in our world. For children of a fallen Angel, if their soul is pure when they reach seventeen years, they become just the same as their parent."

"Meaning she won't have any abilities and she's not immortal, but she will, what, live for goodness knows how long, very slowly aging?"

"Yes. Her body is transitioning; her cells are becoming almost frozen with the trace of light she possesses in her genetic makeup. She will be okay in a few hours. But I'm going to have to explain all this to her."

"You mean you're going to have to tell her that while she's mortal, she will live for thousands of years? Without any abilities to protect herself during all that time?" I paused. "She's not immortal, so she can die, right?"

"She's the same as a fallen Angel. If her heart stopped beating, yes, she would die." Gabriel shoved the chair under the table and walked to the freezer.

"You were glowing when you kissed her," I said matter-of-factly.

Gabriel stopped, and he turned back to me. "She started to glow when the clock struck midnight. Her skin was against mine, so it caused me to do the same." He paused. "Lai, that was all for show. I don't need to tell you that, do I?"

The way he said it made me feel small. For show or otherwise, it had hurt. Right now, I didn't care to dwell on the possibility of what the *otherwise* could mean. And after what had just happened between Jonah and me, I hardly had a leg to stand on.

"You were selling crystals from Styclar-Plena to Sir Montmorency. How did you get them?" I asked.

Satisfied that I was changing the subject, Gabriel rummaged around for an ice tray, but then paused.

"You were listening to my conversation?" he said.

"Yes."

"What were you even doing there?"

I had wanted to keep an eye on Brooke. Fearing she might run into trouble if Fergal slipped up and used her name, *my name*. But, I had also gone to keep an eye on Gabriel and Iona, but I didn't want to say that. Instead I repeated his words back to him. "It's difficult to watch you leave, and all too easy to follow you, Gabriel."

Gabriel's body relaxed a little, as though he understood.

"How did you get those crystals?" I asked him again.

"Orifiel gave them to me when he tasked me again to find you. They were a means of funding my search and aiding my existence here on this plane. I told you before, using our gifts on Earth in the wrong way or in an act of darkness can be very . . . damaging." Ice tray in hand, Gabriel squeezed several cubes out onto the work surface. "He didn't wish for my light to become tainted; he knew it would make it more difficult for me to find you. And now that I have,

I need to ensure that I can afford to protect you in every possible way," he said.

"What, with a big house and a fancy car?"

Gabriel's answer was swift. "No. But houses with high-tech security systems, fast cars, and flights when we can't travel by thought across water cost money, Lailah." Of course, I hadn't considered the detail of the practicalities. But there was having enough and having more than enough. "But it seems that whoever Sir Montmorency was selling the crystals to this evening had no desire to pay for them."

My mind quickly flipped back to Darwin, to his family, and I panicked. "The Vampires . . . did they . . . Sir Montmorency, his son?" I stuttered.

Gabriel took a tea towel off a hook underneath the sink, and I was reminded of the time he had wrapped ice cubes up for my benefit when I had sliced my hand on the lemonade glass. That day felt like a million years ago.

"They are fine, Lailah. I took care of the Vampires."

I breathed a sigh of relief for Darwin. "You suspected something wasn't right. . . . I could tell, when you were with Sir Montmorency. Why did you give him the crystals if you had any doubt over where they would end up?" I challenged.

"Sir Montmorency has been selling my crystals on to dealers for years, Lailah. More perfect than any jewel this world can produce, they are worth a great deal of money." He paused as he finished wrapping up the ice cubes. "The idea of one buyer didn't sit right, no. But it was one last deal to secure our *entire future*. . . . There is no doubt I wouldn't overcome, no risk I wouldn't be willing to take, to keep you safe." Gabriel's eyes hardened in a determined gaze. "I'm far more concerned with what happened when you chased down Azrael when he was making off with the gems." He put down the towel and stared at me. He must have found Brooke, or Brooke him, before he began his search for me. And I didn't know what she had told him.

"I killed him in cold blood," I said. I had to stop hiding who I was, who I was becoming.

Gabriel halted, considering my confession, and then moved across the kitchen to meet me beside the table. He took my hands in his own and kissed them softly. "You were protecting Brooke. I understand. You did what you had to do. I'm so sorry that I didn't get there first . . . that you had to be the one to do it." His eyes were blooming again, his blue roses flowering as though he were offering them to me as some sort of apology.

He drew me in, and I breathed in his citrus scent. Although it wasn't as potent as it had once been, it was still comforting and his embrace calmed me. I faltered, as his love, his light, kindled in me. "Azrael was working for the Purebloods, Gabriel. They wanted the crystals for something. . . . Did you retrieve them?"

"Yes," he answered, and then I remembered.

Jolting back, I placed my hand to my chest, home to the necklace that I was missing. "My crystal."

"It's okay. I have it."

I squeezed a nervous smile, feeling lost without it. "Help Iona, then let's go."

"You're keener than you were," Gabriel mused, taken aback by my sudden desire to leave. He traced every minute movement of my lips, my eyes, expertly reading my defensive body language. Again I assumed he knew what had transpired this evening—knew but was unwilling to utter the words aloud.

"Okay," he murmured. He leaned in and kissed me with such conviction that I nearly believed the message he was trying to convey—the one that used words like "forever."

Dissolving into his kiss created multicolored luminous stripes across my vision, and every last inch of me responded, reaching out and trying to seek Gabriel's heart—the pot of gold at the end of his rainbow.

Somehow, it seemed just out of reach, and a sense of unease crept over me. As I tried to place the reason behind it, I realized that it wasn't the thought of a devious leprechaun trying to steal it away before I found it; I was afraid of a sweet Endlrich Of Elfi who had already taken it for her own instead.

A key turning, followed by the rattle of the front door ricocheting off the wall, broke my thoughts. Fergal prowled through the hall, Brooke behind him, as he searched for Iona.

Gabriel parted from me, giving my waist one last squeeze before swiftly collecting the tea towel and ice cubes. I stopped him as he made his way through the kitchen. "Are you going to tell Fergal, about Iona I mean?" I paused. "When he turns seventeen it's going to affect him, too," I said.

"I won't say anything to Fergal, not until Iona's all right, and not before I have spoken with her alone. I need to be absolutely sure she is Of Elfi before I offer up information to her."

Gabriel directed Fergal into the living room, and I stole the opportunity to take Brooke to one side, knowing that our time here with the Sealgaire was nearly up. I gripped her elbow tightly and ushered her away from the living room door.

"While it's nice to see you alive, I'd remind you what I said about *pushing*."

"I need you to tell me," I said, annoyed that Brooke was now busy straightening out the creases in her dress and only half listening to me. "Brooke."

"Yes, tell you what?" she said.

I caught her eye and whispered quietly, *"Do they know where my mother is?"*

Brooke opened her mouth, but then paused, and finally she wiggled her nose. "No. I'm sorry."

TWENTY-EIGHT

GABRIEL WAS WITH IONA, and so I took myself down into the depths of the grounds and awaited the sunrise. Every inch of my body now felt awake, alert and ready, but now there was an inner turmoil in the mix.

It had been hours, and I had rehashed countless times what had happened with Jonah.

I was bonded to him through his darkness, and I was connected to Gabriel by light. Both of their footprints were stamped across my soul. And somewhere in there was me. But I was too busy hiding in Jonah's shadow or basking in Gabriel's glow to truly find myself.

I was so deep in thought that I barely noticed the sunrise—not until Gabriel's hand squeezed my shoulder. Together, we began to twinkle. But like the last time, Gabriel did not shine with luminosity as I had witnessed in the past. His glow was dull, the struggle between his skin and the warm rays only too easy to see.

He stopped shining and patiently waited for me to do the same.

It took me far longer, but eventually, the white stripes filtering into my being stopped.

I turned to Gabriel, who—now changed—was wearing a more casual white polo shirt and khakis. His pale skin appeared even paler against his collar, and the veins running down his neck were a light gray.

"I'm worried how quickly you stop absorbing the sun," I said.

Before, I had put it down to what he had said about saying good-bye to Hanora—thinking that somehow his sadness had stopped him from shining as bright—but I knew, from the darkness showing in his veins and the thin creases forming around his eyes, that something wasn't right.

Gabriel sighed heavily. "Lai, I have done some things, things that needed to be . . . done." He paused. "An Angel Descendant becomes mortal here if an Arch Angel removes their crystal. But that is not the only way an Angel Descendant can fall."

I looked at him, perplexed.

"I told you, using our gifts here in the wrong way could be detrimental. My crystal is failing because the things I had to do were acts of darkness."

"Wait, what does that mean?"

He looked down to the ground, and then finally met my eyes. "I already told you; you just didn't hear me."

What did he mean he'd already told me? I was about to question him, when I panicked at what he was implying about his crystal failing. I reached for his arms, scanning his body. "You're not fallen. I can still feel your light."

"No, I'm not. I haven't done enough to cause my crystal to completely fail; it's just weaker than it was. I will be fine, I promise." He squeezed my elbows. "I don't want to talk about it, not right now. Please, just come with me."

I considered his request and nodded. He was being honest and upfront, so if he needed some time, I would give it to him. Gabriel took my hand in his, leading me toward the tree line. We walked in silence until we reached a weeping willow tree, which he gestured for me to sit beneath. "I wanted to do this under our tree, but when I arrived there it was no longer standing."

I crossed my legs and looked to the ground, wondering if he was now going to ask for the details of what had happened.

Did he know that was where Jonah and I had been? That I had caused the tree to topple over? But the questions I was expecting never came. Instead, Gabriel pushed his blond hair behind his ears and delved into his trouser pocket.

He knelt down in front of me and took my left hand. His beautiful eyes never leaving mine, he placed something cold in the center of my palm.

I stifled a gasp. My crystal gem was encased in a shiny platinum band.

"I know we are not of this world," he began. "But you, Lailah, have never known Styclar-Plena. You have only ever known Earth. This is your home; the ways and the customs of mortals is what you understand. And so I would ask of you today, what I would have asked nearly two hundred years ago, if I hadn't been too late."

He gently removed the band from my palm and slid it down my ring finger.

"I want you to marry me." He kissed the back of my hand.

My mind raced.

I loved Gabriel. No words could describe the way he made me feel, because it was just that, a feeling.

I considered him. Gabriel had fallen in love with me all those years ago, when my form was human, before our lights had sewn us into each other. He knew I had drunk Jonah's blood, that by doing so I had revived myself with dark energy. If he saw me for who I was now, he would know the girl he had loved was gone, so perhaps that was why he still didn't acknowledge what I had done. And without Gabriel, the part of me I had been clinging to would exist only as a memory—one that belonged to him. And then I would be someone else. And I was afraid of her, because she would go to war.

She would die alone.

"Do you have my chain?" I asked quietly, sliding the ring from my finger.

Gabriel's shoulders slumped as he searched my eyes, but he nodded and took it from his pocket. It dangled from his fingers. I smiled tightly and took it from him, unclasping it and looping the band back through. I finally placed it back around my neck, moving the gem to the center of my chest. "I, just, prefer it on a chain," I mumbled.

I didn't say anything more. I feared what might tumble out of my mouth if I started, so instead I placed my hands around his neck and kissed him. It was all the indication Gabriel needed to assure him of my positive answer, when in fact I had deliberately avoided giving any answer at all.

He enveloped me within his arms, lifting me up and into his lap. He held me as though I were the prize at the finish line of what he had thought to be a never-ending race. And a white sheet surrounded me now, as I let his light stretch and wrap me inside its impenetrable safety.

"When did you . . . how did you?" I reluctantly pulled away, looking down at the band and wondering when he had had the opportunity to have the crystal reset.

"Ruadhan . . . He was a goldsmith, once."

Gabriel hadn't left Iona's side until now; I don't know why I thought he would have. "How long until we leave?" I asked, slipping off his lap and standing before him.

"Iona is still transitioning, but it's not safe here for you anymore. Not after last night." He put his hand to the small of my back, encouraging me to walk with him.

"You should stay until it's over. Have you spoken with her yet?"

We moseyed through the gardens. "No. She's in no state. I was waiting, but it's taking longer than I had first thought." He placed his hand around my waist lightly, pushing my T-shirt up so his skin was against mine.

"She needs to know. When she does, we can leave."

Gabriel considered it. "If I stay, you can't be here. You'll go with Ruadhan; he can take you away for a few hours. If you even remotely sense that Vampires are near, I want you to travel by thought to the cottage on the grounds of the Hedgerley property and wait there until I get to you."

I screwed up my face. "Why? That's the last place I'd go. It can't be secure."

"If they were to come for you, the cottage is the best place you could be." Gabriel took my elbows with his hands. "Hold my arms. Travel there by thought with me."

Before I had a chance to protest, Gabriel's eyes were closed, and the world spun around me as we traveled through a tunnel of light.

It took a moment for the blur of my vision to come back into focus, for the light to stop twirling, but when it did, I was inside the entranceway of the cottage.

"I really don't think it's safe to be here," I said, homing in on the sounds surrounding us.

"Lai, look at the tiles in the floor." Gabriel's fingers trailed down the outside of my arm and he took my hand.

I glanced down to the beautiful sun in the marble flooring. I had thought the artwork to be mesmerizing the first time I had seen it. Now, however, there was a layer of ash coating the bright colors, and I wondered if Gabriel had lit the log-burning stove when he had brought Hanora in here.

Gabriel interrupted my thoughts. "This cottage was my safe house. The design in the tiles of the floor isn't decoration."

I furrowed my brow, not understanding.

"At each point of the sun's rays, and at the center, placed in the marble, is a crystal."

"More crystals?" I asked.

"Yes. They originally came from the necks of Angel Descendants that had asked to fall, and Orifiel gave me plenty. Nearly void of light, they were of little use to him in Styclar-Plena. I didn't sell them all; six are disguised within the design."

I looked to Gabriel, puzzled.

"The same as any crystal found on Earth, they have an optical property known as birefringence. Meaning, when a ray of light hits them, the light refracts and beams back out in strobes. But, unlike Earth's crystals, Styclar-Plena's are more special. If you shine a light on them, hundreds of beams of light will be created—like lasers, Lai. And the sort of light—the energy—that we can produce can end Second Generation Vampires and can at least hold back a Pureblood."

His words took me back to the night I had crawled my way across these tiles with a piece of glass lodged in my navel. Light had engulfed and soothed me. Perhaps the moon had reflected off the crystals embedded in the marble and found the gem around my neck.

"But you can just create a sheet of light to end a Vampire if you had to. I don't get why you'd need to have a safe house."

"Here you only have to concentrate on projecting your light toward the tiles. The light that refracts will keep you in a nebula of strobes. We know the Purebloods are commanding the rifts to open, but they wouldn't be able to create one here among the light."

Something still wasn't sitting right. Gabriel didn't struggle to end more than one Vampire at a time, and he only recently knew about the Purebloods commanding the rifts. "I don't understand. . . ."

"It doesn't matter. All you need to know is that, for the next few hours, if you get any sense that trouble is nearby, you travel by thought to this room. If a Vampire were to somehow follow you, you end them with your light here, where it's safest. The walls are sealed with lead that will contain your light. No one will be able to see it outside of these walls," he told me firmly.

"No one, as in Arch Angels?" I pondered, recalling how my little display with the trees had caught their attention.

"Exactly."

A cold silence surrounded the two of us as I thought over what Gabriel was telling me. "You took Vampires in here to end them, unseen. Not in self-defense, but because you had chosen to take away their existence." I paused, and Gabriel's aura becoming anxious told me that I was right. "You didn't build a safe house, Gabriel; you created an execution chamber."

My words hung in the air.

Eventually, he met my eyes and simply said, "Sometimes there is a need, Lai. Sometimes it's a necessary evil."

I stumbled backward, realizing that he wasn't offering me an explanation—it was a confession. "Hanora . . ."

Gabriel's gaze fell away from mine, but he barely flinched. My arms swayed down by my sides. As my hand loosened in Gabriel's, he clamped his fingers between my own. Hurriedly he said, "I had to, Lai. She wouldn't have let me go; she would have discovered that you were still alive, and she would have told the Purebloods."

I tugged my hand, but Gabriel clutched it even more tightly—still he was unprepared to let me go.

"You said . . ." My thoughts tumbled. "You said that you reminisced with her, that you said good-bye. You lied to me?"

Gabriel shook his head. "I told you the truth. You just didn't hear it, when I spoke it."

"A final good-bye," he'd said, one that cost him a little of his light. I hadn't realized what he had meant because I couldn't conceive the notion that Gabriel would be able to do such a thing.

"They found out anyway." My voice was flat. "They were always going to. You ended her existence to protect me from something outside of your power to prevent." An unconscionable crime had been committed in my name.

"I know it was a terrible thing, but you can understand why I did it. You ended Azrael's life to protect Brooke." Gabriel's voice was raised. He hadn't wanted to end Hanora's existence, and it must have been painful to bring himself to execute an act that went against his very nature. But he had done it—for me. This was the darkness he'd been talking about committing. The reason why his crystal was starting to fail.

"I . . . Gabriel, you shouldn't have. . . . It's different. . . ."

I hadn't killed Azrael under some delusion of protecting a greater good; I had done it in cold blood, because I had wanted to. I realized then that Gabriel would never be able to accept that of me. And I would never be able to come to terms with knowing that he would end another life and risk his own immortality to keep me from harm.

I rehashed the conversation I had overheard between Gabriel and Hanora outside the cottage. He had tricked her into entering. "Why was Hanora wearing a scarf around her head? In Neylis, she had burn marks across her skin. . . ." Gabriel had asked Hanora if she had forgiven him. What had he done?

Gabriel's chest tightened, and I felt giddy as his anxiety swelled through me.

"When I walked into the motel room, she was . . . I reacted badly," he said simply.

Gabriel's body was rigid and I brought myself in closer to him, observing the thin fissures around the edges of his suffering eyes. I brought my thumb up over his eyebrow and stroked the fine lines contemplatively.

"You hit her with your light, didn't you? That's why, on the phone, you asked me how much I had seen. You would have rather I thought something romantic was happening between the two of you than tell me that you had felt anger, that you had committed an act of darkness."

Gabriel bowed his head, bringing his forehead to mine. Finally releasing my hand, he clutched my waist instead. I could comprehend darkness—I was beginning to know it well now—but mine was borne from within me and I owned it. Gabriel's acts of darkness, although they had come by his hand, belonged to me, too. But he would be the one that would pay the price for them.

The cracks were already starting to show, and they had been since he arrived back from his trip. I just hadn't paid enough attention to them. He was living for me, the me whom he had loved all these years, but his love for that person would be the death of him.

"Oh, Gabriel, what have you done?" I stepped back, looking everywhere but at him. The ash was not from the stove. It was Hanora's remains.

Nausea twisted my stomach. "I can't be here." I closed my eyes, thinking of the kitchen in the Henley house; Gabriel reached for my arm as I did.

We arrived back in a blink of an eye.

Ruadhan appeared immediately, his brow creasing as he tried to get my attention. "There's someone here to see you, love," he said, and heavy footsteps slowly approached from behind him. As the floorboards contracted, springing up with each step, finally a figure took up a stance next to Ruadhan.

Malachi.

"What are you doing here?" Gabriel challenged quickly, moving in front of me protectively.

"Nice to see you again, too, Gabriel," Malachi replied with a smooth voice. He proceeded to unbutton his cashmere coat, taking his time and regarding me with that same unreadable expression as I peered around Gabriel's side. "I require an audience with Lailah," he continued, gesturing for me to come forward.

"Shhhh," Gabriel warned, bringing his finger to his lips at the use of my real name.

I moved toward the back of the kitchen, opening up the doors onto the garden. "We can talk outside."

Gabriel shot me an unhappy glance; he clearly didn't want me here anymore and certainly not alone with a fallen Angel. I was almost relieved. I needed space from Gabriel. I needed to think.

"Gabriel, Iona needs you. Go to her," I said. "I'm sure Malachi will only stay for a few minutes."

"I checked him at the door," Ruadhan said, gesturing to Malachi. "He's not carrying anything he shouldn't be."

Iona's whining echoed through the hallway, and Gabriel reacted as he heard her, too.

"She has been asking after you since you left," Ruadhan further pushed, and I wondered if he knew why Malachi was here. Maybe Ruadhan hoped that Malachi would tell me something that would encourage me to fight, to become the savior he hoped for. "I'll be right here," Ruadhan said finally and reluctantly Gabriel conceded.

"You have five minutes," Gabriel said firmly, and Malachi replied with the smallest of smiles.

Once Gabriel had left the kitchen, Ruadhan stood next to the counter. "I'll just be here, love."

"No. Please, Ruadhan, I'm not a child."

Ruadhan took a moment, but then nodded, exiting the kitchen.

Malachi followed me onto the patio, shutting the door behind him. He lined himself up with my body but maintained a distance. His gaze swept from left to right, assessing the surroundings. Finally, he eyed me before he began, "You seem on edge. Something to do with murdering your own father?"

I was on edge all right; I had just learned that Hanora had met her end by Gabriel's hand. "That *man* was not my father, not really." I took a deep breath. "He was working for the Purebloods. So, now you tell me, who are you working for?"

"A good question, child, and not a straightforward one to answer. Let's just say, ordinarily, I work for the highest bidder. But I am no different from your Angel; in a way, he has been working for the Purebloods as well." Malachi's response was easy and unemotional.

"That's a lie," I stated angrily.

"Well, maybe Gabriel is unaware, but he has been, in a way. We all have. Who do you think has ended up in possession of the crystals he's been parting with to fund this lifestyle?"

My forehead creased.

He continued, "The Purebloods have been using those very crystals to command the rifts."

"Those crystals are useless," I said. "Gabriel told me they are virtually void of light, Malachi. And the Purebloods exist in the third dimension. They come through via dark rifts. I saw one form myself."

"You are wrong, child. The third exists in a state of cold, dark matter. When the crystals are taken through the rift, that trace of light from Styclar-Plena reverses and the elements transition into hot, dark matter, allowing Zherneboh and his kind to use them to command and manipulate the rifts—the same way the Angel Descendants do from Styclar-Plena with theirs." He raised his eyebrows. "A recent discovery, I believe, but I would suspect that some of the crystals Gabriel sold have one way or another ended up in Zherneboh's claws. So, we're not all that different."

So that was how they had been commanding the rifts. I bet Orifiel hadn't counted on that when he had parted with them. I shook my head. "Gabriel doesn't know. If he did, then he would never have sold them." Though the words left my lips with conviction, I couldn't be sure if that was true. He had said there was no doubt he wouldn't overcome, no risk that would be too great, to keep me safe. He would sell out this world, any world, anyone and anything because he believed my life was worth more. I could not and would never agree with that. "You need to tell him and tell any others doing the same." I paused, thinking better of what I'd just said. "You work for the highest bidder. . . . I can't trust you or anything that comes out of your mouth. You may as well leave now."

Stepping farther out onto the patio, Malachi placed his hands inside his coat pocket, scanning once again to the left and the right. I couldn't see his face, but it made no difference; I might as well have been looking at his back for all the information I could glean from his empty expression.

"Oh," he said, "but my child, you *can* trust me, for you are priceless. If you don't take the right path, it matters not what anyone would pay me, because this world will not be left in which to spend it."

"And what path is that exactly?" I asked, stepping forward purposefully.

He turned around, now wearing a more solemn expression, as though in some way he pitied me. "I understand it's difficult to choose. Things are seldom ever what they seem. . . . I was one of the first Angels, and I exist here now fallen. But there was a time when I was known as the Ethiccart."

"What do you mean, the Ethiccart?" I asked.

"That was the job title Orifiel bestowed on me. When the

crystal in Styclar-Plena failed, Orifiel brought through the light souls of mortals to fuel it. But it was never the same. I was, shall we say, able to remedy his *situation*."

I didn't understand what he was implying. "Gabriel said the crystal was even more brilliant than it had been, and that there was no remedy needed."

"You must disregard what Gabriel has told you. Through the crystal, he—like the rest—was told a story: the beginnings of Styclar-Plena, Orifiel's brave journey, and the miracle that followed. I know it very well because I was the one that programmed it." He made sure I was looking straight into his eyes as he said, "But that story is a fairy tale, Lailah. Some elements are accurate; lies are easier to believe if they are based on some form of truth, after all."

"Which is what?" I crossed my arms. "What is the truth? What did your job entail exactly?"

"That is something you will need to see for yourself, Lailah."

I shook my head. "I'm not leaving this plane."

Malachi's composed disposition fell away as he began to wave his hands in the air. "You will. You must. For you are the only being that will be able to see through the design I created; the *only being* that can do what must be done."

"Maybe you should just tell me what *you think* that is and save me some time. And I'll be sure to add it to the list," I said with sarcasm.

Malachi clamped his hands underneath my elbows. "Don't be so impudent, child," he said with a sneer. "You need to finish what first began."

I offered Malachi only a blank and bored expression. I wasn't in the mood for riddles.

"The day the darkness fell, it never really left, Lailah. It only became greater."

Still I offered him no reaction.

"Bring the Arch Angels and the worlds they exist in to an end." His tone was now urgent and his pitch heightened as he finished.

I shrugged off his hands. "So you would have me commit genocide against Styclar-Plena? Go after the Arch Angels, slay them all, and then what? Kill the very world that the Angel Descendants and all of Styclar-Plena's inhabitants call home? Leave them for dead, too? Does the third dimension, and the beings that exist there, not concern you far more than a world that exists in light? Would you not have me start there?" Surely the third was a bigger threat to Earth. His statement told me whose side he was on, and it wasn't Styclar's.

"The Angel Descendants and the beings that inhabit Styclar-Plena are innocent in all this. What you choose to do with them is up to you." Malachi brought his finger up under my chin, tipping my face so that I was looking him square in the eyes. "But as I said: Bring the Arch Angels and the *worlds* they exist in to an end."

I blinked rapidly, hearing him properly this time.

Worlds.

Plural.

TWENTY-NINE

MALACHI CERTAINLY HAD MY attention now, but a piercing scream coming from the motor home instantly took me away from the questions rushing to my lips.

Malachi touched his hand to my shoulder, knowing he no longer had my attention. "You need to leave," he said. "But, please, find me again. . . ."

Malachi's accusations of the Arch Angels, of the dimensions, were ineffable. My assumption had been wrong; he was in fact on humanity's side. The vision of the dove transitioning into a raven, when Zherneboh had reached into my mind, came back to me. I believed what Malachi said. But if the Purebloods had once been Arch Angels, and it was not the fallen Angels that had slipped through the rifts and become them, then where were the many fallen Angels now? And how had some of the Arch Angels become Pureblood Vampires? He was right; I needed to know what he knew.

The screams broke through my reverie, and I ran toward them, through the open door of the motor home. Riley and Claire were crowding the hallway. I pushed past them to find Brooke being dragged across the bedroom by Phelan, who had silver chains wrapped around his arms, pressing against her bare skin. She was dressed only in her underwear, and behind her, on the bed, was Fergal, shirtless and wearing only baggy tracksuit bottoms.

He wasn't trying to help Brooke; instead, his chin tipped down as he refastened his cross around his neck.

I tackled Phelan from behind, pulling him away from Brooke; she fell to the floor with a thud. She hissed and bared her fangs, blood smeared around her mouth.

Then I knew why Fergal wasn't trying to help. She'd attacked him.

Brooke whimpered as her skin, now free of the silver, smoldered, and her expression was a mixture of pain and rage.

"Don't touch her!" I shouted at Phelan, who was already lunging back toward her, this time pulling something sharp from the back pocket of his jeans.

"Brooke, leave, now!" I pried her from the carpet, and she turned to Fergal, who was dabbing his neck with his discarded T-shirt.

"Brooke?" Fergal repeated.

Phelan's chest rose as he took a deep breath. I didn't have to tell him my real name; he'd already worked out that I was Lailah. He'd had his suspicions about me all along, and he'd made no secret of his skepticism about Brooke being "the girl." I witnessed the very moment he had worked it out, as the guest at the party had whispered 'voice of an Angel' while I sang. But, that fact was only just this moment dawning on Fergal.

Why hadn't Phelan enlightened him?

Sobbing, Brooke stared up at me. "I'm sorry, Lailah. I was going to tell you. . . . I, I was . . ." Shaking me off, she made for the door behind me. I followed and watched her career into Jonah, who suddenly appeared in the doorway of the motor home.

Cameron, Riley, Claire, and Dylan scattered across the living room, pulling out weapons concealed within their clothing.

I addressed the room. "It's okay, just calm down. Everything's fine."

Brooke was clutching Jonah's waist and crying into his chest. He nudged her away to assess her injures. Scooping her into his arms and stepping through the doorway, he flashed me a quick glance, one that commanded me to follow.

I was only too happy to abide, sensing that our little treaty here was now over, but Fergal's sweet voice made me stop.

"So *you're* Lailah, like?" he said, and despite the fact that a Vampire had just attacked him—and one that was fast becoming his girlfriend, no less—he stretched the widest smile I had seen from him yet.

"I guess so," I answered.

"You're gonna leave now, aren't you?" he asked as Phelan emerged, gesturing for the group to remain still.

"Yes. I'm not sure what just happened in there, but believe me, she wouldn't have meant you any harm. She's quite taken with you," I finished in a whisper.

"Yeah, I know, like," Fergal said, cricking his neck where he was still pressing his T-shirt to his pierced skin. He strolled over to me and squeezed the tops of my arms, his close proximity somehow making me calm. "I need you to come with me," he said quietly.

Over Fergal's shoulder, Phelan's eyes rolled to the floor and then settled back on me. He shook his head with a lack of understanding.

The room was silent; only Riley had moved, repositioning himself next to Claire.

Impatient, Phelan took matters into his own hands as he directed himself to the band of soldiers. "Riley, call Jack; get him back. Time to lock and load, lads."

Phelan marched over to me, taking up a position next to Fergal. "You're coming back to Lucan with us. And I suspect your *friends* are not going to be all too willing to let us take you so easily," Phelan growled.

I looked to Fergal and back to Phelan. They really had no idea what I could do: I only had to think and I could disappear. "I'm not going with you, and it's me you would need to persuade, so tell them to put their weapons away, Phelan!" I hissed.

Taking a cigarette from behind his ear, Phelan lit up. The tip burned a bright orange as he tugged. "We were tasked to seek you out and save you, and that's what we're going to do. Traveling with demons and some sort of double-agent Angel isn't safe. Look at what that thing just did to Fergal." He blew the smoke through his nose. "Fergal, go get Iona. We're going home." He turned away from us.

"You get Iona," Fergal said. "I need to speak with Lailah, alone." He placed his hand across my back and encouraged me to exit the motor home with him.

As I strode through the room, Gabriel's words swirled around my consciousness. *Lai, is everything okay?*

Yes, I answered. I didn't know whether Gabriel had sensed my unease or whether Malachi had spoken with him before departing. Jonah and Brooke hadn't yet returned to the property. They were up ahead, and Jonah was still consoling Brooke.

Tell Iona what you need to and quick. Get the others out—it's time we were leaving.

As I communicated by thought, Fergal tried to lead me around the back of the motor home and I halted, watching Riley sling crossbows into the waiting arms of the young lads. Cameron—the last to receive his—struggled to catch it and bumbled nervously as he tried to grip it in his small arms.

It was definitely time to go.

"Tell them to wait inside. I'm not having a conversation with you while they attack my family, Fergal," I barked.

"Aye," he said, nodding. Shouting now to his group, he said, "Wait inside with that lot, yeah? Don't be forgetting who's in charge, like."

Riley and Dylan exchanged silent glances, but they seemed to listen. Yelling back their acknowledgments, they further rustled around, but then one by one they filtered back inside.

"Let's take a walk," Fergal said.

"No. Say what you have to say here, and do it fast," I insisted, uncomfortable with the situation that was brewing.

Fergal shivered next to me and fingered his bloodied T-shirt, which he still clutched in his hand. Then he pulled it over his head, messing up his white-blond hair as he did. "I really do need for you to come with me. There's someone that's waiting to meet you."

I offered him a weary smile. "I'm sorry. I really do have to go now, but *thank you* for coming for me. And I'm sorry about your father, for all of your family that lost their lives when he did."

Phelan appeared around the side of the motor home. He shoved Fergal in the chest, and I stepped around them, preparing to travel back to the main house.

Fergal's hand found my bare arm, tugging me back toward him. "It's your ma, Lailah."

My mother?

"I arranged a meeting place, a time . . . about half a mile away," he said, pointing in the direction of the tree line. "I was about to take you—Brooke, but seems I'd have been taking the wrong girl," he said smoothly.

Brooke's cries and ramblings about being sorry raced through my mind. She'd discovered that Fergal knew where my mother was, but she hadn't told me. No—she'd lied to me. And I knew exactly why. She'd have had no choice then but to reveal that she wasn't me, and clearly she was unprepared to do that for her own selfish reasons. I guess leopards don't change their spots overnight.

A new wave of hope flowed through me. I wanted to meet my mother, to see that she was still alive, and to seek guidance. Nothing had changed. "Take me to her now," I demanded. Changing direction, I walked toward the forest. Fergal immediately followed.

Phelan trailed us. "What are you talking about? You don't know where the Angel is! I knew you were up to something. What the feck are you doing, Fergal?"

Fergal stopped only briefly to reply. "As much as my pa preferred you, seems yours favored me. He was the one who received the message, and he passed it to me before he died. The only thing I have been *up to* is fulfilling my duties as the leader of the Sealgaire, which don't concern you."

I looked to Phelan over my shoulder, and for a moment he hung back, his face falling; but then his lips formed a narrow line, and he shook his head. "You're full of shite. Lailah—"

"Ignore him," Fergal said.

I hesitated. Now fully fueled, I concentrated on Phelan, and a white-silver outline revealed itself to me, flickering around his form. He was a light soul, and disgruntled and hostile as his disposition was, he hadn't made any dark choices.

"You can trust me. You can't trust him," Fergal said firmly. Taking my arm, he gave me a reassuring squeeze. Once again I was overcome with a sense of peace; there was no indication of anything untoward in Fergal's actions.

I continued on. I was going to meet my mother.

I wanted to reach out and tell Gabriel what was happening, but he'd made it abundantly clear that he trusted no one. He would never allow such a meeting. Hanora's fate only compounded my belief that Gabriel would take away my choice in a heartbeat, if he thought he was protecting me.

"I can't let you take her." Phelan broke my train of thought as he whipped a revolver from behind his back, clicking back the safety in one flush movement.

Fergal sighed, placing his hand on his own back pocket, and I realized then that he had a gun of his own. But instead of brandishing it, he cocked his head toward Phelan. "*He* threw a silver net over you; I didn't. . . . *He* was the one that shot you in that field in Creigiau. Do we really need to waste time playing stick-em-up?"

I paused, turning back to Phelan, who looked up to the sky and back down to the ground, cursing under his breath.

I gulped in terrible understanding. "That's why you were asking about the scar on my shoulder. You thought I was the girl in the clearing that night?" Phelan had shot me, and in the back no less.

"I was trying—"

Fergal interrupted, not allowing Phelan to finish his sentence. "Lailah, she's waiting."

The thought hadn't even fully formed, yet I was suddenly nose to nose with Phelan, my fingers wrapped around the end of the revolver, slinging it far into the distance before he could even blink. I growled a low and sinister sound.

"I didn't mean to shoot you; I was aiming for the Vampire," he muttered under his breath, and for once he seemed unnerved by my actions.

A cloudy red fog appeared across my vision. "I'd say I trust you about as far as I could throw you, but believe you me, I could throw you very, *very* far. Stay away," I hissed.

Phelan remained where he stood, and I marched back to Fergal, gesturing for him to proceed. This time, Phelan didn't try to come after us, taking off back toward the main house. He was going to tell Gabriel, but it didn't matter. By the time Phelan reached him, I would have already met my mother.

Fergal and I continued briskly through the land at the back of the estate, heading toward the tree line. I ran my eyes over Fergal's body; the scent of the fresh blood on his sweater permeated the air. "You couldn't have changed your top?"

"Naw, sorry." He pulled the collar away from his neck and inspected the stains. "I'm gonna have to get it cleaned. It's Iona's gift to me for my birthday. She'll get upset if she sees it ruined."

We were nearing the forest trees that bordered the fields, and as I looked for an opening, Fergal's words broke my concentration. "Your birthday?"

"Aye," he said, nodding.

"I thought it was Iona's birthday today."

"And mine, we're twins. We exchanged presents early; we always do. You're welcome to sing me 'Happy Birthday' by the way." He smiled, but I detected the elevation in his pitch.

If they were twins, then why was Iona transitioning but not Fergal? They had the same mother, a fallen Angel; they were both Of Elfi; and at midnight they both had turned seventeen.

Fergal straightened himself as he placed his hand to the small of my back, guiding me through the tall trees to a clearing. As his body came close to my own, my whizzing thoughts simply slowed, and I felt that sense of serenity that I had felt with him before.

I pulled away, unable to make sense of what I thought I knew, and lingered where I stood. Gabriel had said that if a child of a fallen Angel's soul was pure when they turned seventeen, then they transitioned. *Fergal was not transitioning.*

"What's wrong?" he asked.

I put up my hand and took several steps away from him. "Just, stay there for a minute," I said calmly.

I backed up, only stopping when my heels kicked into bulging roots protruding from the mud. A raven flew from a branch behind Fergal, whipping past my shoulder and momentarily distracting me. Fergal didn't shift and simply returned my stare.

I searched for the glow—for that white-and-silver pulse that should have been gently exuding from his form—but I couldn't focus on the outline of his body; my eye was continually drawn to the cross around his neck, which for the first time I noticed had a slight luminosity to it. Although it would be invisible to the human eye, the glimmer of pure white around the gold was unmistakably the same as the light I had seen stemming from my crystal.

"Where did you get that pendant from, Fergal?" I asked carefully, taking a moment to scan the clearing and the forest of trees behind him.

"What—this? Been in the O'Sileabhin family for generations. Passed down to each leader of the Sealgaire." He paused. "It belongs to Padraig," he said. Distracted, he peered over my shoulder, his eyes no longer meeting my own.

When I was near to Fergal I felt at ease, a sense of complete peace. I had never searched for the outline of light around his form; I hadn't needed to because of the way he made me feel. And there was light, but I realized now that it wasn't coming from him; it had come from the cross he wore around his neck.

I ran over to Fergal, snapping the chain around his neck and launching it far away from the two of us. He glared at me with dipping eyebrows as I shoved him away.

There was no glow.

I felt nothing.

In Fergal's company, Brooke had felt the same as me. He seemed to be a light soul, and she had assumed that to be the reason she hadn't felt the compulsion to drink from him. But he had been refastening his necklace when I had walked into the bedroom.

He wasn't wearing it when she attacked him.

Fergal wasn't a light soul. That was why he wasn't transitioning. Whatever that pendant was, or whatever had been done to it and whether Fergal knew it or not, it had camouflaged him well.

"Fergal, what do you mean, it belongs to Padraig? He's gone," I said.

He didn't answer.

I took a breath. "My mother's not here. She was never going to be . . ."

Fergal's mouth fell open and his pupils swelled to twice their usual size. I mistook his shocked expression as being a reaction to my statement.

I shook my head, ready to disappear from here, knowing now that he had fooled me.

At the same moment that I closed my eyes, canines cracked and pierced the back of my bare neck. I couldn't prevent the paralyzing poison from entering my system before I had a chance to will myself away.

I hadn't seen a rift or heard the Pureblood creeping behind me. No, he had already arrived. He was already waiting.

I should have seen the sign, the warning—the raven.

I remembered this feeling.

THIRTY

THE POISON SWAM THROUGH my veins, and my body stalled. My eyes were frozen open, fixed on Fergal's panicked expression as he tripped over himself, stumbling backward.

"You have her, now give me him." Fergal's words shook, and they left his mouth with a whimper.

I heard the Pureblood's jaw crack before a ghastly screech left his lungs. I couldn't twist or turn my body to see him, but unlike the last time—when I had been poisoned by Eligio—my thoughts, though they dipped in and out, were at least coherent. It wasn't having the same effect on me as it had the last time. But my body was different now; it wasn't human—I was something else.

A figure strode past and finally stood between me and Fergal. A mass of unkempt, shaggy dark hair framed his flawless white skin. I recognized him as the boy from the photo in Iona's locket.

It was Padraig.

The Pureblood's screeching hisses echoed through the small clearing and ricocheted off the trees. He was laughing.

Fergal fell to his knees, covering his face with his hand. "No! I don't understand. . . ."

His brother stood before him, a Vampire.

I was a bargaining chip. Fergal was delivering me in exchange for his brother. He thought Padraig was still alive, and alive he was, but Fergal hadn't counted on them having changed him. But then, why would he have? The Sealgaire thought that Vampires came from Hell itself; they didn't believe that they had been human once. An unfortunate miscalculation for all of us.

Padraig was growling, his irises swirling a dangerous red, and his fangs cracked over the top of his lip. And while Fergal sobbed, all around us rifts were forming. Black slits opened up one by one, as though the scenery were a photograph through which someone was dragging a knife.

Padraig searched behind me, perhaps awaiting a signal. And then it came—a moment later, he was charging toward Fergal, seizing him from the ground and thrusting him against a tree.

I blinked. I was *able* to blink.

I needed to find my light through the poison. I thought of Gabriel, singing astride Uri, and the memory ignited a spark within my chest.

I thought of Gabriel again and once more the white flame flared, but the poison overran it, and the light was extinguished.

As the Pureblood roved ahead of me, the material of his cloak brushed my ear. He extended his clawed hand, which clutched a black crystal.

Malachi had been right. The Purebloods were using the crystals to command the doorways between the third and the second dimension.

Still unable to move, all I could do was watch Fergal struggle as Padraig twisted his arm around Fergal's neck.

A black ribbon of ink began to spill from the crystal in the Pure-blood's palm, feeding into the most prominent rift, which had opened up a few meters away from the tree that Fergal was pinned against.

Black liquid oozed from the crystal and hooked through each rift like thread on a needle, until all the rifts were joined by a dark circle. The pattern repeated, creating a cone shape above us, so that we were all sealed inside this circle of death.

Just then, Jonah and Brooke appeared. They slid to a stop only a few millimeters from the rings of dark matter.

Jonah's eyes met mine. He couldn't pass through. The darkness was seeping from the third. He would be ended if he touched it—his form would dissolve and the darkness that made up his soul would be pulled in.

Jonah's eyes flickered to the largest rift, which was fueling the black spiral around us. His expression was the same one that he'd worn on the day the Vampires descended on the Hedgerley house. The same one he'd worn the night Zherneboh had appeared on the mountaintop. Fear. Fear for me.

Jonah's fear ignited another spark in my chest, but this time the spark didn't die. It roared into a white-and-blue flame until an un-stoppable fire burned within me, consuming all the poison. Jonah was the air the spark needed to grow.

Brooke screamed for me to help Fergal. Even if I could have traveled by thought, I couldn't use that ability to get away from here. I would still pass through the twills, and my form would bleed into them, and I would be stolen away to the third. As I glanced from

Brooke's desperate face to Fergal's, I knew that even if I were somehow able to escape, I couldn't abandon Fergal here to die despite what he had done. Brooke and I might have a difficult relationship, but it was one I had come to value, and she would never forgive me if I didn't help him.

I rose to my feet. The ground beneath me trembled as a tumultuous noise rumbled through the forest.

The Pureblood's Second Generation Vampires were swarming.

They were outside the barriers, and I snapped my head to see the first of an army stampeding toward Jonah and Brooke, who jumped high in the air. As they did, Gabriel appeared in a bright white blur, not far from where they had stood only moments ago.

I didn't have time to exchange even a quick glance with Gabriel; the gurgle of Fergal's blood as Padraig fed on him demanded my attention.

Within a moment, I had Padraig by his neck, ripping him away from Fergal with such force that as the Vampire met the dirt, the ground opened up, making a crater.

Fergal slumped down the tree's side, and the Pureblood hissed behind me. I tore Fergal's T-shirt from around him and used it to apply pressure to his broken skin. My fangs cracked in reaction to the coppery smell, and it was obvious by Fergal's blood drenching through the shirt in a matter of seconds that Padraig had caused too much damage.

In my peripheral vision, sheets of white flashed in succession as Gabriel wielded his light in short sharp bursts, ending wave after wave of Second Generation Vampire outside our cage.

Brooke had made her way around the dark rifts, ducking as a Vampire flew over her head. "Lailah, behind you!"

Padraig had me by the arm, and as he snapped it backward, my bone dislocated from my shoulder. But a second later the injury had repaired.

"Don't hurt him," Fergal said as I spun around to face his brother.

The Pureblood was stalking toward me now, and Padraig was already lunging for my neck.

I clenched my hand into a fist and then opened it away from my body, in the Pureblood's direction. I willed a pulse of light to form. It did.

A whirling ball floated above my palm. I thought of it growing, and it obeyed my imagination. It flashed once, twice, then on the third pulse, it projected and spread, producing a sheet of light, in a similar way I had seen with Gabriel. The light held the Pureblood back. I swept my foot across Padraig's ankles, causing him to plummet back to the dirt. I pressed down on his chest, immobilizing him. He was no match for my strength.

Somehow I needed to command the largest rift to dissipate. If the darkened crystal had opened it, then it could close it, too. But the crystal was still in the Pureblood's possession.

A fierce battle weaved its way through the trees surrounding us. The screech of Vampires being incinerated by Gabriel's light filtered through gaps in the rings.

Jonah was now to my left, behind Brooke. I felt his emotions as he tore out the throats of his attackers. He wasn't struggling, and I wondered if it was my blood in his system that made him more powerful than they were.

The sound of gunfire marked the arrival of the Sealgaire as they took aim at the demons. Ahead of me, a silver-speared arrow sailed through the air, narrowly missing a Vampire as he darted out of the way. It glided to the middle of a ring. Instinctively, I raised my available hand to protect my face, but as the arrow glided through the ink it simply disappeared.

That settled it. We couldn't get out, and nothing could get in.

I had to end Padraig. I exchanged a silent glance with Fergal. He knew what I was about to do, and he shook his head, pleading with me to let his brother live.

My sheet of light was still up, maintaining a wall between the Pureblood and us. Padraig's eyes blazed and his lips spat fire as he thrashed below my foot. He might have been Fergal and Iona's brother once, but there was nothing of who he was left now.

"I'm sorry, Fergal," I apologized quietly as I bent my knee back, allowing Padraig to spring into the air.

The Vampire cricked his neck, but his snarl faded to a surprised whimper. My fist had already broken through his chest, and I coughed back the bile rising in my throat as I spread my hand wide.

The Vampire's eyes drifted to my arm, and then, with a look of incomprehension, they rested on mine. Black lines crisscrossed up his fair skin. They grew up his neck and over his face like branches and then stemmed into blotted thorns. I tore my hand from inside his chest, and he fell backward. The ink seemed to seep through his form, like layers of barbed wire, and his body separated into tiny pieces. So close to the rings, Padraig's remains were pulled inside.

"Lailah!" Jonah's voice dipped in and out, but I was so horrified by the sight in front of me that I smelled the melting silver and lead a fraction too late as a bullet nipped the skin of my lower back.

I reeled around; Fergal was slouched against the tree stump, barely managing to keep his shaking arm steady as he lowered his gun.

My hands fell, and I searched my back. There was a hole in my shirt, and my flesh burned. Pain was all I knew in that moment. I choked, blood rushing up my throat, and the metallic rust seeped in between my teeth.

The protective sheet of light had evaporated, and though the Pureblood was stalking toward me, I fell to my knees, dizzy.

The flashes of light outside had ceased, and Gabriel shouted, powerless to stop what would come next.

"Take the bullet out," Ruadhan commanded. He was straight ahead of me, crouched down outside my cage. His determined gaze locked to mine. "Reach in and take it out, now."

I dug my fingers into my own flesh, feeling for the origin of the searing heat.

The tip of my thumb burned as I found the bullet, and I swallowed back my blood as I dislodged it from my back.

My distorted thoughts reformed as I panted. My skin was mending, but the Pureblood already had me by the scruff. He spun me around to face him, and his fangs ripped through my neck easily. He pumped venom through my system before I could try to defend myself.

I had never felt the sting of this kind of venom. The poison that they had used twice to immobilize me was different; it acted as an anesthetic, freezing me. He held me suspended above the ground, and my legs flailed beneath me.

Gabriel glowed from behind the Pureblood's form, where he was now striking the formation of rings with bouts of white light, but it had no effect on the deadly twills.

If Malachi was right, then the third dimension was purely a state of cold dark matter from which the black ribbons were originating. Gabriel's light might hold back the darkness, but here in the second dimension, it couldn't overcome it.

The Pureblood's venom invaded me.

I was defeated.

The Pureblood cracked his jaw. Fighting was useless, and my heavy head fell forward. But then, I saw: There was no mark above this Pureblood's eyebrow. Zherneboh hadn't come himself; he had sent another. Why?

The Pureblood's claws scraped down my arm, creating streaks of my blood, and then he punctured my wrist as he lifted it to his vile maw.

And as venom slowly traveled down my veins, my arm began to blacken. Tattoolike markings formed across my skin.

He was trying to resurrect the girl in shadow. She was different from me. They thought she would abide them with no question, with no moral conscience of any kind. They thought she would be their weapon to wield. He didn't know that if my soul was painted black, I would be ended.

In the background, Jonah shouted, "Emery!"

The Gualtiero Emery.

This was Jonah's maker.

That name made my eyes flare red. This was the Pureblood that had changed Jonah, who had stolen his life from him.

That name was like an anchor, weighing me down.

That name made me want to fight.

Jonah's words returned to me: *Embrace all that you are, and you will be untouchable. . . .*

It had been easy to embrace the light, but I hadn't wanted to embrace the darkness. Because I was too afraid that what I would gain would pale in comparison with what I stood to lose. But I had absorbed the sun and taken the dark energy from Jonah's blood. I was now fully loaded—all I needed was the courage to fire.

Grabbing me by my T-shirt, the Pureblood lifted me higher into the air and drew me back toward his body. His split tongue spat over his bottom lip as he licked my neck, tasting my skin, preparing to finish what he'd started.

I needed to be brave.

I had to stop living for Gabriel and start living for me instead. Or I wouldn't live at all. I was finally ready to embrace what and who I was.

I closed my eyes. I stopped fighting the dark venom and simply welcomed it. I inhaled, locked in concentration, encouraging it not to overrun my soul but instead to dilute and merge with my gray being. My inner storm grew as the darkness formed with the rest of me. I let my body absorb it, and with all my will I commanded it with the power of thought to reach a natural balance.

I flashed my eyes open.

"No," I said coolly.

The Pureblood withdrew; he was a millisecond away from splitting the skin above my collarbone. He looked to my arm, and his huge black orbs grew even wider as the tattoo markings disappeared from my skin.

An upsurge of power exploded, coursing through my entire being, wonderful and wicked.

I was unbreakable. Unstoppable. *Untouchable.*

Emery released me, but I didn't clatter to the ground; I remained levitating in midair and I parted my lips slightly, growling in a low hum.

"Zherneboh didn't come for me himself." I paused, listening to the sound of Fergal's chest barely rising and falling. "Because he knows what I am capable of."

I gestured to the darkened crystal still held in Emery's palm. "Close it. Now." I tipped my chin toward the most prominent rift.

A sinister hiss sounded through Emery's pointed fangs. I anticipated his next move as he slinked away, preparing to jump back through the gateway. Within a blink, I had my hands at the top of his cloak, holding him to the spot, still several feet from the cold ground.

Suddenly, it was no longer enough to simply escape. No—I wanted vengeance.

"I would tear your heart out for all you've done, but I doubt you have one." I rolled the tip of my index finger over Emery's chest, bringing it to his chin and forcing it up so his eyes were unable to escape mine. "Throw it in," I commanded.

This time the Pureblood obeyed me, and as the crystal flew through the air, the rift pulled it inside. Once swallowed up, the black spiral started to uncoil from the top down. The sun broke through and shone onto Emery's deformed face, making him flinch.

The Second Generations halted, witnessing their Master answering to me. They shrieked and began to scatter across the landscape. The Sealgaire capitalized, firing rounds of shots. I tightened my lips into a hostile, hateful grin.

I didn't need to close my eyes to witness the storm across my vision. The sky above had transformed into a canvas of white and black bolts that electrified the sky.

Lightning streaked and forked into three.

I ascended high into the air, and with one hand I dragged Emery up with me.

The Pureblood's shrill cry fell against the stillness. There was no wind or rain, but I could see in the distance a flock of ravens flying away from his desperate hysteria.

Inside my palm, I willed my essence, and it came in the form of a plume of smoke, only this time the smoke was not black. Instead, it was the color of my soul. It was gray. The Pureblood snapped his jaw closed, so I willed the smoke to travel to his orifices instead.

I knew then that I was capable of what they were not. I was an impossible palette. I was what they could not be. I was the in-between, just like this dimension, and Earth was my home, not theirs. Here, I could prevail.

As my essence filled him in the form of smoke, it suffocated his dark being, assailing his insides and manipulating his makeup with my own gray matter. He would never win this fight. I watched his expression flash as he began to battle with himself. "Let's see if you will live or die, shall we?"

The thunder pounded in waves of two.

A glow warmed my neck as a tear formed in the air behind me. I had attracted the attention of the Arch Angels. Still, I focused intently on the Pureblood—if the Arch Angels were coming, then they were welcome to watch.

The Pureblood's tattoos, which ran in quill shapes across his face and down his neck, wobbled as though they were separate from his skin. They began to fade, and as they transcended his form, they grew into feathered wings behind his back.

I stifled a breath.

Emery's body flitted in and out of focus, and I tightened my clenched fist gripping his cloak. He opened his mouth, his fangs still prominently displayed, and the smoke leaving my raised palm ceased.

I looked over my shoulder. A single, towering figure hovered in front of a golden splinter in the air. The Arch Angel had magnificent white wings that curled almost hypnotically behind his back. He inched forward, and I commanded the gray smoke once again within my palm. He raised his hand and stopped, maintaining his distance.

I turned my attention back to Emery. Black fissures had splintered across the sclera framing his now-sapphire gems, and gradually they became nothing more than dirtied, soaking puddles. His eyes burst, bleeding down his cheeks, robbing him of his sight.

His skin was tearing away, leaving his decaying, flesh-colored muscle exposed. The stringy veins growing up his hands grew thicker and then ruptured. Black oil spewed from them.

His inner conflict raged. He couldn't accept the light and the dark mixture; it was a cancer, eating away at him from the inside out.

"Mercy!" he spat.

His skeletal hand lashed in the air as he searched for my own and finally his fingers crept around my wrist. As he squeezed, his digits broke apart against my hard skin.

I stared at him, knowing that what Malachi had said was absolutely true; knowing that Emery was begging for a quicker demise, perhaps to leave in light the same way he had come.

He was not worthy of such an end.

His wings began to wilt, and finally the thinning feathers depleted and then fell away.

The anguished sound reverberating from his throat was one of torture.

I wavered for the briefest moment, but then I thought of Jonah and what Emery had done to him, and hundreds, maybe thousands more. I would see his execution through on their behalf; they deserved their revenge, and so did I. He would provide me with my gratification.

Self-appointed judge and jury, I would ensure justice was done. My eyes slanted, and I tipped my chin, staring at the Arch Angel over my shoulder. Speaking to him directly, I delivered my final verdict—one that was intended for both Emery and the Arch Angels.

"No mercy."

Emery gurgled in the back of his throat and the last of his skin slowly dripped from around his face. The sound stopped as his lizardlike tongue melted away; blind and mute, he could no longer plead. His extended suffering bolstered my resolve, and I only uncurled my knuckles from around his cloak when he had finally finished burning.

Embers of gray ash rained down now from the heavens to the Earth.

The silence fell at once.

THIRTY-ONE

It was as though sound no longer existed. The world, acting as my audience to Emery's execution, had sucked it all away, taking a horrified gasp as it watched me.

The warmth on the back of my neck had left, along with the Arch Angel, and the rift he had created in the sky sealed.

I drifted down to the ground. I found my feet, but my body was shaking, as the adrenaline petered out. I stared up to the heavens, the sky in between the swaying treetops swirling back to a pastel blue, the sun stretching its rays and lighting the clearing.

The black threads had looped their way back into the third, and the most prominent doorway was the only one that remained. It had decreased in size and was slowly diminishing.

Next to the rift, Brooke hunched over Fergal, and, like a waterfall cascading over a cliff, her cries rushed to me. The Sealgaire, Ruadhan, and Gabriel were gaping at me, transfixed. Relieved, shocked, appalled, maybe, by what they had seen me do to Emery. Phelan broke his gaze away from me long enough to attempt to help Fergal.

Gabriel's expression was one of distress; who knew what he thought of me now that he had seen me do what I had once thought myself incapable of.

I sought out Jonah, but he was already making his way across the clearing, watching as Phelan tried to pry Brooke from Fergal.

Jonah wrapped his arms under Brooke's, dragging her backward, allowing Phelan to get to his cousin. Desperate, Brooke knocked him with a frenzied force. He staggered backward and stood unbalanced in front of the diminishing rift.

Brooke yanked Phelan off Fergal, and I wasn't sure at that moment which of her impulses was more prominent—the need to get him to help or the desire to drink his blood. Brooke hauled Fergal over her shoulder in a clean, quick movement and fled deep into the forest.

Jonah's conflicted eyes stewed with indecision. Why wasn't he going after her? There was nothing to keep him here.

Jonah looked up at me, and I locked my stare with his. I felt his anxious, hesitant feelings swelling low in my gut.

Gabriel was immediately behind me, his hands clasped around my chest, and he nuzzled into my neck. He was whispering something in my ear, but I didn't respond. My attention instead was ahead of me, placed firmly on Jonah, who was flicking up the hood of his jacket.

Gabriel took my hand, but my eyes didn't meet his. I felt his grip tighten as he looked from Jonah to me. His fingers began to dig into my skin.

You were wearing Jonah's jacket. . . . Gabriel spoke to me in private.

Now, I turned to him. My eyes darted over his face, taking in

349

every twitch of his muddled expression. I thought he had known that I had drunk from Jonah, but that he hadn't wanted to utter the words aloud.

I had been wrong.

His lips parted ever so slightly, but he didn't speak; instead I heard him in my mind.

It wasn't Azrael's blood. . . . It was Jonah's.

Every muscle in Gabriel's body tensed. I tried to speak to Gabriel's mind in return, but all I could hear as I reached out was the final verse of our song, the verse I had been unable to recall, his voice singing:

*When e'en the wreaths in which I dress thee, are sadly mixed,
half flowers half chains.*

They had always been Gabriel's lines; he had sung them to me. Unable to stop the image of my lifeless body laid on top of straw, the memory appeared in his mind and transferred into my own. I was lying there, still, with a crown of red and white rose petals placed delicately across my forehead.

I didn't have an opportunity to explore any further; Gabriel looked to the left and then his hands rose to his torso. Before I had a chance to consider why, he had thrust them to my chest and sent me sailing away from him.

I was pushing my body out of free fall when I caught glimpses of a tremendous surge of light pulsing from where I had just been. I regained control of my tumbling body and landed on my tiptoes. I raised my palm to my forehead as a pounding beat sounded in my mind.

Ruadhan appeared instantly and blocked my line of sight. Spinning me around, he enfolded his arms around my back, pressing me protectively to his chest, where he tried to hold me captive.

I quickly broke away to see Gabriel's hands stretched out in front of him, fragments of yellow electrifying the particles of air. I followed their path: They led to the last remains of the black smudge that had been the rift to the third. It swallowed itself whole, disappearing completely.

The rumble in my temple faded, leaving behind a low thud.

To the right, Phelan was bent over, hands clamped over his head as though bombs had fallen from the sky. Members of the Sealgaire were scattered around the broken trees, mouths agape, looking on with astonishment.

I searched the clearing, trying to ascertain what had just happened. Maybe something had tried to reemerge from the rift from behind where Jonah had been standing. Gabriel must have seen and pushed me away before expelling his light, to catapult it back through, causing the rift to dissolve even faster. I decided that Jonah must have fled. We'd said our final farewell, and I was glad—I couldn't bear another one.

Gabriel's arms were trembling.

Gabriel, I called over the top of the thud reverberating inside me.

He didn't answer.

I tried to speak to him again, but still he didn't reply. There was no sheet of light; he wasn't blocking me. He was just . . . absent.

Gabriel dropped to his knees, his shoulders hunched, and his hands fell to the top of his legs. I rushed forward, stooping to the ground, and took him in my arms. "What happened?" I asked.

Ruadhan's palm spread at the nape of my neck. "Ruadhan, you should go after Brooke. You need to help Jonah," I instructed, presumptuously.

He didn't shift from me.

"Please! Go!" I commanded.

Ruadhan parted from me, but he didn't leave.

I cupped Gabriel's face with my hands. "Gabriel, please. Tell me, what happened? Are you hurt?"

His skin was like dry ice against my palms. I tried to connect to his aura, but I could no longer feel him.

Then he reached for my waist, finally meeting my gaze.

His Adam's apple bulged as he swallowed. I stifled a whimper at the sight of his eyes. They were empty; the light behind them had vanished. The lines across his skin were deeper, stretching farther, and as I glanced down to his hands, there were hundreds of dark spots speckled over his skin.

"You've lost your light. . . . You've fallen," I whispered, disbelieving. My breath caught in the back of my throat. "No." I froze.

Gabriel shifted, pressing his thumbs to my hip bones. He tugged the hem of my T-shirt as he placed his cheek in my lap.

"There was no demon. . . ." I pushed Gabriel away by his shoulders, and my weight tipped forward to the ground. Disoriented, I crawled across the mud, digging my fingernails into the dirt, over to where Jonah had been only minutes ago.

I tore at the top layer of earth underneath my palm, searching. There was no ash, no sign he had ever been here at all. He was just gone.

Gone.

My insides hollowed, my head spun, and the only thing that remained was a dull echo that ricocheted off my empty walls.

I don't know why, but I began to claw at the ground, as though I were trying to burrow a way to wherever he might be.

Infuriated, crimson tears poured down my cheeks. My blood was his blood; he'd sacrificed it only hours ago, and I knew that every drop that left me was irreplaceable.

I felt Ruadhan's hands pulling me up. "Enough, now," he said somberly.

I struggled beneath him, thrusting my weight back to the ground. I pummeled the dirt, wishing that I could feel physical pain, but there was none.

Ruadhan bent down and whispered in my ear. "I'm so sorry, love. Please—"

I allowed him to pull me up and lock me in tight. A faint, pitiful squeak escaped my lips. The taut muscles in my torso unclenched, and my arms fell loose. My clay-covered fingernails dropped wearily down at my thighs.

"We have to leave now," Ruadhan said eventually, placing me steadily on my feet, but he continued to clutch my waist, supporting me.

I glanced over my shoulder, to where Gabriel sat on his knees, but I couldn't bring myself to meet his eyes.

The Irish lads remained where they stood, entirely still, heads down. They didn't make a sound. This was what people did for the dead, but it was to me they were showing their respect—not to a demon, not to Jonah.

I stared blankly up at the sky. My jaw unhinged and with an ear-splitting scream, I cried for him.

I sat hunched over on a stool in my bedroom. Many hours had rolled over, and Ruadhan had attempted to pry me away several times. Somehow it felt as though if I left this place, I was leaving Jonah behind; I was accepting that he was never coming back. I wondered if that was why Jonah hadn't left before I did, if he had felt the same way about me.

It was the early stages of twilight, and I'd traced the outline of the small chandelier hanging from the ceiling over and over, trying to distract myself from the pain of reality.

I was sick of it, sick of this.

Gabriel was fallen now, and like Iona he would wear away slowly—like an aging building, completely vulnerable to anyone who wanted to bulldoze it. And Jonah was gone. I had doomed them both to terrible fates.

My desire to meet my mother had cost me more than I was able to bear. What was I thinking?

I knew exactly what. I had wanted her to tell me what to do, which path to take, because I didn't trust myself to make that decision.

I couldn't hide from the gut-wrenching thoughts that persisted.

This was where the truth really lived.

I held my new ring in between my fingertips, finally sounding out the reason I had threaded it back to the chain. It was not out of comfort, as I had said; it was because I hadn't been brave enough to say no.

I pushed myself off the stool and wandered over to the door.

When I opened it, Gabriel had his back to the wall, slouched down—waiting for me. I wished he weren't.

"Lailah," he said, ushering me back inside. He reached for the light switch, but I pushed his arm down, shaking my head.

"Don't turn it on. There's no place for light in this room. I want to be in the dark," I spat.

He looked at me wearily and then gestured for me to sit, but I remained standing. He had changed; now dressed in a high-neck sweater and jeans, his face looked washed out.

"We need to move on," he said quietly.

I shifted my weight where I stood and looked him square in the eyes. "Are we really not going to talk about him? About what you did?" I took a deep breath. "You killed Jonah, Gabriel. Why? Why did you do it, to him and to yourself?" I demanded coldly. Though my words were fraught, I felt detached, as though it hadn't really happened.

Gabriel cleared his throat and took my hands in his. "Lai, I was fortifying your life. You drank his blood, you bonded yourself to him, and he was bonded to you. It was too dangerous; you'd have ended each other." He spoke softly, squeezing my hands inside his.

"You killed him because you were protecting me? Not because you were angry, or jealous, or . . ." My stomach somersaulted. I thought Gabriel had reacted in fury, lost control maybe, but that wasn't the case. He took Jonah's life in an attempt to preserve mine. And as it had been with Hanora, it was a selfish act—who was he to decide whose life was worth more? The last of his light had drained away by his action. I retreated from him, my palm meeting my cheek as I closed my eyes in horror.

"Everything I have done has always been for you, Lailah," he said flatly, as though this information should not be news to me.

"No, stop saying that, just stop!" I shouted.

Gabriel moved around my side and placed the back of his hands against my neck, brushing them up and over my jaw, finally cupping my cheeks. "I love you. You do what you must for the one you love."

My eyes prickled and one single tear fell—that was all I would allow. "*Oh, Gabriel* . . . You said you would tear down everywhere, until all that was left was nowhere and you would save me." I took a sharp breath. "And all this time, that's exactly what you've been doing: tearing everything, *everyone*, down. Hanora, Jonah, even yourself. And you're doing it to try and save someone who is already dead." I threw his hands off me.

Gabriel's brow dipped. "You're not dead, Lailah."

"I'm *so sorry*, Gabriel. The girl you loved is gone. It's time to let her go."

"What are you saying? I love you, please—" he begged.

I hesitated. I would always love Gabriel, but my choices—his choices—had inadvertently led us away from each other. And in a way I was relieved. I knew where my final destination would be; I think I had always known.

Taking his elbows, I said, "I am the reason you are fallen. Your crystal failed because you acted in darkness and every bit of it belonged to me." I stopped, trying desperately to will the words I thought I would never say to leave my lips. "You were where my life truly began, but you can't follow me anymore. I am heading toward the end, and I will not be the reason for yours. . . . Go to Iona," I said, my voice shaking.

Gabriel faltered when I said her name. "I don't love Iona."

I reached for his temple, pushing his blond curls away from his face, and stroked the deep-set lines stemming from his eyes with my thumb. "You will. I watched you glow when you kissed her, before it turned midnight, before her light met your own. . . ."

Gabriel grimaced, ready to protest, but I pushed on. "The thing about light is that it can be just as blinding as the dark. Maybe you don't see it—maybe you don't want to see it—but you need to take her hand. She will guide you back to the light." My eyes defied me, swelling and becoming puffy.

Gabriel tried to respond, but I pressed my finger to his lips. "She will save you, where I cannot."

"I don't understand. You're sending me away because you're trying to *save me*? Or are you just saying all this because you don't want me anymore?" He fidgeted with the cuffs of his sweater, tugging them over his blemished hands, waiting for my answer.

I pushed up his sleeves, revealing the freckled spots growing up his skin, and he immediately pulled them back down.

"Phelan says that our scars show us to be righteous warriors— heroes, I guess. These are yours, you said so yourself. If you were comfortable with what you did, you wouldn't hide them."

"I only cover them so that there's no confusion over who the hero of this story is, Lailah," he replied quickly.

I watched his top lip tremble. I might not share a connection with him through light anymore, but I didn't need to in order to know that he wasn't being honest. "No, you mask them because you believe they brand you as the villain. And we both know that's not who you are, but it's who you become when you're with me."

He didn't respond, and I knew then that everything I was thinking—everything I was saying—was right. I took his hands in my own and held them tightly. "*'When e'en in wreaths in which I dress thee, Are sadly mixed, half flowers half chains.'* You used to sing those words to me, and later you thought they were about me, didn't you? You placed a crown of roses across my forehead that day." I paused, my mind making sense of it all. "But I think those words were really meant for you. . . . And they always will be, if I don't rewrite them," I murmured.

Silently we watched each other. No more moves to make, it felt like our game was at an end.

I found his lips and kissed him. I savored the moment for as long as I could. Immortal or not, he was my Heaven. That had never changed and never would.

Reluctantly, I pulled away, but his hand swooped to the small of my back and he crushed me into his chest. His kiss was desperate and bittersweet. His eyes brimmed with sadness, and the acidic taste of his lemon tears wet my lips as they spilled, causing my own eyes to water. He brought the tip of his nose up and gently circled my own. Still he clung to me. "I want to be the person you look to, Lai."

A whimper left me as I said, "I have no doubt that one day I will look to you again, Gabriel, but I hope that when that day comes, you will choose instead to look to Iona." My skin tingled as a chill crept up my spine, as though someone were walking over my grave.

He held me in his arms, breathing in the scent of my hair, and I knew that if I didn't do it now I never would.

I released him.

I wobbled toward the door, hardly sure if my legs would be able to carry me.

"Wait!" Gabriel shouted after me. "I can't let you go, if the only reason you are walking away is because you are trying to spare me, Lai." His voice was hoarse.

I stopped.

"How can you even think it would be *possible* for me to love someone else. . . ." His voice dipped as he trailed off. "Because you loved him, didn't you?" He paused. "Tell me you choose him. Even in death, you choose him over me."

I peered over my shoulder but bowed my head. Here, in the twilight of truths, he received the agonizing answer to his quietly spoken question.

"When?" he asked in a murmur.

I stifled a breath, finding myself unable to speak.

"*When* did you fall in love with him?"

I blinked hard and heavy and then met his eyes, revealing the gleam Jonah had left in mine. "Once upon a time, underneath a Christmas tree."

THIRTY-TWO

I AMBLED DOWN THE hallway to Jonah's bedroom. I clicked the door shut before making my way to his bed. I would have to leave here, but not quite yet.

I swayed as I climbed up onto the sheets, and I took his pillow beneath my arms, burying my head in its center. I cried for him like I had never cried before.

I cried for Gabriel, too. For what he'd become. For whatever part I played in what he had become. I cried for Brooke, who had not returned after fleeing. Not knowing if Fergal was dead or alive, I cried for him, and for what that meant for Iona, too. And I cried for me. But mostly I cried for Jonah.

Exhausted and spent, I pushed the pillow aside, but my arm caught on something as I did. I sniffled and then reached inside the pillowcase next to the one I had rested my head upon.

A book was hidden within the cotton case. Cautiously I pulled it out. The bindings were suede leather, and I ran my fingertips across the softness. Untying the string holding it closed together, I unfolded the pages.

The first merely had Jonah's name across the top. My heartbeat quickened, thumping in time to the fading sound of the thud still resounding inside me. I crossed my legs and held it, staring at his full name: Jonah Cyrene. I hadn't even asked him what his surname was, because ever since I met him, everything had always been about me.

Finally, I flipped open the first page and on a sheet of white was a charcoal drawing of a couple holding hands. The woman bore a likeness to Jonah, and I realized then that I was looking at a portrait of Jonah's parents. I hadn't known that he had been some sort of artist; he'd never mentioned his affinity with such a pastime. Tentatively, I slid my index finger behind the sheet and flipped over to the next drawing.

I dropped the sketchbook and bounced back as though I had seen a ghost. Slowly, I picked it back up and ran my eyes over every curve of the young girl's image. Her wide smile made her leap off the page, bringing her to life.

It was the butterfly girl.

Her eyes depicted star shapes as they searched the sky. She was dressed in a cardigan, shaded in black charcoal, over a long dress that swept her ankles. I traced every inch of the drawing, and in the bottom right-hand corner I found a date. It was the same day that I had had the vision of her under the willow tree. I had to turn the book in my hands to read *"el efecto mariposa,"* "the butterfly effect," the words the girl had spoken to me written horizontally on the sheet.

I desperately tried to piece together why he had a sketch of the girl who had come to me in my vision, along with the words she had imparted to me. Jonah had said "*el efecto mariposa*" was a sign to him, one that gave meaning to the chaos. I was missing something. It didn't make sense.

I was searching the next page, looking for more pictures of her, when I stopped.

There was a drawing of me, the way I looked before I had re-awakened from my cocoon. Everything about the way I appeared was the same as the reflection I had once seen in the mirror; the only difference was the color of my eyes and hair. But the detail that held me captivated was the smile he had given me, stretching high as though I were laughing. This was the girl Jonah had chased after, the one he protected and the one he wished had never left. As I turned page after page, images of me filled his book. I stopped when I reached one where I was different.

He had drawn me with my hair in a long bob drifting above my shoulders and a distant look across my face. The girl on the sheet was beautiful.

I didn't understand. Jonah had angrily stripped me away, layer by layer, yet he had portrayed me here in a delicate and attractive form.

I pawed through the pages. There were more just like it. I stalled on the last picture—the only one outlined in pencil and painted with oils. Red and white roses were scattered across my bare skin and my confused eyes stared right back at me. Dated today, not yesterday, he had sketched this after he rescued me, and only hours before he had met his end.

This image didn't illustrate revulsion or rejection; it only showed love.

A knock on the door startled me. Then, Ruadhan stepped

through. "Sweetheart, we need to chat," he said, making his way over to me and perching on the end of Jonah's bed.

I cleared my throat, trying to breathe. But I knew that with Jonah gone, I would never be able to breathe easily again.

I sat next to him, draping my legs over the foot of the bed. "Ruadhan," I whispered. "Jonah didn't hate me, did he?"

My makeshift father cuddled the tops of my shoulders, rubbing my back reassuringly. "No, love, of course not."

"No. I mean, he said some things—some dreadful, hurtful things. Do you know what I'm talking about? The way I looked, the way I *felt* to him?" I asked, seeking the truth.

"Aye." Ruadhan brushed the stubble on his chin, appearing awkward.

"He was lying, wasn't he?"

Ruadhan didn't answer me immediately, my question making him uncomfortable. "He was very upset, love. But no, he didn't mean *those* things." He sighed. "I don't want you to think ill of the lad. He felt . . . Well, we all felt you needed to leave him behind. After what happened, he decided that you'd stand a better chance with Gabriel and no *distractions*." Ruadhan paused before offering an apology: "I'm sorry, love."

The conversation I had overheard between Gabriel and Jonah came to my mind; I'd been too fixated on what Jonah had implied about Iona to pay much attention when they had argued over whom I was safest with. It still didn't explain why he had denied me when I tried to kiss him, though, and now I would never know.

"Jonah spoke with you sometimes, didn't he?" I posed.

"Aye, love. On occasion."

I reached for the sketchbook behind me and placed it on my lap. "Did you know that Jonah was an artist?" I asked.

Ruadhan scratched his neck and didn't answer my question. Instead he said, "Lovey, we need to move forward now. We have to leave—tonight."

"Ruadhan, please. Did you know?" I asked again.

He huffed, but then looked at my downturned lips and gave in. "Never really said much about it. I knew he liked to sketch a long time ago, but he stopped. Something about it he found too difficult, I think."

I nodded and carefully tipped the book open to the drawing of the butterfly girl. Ruadhan's bushy eyebrows arched, and he looked from her to me.

"Do you know who this is?" I asked.

Ruadhan shook his head. "No, sweetheart, I don't."

I turned the leather bindings horizontally and pointed to the words in the left corner. "*El efecto mariposa*. Mean anything to you?" I asked, hoping for a glimmer of recognition.

"Aye. Well, some of it at least. Mariposa was Jonah's sister's name. That must be a portrait of her."

Mariposa. Jonah's sister.

The book fell from my grip, and Ruadhan caught it before it hit the floor.

"Don't you dare make her death count for nothing," Jonah had said. I knew who he meant now—Mariposa. Jonah believed his sister had died in order to set off a chain of events that would lead him to me, chaos that had meaning . . . the purpose of which was to save me.

A thousand thoughts tumbled, turning over in my mind. But it was hard to focus on any of them with the drumming sound still beating in the background.

The realization found me, overcoming all other thoughts.

The pound of the drum.

I launched myself from off the bed as though I'd just been shocked. "He's not dead!" I roared.

Ruadhan sprang up, bringing my waving arms down to my sides, trying to calm me. "Love, it's okay to be upset; we are all upset. But he is *gone*."

"No, no he's not!" I tugged away. "Ruadhan, please, what did you see when Gabriel expelled his light? What happened?" I demanded.

"You know what happened. Come on now, stop."

"Ruadhan, *tell me*." I grasped him by his shirt.

"Gabriel struck him with his light. He fell backward and then . . . Sweetheart, please, you don't need to do this to yourself," he said, squashing his large hands over mine.

"He fell backward, and then what? There was no ash, no dust, not a trace. . . . Ruadhan, *he didn't burn*," I stated.

"Love, it's over. He's lost to the darkness now."

His words caused the spark in my subconscious to grow. I paced around the room in a small circle, my head held down as I contemplated. "Gabriel's light propelled him backward, and he fell through the rift before it could end him," I said, sounding out my thoughts.

"Even if that were so, he would have lost his form the moment he touched the dark matter." Ruadhan was following my route around the room, trying to stand in my way.

I couldn't argue with Ruadhan—Jonah should have lost his form—but the echo inside me belonged to him. I had thought it to be the remnants of a cry from within Gabriel as his crystal failed, but I was wrong. It had come from Jonah.

Jonah had drunk from me on several occasions; he'd taken my dark matter through my blood. Whatever I had inside me that allowed me to keep my form in all worlds—perhaps this singlet particle that Darwin had told me about—could have just as conceivably transferred to Jonah, too. And his soul was dark; it matched the third. . . .

Jonah was lost to his darkness all right—he was in the third dimension.

But the beat had been fading with every hour that had passed. I didn't have a dark crystal; I couldn't command a rift to the third to open. Was there another option? There was the fixed gateway in Lucan that Gabriel had told me existed. But if I couldn't travel by thought across water, it might be too late by the time I found it.

Ruadhan seized me by my shoulders. He stroked my short hair, tucking the loose strands behind my ears. "You will be okay, I promise. Time heals all things."

I snapped my eyes to his.

"Time. Heals. All," I repeated calmly.

Ruadhan had just given me the solution to an impossible problem.

I knew what I had to do then.

"Love . . . Are you feeling okay? You've been through a lot. We should talk about that, talk about what we're going to do next—"

I cut him off. "I have to go."

"What do you mean? Where to?" he asked.

I cast my gaze back down to the sketchbook, focusing on it as I was flooded by the enormity of what I was about to attempt.

"Lailah."

I grabbed him in a bear hug, kissing him roughly on the cheek, and I smiled at the familiar scratch of his stubble. "Thank you."

I closed my eyes and thought myself away.

I WAS BACK AT the entrance of the forest within a matter of moments. Dusk was fast approaching, twilight was dwindling, but right this moment it matched the color of my soul.

I jumped over the fallen tree trunks and pushed my way through the carpet of bloodied leaves and broken branches. I hadn't taken much time to fully observe the destruction that marked the nightmarish events of this morning, but as I stood on the outskirts of the clearing, a sense of eerie serenity soaked the scenery.

The ground was covered in thick coatings of ash and puddles of goo that were sticking to my shoes. I picked my feet up, marching to where I had stood next to Gabriel. Pressing my palm to my crystal gem, I took comfort from its coolness.

Staring at Jonah's sketchbook, a small voice in the back of my head argued that it wasn't possible, and if it were, who was I to think I could change the past? But I had ended a Pureblood right here—an inconceivable feat.

I steadied my nerves and shut my eyes tightly. I pictured the scene: Jonah positioned ahead and Gabriel behind me. I ran the memory through my mind, looping it over and over, and at first nothing happened. I tried again, this time seeking out the feel of Gabriel's skin on mine.

Warm, sunny shades replaced the drab colors of early dusk, gradually returning me to the echo of this morning.

In my mind's eye, Gabriel sidestepped me, his fingers digging into my skin as he looked from me to Jonah.

As Gabriel raised his hands, I focused as they met my chest. I stretched my mind, reaching out for the feel of his force.

The scene rippled, the colors in the clearing absorbing me into them as I became painted back into the picture.

I let the pressure to my chest travel through me.

I was reliving.

When this had happened to me before, I had wondered whether I was merely trapped inside the events that had come to pass or whether I could somehow change things. Now was the time to find out. Jonah wasn't dead—he was lost, and I was the only one who could rescue him.

I fought hard and swung my body up and away. I landed next to Jonah in a hazy blur. I extended my hand. "No."

Static vibrated in tiny particles, gently bouncing the picture up and down. The pigments of color faded, and my gray bled into the portrait, spilling across the scene. The fractured air hung dubiously, as though Gabriel's light ahead was opposing me. I willed time to remain at bay, and reached for Jonah's jacket. I thrust my weight into his side in an attempt to push us both away. But he didn't budge. I wrapped my arm across his back and tried again, this time bending my knees and jumping. Still he didn't shift.

Flecks of yellow electricity surfaced at the ends of Gabriel's light and the strobes oscillated erratically, beginning to creep nearer.

I cursed myself for my arrogance—and then I thought back to Darwin's theory, and I cursed the man wearing the jacket.

I recalled what Darwin had said: The universe didn't give without taking; all things must be equal.

A small, sarcastic snort left me, and, aware that I was beginning to lose the fight with time, I was left with one final thing to accept and embrace: the exchange.

I unclasped the ring from around my neck and fastened it around Jonah's instead. I was leaving it for Gabriel, giving him the only thing I had left to offer: a second chance.

The sparks lunged forward, streaking into my gray, and I turned to meet Jonah. His eyelashes fluttered ever so gently as the color in his face returned, moving down over him and past his cheekbones.

I whispered quickly in his ear, pausing to see his renewed hazel eyes slowly slide to the corner. He could hear me. Finally, I took the easiest breath of my life, and said, "I came back for you, Jonah."

The only part of this masterpiece that I cared to now regard was his lips. I kissed them for one last time, and I thought for a fleeting moment that he squeezed back.

Gabriel's light—now a mere inch from us—flamed in a luminous fireball and began shooting through the last of my gray.

I thought the action, and it happened instantly.

Jonah rocketed away from me.

The whip of air as he left dried the last of the wet paint, time wobbled and then fully restored.

I had been time's prisoner once, and yet here I had wielded the hands of the clock. But it didn't matter whether I was the one stealing or the one being stolen; it all led to my incarceration. Time was never on my side.

Now I would be sent to the one place that the nowhere itself didn't dare enter. And if I couldn't escape, then neither would the Purebloods. Zherneboh had made me a weapon, and I would make sure he watched the bomb he had created detonate at his feet.

This morning, I had found the strength to live for me.

By dusk, I had decided to die for everyone else.

Ruadhan might well get his savior after all.

A last smile creased my cheek as I thought of Jonah, and Gabriel's wave of light smacked me with all its might.

Carrying me away in its ferocious tide, his light sent me crashing toward the shores of Hell.

EPILOGUE

THE SHEET OF LIGHT in the distance flickered and then faded. My back smashed into a tree hard enough that I was able to bring myself to a jarring halt. Dazed, I raced back to the clearing.

"Lailah!" I roared, my attention locked to the black smudge of the rift that was shrinking. I searched for her, but she was gone.

"Lad, you're . . . How did you?" Ruadhan's question met me like an accusation.

Gabriel was crouched low to the ground; he raised his face, which fell in a confused expression when he found me standing in one piece. He got up then, his glare leaving me and fixing on the rift instead.

Anguish streaked down me. I careened into Gabriel, and to my surprise he went down with ease. The kid farmers scattered around the side of us, reaching for their weapons, and I hissed, brandishing my fangs.

"What the hell did you do?" I shouted, holding Gabriel by his throat beneath me. I waited for a reaction, anticipating the Angel's retaliation, but it didn't come. Something was wrong; the quiver of his top lip and his aggrieved expression told me that he wanted to hurt me, but his weak eyes gave away his inability.

Ruadhan pulled me off him, bumping me to the side, and then helped Gabriel to his feet.

"Where is she?" Gabriel sounded, his pitch heightening.

I chewed the inside of my cheek, turning to view the diminishing rift.

Both Gabriel and Ruadhan followed my sight and Gabriel cried, "No! That's not possible. I pushed her away. . . . Lailah!" he bellowed.

But he was met with no reply.

He was unsteady on his feet as he lunged at me, smacking my chest, but then he stopped. "Her ring," he said, reaching for it around my neck.

I peered down and, sure enough, there it was. I couldn't recall when she had passed it to me, but the things she whispered in my ear were ringing loud and clear.

"She left this for you," I said. Grinding my teeth, I unclasped it, but instead of handing it to Gabriel, I gave it to Ruadhan. "She said your crystal would fail, and to give you this when you once again found your light. I guess she was right."

I almost didn't want to part with the information; I wanted to leave him in the dark, see how he liked it for a change, but I knew she would have never forgiven me.

"I don't understand." His voice was small.

"She said you should go to Iona. Some crap about light being love, and when you love her, your immortality would be restored with that." Stupid piece of rock . . . I should have launched it a thousand miles away. But then I'd rather he live forever, suffering with the knowledge of what he'd done. Although, he had lost his light, which meant he was fallen. I could just kill him. . . .

"What? Why would she say that? When would she have even had the chance? You should be dust, and she should be here!" Gabriel began drifting toward the rift, but the third dimension was the one place where he couldn't chase after her.

I knew what it was like, for her to be so out of reach, and reluctantly I relented. I took up position beside him. "I don't know how she did what she did, but, Gabriel . . ." I commanded his attention. "She said to tell you that inevitability means nothing when there is choice, and that her choice was *me*." I let the words hover, not fully understanding all of what she had said, and not entirely sure that I believed what I thought she was trying to say.

Gabriel stepped backward, Ruadhan's hand finding his shoulder, and to my surprise he didn't argue. "Did she say anything else?"

I looked from the rift back to him, sparing only a moment to glare in warning at the young lads who were daring to come toward us. I reserved a special flare of flame in my eyes for Phelan. "She told me not to follow her."

"You couldn't even if you wanted to, lad; none of us can follow her there. She must stand alone now." Ruadhan's tone oozed a sense of pride and it irked me. How dare he be proud of her sacrifice for me, for them, for *anyone*? Why did she have to fight, to fall? Why her? She deserved more than the little this life had offered her.

Anger flooded me. Somehow she had spared me from Gabriel's wrath, and she'd doomed herself to do it. And she'd done so despite all the things I had said to her, and they had cut deep.

I knew Lailah; she would meet her end if she had to, and she would meet it alone. Stupid, stubborn girl . . .

I didn't want to remember the things she'd whispered in my ear, thinking they were the last words she'd ever say to me. But I forced myself to focus, searching for something, anything. . . . She had reminded me one last time to run from the hurricane, *to not dare follow her.*

Wait . . .

A triumphant grin edged my lips as it dawned on me what that really meant. "Why would she tell me not to follow her if there was no way I could?" My words hung in the air, and both Ruadhan and Gabriel stared blankly at me. "She had no warning, and yet somehow she was able to keep your light at bay. She told me she came back for me, but how could she have if she never left?"

My attention turned to the collapsing rift. In a few moments, it would disappear completely, and then the possibility—the opportunity—would be lost.

I flipped my hood over my head and crouched low, readying myself.

"Lad, no—" Ruadhan surmised my intention, but Gabriel cut him off.

"Bring her back, Jonah." Gabriel's face was a mix of pain and desperation.

I stared at the rippling ink of the gateway, hoping that I was right; it wasn't like there was another option. I could stay here, without her, and merely exist alone in my darkness, or I could try. And if my soul drained into the dark matter, then the result was no worse.

Either way, I'd be lost.

The light at the end of the tunnel was through that rift.

I would find her, and I would bring her home.

I ran and leaped into the center of the black liquid, and it spilled around me as I fell through.

If she was a hurricane, then I was bound now for the eye of the storm.

ACKNOWLEDGMENTS

MOM & DAD—WHO TAUGHT me that life is limitless.

Because of you both, I, too, believe that "the truth is out there."
I'm guess I'm trying to find it by telling these stories.

Gillan—"I wish there was a way to know you're in the good old
days before you've actually left them."—Andy Bernard, *The Office* . . .
Because of you, know that I knew.

Pat-Dad—For Gillan and me, you took a house and transformed it
into a real home. Though we might now be living farther away, I don't
think we've ever been closer. You did that, and we are so glad you did.

Jen—A beautiful person, inside and out. You made all the difference, and right when we needed it the most.

Penny—Very few people enrich the lives of others the way you
do; even fewer do it without realizing. I hope you know how very
special you are.

Gill—Thank you for cheering me over yet another finish line!

Ken—Your job title has officially been upgraded from Wine
Waiter to Muse. I'll get you a badge. . . .

My dearest friends—The tea flag is still at full mast, ladies! As ever, grab the Jammy Dodgers and let's swap some stories.

The Wattpad readers—Thank you for continuing to *fist pump* and *face palm*! Your messages and comments make my day, every day.

My Wattpad HQ family—With special thanks to Ashleigh, Caitlin, Maria, Danielle & Gavin.

The Wattpad Retirement Home—A special group of writers who I know are destined for great success!

Claire Jacob—I will never forget your words written in response to mine. That day, I felt like my voice had been heard. Thank you.

Beth Collett—My personal proofer and uber-Brummie friend . . . I look forward to reading your first novel someday soon!

Lori Goldstein—A wonderful writer who brought *Becoming Jinn* to the world, my trusted beta reader, and a very good friend. Being on this journey with you has made it so much more fun! It is truly a privilege to know you.

Macmillan / Feiwel and Friends—How very lucky I am to be able to work with such an incredible team! Every day I am grateful to Jean Feiwel, who welcomed me so warmly into the F&F family, and to Liz Szabla, who quite frankly changed my life.

Special thanks to—Angus Killick, Anna Roberto, Christine Barcellona, Holly West, Lauren Burniac, Lauren Scobell, Bethany Reis, Molly Brouillette, Ksenia Winnicki, Caitlin Sweeny, Kathryn Little, Rich Deas, Anna Booth, Dave Barrett, Nicole Moulaison, Gabby Oravetz, Allison Verost, and Elizabeth Fithian.

My Fierce Reads tour mates—Marissa Meyer, Gennifer Albin, Jessica Brody, and Lish McBride. With special thanks to Mary Van Akin.

Martina Boone—Who loved *Lailah* enough to blurb the book, and who has been a fantastic support to this newbie!

Anasheh Satoorian and Patricia Lopez—Who did the most awesome job of hosting *Lailah*'s blog tour over on *The Fantastic Flying Book Club* blog, and who became my best book buddies in the process!

The Styclar Street Team Founders—What can you say to the most wonderful and supportive group of bloggers that ever existed? Thank you for devoting your time and putting in so much effort to spread the Styclar word out in the bloggersphere and beyond! To you I give #AllTheHugs.

The Styclar Street Team Founders are made up of the following bloggers. Be sure to check out their sites for all things YA!

Amber and Jessica—*The Book Bratz*

Anasheh—*A Reading Nurse*

Andrew—*Endlessly Reading*

Beth—*Curling Up With A Good Book*

Britt—*Please Feed the Bookworm*

Crystal—*Bookiemoji*

Dana—*DanaSquare*

Danny—*Bewitched Bookworms*

Genissa—*Story Diary*

Octavia and Shelly—*Read.Sleep.Repeat.*

Patri—*The Unofficial Addiction Book Fan Club*

Pili—*In Love With Handmade*

Rachel—*A Perfection Called Books*

Ri—*Hiver & Café*

And a very special thank you to all the readers, old and new—you make all this possible!